PENGUIN BOOKS
THE READ-ALOUD HANDBOOK

Jim Trelease works full-time addressing parents, teachers, and professional groups on the subjects of children, literature, and television. A graduate of the University of Massachusetts, he was for twenty years an award-winning artist and writer for *The Springfield* (Massachusetts) *Daily News*. His work has also appeared in *The Reading Teacher* and *Parents Magazine*. The father of two grown children, Trelease lives in Springfield, Massachusetts, with his wife, Susan.

Initially self-published in 1979, *The Read-Aloud Handbook* has had four American editions, and has been published in Britain, Australia, and Japan. Mr. Trelease is also the editor of two read-aloud story anthologies, *Hey! Listen to This*, for grades K–4, and *Read All About It!*, for preteens and teens; both books are available from Penguin.

Jim Trelease's lectures are available on both videocassette and audiocassette. For more information, write Reading Tree Productions, 51 Arvesta Street, Springfield, MA 01118, or visit his Website at http://www.trelease-on-reading.com.

The Read-Aloud Handbook

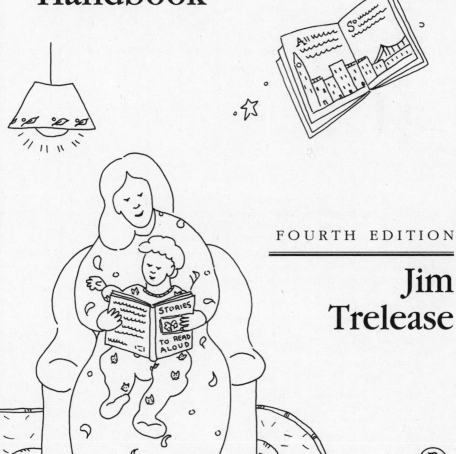

FOURTH EDITION

Jim Trelease

PENGUIN
BOOKS

PENGUIN BOOKS
Published by the Penguin Group
Penguin Books USA Inc., 375 Hudson Street,
New York, New York 10014, U.S.A.
Penguin Books Ltd, 27 Wrights Lane,
London W8 5TZ, England
Penguin Books Australia Ltd, Ringwood,
Victoria, Australia
Penguin Books Canada Ltd, 10 Alcorn Avenue,
Toronto, Ontario, Canada M4V 3B2
Penguin Books (N.Z.) Ltd, 182–190 Wairau Road,
Auckland 10, New Zealand

Penguin Books Ltd, Registered Offices:
Harmondsworth, Middlesex, England

The Read-Aloud Handbook first published in the United States of America in
Penguin Books 1982
First revised edition published 1985
Second revised edition (under the title *The New Read-Aloud Handbook*)
published 1989
This third revised edition published 1995

10

Portions of this work were originally published in pamphlet form.

Grateful acknowledgment is made for permission to reprint an excerpt from
"TV: Checking for Intelligent Life on Earth," *USA Today*, November 4, 1993.
Copyright 1993, USA Today. Reprinted with permission.

Library of Congress Cataloging-in-Publication Data
Trelease, Jim.
    The read-aloud handbook / Jim Trelease.—4th ed.
      p. cm.
    Rev. ed. of: The new read-aloud handbook, 1989
    Includes bibliographical references and index.
    ISBN 0 14 04.6971 0
    1. Oral reading.   I. Trelease, Jim. New read-aloud handbook.
  II. Title.
  LB1573.5.T68   1995
  372.6—dc20   95-2269

Printed in the United States of America
Set in Garamond Light
Design and Illustrations by Virginia Norey

To Elizabeth, Jamie, and now Connor, too—
the best audiences a reader-aloud could hope to find.

And to Alvin R. Schmidt, a ninth-grade English teacher
in New Jersey who found the time forty-one years ago
to write to the parents of one of his students
to tell them they had a talented child. That vote of
confidence has never been forgotten.

Acknowledgments

This book could not have been written without the support and co-operation of many friends, associates, neighbors, children, teachers, and editors. I especially wish to acknowledge the memory of Mary A. Dryden, of Springfield, Massachusetts; she began it all by convincing me to visit her class twenty-eight years ago at Veterans Memorial School (now Mary Dryden Memorial School).

I am also deeply indebted to Dick Garvey and Carroll Robbins, my former editors at *The Springfield* (Massachusetts) *Daily News*, for their long-standing support of staff involvement with the community's school-children. It was this policy which provided the early impetus for my experiences in the classroom. At the same time, I am particularly grateful to my dear and trusted friend Jane Maroney, whose guiding hand and early enthusiasm helped shape the initial concept of this book.

In addition, I would like to thank my neighbor Shirley Uman, whose enthusiasm for my idea spilled over at a family reunion ten years ago within hearing distance of a fledgling literary agent, Raphael Sagalyn, who carried it home to Penguin Books; Bee Cullinan of New York University for her early encouragement; my editor at Penguin, Kathryn Court, for her continued faith and support; Stan Reeves, lifetime reader extraordinaire; and a lovely woman named "Florence of Arlington," who wrote a fateful letter in 1983 that changed the Treleases' lives forever.

It is impossible to express adequately the gratitude I feel toward the hundreds of individuals who, over the last fifteen years, have taken the time to share with me their personal experiences with reading and children, only a fraction of which I can use in each edition. For this edition, I am grateful to Kathy Bryson Nozzolillo, Jeff Smoker, Dr. Hazel Fisher, Janet Moylan, Michel Marriott, Dr. Alexander Randall IV, Sandra C. Odom, Marcia, Mark, and Jennifer Thomas, Rodney T. Snell, Kelly Kline, Linda Kelly-Hassett, Mary W. Williams, Betty Frandsen, and Thomas P. O'Neill, Jr.

For the many clerical and manuscript needs that accompany a revision, I thank my long-suffering assistant Linda Long, as well as Kathy and Kelli Botta, and Carma Sorcinelli.

And, finally, I thank my family—near and far—for their patience and understanding during the long absences required for each revised edition.

Contents

Introduction

If we could get our parents to read to their preschool children fifteen minutes a day, we could revolutionize the schools.
—Dr. Ruth Love, Superintendent, Chicago Public Schools (1981)

Taped inside my copy of *Charlotte's Web* are a note and a photograph of a little boy beside a cake. They were sent to me by a stranger named Kelly Kline, a parent in Cleona, Pennsylvania: "Dear Mr. Trelease—I heard you speak at Lebanon Valley College, Pennsylvania, last month. I was the mother who had just finished reading *Charlotte's Web* to my three-year-old son, Derek. We thought you would get a kick out of our 'Wilbur' cake. I forgot to mention, when I finished reading the book, his next four words were, 'Mom—read it again!' Guess what we're doing? You got it—we're on Chapter 17."

Upon investigation, I learned that Derek's mother did not start reading to him when he was three. Beginning with the day he was born, she did not let a day go by without a book—often more than one. She began with Jack Prelutsky's *Read-Aloud Rhymes for the Very Young*, along with nursery rhymes. What started as a handful of books from the library grew into bagsful of books, so by three he was ready for his very first novel.

By four years of age, he had taught himself to read. Not with a commercial phonics program, however. One thing can be said in favor of such products: they're right when they say, "There are only forty-four sounds in the English language." And all of those forty-four sounds—every ending, blending, and diphthong—can be found in *Goodnight Moon* and *Make Way for Ducklings* and *Charlotte's Web*. Which is just the way Mrs. Kline gave them to Derek. Although she was trained as a teacher, she did no formal teaching with Derek other than to answer his questions and read to him.

Now I want you to jump ahead to the day Derek sat down at the kindergarten learning table for the first time. Think about the dozen novels he'd heard by that day; the thousand picture books he'd heard, as well as the ones he'd read himself; and the tens of thousands of words he knew from all those readings. And then I want you to think about the child on his left and the one on his right—who, if they were typical American kindergarten children, had heard no novels and only a handful of tired picture books over the last five years.

Which child had the larger vocabulary with which to understand the teacher? Which one had the longer attention span with which to work in class? And which child had a parent who would be the least likely to ever have to call Hooked on Phonics, 1-800-ABCDEFG?

Mrs. Kline brought a child to the classroom ready and willing to learn. Did she have to invest $230 in a seventeen-pound box of flashcards and phonics tapes? Did she have to enroll him in an elite and expensive preschool? Did she have to bring him down to the computer store and plug him into expensive software? All Kelly Kline needed—all anyone needs—is a free public library card and the determination to invest her mind and time in her child's future. Nothing on Wall Street ever will pay dividends as rich as that.

I recently called Kelly Kline to see how Derek was progressing at age six. He now reads picture books to his mother and she does novels with him. They'd just finished *Maniac Magee* by Jerry Spinelli and Roald Dahl's *Matilda*.

Imagine how bright a world we would have if all parents behaved like Derek's. Extensive research has proven that reading aloud to a child is the single most important factor in raising a reader. It is also the best-kept secret in American education. This inexpensive and pleasurable fifteen minutes a day—either in the home or in the classroom—is more effective than worksheets or any other method of reading instruction.

With that in mind, this is a book for new parents, veteran parents, grandparents, teachers, principals, day care providers, and librarians— anyone who feeds the minds and affects the lives of children and thus the future.

New parents care deeply about nothing as much as their newborn. Next they care about the child's future. They want him or her to be happy, healthy, and have the brightest future. Most parents do every- thing they know to ensure that future, often making great sacrifices to- ward that end. Nonetheless, 25 percent of children do not succeed and another 25 percent don't come close to achieving their potential. Among those who don't succeed, a major portion end up in poverty and/or prison. Sixty percent of American inmates are illiterate.

Perhaps some parents aren't doing what they should, something they don't know about. What goes on in the homes of children who succeed? It can't always be a case of money, because some of the most success- ful children come from poor homes. Are there magic potions that parents feed successful kids? In a word, yes, and this book is about those potions.

As for educators and parents of children already in school, this is a book of resources. Here are the things that work—I'll not bore you with fanciful theories. I'll give you the facts about reading aloud and its im- pact on learning; you take it from there. But if you decide to take it further, to go out and make converts of the people in your community or fight to introduce read-aloud programs in your schools—as at least three states have done—then this can be your handbook of *proof.*

One note of caution for parents and teachers: This is not a book about teaching a child *how* to read. It's about teaching children to *want* to read. "What we teach children to love and desire," goes an education adage, "will always outweigh what we teach them to just do." And while this is going on, the emotional bonding that occurs between reader and listener is magnified and strengthened.

You should also know that *The Read-Aloud Handbook* is two books in one. The first half is the evidence in support of reading aloud and the second half is the Treasury of Read-Alouds, a beginner's guide to recommended titles, from picture books to novels. The listing is in- tended to take the guesswork out of reading aloud for busy parents and teachers (many of whom were never read to in their own childhoods) who want to begin reading aloud but don't have the time to take a course in children's literature. Since the Treasury is annotated with age and grade levels, it doesn't have to be read all at once. Before using the Treasury, however, you might find it helpful to read Chapter 9 (How to Use the Treasury).

For those returning readers who wonder how this edition differs from previous ones, I assure you none of the fundamentals have changed. Statistics have been updated and exciting new research and anecdotes added. Since the last edition, major national and international studies have been done on reading, one involving more than 210,000 children. What the researchers found are certain patterns among the children from around the world who read best. Similarly, two college researchers published their work after thirty years of reading "autobiographies" written by college students, documenting what they liked about reading as children and what they hated—what worked and what didn't. I've included those surprising findings here, along with many others. In addition, more than 15,000 new children's books have been published since the last edition and I've collected what I hope are some of the best read-alouds from that total and added them to the Treasury.

There is also a chapter on television. It's a reasoned and, I hope, enlightening one, to be used in controlling the abuse of the medium, not eliminating it. I will give you the research showing that if you control it, you can positively affect student achievement; left uncontrolled, it will severely diminish achievement. I'll address many of your TV concerns: How much is okay and when does it become harmful? Are some shows better than others for a child to see? How do I get out of the role of video-cop, fighting with them to turn it off and do their homework? Yes, there are inexpensive devices that will accomplish that for you.

In writing each edition, my foremost perspective has been that of a parent—because that is how I came to write this book in the first place. But in the intervening years, half of my time has been spent working with classroom teachers—the people who must pick up the pieces when parents don't do their job. More than fifty colleges and universities now use this book in their education classes. Therefore I have included annotations for those who require such data for their research or classes, but have placed most of it in the Notes so it will not intrude on the normal reading process.

Where It All Began

Back in the 1960s, I was a young father of two children and working as an artist and writer for a daily newspaper in Massachusetts (I am now a grandfather as well). I was reading to my daughter and son each night, unaware of any cognitive or emotional benefits that would come of it. I had no idea what it would do for their vocabulary, attention span, or interest in books. I read for one reason—*not* because of any education courses I took in college (I'd taken none as an English major), and *not* because the pediatrician or principal told me to (they hadn't). I read because *my* father had read to *me*. And because he'd read to me, when my time came I knew intuitively there is a torch that is supposed to be passed from one generation to the next.

As a school volunteer in Springfield, Massachusetts (I'd been visiting classrooms on a weekly basis for several years, discussing my careers as artist and writer), I was invited one day to speak to a sixth-grade class.

After spending an hour with the class, I gathered my materials and prepared to leave when I noticed a book on the shelf near the door. It was *The Bears' House*, by Marilyn Sachs, and it caught my eye immediately because I'd just finished reading it to my daughter.

"Who's reading *The Bears' House?*" I asked the class. Several girls' hands went up.

"I just finished reading it," I said. Their eyes lit up. They couldn't believe it. This man, who had just told them stories about how he got started in newspapers, this man, whose drawings and stories they had been clipping out of the paper for the last month—this man was reading one of *their* books?

So I explained about my children, Elizabeth and Jamie, and how I read to each of them every night. I told them how, when my children were little, they were most interested in the pictures. That was fine with me because I was an artist and I was interested in the pictures, too. I told them how much we enjoyed Maurice Sendak's *Where the Wild Things Are* because of how he drew the monsters. I loved to read the *Little Tim* books to see how Edward Ardizzone drew the ocean and *Make Way for Ducklings* to see how Robert McCloskey drew the ducks.

"And did you know," I said when I saw them perk up at the mention of the *Ducklings* classic, "that Mr. McCloskey had a dreadful time trying to draw those ducks? He finally brought six ducklings up to his apartment in order to get a closer look. In the end, because they kept moving around so much, do you know what he did? You may find this hard to believe, but I promise you, it's true: in order to get them to hold still, he slowed them down by getting them drunk on red wine!"

The class clapped their approval of McCloskey's unorthodox approach.

Then we talked about *The Bears' House*: what it was about (for those in the room who had not read it); what the students liked about it; and what else they had read by the author. I asked the rest of the class what they had read lately. There was a forest of hands and a chorus of books. It was forty-five minutes before I could say good-bye. I stepped out into the corridor, where the teacher thanked me for coming. "But most of all," she said, "thank you for what you said about the books. You have no idea what it means for them to hear it from someone outside the classroom."

In the days following the visit I pondered what had happened in that classroom. The teacher subsequently wrote to say that the children had begged and begged to go to the library that afternoon in order to get the books I'd talked about. I wondered what it was that I had said that was so unusual. I had only talked about my family's favorite books.

All I was doing was giving book reports. As soon as I called it that, I realized what was so special about it. It probably was the first time any of them had ever heard an adult give a book report—an unsolicited one, at that. I thought of how few of them had ever heard a teacher say, "You'll have to bear with me today, class, I'm a little fuzzy-headed this morning. I stayed up until three o'clock this morning reading the most wonderful book. I just couldn't put it down. Would you like to hear what the book was about?"

I'd piqued the children's interest by giving them a book report. But an even better description of it would be "a commercial." I'd started by selling them on newspapers and a career and concluded by selling them on books and reading.

So I made a resolution: from then on, whenever I visited a classroom, I would save time at the end to talk about reading. I'd begin by asking the class, "What have you read lately? Anybody read any good books lately?" In the ensuing years, to my dismay, I discovered they didn't read. They weren't reading much either in the remedial classes or in the classes for the gifted and talented. Nor was there any difference between the public schools and the parochials. But slowly I began to notice one difference. There were isolated classrooms where the kids were reading—reading a ton! How is it, I wondered, that these kids are so turned on to reading while the class across the hall (where I was the previous month) wasn't reading anything? Same principal, same neighborhood, same textbooks. What's up?

When I pursued it further I discovered the difference was standing in the front of the room: the teacher. In nearly every one of the turned-on classes, the teacher read to the class on a regular basis. Maybe there is something to this, I began to think—more than just the feel-good stuff I got from reading to Elizabeth and Jamie. So off to the libraries of the local teachers colleges I went, looking for answers. And there I discovered the research showing that reading aloud to children improves their reading, writing, speaking, listening—and, best of all, their attitudes about reading. There was one big problem with the research: the people who should have been reading it weren't reading it. The teachers, supervisors, and principals didn't know it even existed. Indeed, as I was soon to discover, there were many schools where teachers were forbidden to read aloud to students, a rule created out of the misconception that such behavior was a waste of instructional time and would make the children lazy.

I also found that most parents and teachers were unaware of good children's books. When I pressed some of my newspaper colleagues (most of whom were college graduates) about reading to their children, I'd get answers like, "Oh, I tried that, but the books are so boring neither of us could stay awake."

In the late 1970s, when I realized there was nothing generally available for parents and teachers on reading aloud, not even book lists (except those included in children's literature textbooks), I decided to compile my own. As a result of working at the newspaper, I had access to modern typesetting equipment, so the task was relatively simple: I'd write a short how-to booklet on reading aloud to children, half the book being a list of recommended titles. To be candid, I never imagined the events that were to follow. Initially, it was a modest self-publishing venture (costing me $650 for the first printing—the family vacation money for one summer), with local bookstores taking copies on consignment. Within three years the booklet sold more than 20,000 copies in thirty states and Canada. By 1982, Penguin Books had seen a copy and asked me to expand it into the first edition of the book you are reading now. The book you are reading is the third American revision. There have been British, Australian, and Japanese editions as well.

Even in this—the growth of this book—we can see the metaphor of "passing torches." A few months after the first Penguin edition of *The Read-Aloud Handbook* was published, someone gave a young graduate student a copy of the book on the occasion of his becoming a new parent. He was also doing part-time carpentry work, and he was hired by an Arlington, Virginia, couple to do some work in anticipation of their new baby. He gave them a copy of the book. This Arlington mother, though, did more than just read it. She wrote an unsolicited "book report" about it to a national syndicated columnist—a woman named Abigail Van Buren. And when her letter appeared with "Abby's" response on February 23, 1983, almost overnight Penguin had orders for 120,000 copies of the book. As you can imagine, she's now known in our house as *"Dear, Dear Abby."*

I share that background with you not in a self-congratulatory way but rather as evidence in support of a major thesis of this book. The cultural problems of our nation are not insurmountable. We know how to cure many of them, and you can help. I propose that you—one parent, one grandparent, one teacher, or one librarian—can make a lasting difference. So sprinkled throughout the first half of this book are examples of people who made the world a better place for one child, a dozen, hundreds, and thousands. Few of them are famous. Most are folks you probably never heard of—like Kelly and Derek Kline—but I think you'll remember them after you've met them here.

Changes in School and Out

Since that first edition back in 1982, there have been many changes in our world—especially in classrooms and homes.

Major alarms have been sounded by government and business over the decline in student scores. These, in turn, have prompted national reform movements. Nearly all states have raised both graduation requirements and teacher salaries, toughened curricula, and strengthened teacher-training programs. Some have instituted teacher competency tests, and almost a third of the states began spending tax dollars to educate four-year-olds. For those who wonder how much of a difference there is between student scores today and those of the "good old days," you might be interested in the Appendix.

Yet, for all the reform, student reading scores remain unchanged over the last twenty-five years—with the exception of minorities, whose scores have crept upward but still remain far behind those of whites.[1] One can only conclude: Something is missing. This book is about what's missing.

We also must consider how much social change has occurred in the last fifteen years:

- Weapon detectors are now used in 25 percent of urban schools.
- The opening of the 1994 school year found gun-sniffing dogs patrolling the lockers of Corpus Christi schools, while other school districts were eliminating lockers or forbidding book bags in an attempt to reduce the number of hiding places for students' weapons.[2]
- Some inner-city schools have taken to issuing dog tags to their students and building bulletproof walls around their playgrounds. The hottest "must-have" item on college campuses in the fall of 1994 was pepper spray, a self-defense chemical spray.[3]

The changes within students' homes have been just as dramatic. When the first edition was published, most students in America had not attended preschool or day care. Few had mothers who worked outside the home. There was no video rental store nearby and there was no cable TV. Over one decade, all these have become common experiences. Where there used to be a single shopping mall, open six days a week, there are now mega-malls open seven days and six nights a week.

And out-of-school havens are proving to be as dangerous as school:

- On California beaches that used to be the subject of *Beach Blanket Bingo* movies, the lifeguards now wear bulletproof vests.
- The largest toy-store chain in America decides to stop selling one of its hottest items—realistic-looking toy guns.[4]
- Major American cities are imposing teen curfews, as are shopping malls that fifteen years ago were courting teen shoppers.
- Sales for house alarms are at record highs.
- Neighborhood video stores now carry the uncut versions of films that Hollywood once deemed too violent to show on the big screen.

New Parent Interest

One hopeful sign in all this is a growing interest on the part of new parents in the parenting process. Born in the rudderless sixties and early seventies and better educated than their predecessors, these parents seem determined to correct the mistakes of their own parents by devouring the hundreds of parenting books now in print. To the relief of educators who watched parent-teacher associations (PTAs) decline for twenty years, membership has been rising since 1983.

There are two rubs in this. First, parents most in need of help (the ones who bring the largest number of at-risk children into schools— young, poor, undereducated mothers and fathers) either won't or can't avail themselves of these tools; and second, a growing number of afflu- ent, fast-track parents are using education as a pressure cooker to pro- duce an instant adult.

The challenge posed by both kinds of parent is addressed here. As for those parents (and educators) bent on raising "superbabies," I offer this caution: The four-year-old who is forced into reading might be a gifted child. *Might* be. More likely the child is the product of a pushy, insecure parent intent on impressing the neighborhood or office with a four-year-old reader who "barks" at type. I will explain later the differ- ence between children who arrive at reading naturally as a result of being read to and those who arrive prematurely as a result of "hot- housing."

Suffice it to say, the business of childhood is play; the prime purpose of being four is to enjoy being four—of secondary importance is to prepare for being five. What the pressuring parent needs to do is read Dr. David Elkind's two books, *The Hurried Child* and *Miseducation: Preschoolers at Risk*, which clearly document the dangers of what many principals call "suburban child abuse." It is sobering research and commonsense reading.

If parents really want to help their child in a way that is developmen- tally appropriate, they should send for a little publication out of the U.S. Department of Education called "Helping Your Child Get Ready for School," by Nancy Paulu. It discusses the skills that a child should have at successive ages from one through five, and lists simple activities that will build those skills. Send fifty cents to: Consumer Information Center, Department R.O., Item # 372A, Pueblo, CO 81009-0011.

The Time Myth

Here's one of the most common responses I hear from parents: "Sure, I know I should read to my child, but who's got time today? We're both working, and when we're not working or commuting, we're driving the kids to day care or soccer practices or the orthodontist. Nobody's got time today!" For those parents, I remind you: We're talking about only fifteen minutes a day (unless you and the child opt for more). Surely you can afford *that*. If nobody had any time, the shopping malls would all be empty; cable television would be bankrupt; video stores would become antique shops. Who's kidding whom here?

The *real* question is: How do we spend the time we have? Male and female adults each spend an average of six hours a week shopping,[5] and each averages thirty hours a week watching television. Contrast those figures with the 1981 time-study of double-income and single-income two-parent families in which parents' time with children was monitored. The researchers wanted to see if there were any significant differences.

In homes of school-age children, daily "educational interaction" (like playing with or reading to the child) averaged:

- 12.2 minutes for the "at-home" mother, 7.0 minutes for father;
- 11.7 minutes for the "working" mother, 5.6 minutes for father.

In one-to-one conversation with the child:

- 9.5 minutes for "at-home" mother, 7.8 minutes for father;
- 10.7 minutes for "working mother," 4.0 minutes for father.

Weekend figures either stayed the same or declined a few minutes (in the case of fathers). For families with preschool children or younger, the amount of time spent tripled but the ratios remained the same. So, despite the differences in the time available to them, there are only a few minutes' difference between what dual- and single-income two-parent families spend with their children. In other words, it is not time but *dedication to parenting* that makes the difference. (In a separate project, however, researchers studied preschoolers recommended for speech therapy and found surprising differences between the language skills of children from single- and two-parent families—see page 40.)

The problem is not time. With few exceptions, it is a matter of priorities. Most parents find the time to put in a full workday, take a full complement of coffee breaks, eat lunch and dinner, read the newspaper, watch the nightly newscast or ball game, do the dishes, talk on the phone for thirty minutes (mostly about nothing), run to the store for a pack of cigarettes or a lottery ticket, drive to the mall, and never miss that favorite prime-time show. Somehow they find the time for those things—important or unimportant as they are—but can't find time to read to a child. My task in this book is to convince you that reading to a child is more important than all the other items on your leisure priority list.

Where Fathers Strike Out

There is one particular group I wish a word with in this introduction—fathers. While I confess to having a special feeling for them, too often the feeling is disappointment. One of my personal goals is to convince as many fathers as possible of their powerful influence, to build not only better athletes but literate ones, too. Standing in the lobbies of American libraries, you would think fathers were an endangered species. Consistently, whether I am in Hawaii, Louisiana, Georgia, Alaska, or Massachusetts, men make up less than 7 percent of my parent audiences. Educators tell me this is the same figure for male turnout at PTA meetings.

But there is never a shortage of males in our remedial reading classes, where boys make up more than 70 percent of the enrollment.[6] In *American* remedial classes, that is. Boys *don't* constitute 70 percent of the remedial students in many other countries. In Israeli remedial classes, there are *no* gender differences.[7] In Finland, England, Nigeria, India, and Germany, the girls outnumber the boys.[8] So the old genetic argument that boys develop more slowly than girls doesn't fly here—unless they're making little boys differently in Nigeria and Israel than they are in the United States. What *is* different is our cultural values. Many American boys are sentenced to remedial classes by fathers who convince the child that the most important things in life are the things we throw and catch. "The important things in *my* life, son, are the things you see me get excited about—the Cowboys and the Forty-Niners, the Knicks and the Bulls, the Braves and the Blue Jays. You don't see me getting excited about *Charlotte's Web*, do you?"

In elementary schools, 88 percent of the faculty is female.[9] If a boy seldom sees an adult male reading in school and seldom one at home, he's liable to think reading isn't for males—like himself and his dad. Somehow we have to short-circuit that dangerous connection by convincing American males that it is not only possible but *preferable* for fathers to be both athletically and intellectually involved in their children's lives. A father can play catch in the backyard after dinner and, on the same night, read to the child for fifteen minutes. He can take him to the basketball game on Friday night and to the library on Saturday morning.

The sports world, in fact, is analogous to the world of reading. Consider the role of fathering in professional baseball. The structure of the sport, with its slow, nonviolent nature (like that of reading), allows for an intimacy between father and sons that has resulted in the highest father-son ratio in professional sports—by one count, sixty-five players in professional baseball had fathers who were major leaguers.[10] Thus the odds against Bobby Bonds's or Ken Griffey's son making it to the majors were only 500 to 1, as opposed to those of a boy whose father did not play in the majors—for whom the odds were 25,000 to 1.[11] The reason the odds favored Ken Jr. is that he hung around with a major leaguer, played catch with him in the backyard, went to spring training with him, even sat in the dugout with him.

Now compare the odds of success for a boy or girl whose main role model is seldom if ever seen or heard reading, versus the odds for the child who hangs around with a reading parent, a parent who curls up in bed with child and book, who takes the child to the library, who is seen reading a daily newspaper—even shares parts of it with the child. Who stands the best chance of becoming a lifetime reader and, consequently, a lifetime achiever?

These role-modeling principles apply to school. We see a significant decline in boys' scores when their fathers are absent from the home.[12] (Yet, as you will find in Chapter 7, the life of Ben Carson proves that courageous, commonsense parenting can more than compensate for the harm of an absent father.) A 1991 study of 57 fourth-, fifth-, and sixth-grade boys in Modesto, California, found that:

1. Boys who were read to by their fathers scored significantly higher in reading achievement.
2. Fathers who read recreationally had sons who read more and scored higher than boys whose fathers did little or no recreational reading. In a survey of all the fathers, only 10 percent reported having had fathers who read to them when they were children.[13]

But be you a father or a mother, it is important you know how essential your role is in education. In 1991, the Carnegie Commission's *Ready to Learn* report indicated that kindergarten teachers estimate 35 percent of their students were not ready for first grade. Seeing as how the teacher had had each child for less than 700 hours and the parent(s) had had the child for 52,000 hours, his entire six-year-old life, which "teacher" do you think is responsible for the child being unprepared?

One-third of American parents do an outstanding job, one-third do a good job, and one-third do less than lousy! And it is this bottom third that breaks the backs of American teachers every day. Children who come into the classroom from troubled homes find themselves overwhelmed from the first day. And if the child is overwhelmed, imagine how the teacher feels. One kindergarten teacher in Lodi, California, described for me her daily challenges: Thirty-one children speaking ten different primary languages. For a variety of reasons, but none provable, she suspects several of the children are being abused at home. Most of the families subsist at a level of poverty unimaginable to America's middle and upper classes. "One child wanted to show me all the words he could write but had no paper at home to write on. In desperation, he finally found a light-bulb wrapper. Then, ever so carefully, so as not to rip the corrugated paper, he printed and printed until he had filled the entire surface with his words."

Such a child represents both the challenge in our classroom community *and* the possibilities. For that child whose parents cannot or will not do the job, the classroom teacher becomes the last hope, the "last stop for gas before the beltway of adulthood," as Phyllis Theroux once put it. If the teacher finds a way to turn the child on to the joy of reading and creates a lifetime reader, that student has a much greater chance of growing up and doing the right things with his or her child. And that will make a future teacher's burden less heavy. At the same time, the teacher is creating a smarter, less desperate America.

Social Ills and Reading

The boldness of the headlines and the blood-in-the-streets reports on the eleven o'clock news would lead some to believe we are hitting new lows in America. Not so, but it might be helpful to look at what has bailed us out in the past. Today's homicide rates are not at record highs—those in the 1800s were higher. Our homeless numbers cannot compare with the 10,000 homeless and abandoned children living in New York or London in the 1880s. But the last century may hold the cure for today's ills.

It was in response to growing lawlessness caused by the polarization between the rich and the poor in the 1830s that compulsory education was born in Massachusetts. In the wake of public riots and lynchings, Horace Mann reasoned that the only way to close the gap between the top and the bottom is education. "Education, beyond all other devices of human origin, is the great equalizer of the conditions of man," he wrote. "It does better than disarm the poor of their hostility towards the rich: it prevents being poor." This was the philosophy that led to compulsory education in America.[14]

And reading is the heart of education. The knowledge of almost every subject in school flows from reading. One must first be able to read the word problem in math in order to understand it. If you cannot read the science or social studies chapter, you cannot answer the questions at the end of the chapter. One can arguably state: Reading is the single most important social factor in American life today. Let me tell you why I believe this is so:

1. The more you read, the more you know;[15]
2. the more you know, the smarter you grow;[16]
3. the smarter you are, the longer you stay in school and the more diplomas you earn;[17]
4. the more diplomas you have, the more days you are employed;[18]
5. the more diplomas you have, the more your children will achieve in school;[19]
6. and the more diplomas you have, the longer you will live.[20]

The converse, therefore, would also be true:

1. The less you read, the less you know;
2. the less you know, the sooner you drop out of school;
3. the sooner you drop out, the sooner and longer you will be unemployed;
4. the sooner you drop out, the greater your chances of going to jail.

The basis for that formula is firmly established: Poverty and illiteracy are related—they are the parents of desperation and imprisonment.

- 82 percent of prison inmates are school dropouts.[21]
- 60 percent of inmates were raised in poverty.
- 60 percent of inmates are illiterate.[22]

Why are our children failing and dropping out of school? Because they cannot read—which affects the entire report card. Change the graduation rate and you change the prison population—which changes the entire climate of America. The higher a state's high school graduation rate, the *smaller* its prison population.[23]

So common sense should tell us that reading is the ultimate weapon —destroying ignorance, poverty, and despair before they can destroy *us*. A nation that doesn't read much doesn't know much. And a nation that doesn't know much is more likely to make poor choices in the home, the marketplace, the jury box, and the voting booth. And those decisions ultimately affect the entire nation—the literate and the illiterate. The challenge therefore is to convince future generations of children that carrying books is more rewarding than carrying guns. This book is about meeting that challenge.

One note of caution to the reader: The statistics you find in the early chapters of this book can easily be interpreted to mean that today's student is significantly less intelligent than students of fifty years ago. Such conclusions are erroneous. Today's average student is, in fact, as smart—if not smarter—than his predecessors. If you wish to read the evidence, see the Appendix. The critical difference is not in the student scores but in the world—it's now a lot more complicated. Yesterday's scores—as good as they might have been—are not good enough today.

The Read-Aloud
Handbook

1

Why Read Aloud?

Perhaps it is only in childhood that books have any deep influence on our lives . . . in childhood all books are books of divination, telling us about the future, and like the fortune-teller who sees a long journey in the cards or death by water, they influence the future. I suppose that is why books excited us so much. What do we ever get nowadays from reading to equal the excitement and the revelation of those first fourteen years?

Graham Greene,
The Lost Childhood and Other Essays

In this chapter, we will examine both aspects of WHY: why it is so important for us to read to children at this particular point in history; and why reading aloud is so effective.

A few years ago on a lovely autumn morning, I visited the same kindergarten room I had attended as a child at Connecticut Farms Elementary School in Union, New Jersey. Gazing up at me were the upturned faces of about fifteen children, each of them seated expectantly on their story rugs. "How many of you want to learn to read this year?" I asked.

Without a second's hesitation, every hand shot into the air, many accompanied by boasts like "I already know how!" Their excitement matches what every kindergarten teacher has told me: Every child begins school wanting to learn to read. In other words, we've got 100 percent enthusiasm and desire when they start school.

Several months later, the National Reading Report Card told the rest of the story:[1]

- Among fourth-graders, 45.7 percent read something for pleasure each day.
- Among eighth-graders, only 27 percent read for pleasure daily.
- By twelfth grade, only 24.4 percent read anything for pleasure daily.
- Fourth-grade weekly library use is 40 percent, but this number drops to 10 percent by senior year.

Simply put, we have 100 percent in kindergarten and lose 75 percent of our potential lifetime readers by senior year. Any business that lost 75 percent of its customer base would be in Chapter 11 overnight. That, in a nutshell, is the crisis facing America today.

Our objective is to create lifetime readers—graduates who continue to read and educate themselves throughout their adult lives. But the reality is we've created schooltime readers—graduates who know how to read well enough to graduate. And at that point the majority take a silent vow: If I never read another book, it'll be too soon.

You would be hard-pressed to find a parent, teacher, politician, or businessperson who did not believe we are in the throes of a cultural and social crisis.

In the dawning hours of our awareness, 1983, a national commission was created to discover the causes of the crisis and produce a solution. It was called the Commission on Reading, organized by the National Academy of Education and the National Institute of Education and funded under the U.S. Department of Education. It consisted of nationally recognized experts in how children develop, how they learn language, and how they learn to read. Since nearly everything in the school curriculum rested upon reading, reading was at the heart of both the problem and the solution.

As the most important discipline in education, reading has generated more than 1,200 research projects annually in recent years. It took the Commission two years to evaluate the more than 10,000 research projects that had been done in the last quarter century in order to discover what works, what might work, and what doesn't work.

In 1985, the Commission issued its report, *Becoming a Nation of*

Readers. It is, in my opinion, the most important and commonsense education document in twenty-five years. Among its primary findings, two simple declarations rang loud and clear:

- "The single most important activity for building the knowledge required for eventual success in reading is *reading aloud* to children."[2]
- The Commission found conclusive evidence to support the use of reading aloud not only in the home but also in the classroom: "It is a practice that should continue throughout the grades."[3]

What the experts were saying was that reading aloud was more important than worksheets, homework, assessments, book reports, and flash cards. One of the cheapest, simplest, and oldest methods of teaching was being promoted as a better teaching tool than anything else in the home or classroom. What exactly is so powerful about something so simple you don't even need a high school diploma in order to do it?

Marketplace Reasons for Change

Before I give you the reasons it works, it might be helpful if I gave you proof that the old methods haven't worked. These six examples will simultaneously support my thesis that we desperately need to change the way we raise readers in the home and in the classroom.

1. Every workday afternoon a courier shows up at the door of the fifth largest insurance company in America, New York Life. There he is handed a satchel of insurance claims, which he drives to JFK Airport. The satchel is then loaded aboard an Aer Lingus jet and flown to Dublin, Ireland, where American insurance claims will be processed by another people in another country.[4] Why? Because New York Life cannot find enough young people in the metropolitan area, between the ages of twenty and thirty, who know how to read, write, and think clearly and critically enough to process insurance claims. Ireland has them.
2. In 1988, 44 percent of the job applicants at Prudential Insurance in Newark, New Jersey, could not read on a ninth-grade level. As Prudential's CEO said, "They are seventeen years old and virtually unemployable."[5]

3. When New York Telephone advertised several hundred full-time job openings, they received 117,000 applications. Less than half qualified to take the basic exam and only 2,100 passed. The situation is no better elsewhere in America. BellSouth Corporation in Atlanta, looking for directory assistance operators and clerical workers, found that only 1 in 10 applicants could meet their entry requirements.[6]

4. At the Motorola electronics company in Schaumburg, Illinois, in 1992, officials found that 50 percent of job applicants failed to achieve seventh-grade reading and fifth-grade math levels.[7] Nationally, Motorola discovered 80 percent were unable to read on at least a seventh-grade level.[8]

5. On Long Island, New York, a bank reports that only 2 in 15 applicants can pass a simple math test.[9]

6. Thirty percent of the nation's largest companies (and many of its smaller ones) are collectively paying $25 billion a year teaching remedial math and reading to entry-level employees.[10]

What, you might ask, does this have to do with *reading*? It can be reduced to a simple, two-part formula:

- The more you read, the better you get at it; the better you get at it, the more you like it; and the more you like it, the more you do it.
- And more you read, the more you know; and the more you know, the smarter you grow.

Contrary to what alarmists would have us believe, we are not a nation of illiterates. The average American student *can* read. And 95 percent of twenty-one- to twenty-five-year-olds, our alumni, can perform routine tasks using printed information (one paragraph of simple sentences).[11] Sixty-three percent go on to advanced education, compared to only 20 percent in 1940. As I explain in the Appendix, today's students probably do not think any less or any slower than their grandparents did. But the needs of today's world are far more complex than those of 1940, and are growing more complex by the hour. Seventy percent of the reading material in a cross section of jobs nationally is written on *at least* ninth-grade level.[12]

The World's Growing Complexity

The contrast between yesterday and today in America can be seen in Baltimore, Maryland, in the life of a forty-two-year-old resident that *The New York Times* described as Joe, and that of his son, Joe Jr. Back in 1965, Joe Sr. had no trouble landing a full-time job with the biggest employer in Baltimore, Bethlehem Steel, despite literacy skills that allowed him to read only the simplest of sentences. Today, twenty years later, his son is job hunting with the same reading skills his father had, and the difference is staggering. First, Bethlehem Steel is gone. Second, the largest employer in Baltimore is Johns Hopkins University Medical Center. And third, even a college diploma won't guarantee a job at Johns Hopkins. The challenge to America is that there are 150,000 young Joes living in Baltimore, a situation duplicated in every urban center across America, to say nothing of rural America.[13]

Sometimes a job's complexity changes so fast, it turns blue-collar requirements into white-collar almost overnight. Witness the so-called 72-hour Gulf War that put to rest the adage "An army marches on its stomach." Marching armies no longer win wars—their technologies do. The high-tech equipment that allowed the United States to direct its radar missiles down chimney holes requires an IQ equal to that task. As a result, America's first large equal-opportunity employer no longer has opportunities for anyone without a regular high school diploma.

- In 1980, 50 percent of army recruits were among those scoring in the lowest quarter on the entrance exam. By 1992, only 2 percent were accepted from that quarter.
- The army's task is so complex it no longer accepts a General Equivalency Diploma (GED), even though the army invented it for World War II. "Forty years later we don't accept the thing that we made," sighs one recruiter who has to turn away fifteen to twenty high school dropouts a month.[14] A major factor in that decision was that GED recruits flunk basic training twice as often as high school graduates.[15]

But the changing world versus the unchanging reading patterns of young Americans is only *part* of the problem. Equally important is the out-of-sight problem: While American children are not getting any smarter, those in other countries *are*. Nations we left in our academic dust in the past are now on equal footing, thanks to their educational improvements. And I don't just mean obvious competitors like Japan.

What effect would a rise in, let's say, India's scores have upon the U.S.? In the 1960s, America had a healthy lead in engineering and math skills. Then India's scores began to rise. As soon as they neared us, companies like Motorola, IBM, and Texas Instruments shipped them business. By 1993, most of the state-of-the-art components for Motorola's hand-held satellite telephone system (invented in the U.S.) were being made in India by engineers now as skilled as ours but willing to work for much less. Thus 10,000 computer jobs went out of the country.[16]

Not Making the Grade

Couple the above examples with these classroom problems:

- Only 5 percent of twelfth-graders are able to write on the level of a college freshman.[17]
- Less than 5 percent of high school seniors can read material on the level of *The New York Times*, and 63 percent are not reading at the level of a tabloid newspaper. More than 75 percent, however, can read on at least a fourth-grade level.[18]
- In its 1986 evaluation of third- and fourth-grade students, the National Assessment of Educational Progress (the nation's report card) found 90 percent of the students had not read a book or story recently.[19]
- In 1988, the U.S. Department of Education did the first longitudinal study of American eighth-graders, 24,599 in 1,000 schools.[20] More than half (53 percent) had no risk factors at home—latchkey, single parent, parent without diploma, poverty level, limited English. Among its findings:
  - ✔ *Sixty-six percent were unable to summarize what they read.*
  - ✔ *They averaged 21.2 hours a week of television watching.*
  - ✔ *They averaged 1.9 hours a week of reading (outside school, but including homework).*
- When literate fifth-graders were monitored for how they spent their free time, 90 percent devoted less than 1 percent of their time to reading and 33 percent of the time to watching television.[21]
- In comparing 1992 reading and writing scores with those of 1972, there was little or no improvement in student scores, despite at least fifteen years' worth of standard-raising and curriculum

changes. The only appreciable changes were improvements in minority scores, though these were still well below those of majority
students.[22]

The lack of interest in reading is evident not only at the bottom or
middle of the class; it is there at the top as well. Scholar and author
Jacques Barzun writes of a committee interviewing 150 young people
—three top students from each state—to award ten full scholarships
worth $60,000 each. "One member of the committee asked every can-
didate this question: 'Did you, during the past year, read a book that
was not assigned? If so, please tell us a little something about that book.'
Only one student out of the 150 was able to comply."[23]

If you think things are better with the grown-ups at home, think again:

- Forty percent of U.S. households did not buy a single book (hardcover or paperback) in 1991, with young adults showing the least
  interest.[24]
- Most of the book buying and reading is done by a hardcore 30
  percent of the public.[25]
- In 1967, 73 percent of adults classified themselves as daily newspaper readers; by 1989 that figure had dropped to 50 percent.[26]
  Among the top twenty nations for per capita newspaper circulation, the U.S. places nineteenth—behind nearly all the modern
  industrial powers.[27]
- Sixty-eight percent of U.S. adults report television-viewing as their
  greatest pleasure—outweighing even friendships and vacations.[28]

Simply put, the scores are telling us our students know how to read.
But their behavior as children and adults tells us they don't like it enough
to do it very often. We've taught children *how* to read but forgotten to
teach them to *want* to read.

If a nation doesn't read much, it doesn't know much. Thomas Jefferson explained the danger in that when he wrote: "If a nation expects to
be ignorant and free, in a state of civilization, it expects what never was
and never will be."[29]

An ignorant but entertained populace is especially dangerous in a
democracy, where the ignorant majority—basing their votes on thirty-
second TV commercials—can outvote the educated minority. Similarly,

ignorant jurors will find legal arguments and DNA-testing too complicated to understand and will subsequently vote their prejudices in the
jury room. Such a situation puts our entire society and way of life at
risk, not just the gross national product.

So where do we go from here? We follow the advice of the man who
founded compulsory education back in the 1830s, Horace Mann: "Men,"
he wrote, "are cast iron; but children are wax."

We begin with the "wax"—children—and we use the findings of the
Commission on Reading to shape them: We read aloud to them throughout the grades. Simple. And unlike most reforms, it will not increase the
tax rate one percent!

Reading Facts of Life

What is it about this simple act of reading aloud that accounts for its
success? How could such a simple habit create what billions of workbook pages could not?

We read to children for all the same reasons you talk with children:
to reassure, to entertain, to inform or explain, to arouse curiosity, to
inspire. But in reading aloud, you also:

- Condition the child to associate reading with pleasure;
- Create background knowledge;
- And provide a reading role model.

Let's look at how we create lifetime readers.

There are two basic reading "facts of life" that are largely ignored in
many education circles; yet without these principles, little else will work
in education.

Reading Fact No. 1: *Human beings are pleasure-centered.*
Reading Fact No. 2: *Reading is an accrued skill.*

Each feeds off the other. *Human beings are pleasure-centered.* Human
beings voluntarily will do over and over *only* that which brings them
pleasure. If we hate the taste of something, we don't eat it or drink it.
People who hate mowing the lawn look for excuses to avoid mowing
the lawn. But if we *like* something, we go to great lengths to do it, eat
it, or drink it. Far from being a theory, this is a physiological fact and is
reinforced by the discovery in the 1950s of "pleasure" and "unpleasure"

WHY READ ALOUD? **9**

centers in the brain. When our senses send electrical messages to either of these centers, we respond positively or negatively.

We all know the meaning of pleasure, but what exactly is "unpleasure"? It is not the same as pain. Most of us can go weeks without experiencing a moment of pain. "Unpleasure," on the other hand, is far more common and therefore a force to be reckoned with in education. "Unpleasure" is the uneasy feeling you have before a dreaded appointment with the dentist, the feeling you have when you are very hungry or thirsty, the feeling a naughty child experiences while sitting isolated in a chair for a "time out." It's not pain but it's not pleasure either—it's "unpleasure," and it is essential to understand its motivational relationship to reading.

One science writer explained it this way: "Much human behavior is more easily understood when we bear in mind that we have two motivational systems which can be in opposition. We constantly trade off losses and gains: the effort of climbing a mountain against the pleasure of reaching the top."[30] In the case of reading, the effort in sitting still and decoding all those words against the pleasure of a satisfying story.

Indeed, the eminent animal psychologist Theodore Schneirla of the American Museum of Natural History went so far as to reduce all behavior to two simple responses: approach and withdrawal. We approach what causes pleasure, and we withdraw from what causes unpleasure or pain.[31]

These are also the sustaining principles of advertising: Promote the pleasures, downplay the unpleasures.

Every time we read to a child, we're sending a "pleasure" message to the child's brain. You could even call it a commercial, conditioning the child to associate books and print with pleasure. There are, however, "unpleasures" associated with reading and school. The learning experience can be tedious or boring, threatening, and without meaning. There are endless hours of worksheets (a thousand a school year for most elementary students), hours of intensive phonics instruction, public performance that risks embarrassment (round-robin reading in front of the class), and hours of unconnected test questions. If a child never or seldom experiences the "pleasures" of reading and meets only the "unpleasures," then the natural reaction will be withdrawal. Which brings us to Reading Fact No. 2.

Reading is an accrued skill. That means reading is like riding a bicycle, driving a car, or sewing: in order to get better at it you must do it. And the more you read, the better you get at it; and the better you get at it, the more you like it; and the more you like it, the more you do it and the better you get at it, ad infinitum.[32] Major reading research in the last twenty-five years confirms this simple formula—regardless of sex, race, nationality, or socioeconomic background. Students who read the most, read the best, achieve the most, and stay in school the longest. Conversely, those who don't read much *cannot* get better at it. And most Americans (children and adults) don't read much, and therefore aren't very good at it.[33] Why don't they read much? Because of Reading Fact No. 1 (human beings are pleasure-centered). The "unpleasure" messages they received throughout their school years have outweighed the "pleasure messages." They avoid books and print the same way an adult avoids eating greens after being forced to eat overcooked vegetables throughout his childhood.

Who Reads Best and Why?

None of this is theory. It is thoroughly documented in the studies done nationally and internationally over the last twenty-five years, one of the most comprehensive of which was conducted in 1990–91 in thirty-two countries, including Finland, the United States, France, New Zealand, Hong Kong, Spain, East and West Germany, Indonesia, and Venezuela, assessing 210,000 nine- and fourteen-year-olds.[34] Which children read best?

For nine-year-olds, the four top nations and their scores were Finland (569); U.S. (547); Sweden (539); and France (531).

But the U.S.'s position dropped to a tie for eighth when fourteen-year-olds were evaluated. This demonstrates two things: American children *begin* reading on a level that is among the best in the world. But since reading is an accrued skill and since American children appear to do less of it as they grow older, their scores begin to decline when compared with countries where children read more as they mature.

Finland's high reading achievements should give pause to those who think an earlier reading start ("hothousing") will produce better results. There was only three months' difference in age between the first-place Finnish children and the second-place American students. Significantly, the Finnish children were introduced to formal reading instruction only at age seven, two years later than American children, yet they still managed to outscore them by age nine.

Here are two of the factors that produced higher achievements around the world (two others will be found in the library chapter):

- The frequency of teachers reading aloud to students.
- The frequency of SSR (sustained silent reading/pleasure reading in school). Children who had daily SSR periods scored much higher than those who experienced SSR only once a week.

So wherever in the world it is done, in the home or in the classroom, reading aloud serves as a kind of commercial for the pleasures of reading. This in turn serves as a catalyst for the child wanting to read on his own. But it also provides a reading foundation by nurturing the child's listening. *Listening comprehension comes before reading comprehension.* Take, for example, the word "enormous." If a child has never heard the word "enormous," he'll never say the word. And if he's neither heard it nor said it, imagine the difficulty when it's time to read it and write it. The listening vocabulary is the reservoir of words that feeds the reading vocabulary pool.

Background Knowledge

Most teachers are aware of how "background knowledge" works, but few parents understand its importance. Background knowledge is the tool we use to make sense of what we see, hear, and read. Most of the mental energy required in reading, let's say, a recipe for brownies, is divided between three activities: (1) decoding the words you are reading; (2) recalling your background knowledge of cooking; and (3) comparing the new knowledge with the background knowledge.[35]

If a person's background knowledge (which includes vocabulary words) is shallow or faulty, then the new material—even if read correctly—will not make sense. For someone unfamiliar with recipes, a brownie recipe can be as difficult as Latin. The less we know about a subject, the slower we read, and the less we understand.

That is one reason why children who read the most (and/or who travel the most) are the most well-rounded students in the classroom. They bring the largest amount of background knowledge to the table and thus understand more of what the teacher or the textbook is teaching. When students at the University of Virginia, ranked among the best in the United States, had to read sections of Hegel's *Metaphysics*, their speed and comprehension slowed considerably. But they had no difficulty in reading an account of Lee's surrender at Appomattox, Virginia —because they had background knowledge of the persons, places, and events involved in the latter reading.

On the other hand, students at a community college in Richmond, Virginia, experienced comprehension problems with even the Appomattox account. Researchers found most of the students were not only ignorant of Generals Grant and Lee, but of the name "Appomattox" as well. And these were students living in the state of Virginia![36]

Even a newspaper becomes difficult reading without background knowledge. For example, one randomly chosen edition of the *Los Angeles Times* produced three items that would have been inaccessible to someone without background knowledge:

1. A "Peanuts" cartoon in which Charlie Brown is reading to Sally: ". . . But David won the fight when he hit Goliath in the head with a stone . . ." To which Sally replies, "What did Goliath's mom say about that?"
2. Sports columnist Jim Murray, writing about Bob Beamon's historic · long jump in the 1968 Olympics: "Beamon was in the air just shorter than the Wright Brothers."
3. The headline above an editorial page column: "Beware the Trojan Horse in INF 'Inspections.' "

Without background knowledge, you cannot understand the editorial page, the sports page, or even the comics page. If you don't know the story of David and Goliath, or of the Wright Brothers, or of the Trojan Horse, you are not going to understand any of those references. The expression that was coined for this situation is "I don't get it!" The more Americans "don't get it," the deeper our troubles become.

An important part of background knowledge is familiarity with the background words. A little girl in Arizona may not have ever heard the words "Paris," "vines," and "appendix," but after experiencing Ludwig Bemelmans' *Madeline* she will have these as part of her background knowledge. Children who have been read to come to books with a larger inventory of sounds, words, and experiences—and thus hold an advantage. Reading and background knowledge feed off each other. The larger your vocabulary, the easier it is to understand what you are reading. And the more you read, the larger your vocabulary grows.[37]

Reading Commercials

Each time you read aloud to a child or class, you offer yourself as a role model. One of the early and primary abilities of children is imitation.[38] They imitate much of what they see and hear, and it is this ability that allows a fifteen-month-old child to say his first words. By age two, the average child expands his vocabulary to include nearly three hundred words. That figure is more than tripled again in the next year, at the end of which the child already understands two-thirds to three-quarters of the words he will use in future daily life.[39] Once he learns to talk, he will average as many as ten new words a day—not one of which is on a flashcard.[40] Much of that pace is determined, however, by the amount and richness of the language he hears.

Most young parents are unaware of their role as prime models for language; they think children are somehow programmed to speak the language automatically. Most, however, express surprise at how quickly the child imitates what he sees on television—especially the commercials. No matter how often children see a particular commercial, the same fascination is reflected in their eyes each time.

The commercials are carefully calculated to have just that effect. Advertising agencies pay upwards of $50,000 a minute to ensure that your child is enraptured by the commercial. That enchantment is based upon an unofficial but guiding formula devised in the 1950s:

1. Send your message to the child when he or she is still at a receptive age. Don't wait until he's seventeen to try to sell him chocolate breakfast cereal. Get him when he's five or six years old.
2. Make sure the message has enough action and sparkle in it to catch and hold the child's attention. Avoid dullness.
3. Make the message brief enough to whet the child's appetite, to make him want to see and hear it again and again. It should be finished before the child becomes bored.

We would do well to learn from Madison Avenue and adapt the formula to sell a product called READING:

1. Read to children while they are still young enough to want to imitate what they are seeing and hearing.
2. Make sure the readings are interesting and exciting enough to hold their interest while you are building up their imaginations.
3. Keep the initial readings short enough to fit their attention spans and gradually lengthen both.

Neither books nor people have Velcro sides—we don't naturally attach to each other. In the beginning there must be a bonding agent—parent, relative, neighbor, teacher, or librarian—someone who attaches child to book.

None of this is complicated. Anyone who can read can do it with a child, and even illiterates can do it with the right technology (like books on tape from the library). And when you look at all the arguments in its favor, how could we *not* read aloud to children? Nonetheless, the Carnegie Foundation found that "only half of infants and toddlers are routinely read to by their parents, and many parents do not engage in other activities to stimulate their child's intellectual development. It is not surprising, then, that teachers report that 35 percent of American kindergarten children arrive at school unprepared to learn."[41]

Nor does the pattern improve much with the child's age. Looking at children in general and not just toddlers, a 1990 survey showed only 20 percent of parents had a daily involvement with reading to their child; if you include the ones who involved themselves two to three times a week, the figure improves to only 42 percent.[42]

What keeps us from doing it? For some people, it appears too simple and too pleasurable to be effective. I can guarantee, if reading aloud cost $129, we'd have it half the homes in America, and if the kids hated it, we'd have it in every classroom!

The "Coppedge Effect"

For the child who is not read to in the home, the first meeting with meaningful print comes in school. Usually that is when he has his first taste of reading "unpleasure" as he goes into business for himself—sound by sound, syllable by syllable, word by word—learning how to read. The danger is that, with nothing to compare it to, the child begins to think *this* is what reading is all about: skill sheets, workbooks, flash cards, and test scores. And those are not motivators. Have you ever heard of a parent who walked into a child's room late at night and found the child in bed, under the covers, with a flashlight—and a workbook?

Children cannot fall in love with drill and skill because they are lifeless. But not pointless. Initially, worksheets were created as an assessment tool—to help the teacher assess who understood the lesson and who didn't. So she passed out the sheets, collected them, and corrected them. At that point she knew that "Janie," "Tommy," and "Anthony" didn't understand. But in order to work individually with those three, she had to find something to keep the rest of the class busy—so she passed out more worksheets. Perhaps if there were not such a universal prejudice against pleasure in the classroom in those days, she might have hit upon the idea of letting the class read for their enjoyment.

So what began as an intelligent assessment tool degenerated into a crowd-control device. And as class size grew, so too did the worksheets. By the 1980s, the average elementary school child was spending 70 percent of the school day doing "seat work" with 1,000 worksheets a year (about six a day).[43] So by fourth grade, the student had already begun to think that worksheets are what reading is all about.

The danger in such thinking is what I call the "Coppedge Effect." One day I was having lunch with Rex Coppedge, a retiree in Plano, Texas. He couldn't make up his mind about what to order and I suggested the chicken. He looked at me over his menu and scowled. "Never eat it. I hate chicken."

He hates chicken? What's to hate? I could understand hating Italian or Mexican food, even seafood. But chicken? There's not enough taste to hate. As we waited for our food to arrive, I asked him why he hated chicken. This is what he told me:

"I grew up in Bonham, Texas, where my grandfather was a former Methodist circuit rider and a distinguished member of the Methodist community. Every Sunday the church elders would descend on Grandfather's home for a chicken dinner. Now, I was an only child, and as such I expected to be as important on Sundays as I was during the week at home. But not so. Every Sunday I would be shunted into the kitchen to eat among the chicken smells, away from the adults." The more Rex Coppedge came to associate his isolation with the smell of chicken, the more he grew to hate chicken. And so it is with children who come to associate worksheets or intensive phonics drills or book reports with reading. The end result can easily be a lifelong loss of reading appetite.

Nonworking Worksheets

The most frustrating aspect of all this is that educational research has shown for nearly twenty-five years that worksheets don't work, that there is no correlation between the number of worksheets a student does in school and how good a reader the child eventually becomes.[44] Nonetheless, many schools continue to ignore the research. School districts like Dallas advise principals that a school of 500 students should plan for 60,000 sheets of paper for duplication of worksheets each month.[45]

Since 1972, the National Assessment of Educational Progress (NAEP) has tracked the reading scores of fourth-, eighth-, and twelfth-graders. They have found the students who scored highest were the ones who were taught with trade books (as opposed to basal textbooks) and those who did the most pleasure reading. With those findings in mind, how are we supposed to react to NAEP's 1992 report that found 41 percent of the fourth-graders were below even the *minimal* level of reading achievement, one-third of all students were using workbooks and worksheets on a daily basis, and more than 50 percent of the fourth-graders had no regularly scheduled SSR time?[46]

The lack of SSR time and the continued reliance upon worksheets to improve student reading skills is like the drunk looking for his keys under the streetlight. He knows he didn't lose them there—but the light is better. We know the scores haven't risen with worksheet use—but they're easier for teachers to use. And parents don't help matters when they complain to the teacher, "Jessica brought home only five worksheets last week. Don't they have reading anymore?"

For the moment, let's put aside what this costs in the way of potential readers slipping down the education drain. What do worksheets cost in tax dollars? In 1989, three researchers at the State University of New York at Albany tabulated the costs of one year's worth of worksheet instruction for a second-grade child. Not including the cost of the school building's utilities (heat, etc.) and the salary of the teacher, it still came to an average of $59.98 per child. The researchers' conclusion was that most schools find it easier to make 25 copies of a piece of paper than to purchase books. The approximately $60 spent on worksheets could purchase 20 children's trade paperbacks for the child, or 500 for the entire class.[47]

When parents and educators wonder why the students' scores don't improve, even when they are placed in remedial classes, they need to know how that time is spent: Remedial readers spend more time doing seat work and reading exercises aloud to the teacher than do better readers, and they spend less time reading without interruptions than do better students;[48] the pattern persists into the secondary level, where remedial eighth- and ninth-graders do grammar exercises 2.6 times more often, write reports 2.4 times more often, and fill in blanks 5 times more often than do students in classes of high achievers.[49]

The end result is what researchers call the "Matthew effect": Rich readers get richer and poor readers get poorer. "Matthew" refers to the Gospel According to Matthew: "For unto every one that hath shall be given, and he shall have abundance: but for him that hath not shall be taken away even that which he hath."[50] So we're back to that formula again: You can't get better at reading unless you read, but we keep putting impediments in the path of slow readers and wonder why they're so slow. Even if they wanted to, who could improve with all those questions and assessments hanging around their necks?

Therefore, if we truly wish to revolutionize American education, we must put far more pleasure into the reading experience. And the most effective and time-honored way of doing that is by reading aloud to the child, the family, and the class.

The education of a parent significantly affects—for better or worse—a child's school success. Children of high school dropouts do worse than those whose parents graduated, and college graduates proportionately produce more college graduates. There are, of course, success stories in which achievers come from poorly educated families, but it is the fact that they beat the odds that makes such stories so inspiring.

What are the stumbling blocks for undereducated parents? Because they haven't experienced school success, they don't know the importance of homework, of being read to, of a library card or books in the home, of a chalkboard or a daily newspaper, of endless conversations with a child. Children who achieve *usually* come from such advantages and, in turn, tend to do these same things with *their* children when the time arrives. We become a chip off the old block by hanging around with the old block.

Chips Off the Old Block

My favorite example of this is a remarkable study of thirty men who were identified as growing up in working-class, blue-collar families: Fifteen of them eventually became college professors and fifteen remained in blue-collar careers. In hand-picking the thirty, the researchers made sure all came from similar socioeconomic childhoods with similar family traumas (family alcoholism; parent death; divorce; etc.).

If the thirty men began life in similar circumstances, how to explain the fifteen who rose so far above their families' status? In extensive interviews with the thirty, significant differences appeared regarding books and reading as children.

- 12 of the 15 professors were read to or told stories by their parents, compared with only 4 of the blue-collar workers.
- 14 out of the 15 professors came from homes where books and print were plentiful; among the blue-collar men, only 4 had books.
- 13 of the professors' mothers and 12 of the fathers were identified as frequent readers of newspapers, magazines, or books; blue-collar workers identified 6 mothers and 4 fathers.
- All of the 15 professors, compared with only 3 of the blue-collar workers, were encouraged to read as children.

A significant part of the study was what the fifteen professors found motivating or interesting in their childhood reading. They found answers or information relating to problems in their lives. The book, in a manner of speaking, became food for the starving child. Typical in this respect was Professor Respondent #2, "a sociologist, whose mother died when he was seven years old with the result that the respondent was put into an orphanage where he stayed until he was 'on his own' at about age 17. This respondent experienced great anxiety at being put into an orphanage and he identified the chief problem as being the 'uncertainty of what happens to orphans.' "

He explained: "All of a sudden my mother was dead and I was in this place. I felt I didn't know what would happen to me. I was scared and had continually in my mind the question of what would happen to me and to others in that place. What happened to kids in orphanages?"

"In the orphanage library, at about age 8, this respondent discovered the Horatio Alger books. The discovery had a profound impact on him because all of a sudden he realized that he could create his own life even if he was in an orphanage. He had been looking for an answer to the question of what would become of him and now he *realized that what would become of him was up to him.* Horatio Alger books provided him with the *model of a boy whose life was his own* and who could create it as he chose."[51]

Such life stories remind us how easy it is to overlook the very purpose of literature: to provide meaning in our lives. That, of course, is the purpose of all education. Child psychologist Bruno Bettelheim says that finding this meaning is the greatest need and most difficult achievement for any human being at any age. Who am I? Why am I here? What can I be?[52] In his widely acclaimed *The Uses of Enchantment*, Bettelheim writes that the two factors most responsible for giving the child the belief that he can make a significant contribution to life are parents/teachers and literature.

Literature is considered such an important medium because—more than television, more than films, more than art or overhead projectors —literature brings us closest to the human heart. And of the two forms of literature (fiction and nonfiction), the one that brings us closest and presents the meaning of life most clearly to the child is fiction. That is one reason most of the recommendations for read-alouds at the back of this book are fiction.

What is it about fiction that brings it so close to the human heart? Three-time Pulitzer Prize–winning novelist and poet Robert Penn Warren said that we read fiction because:

- We like it.
- There is conflict in it—and conflict is at the center of life.
- Its conflict wakes us up from the tedium of everyday life.
- It allows us to vent our emotions with tears, laughter, love, and hate.
- We hope its story will give us a clue to our own life story.
- It releases us from life's pressures by allowing us to escape into other people's lives.[53]

From Worst to Best

Just as parents in low-income situations need to be reminded that their task is not insurmountable, so too do educators who work with children coming from those homes. Reading achievement and "pleasure" do not have to be mutually exclusive. During his ten years as principal of Boston's Solomon Lewenberg Middle School, Thomas P. O'Neill, Jr., and his faculty proved it. The pride of Boston's junior high schools during the 1950s and early 1960s, Lewenberg subsequently suffered the ravages of urban decay, and by 1984, with the city's worst academic record and Boston teachers calling it "Loonybin" instead of Lewenberg, the school was earmarked for closing. But first, Boston officials would give it one last chance.

The reins were handed to O'Neill (no relation to the former Speaker of the House), an upbeat first-year principal and former high school English teacher whose experience there had taught him to "sell" the pleasures and importance of reading.

The first thing he did was abolish the school's intercom system ("As a teacher I'd always swore someday I'd rip the thing off the wall. Now I could do it legally") and then set about establishing structure, routine, and discipline. "That's the easy part. What happens *after* is the important part—READING. It's the key element in the curriculum. IBM can teach our graduates to work the machine, but *we* have to teach them to read the manual." In O'Neill's first year sustained silent reading (see Chapter 8) was instituted for the nearly four hundred pupils and faculty for the last ten minutes of the day—during which everyone in the school read for pleasure. Each teacher was assigned a room—much to the consternation of some who felt those last ten minutes could be better used to clean up the shop or gym. "Prove to me on paper," O'Neill challenged them, "that you are busier than I am, and I'll give you the ten minutes to clean." He had no takers.

Within a year, critics became supporters and the school was relishing the quiet time that ended the day. The books that had been started during SSR were often still being read by students filing out to buses—in stark contrast to former dismissal scenes that bordered on chaos.

The next challenge was to ensure that each sixth-, seventh-, and eighth-grade student not only *saw* an adult reading each day, but also *heard* one. Faculty members were assigned a classroom and the school day began with ten minutes of reading aloud—to complement the silent ending. Soon reading aloud began to inspire awareness, and new titles sprouted during SSR. In effect, the faculty was doing what the great art schools have always done: providing "life" models from which to draw.

It's nice they were all enjoying themselves, you say, but what about the reading scores? In the first year, Lewenberg's scores were up; the second year, not only did the scores climb but so, too, did student enrollment, in response to the school's new reputation. By 1988, Lewenberg's 570 students had the highest reading scores in the city of Boston, there was a fifteen-page waiting list of children who wanted to attend, and O'Neill's approach was offered by *Time* as a viable alternative to physical intimidation, in its cover story on Joe Clark, the bullhorn- and bat-toting principal in Paterson, New Jersey.[54] In 1995, O'Neill became principal of Bigelow Middle School in Newton, Massachusetts.

Lewenberg's success was no accident. When you consider the broad areas stimulated by reading aloud, one can only wonder why it is not done in all classrooms. It exposes the student to:

- A positive reading role model
- New information

- The pleasures of reading
- Rich vocabulary
- Good grammar
- A broader variety of books than he'd choose on his own
- Richly textured lives outside his own experience
- The English language spoken in a manner distinctly different from that in television sitcoms or MTV.

At the same time, the child's imagination is stimulated, attention span stretched, listening comprehension improved, emotional development nurtured, the reading-writing connection established, and, where they exist, negative attitudes reshaped to positive ones. Outside of all that, reading aloud doesn't do much!

Portraits of Four Student Families

If you read it carefully, the most insightful and detailed portrait of America can be found in a daily newspaper. Beside its lurid or dramatic headlines are the minutiae that make up who and what we are as a people. Most of us are not the murderers or politicians pictured in the headlines; our portraits are painted in the small stories—birth announcements, obituaries, want ads, personals, honor roll reports, wedding announcements, and graduation stories. That's why I love to read local newspapers when I'm traveling.

One evening after lecturing in New Jersey, I was paging through a local newspaper and in the space of a few pages I encountered four young people who represent the hope and despair in America today.[55] They also happened to exemplify the dos and don'ts of reading.

The day's lead story was a profile of two high school students, written on the eve of the fortieth anniversary of the 1954 Supreme Court desegregation ruling, *Brown vs. Board of Education.* The two boys, who had known each other through sports for years, were competing against each other in a local track meet. In a few years, they will be competing for employment. In each case, there will be winners and losers, depending on the talents one brings to the field.

One of the students, Darnell, came from an inner-city community, attended a high school that was 93 percent black; the other, Mark, lived six miles away and attended a school that was 97 percent white. The black community's average income was $20,754, the white community's was $43,601.

Forty percent of Darnell's classmates, including himself, took at least one remedial class. Although his school provided no advanced placement (college level) classes, it did broadcast "Channel One," the twelve-and-a-half-minute daily television news and features show. His school's graduation rate was 62.8 percent.

Mark, on the other hand, was in a school with a 91.6 percent graduation rate; he took nine straight classes a day, including three advanced placement classes and no remedial classes. The nine classes allowed him no time for lunch, but that was Mark's choice, not the school's. "Channel One" was not broadcast.

Obviously, there were dramatic differences in the quality and quantity of education offered to these two students. Despite *Brown vs. Board of Education*, they were still separate and unequal. But that inequality began long before each reached school age. It began in their homes. Mark was the older of two children and lived with his mother (a real estate broker and former teacher) and father (a math teacher). Ten years earlier, Darnell's mother had determined she was unable to raise him and his five brothers and sisters and turned them over to her mother-in-law, already the mother of six children, who were older. She had cared for them ever since and recently adopted four of them. Her home, "a gathering place" for family (including twenty-one grandchildren and two great-grandchildren), was obviously a place of deep caring. But was it a place that encouraged learning as Mark's did?

Mark grew up in a home that was both nurturing and structured. Television was strictly monitored and limited. Although there were always two television sets in the house (family room and living room), he saw little of it in his early years, outside of PBS's *Mr. Rogers, Sesame Street,* and *1-2-3 Contact.* As he grew older, his school schedule left little time for television. His mother was a firm believer in early bedtimes for children, as well as in the power of books. Consequently, Mark and his sister found a new book under their pillows on most Friday evenings or Saturday mornings when they were growing up. He also had a bedroom and desk of his own.

Because of the crowded conditions in Darnell's home, he had no place upstairs where he could sit and do homework. Upstairs he could only sit on his bed. Downstairs there was a table, but it was surrounded by four television sets in the room, two of which were running separate shows on the occasion of the reporter's visit (*Barney* and a talk show featuring a discussion about men who date other women when their wives get too fat).

The front-page article about Darnell noted that his nightly homework amounted to half an hour, which he did while surrounded by the constant blare of television.

Continuing to page through the day's newspaper, I found an article four pages later about a New Jersey high school senior, Thomas J. Farmer, who had just graduated with an associate's degree from Brookdale Community College, one month *before completing high school.*

Thomas's mother was a former teacher and his father a doctor. An exceptionally bright student, he had been taking college courses of one kind or another since he was in seventh grade. He did four hours of homework a night. Thomas could name a favorite author, favorite composer, even a favorite science writer, but not a favorite television show. He was class president, prom king, newspaper editor, and an Eagle Scout, and he took piano lessons. His four siblings had similar success stories.

What's the secret? What was the parents' role in raising such exceptional children? Was it in the genes? What they did was simple and cheap—things that could be done by almost any family, regardless of their income. First, they limited television viewing for all their children. There were no private TV sets in the bedrooms. There was one in the living room but this was rigged so it could be turned off from the parents' bedroom.

Another secret was to find out what interested each child and then explore it together as often as possible. The local free public library became a weekly, and often daily, experience in the life of the children. Indeed, when he was in sixth grade, Thomas's mother took him to the library *every day* for an hour. Was that inconvenient at times? Certainly, but good parenting is not about convenience.

Anyone who waits for the government or the local schools to break the cycle of inequality within our communities or homes is going to have a long wait. It probably won't happen even in our lifetimes. On the other hand, if you start in the home and begin with reading, you can change it in less than a lifetime. Students who succeed in school don't drop out of school. They learn more, earn more, and even live longer.[56]

And what does it cost? Some time to read to a child, a library card, some space the child can call his or her own—a small corner for an old table, some used books, and a limit on distractions like television. Unfortunately, many low-income parents or care-givers are unaware of the impact of such things. They missed out on this parenting when they were children, and the problem is perpetuated generation after generation. And that is where parent education can play an essential role. But it is also where teachers can play a pivotal role as well.

For the child whose parents cannot or will not do the job, the classroom teacher is his last hope. Teachers who complain about unqualified parents must be reminded there is one place where we have required attendance for all parents: your classroom. All of *tomorrow's* parents are sitting in your classrooms today. By law, tomorrow's parents *must* attend first grade, second, third, fourth, fifth, etc. If somewhere in those required classes we turn the child into a lifetime reader, we greatly enhance the chances of filling the void left by dysfunctional homes—which now approach the 30th percentile. Once children become confirmed and loyal readers, they hold the power not only to educate themselves but also to overcome the most deprived circumstances—as in the case of Rodney Snell, the last student I found in that day's newspaper.

His story was buried in the news article on the graduation at Brookdale Community College (the same school that graduated Thomas Farmer). Pictured with the article was the college president and one of its distinguished new graduates, twenty-eight-year-old Rodney T. Snell. Like Darnell, Snell was black and raised by grandparents—former Georgia cotton workers.

He had been elected to give the graduation address for his Brookdale classmates and he was an obvious choice: he had won more than forty awards while leading Brookdale's formidable speech team to a national "top ten" ranking, even beating Ivy League colleges. He would *not* have been an obvious choice eleven years ago when his high school handed him an equivalency diploma in exchange for quickly removing himself and his troublesome ways from the school. Snell's high school days had been filled with truancy, drinking, and smoking pot with "a bad crowd," much to his grandparents' dismay. They'd been warning him since junior high that he was heading down a dead-end street but, like many teens in his situation, he ignored their entreaties.

The years after high school were spent selling clothes and records, getting fired, and collecting unemployment. Finally, at age twenty-five, he began to see the wisdom in his grandparents' warnings and took some courses at Brookdale. "I wanted to do something with my life," he says. The newspaper article noted that he would be attending Emerson College in Boston to study English, with an eye on becoming a college professor.

"Wait a minute," I thought. One doesn't simply step from the unemployment line with a courtesy GED to the status of commencement star. Something is missing here, I said to myself. And when I interviewed Rodney Snell, I got the rest of the story.

In stentorian tones and with a wisdom that belied his age, he told me about being raised by his grandparents as the only child in a lower-middle-class family, nestled in Long Branch, a blue-collar, largely Italian-American community on the New Jersey shore. He seldom saw his grandparents reading anything, and there were no magazines or news-papers in the home.

But in school he learned to read. And he learned in a way that brought him more pleasure than pain. Reading quickly became a favorite activity. "One big factor in that early addiction to reading may have been that I had no regular access to television until I was twelve years old," he related. Up to that time, the only television set in his home was in his grandparents' bedroom, and that was largely off-limits to him. When they finally bought a television for the family room, Rodney was entering junior high, and he quickly became addicted to it; his schoolwork began to decline.

Between first and sixth grades, though, he was a devoted reader. He cannot point to any one reason other than the fact it brought him plea-sure, though he credits his aunt Jane with keeping him supplied with books of his own. His family traveled often and when they stopped along the way, someone usually had enough money to buy him a comic book to pass the time. Fortunately for Snell, the love of reading had been planted early enough to take deep root. It would stay with him even during his troubled adolescence, and his bedroom was always filled with books.

"My problems in junior high and high school really boiled down to the structure," he said in hindsight. "We were shuttled from one class to another, no one paying any individual attention to us. I just wanted someone to pay attention to me, and no one in school would do that. So I acted up to get attention—the wrong kind.

"But I never stopped reading," he explained. Asked where he devel-oped a vocabulary that would allow him to win college speech awards, he replied immediately, "Reading and reading and reading."

From Homeless to Harvard

A freak situation, you might say. Then consider this last example, carried by the national news services a few weeks later. It is the tale of

Lauralee Summer, a shy, fatherless child who spent a major portion of her childhood in homeless shelters, as well as in foster homes. Even when she was able to attend school, her home situation separated her from classmates, leaving her so isolated she often chose not to attend school at all. What put her on the news wires was that she had just been accepted at Harvard University.

Lauralee's mother was a nurse's aide and, by the child's own description, "a dreamer with many castles in the air, but few foundations under them." One of her mother's few foundations, however, was a respect for books. "She was about twenty months old," recalled the mother, "when I began reading to her every single night" from a well-worn volume of nursery rhymes, the only book they owned.

This early pleasure connection with print was powerful enough to motivate Lauralee to spend the money from her fourth birthday on a "see and say" book she eventually used to teach herself to read. As she and her mother moved from state to state, they always sought out the public library, and the child surrounded herself with borrowed books. When adults would awaken early in the morning at a Salvation Army shelter, their movements and the lights would awaken Lauralee. At that point she would simply pick up one of her books and begin her day's reading. The voracious appetite for print continued right through her high school years, which she spent in Quincy, Massachusetts, living with her mother in the home of a woman who took them in as part of a church program. Beyond the emotional grounding it provided her in a transient childhood, Lauralee's reading allowed her to finish sixteenth in a class of 292 students at Quincy High School, and her SAT score was 1,460 out of a possible 1,600. Another foundation in her homeless childhood was religion, and she has chosen comparative religion as a major at Harvard.[57]

As the above examples demonstrate, language is the basic ingredient of school and community success. And nothing nurtures language skills as well as reading aloud to a child—regardless of the family income or the parent's education level.

2

When to Begin
Read-Aloud

*In every task the most important thing is the beginning . . .
especially when you deal with anything young and tender.*

—Plato,
The Republic

"**H**ow old must a child be before you start reading to him?" That is
the question I am most often asked by parents. The next is: "When is
the child too old to be read to?"

In answer to the first question, I ask one of my own. "When did you
start *talking* to the child? Did you wait until he was six months old?"

"We started talking to him the day he was born," parents respond.

"And what language did your child speak the day he was born? English? Japanese? Italian?" They're about to say English when it dawns on
them the child didn't speak *any* language yet.

"Wonderful!" I say. "There you were holding that newborn infant in
your arms, whispering, 'We love you, Cindy. Daddy and I think you are
the most beautiful baby in the world.' You were speaking multisyllable

words and complex sentences in a foreign language to a child who didn't understand one word you were saying! And you never thought twice about doing it. But most people can't imagine *reading* to that same child. And that's sad. If a child is old enough to talk to, she's old enough to be read to. It's the same language."

Obviously, from birth to six months of age we are concerned less with "understanding" than with "conditioning" the child to your voice and the sight of books. Dr. T. Berry Brazelton, the longtime chief of the child development unit of Boston Children's Hospital Medical Center, says that new parents' most critical task during these early stages is learning how to calm the child, how to bring it under control, so he or she can begin to look around and listen when you pass on information.[1] Much the same task confronts the classroom teacher as she faces a new class each September.

We have long known that the human voice is one of the most powerful tools a parent has for calming a child. And what many previously suspected now has been established in new research indicating that the voice's influence starts *even earlier than birth*. University of North Carolina psychologist Anthony DeCasper and his colleagues explored the effects of reading to children in utero, thinking that infants might be able to recognize something they had heard prenatally. He asked thirty-three pregnant women to recite a specific paragraph of a children's story three times a day for the last six weeks of pregnancy. Three different paragraphs were used among the thirty-three women, but each woman used just one passage for the entire recitation period. Fifty-two hours after birth, the newborns were given a special nipple and earphones through which they could hear a woman (not the mother) reciting all three paragraphs. By measuring each child's sucking rate during the listening period, researchers concluded the infants recalled and preferred the passages their mothers had recited during the third trimester.[2]

"The babies' reactions to the stories had been influenced by earlier exposure," DeCasper concluded. "That constitutes learning in a very general way." In a similar experiment with reading to fetuses during the two and one-half months before birth, DeCasper found the child's heartbeat increased with a new story, decreased with the familiar one.[3] Both of these experiments clearly establish that a child becomes familiar with certain sounds while in utero and begins associating those tones with comfort and security. The baby is being conditioned—his first class in learning. Imagine how much can be accomplished when a child can see and touch the book, understand the words, and feel the reader. The possibilities are limitless—as the case of Cushla Yeoman demonstrates.

Cushla, Jennifer, and Steven

In *Cushla and Her Books*, author Dorothy Butler describes how Cushla's parents began reading aloud to her when she was four months of age.[4] By nine months the child was able to respond to the sight of certain books and convey to her parents that these were her favorites. By age five she had taught herself to read.

What makes Cushla's story so dramatic is that she was born with chromosome damage, which caused deformities of the spleen, kidney, and mouth cavity. It also produced muscle spasms—which prevented her from sleeping for more than two hours a night or holding anything in her hand until she was three years old—and hazy vision beyond her fingertips.

Until she was three, the doctors diagnosed Cushla as "mentally and physically retarded" and recommended that she be institutionalized. Her parents, after seeing her early responses to books, refused; instead, they put her on a dose of fourteen read-aloud books a day. By age five, Cushla was found by psychologists to be well above average in intelligence and a socially well-adjusted child.

The story of Cushla and her family has appeared in each edition of *The Read-Aloud Handbook* and each time it was my hope it would inspire an unknown reader someplace. Thus it was with tremendous pleasure that I one day read this letter from Marcia Thomas, then of Memphis, Tennessee:

> *Our daughter Jennifer was born in September 1984. One of the first gifts we received was a copy of* The Read-Aloud Handbook. *We read the introductory chapters and were very impressed by the story of Cushla and her family. We decided to put our daughter on a "diet" of at least ten books a day. She had to stay in the hospital for seven weeks as a result of a heart defect and corrective surgery. However, we began reading to her while she was still in intensive care; and when we couldn't be there, we left story tapes and asked the nurses to play them for her.*
>
> *For the past seven years we have read to Jennifer at every opportunity. She is now in the first grade and is one of the best readers*

in her class. She consistently makes 100 on reading tests and has a very impressive vocabulary. She can usually be found in the reading loft at school during free time, and at home she loves to sit with my husband or me and read a book.

What makes our story so remarkable is that Jennifer was born with Down syndrome. At two months of age, we were told Jennifer most likely was blind, deaf, and severely retarded. When she was tested at age four, her I.Q. was 111.

For this edition of my book, I needed Mrs. Thomas' permission to use her letter. Since the family had moved in the intervening years, it took me a while to find them, but finally I did. And on the summer afternoon I called, Jennifer—who was about to enter fourth grade and is reading on grade level—was entertaining her former third-grade teacher for lunch, sharing some of her favorite books.

A Worcester, Massachusetts, newspaper editor once looked at my evening's audience and whispered to me, "Well, here it is—another night and Jim Trelease is out 'saving the saved.' " And he was right. Like a Sunday preacher, I'm often preaching to the converted—the parents and teachers who least need to hear me, the ones who are already reading to their kids. The ones who most need to hear me or read my book—they're usually at the mall or home watching *Wheel of Fortune* or *Hard Copy*. And then along comes a Marcia Thomas.

Or a Geri Kunishima. Of all the parents I've ever had in my audience, the one who *least* needed my message was Geri Kunishima in Honolulu, Hawaii. Nonetheless, there she was in 1992 and again in 1993. A classroom teacher as well as a parent, Geri and her husband, Lindy, have three children—two girls and a boy. Six months after Steven was born, Geri began to suspect something was wrong with him; the doctors told her to relax.

At eighteen months, still unable to walk or talk, the child was found to be suffering from hypoplasia of the vermis. To put it simply, the transmitter for the brain's messages had not developed—and never would. The doctor's verdict left no room for hope. "He will never walk or talk, or do much of anything that requires muscle control. He will be profoundly retarded, ineducable in all but the simplest tasks," the doctor explained, and then suggested eventual institutionalization.

When Geri Kunishima recovered from the initial shock and depression, she recalled that she and Lindy had read aloud to the girls when they were Steven's age. The older daughter, Trudi, claimed to see a spark in the boy's eyes—something waiting to be reached. Maybe a daily read-aloud would help.

So began a nightly program: someone sat and read with Steven each evening while dinner was being prepared. Cushioned by floor pillows that supported his head so he could see the pages, he was read to. Book after book, night after night. Nothing seemed to register. There was no reaction from Steven, just a blank stare.

And then one day, three months later, when Trudi announced it was time for a story, she was amazed to see him begin to pull himself across the floor to the bookcase. Pawing at the books, he smacked one until it opened. Then he stared at the animals on the page. The scene was repeated the following night—same book, same page. "He's got a memory!" the family exulted.

The Kunishimas then increased their efforts. There were more books, and muscle exercise, too. The brain often compensates for damage in one area by opening alternate routes, Geri reasoned, and this may be happening with Steven. His progress was slow and painful, but the work bore fruit. Though unable to speak words at age four and a half, he was speaking a few within a year. And more the next. Walking and school-work amounted to climbing mountains, but the Kunishimas never quit. By age thirteen, Steven was walking and talking, and played a little basketball—though not very well. More important, he was reading and writing—on grade level.

Geri Kunishima didn't need to hear what I was saying in those Hawaii lectures. She and her family were living proof of the power of reading to children.[5] Now if the Yeomans, the Thomases, and the Kunishimas could accomplish all they did with their children, imagine how much can be realized by the average family if they begin reading to a child early and in earnest.

A Baby's Reading Diary

Erin had no idea what a lucky girl she was the day she was born to Linda Kelly-Hassett in 1988—but she soon found out. A few years later, I found out, too, when Erin's mom shared with me her journal of reading experiences. Since I didn't keep such a document with my own children and since Linda began even earlier than I did (ignorant parent that I was back in those days), I think her remarks will speak louder than anything I might write in this space. Linda was a third-grade teacher before Erin was born, and a devoted reader-aloud to her students. Everything she did in class, and recommended to the parents of her students, she applied to Erin. Not every parent has the time to do all that Linda did, but if they did even half as much, all children's futures would be brighter. You should note especially the unforced and gradual manner in which books were introduced to Erin, and the way in which they were tied to everyday events.

> *Erin's first book, on her first day of life, was* Love You Forever, *by Robert Munsch. My husband videotaped me reading it. He was unfamiliar with the story and was moved to tears as we rocked "back and forth, back and forth." That video went to relatives and friends, helping to bring Erin into their lives in a special way, and it also went to my former class of third-graders—planting a seed for the next generation.*
>
> *Erin's first four months saw mostly soft chunky books, board books, and firmer-paged, lift-the-flap books. These were not only read but tasted and enjoyed. When she was four months old she began to enjoy time in her Johnny-Jump-Up, often spending forty-five minutes at a time, two or three times a day, jumping happily to poems, songs, and pop-up books. Over and over we read poems from* Read-Aloud Rhymes for the Very Young, *by Jack Prelutsky, sang along with the* Wee Sing *tapes, and played with books like* Who's Peeking at Me?, *by Kees Moerbeek.*
>
> *The enjoyment of Johnny-Jump-Up diminished around eight months when crawling and seeking her own entertainment took over. She loved tearing paper at this time, so we put out lots of magazines, but only very durable books. At reading time we stayed with the same kind of book until she was around ten months. At this stage, I became so eager to read story books to her that I decided to read these to her while she was in her high chair (so she couldn't tear the pages). It worked beautifully and provided some surprises.*
>
> *For starters, we never had any food battles because I was too busy reading to let myself become overly concerned with her food intake. As I read, she ate her finger foods while I spooned in some baby fruit and veggies. Mealtime was fun, positive, and usually ended with her pointing to the bookshelf and requesting another "boo(k)." This practice set a precedent that has followed through her four years. I continue to read to her at breakfast and lunchtime. When she has friends over, we always have a story or two at snack time. Using big books from my teaching days is a special treat.*

Several memorable events happened during this period of early reading. My husband was transferred to the East Coast and got home every other weekend. Between Erin's tenth and fifteenth months, we were pretty much by ourselves when eating, so mealtime reading grew in length. It was nothing for her to actively listen to stories from 20 to 40 minutes after a meal. A note in my journal for February 4, 1990 reads: "9 books after breakfast; 10 books and 4 poems after lunch; 7 books after dinner." This was not an unusual day's reading.

Ten days later, February 14, 1990, I wrote this entry: "After breakfast, Erin asked for a book. Since we were moving at the end of the month, I read her Goodbye House *by Frank Asch. She kept asking for another book as soon as I finished one. I ended up reading for 75 minutes, covering 25 books. At fourteen months of age she had sustained interest in the stories—actively listening, pointing, saying words, and making sounds.*

"I want to note that all these books were familiar to Erin. She did not immediately take to a new book. I would introduce it to her over a period of days. The first day we would look at the cover and 'talk' about it. On the second day, I would then proceed to read the first page or so. I would read a few more pages each additional day until about the fifth or sixth day, when the book would be familiar enough for me to read it in its entirety.

"Another memorable event occurred a month earlier, when she was thirteen months. On the evening of January 17, 1990, we had a snowstorm. The snow fell in big fluffy flakes and we sat in front of the patio window to watch them. Erin kept raising her arms over her head, indicating that the snow was falling from the sky.

"She ran to the kitchen and pointed to the calendar picture of the dog in the snowstorm. She then ran to the window and pointed to the snow. Then back to the kitchen to point to the calendar. She did this over and over. Finally, tired out, she sat on the floor near the coffee table where I had a book catalog. She saw the small picture advertising The Snowman, *by Raymond Briggs, and pointed it out to me. I remarked, yes, that was a snowman made from snow.*

"I told Erin that we had a copy of the wordless book The Snowman *over on the bookshelf. She got so excited that she actually began to quiver all over. She ran over to me as I got the book down and when I showed her the cover she radiated such delight it was as if the snowman had come to life.*

"Erin reverently took the book from me, held it to her chest, and walked slowly over to the window. For the next twenty minutes we sat at the window, looking through the book and glancing at the falling snow. I will never forget the warmth of that night and how the book made it feel so connected. The Snowman *became a favorite for the next year and hardly a day went by without a telling of the story.*

"Shortly after our move to Pennsylvania, I was reading her The Very Hungry Caterpillar, *by Eric Carle—as I had been doing for the last six months. This time, during the reading of the second sentence—'One Sunday morning the warm sun came up and—pop!—out of the egg came a tiny and very hungry caterpillar'—while I was still forming my mouth to say 'pop,' Erin said the word 'pop!' and with perfect inflection. She was seventeen months that day and it was the start of her inserting words into familiar stories. What an addition to an already pleasant experience."*

Beyond the love of reading nurtured by these parent-child experiences, Erin's verbal skills were growing. She spoke in complete sentences at twenty-one months and had a vocabulary of 1,000 words by twenty-four months—all achieved without flash cards or "drill and skill." Erin's father wasn't excluded from the readings, and the two had a collection of books she labeled "Daddy Books" that became a personal cache.

With all of this reading, Erin's attention span and interests grew by leaps and bounds. By four and a half years of age, she had enjoyed the complete texts of novels like *Charlotte's Web*; *James and the Giant Peach*, by Roald Dahl; the *My Father's Dragon* series, by Ruth Stiles Gannett; the *Mouse and the Motorcycle* series, by Beverly Cleary; every *Littles* book, by John Peterson, that her mother could locate; and three of the *Little House on the Prairie* volumes, by Laura Ingalls Wilder. Family friends noticed Erin's affection for the latter books and made her a complete Laura Ingalls outfit, which she delights in wearing to act out favorite parts from the novels.

Erin's advantages are what the Albany (New York) Area Reading Council had in mind in their little brochure for new parents:

"All babies are born equal. Not one can . . . speak, count, read, or write at birth. . . . But by the time they go to kindergarten they are *not equal!*"[6] The difference, of course, is between the parents who "raise" their children, as opposed to parents who "watch" them grow up.

Pushy Parents: Relax!

Of course, admirable as it might be, such interest in a child's intellectual growth can be taken to extremes. You can expect negative consequences if this interest takes the form of an obsession with teaching your child to read, says Brazelton, who, along with his hospital work, research, and writing, was a practicing pediatrician in Cambridge, Massachusetts, for more than thirty years.

"I've had children in my practice," Brazelton explained to John Merrow in a National Public Radio interview, "who were reading from a dictionary at the age of three and a half or four, and had learned to read and type successfully by age four. But those kids went through a very tough time later on. They went through first grade successfully, but second grade they really bombed out on. And I have a feeling that they'd been pushed so hard from outside to learn to read early, that the cost of it didn't show up until later."

Testimony to the importance of an *unforced* learning schedule in these formative years comes from all corners of the fields of psychology and education—including one that dates back nearly three thousand years: "Avoid compulsion and let early education be a matter of amusement. Young children learn by games; compulsory education cannot remain in the soul," was the advice offered by Plato to parents. Many of the parents who are rushing to buy commercial phonics programs often are ignorant of the fact that most three- and four-year-olds are incapable of making the subtle sound distinctions in intensive phonics instruction. More often than not, the child ends up "barking" at type to please the parent, but feeling like a trained seal. That's hardly a pleasant introduction to the world of print.

None of these experts is saying that "early reading" is intrinsically bad; rather, they feel the early reader should arrive at his skill naturally, on his own, without a structured time each day when the mother or father sits down with him and teaches him letters, sounds, and syllables. The "natural way" is Erin Hassett's way or the way Scout learned in Harper Lee's *To Kill a Mockingbird*—by sitting on the lap of a parent and listening, listening as the parent's finger moves over the pages, until gradually, in the child's own good time, a connection is made between the sound of a certain word and the appearance of certain letters on the page.

The Ultimate Copycats

Whether you are reading to infants or to schoolchildren, each read-aloud feeds the listening vocabulary, which, in turn, feeds listening comprehension, which feeds the speaking, reading, and writing vocabularies. It starts in infancy with hearing and proceeds into school years with writing. Jacques Barzun explained it this way: "Both speech and writing are ultimately copycat experiences—words get in through the ear or eye and come out at the tongue or the end of a pencil."[7] Therefore, the richer the language a person hears and reads, the richer and clearer will be the person's speech and writing. You don't use words you've never heard or read. Simple.

The best "copycats" on the face of the earth are children. Nothing demonstrates it better than the following research project and two anecdotes:

In the first instance, researchers found that deaf babies of deaf parents, having watched their parents using sign language, begin imitating this communication behavior by using significant hand gestures at ten months of age. These hand gestures are used in the same way that hearing children string together certain sounds or noises like "bababababa" or "dadadada." For deaf children, these as yet meaningless gestures would be the equivalent of hearing children's "babbling."[8]

Even our subtlest behavior with print can be absorbed by children. Linda and Frank Van Hoegarden approached me after a lecture one evening at Maerker School in Westmont, Illinois, and told me about their page-ripping daughter, Ann. From the day Ann was born, there had always been a wealth of reading material in the Van Hoegarden home —books, magazines, newspapers. And from the very beginning, her parents read to her. However, at fifteen months of age, she began to exhibit a disturbing habit. She'd pick up books, carefully turn two or three pages, then rip out the next page, throw it aside, turn a few more pages, rip out another page and throw it aside. She did this with books, she did it with magazines, and in each case she did it methodically.

Her parents patiently explained this was "naughty." They went out of their way to demonstrate the gentle way to handle a book. It did no good. As soon as she was alone with a book, she would rip into it with the same enthusiasm and determination. Losing their patience, the parents scolded, "No, Ann. We don't do that with books! No, Ann! That's naughty!" It did no good. They'd heard of children eating books, even ripping pages while trying to turn them, but they couldn't understand a fifteen-month-old ripper who approached the destruction with such *confidence*.

Then late one evening, the parents were relaxing, watching TV, when Linda looked over at Frank and it all came together. There was Frank casually paging through a magazine that had come in the mail that day. He turned a few pages, ripped out one of the stiff advertisement inserts, threw it aside, turned some more pages, and ripped out another. Linda had finally discovered their daughter's "ripping role model."

Reading specialist Theo Spewock does home liaison work with children at risk in poor families near Altoona, Pennsylvania. She reads to the child and demonstrates to the parents how it should be done. In this case, the child was Tyrone, whose father was unemployed most of the time but did manage to pick up some part-time work repairing truck engines. One day Tyrone's mother heard him talking in his bedroom and when she looked in, she saw the boy reading to his trucks, just as he saw his father do. What? You never saw a man reading to his truck? What else would a three-year-old think if he saw his father bent over an engine with a repair manual and talking to himself? He must be reading to his truck!

Everyone's Favorite Word

The most important copycat experience is language, most of which we learn by copying. Consider the most frequently used word in the English language: THE. I always ask my lecture audiences if there is anyone present who thinks this little three-letter word is a difficult word to understand, and out of three hundred people I'll get about five who raise their hands—amid snickers from the rest.

I then ask those who *didn't* raise their hands "to pretend I am a Russian exchange student living in your home. It's also important to know there is no equivalent word in Russian for 'the,' as we use it. Indeed, many languages don't have such articles—Chinese, Japanese, Korean, Farsi, Polish, Punjabi.

"Now, as the Russian exchange student, I've been living in your home and listening to you and your family for three weeks when one day I come to you and say, 'Don't understand word you use over and over. What means word "the"?' "

How would you begin to explain the meaning of the word to this person? No one ever volunteers to explain it, and everyone laughs embarrassedly. Explaining this simple word turns out to be extremely complex. Nevertheless, we do know how to *use* it. And we knew it before we ever showed up for kindergarten.

How did you learn it? One morning when you were three years old, did your mother take you into the kitchen, sit you down at the table with a little workbook, and say: " 'The' is a definite article. It comes before nouns. Now take your green crayon and underline all the definite articles on the page." Of course not.

We learned the meaning of this tiny but complex word by *hearing* it. In fact, there were three critical factors involved in our learning it:

1. We heard it over and over and over (immersion);
2. We heard it being used by superheroes—Mom, Dad, brother and sister (role models);
3. And we heard it in a meaningful context—the cookie, the nap, the crayons, and the potty.

Concept and Attention Span

A prime ingredient in the success of reading aloud to very young children is that most often it is done one-on-one, by far the most effective teaching/bonding arrangement. In studying methods to reverse language problems among disadvantaged children, Harvard psychologist Jerome Kagan found intensified one-on-one attention to be especially effective.[9] His studies indicated the advantages of reading to children and of listening attentively to their responses to the reading, but they also point to the desirability of reading to your children separately, if possible. I recognize this approach poses an extra problem for working mothers and fathers with more than one child. But somewhere in that seven-day week there must be time for your child to discover the specialness of you, one-on-one, even if it's only once or twice a week.

One-on-one time between adult and child—be it reading or talking or playing—is essential to teaching the *concept* of books or puppies or flowers or water. Once the concept of something has been learned, then the foundation has been laid for the next accomplishment: attention span. Without a concept of what is happening and why, a child cannot and will not attend to something for any appreciable amount of time.

Here, for example, are two concepts entirely within the grasp of a three-year-old:

- The telephone can be used to make and receive calls;
- Books contain stories that give me pleasure if I listen and watch.

A nursery school teacher told me once of her experiences on the first day of school with these two concepts. All morning the three-year-olds in her new class used the toy telephone to make pretend calls to their mothers for reassurances that they would be picked up and brought home. They dialed make-believe numbers, often talked for extended periods of time, and used telephone etiquette. Understanding the *concept* of the telephone, these children were able to use and enjoy it for a considerable length of time. Their telephone attention span was excellent.

Let's compare that with story time in the same class. Thirty seconds after the story began, several of the children stood up and moved away from the circle, obviously bored. More children quickly joined them. Within two minutes, half the children had abandoned the story.

The difference between the attention spans for each of these two activities is based on the *concept* that each child brought to the activity. Where a child had little or no experience with books, it was impossible for him to have a concept of them and the pleasure they afford. No experience means no attention span.[10]

Short attention spans among three-year-olds are not unusual, but when they continue into the early primary grades, there is cause for alarm. With parents averaging about eleven minutes a day of one-on-one time with a child, it's little wonder I receive letters like this from a speech and language clinician in a Massachusetts school system:

> *My language development program is focused on reading aloud to my students. The impetus for this began when, much to my dismay, my caseload of language-delayed kids was rising by leaps and bounds. Before coming to this city, I had worked extensively with culturally deprived and abused children; their language delays were understandable. But why, in this middle-class to upper-middle-class community, was there a rising number of primary children who lacked vocabulary development, memory skills, processing abilities? They often seemed to lack motivation, had limited imaginations and attention spans, and found it difficult to follow*

directions. In addition, only a handful were diagnosed as learning disabled.

As I became more familiar with the children and their family situations, several possible causes appear. Many of them have been in child care from infancy and/or early childhood. Many presently go to a child care situation after school. Many parents admitted they had little time or energy to read to them. Nor did they have the patience to answer . . . the unending questions of a curious 3- or 4-year-old. Television served as a babysitter and pacifier.

Some parents were quick to point out the children were read to in child care and had good experiential learning activities in their centers. But somehow, without the cozy, one-on-one giving of a parent or primary care-giver, the "group" experience had lost meaningfulness for many of the children.

Good News for Single Parents

Undergraduate speech pathology students at Baldwin-Wallace College in Berea, Ohio, were alarmed by the increasing number (35 percent) of preschool children who were being diagnosed with speech delays of six months or more. Interestingly, there had been little or no previous research on this subject. After screening out children with hearing deficiencies and those from limited-English situations, the study focused on 311 preschoolers, ages three to five, from lower- to upper-middle-class families. The results showed that children coming from homes with two working parents were almost *twice as likely* (44 percent to 25 percent) to have speech delays than were children coming from homes with working single parents. A follow-up study in 1994 produced the same results.

Professor Deirdre P. Madden describes the study's conclusions: "When single parents come home from working, the only person present with whom to discuss the day's events is the child. This presents a unique opportunity for the child to practice formulating and expressing thoughts as well as practice recall. On the other hand, married parents returning from work may quite naturally turn to each other for such discussion and leave the child to watch cartoons and engage in some other form of self-entertainment. Because the day care situation may not encourage verbal expression, particularly for a quieter child, it is plausible that just the difference in amount of time offered the child by the parents may have created the results."[11]

That 35 percent in the Baldwin-Wallace study rang some bells with me when I read it. And sure enough, after a little searching, I found this: According to the 1991 Carnegie Commission's *Ready to Learn* report, kindergarten teachers estimate that 35 percent of students were not ready to start school.

Kids Who Read Early

Most of us are intrigued by the success secrets of famous people—like Michael Eisner, the Disney CEO, being required as a child to read for two hours for every one hour of television viewing, or a teenage Michael Jordan daily practicing in the dark on a neighborhood playground after being cut from his high school team. Achievers are not born successful, and readers are not born readers. So let's look at the childhood patterns of three groups of successful readers. First we'll look at the superreaders—the kids who show up for school already knowing how to read, what educators call "early readers."

During the last thirty years major studies have been done on these children.[12] The majority of these students, I might add, were never formally taught to read at home, nor were they hooked up to any commercial reading programs.

The research, as well as studies done on pupils who respond to initial classroom instruction without difficulty, indicates four factors were present in the home environment of nearly every early reader:

1. The child is read to on a regular basis. This is the factor most often cited among early readers. In Dolores Durkin's 1966 study, *all* of the early readers had been read to regularly. Additionally, the parents were avid readers and led by example. The reading included not only books but package labels, street and truck signs, billboards, et cetera.
2. A wide variety of printed material—books, magazines, newspapers, comics—is available in the home. Nearly thirty years later, National Assessment of Educational Progress (NAEP) studies report the more printed materials found in a child's home, the higher the student's writing, reading, and math skills.[13]
3. Paper and pencil are readily available for the child. Durkin explained, "Almost without exception, the starting point of curiosity about written language was an interest in scribbling and drawing.

From this developed an interest in copying objects and letters of the alphabet."

4. The people in the child's home stimulate the child's interest in reading and writing by answering endless questions, praising the child's efforts at reading and writing, taking the child to the library frequently, buying books, writing stories that the child dictates, and displaying his paperwork in a prominent place in the home.

I want to emphasize that these four factors were present in the home of nearly *every* child who was an early reader. None of these involved much more than interest on the part of the parent.

The Three "B's"

Next we'll look at the responses I received from adult "lifetime" readers—my friends and associates. Since parents often think there are "quick fixes" they can buy, some kind of "kit" to help a child do better at school, several years ago I began asking my associates, "What did you have in your home as a child that helped you become a reader? Things your folks had to *buy.*" Besides the library card they all named, but which is free, their responses form what I call the "Three B's," an inexpensive "reading kit" that nearly all parents can afford.

The first B is BOOKS: Ownership of a book, with the child's name inscribed inside, a book that doesn't have to be returned to the library or even shared with siblings. I still have the first book I ever bought, the first I ever won, and one of the first I ever received as a gift.[14]

The second B is BOOKBASKET (or magazine rack)—placed where it can be used most often. There is probably more reading done in the bathrooms of America than in all the libraries and classrooms combined. Put a bookbasket in there, stocked with books, magazines, and newspapers. Put another one on or near the kitchen table. All those newspaper coin boxes aren't standing in front of fast-food restaurants as decorations. I am convinced that human beings want or need to read when they're eating alone. And with more and more children eating at least one daily meal alone, this is a prime spot for recreational reading. If there's a book on the table, they'll read it—unless, of course, you're a foolish enough parent to have a television in your kitchen.

And the third B is BED LAMP: Does your child have a bed lamp or reading light? If not, and you wish to raise a reader, the first order of business is to go out and buy one. Now you can say to your child,

"Elizabeth, we think you're old enough now to stay up later at night and read in bed like Mom and Dad. So we bought this little lamp and we're going to leave it on an extra fifteen minutes [or longer, depending on the age of the child] IF you want to read in bed. On the other hand, if you don't want to read—that's okay, too. We'll just turn off the light at *the same old time*." Most children will do anything in order to stay up later—even read.

Parents who worry about the impact reading in bed will have on children's eyesight—that it might adversely affect their vision—should relax. When I asked such questions of Dr. Eugene Folk, former director and chief pediatric ophthalmologist of the Vision Clinic at the Eye Center of the University of Chicago College of Medicine, he chuckled and replied, "There is no evidence to support *any* connection between reading in bed as a child and future vision. It's an old wives' tale." He also notes that even reading small print will not damage the eye—not even for people who already have poor vision.

And then there are the parents (mostly moms) who worry about the children abusing the bedtime reading privilege. "I've got a child who would read until two in the morning and then I can't get him up in the morning for school. How do you handle that?" they ask. Until recently there was no solution, short of parental supervision, but new lighting technology has come up with a kinder, gentler answer. IQ Lighting or Smart Bulbs can be found in your local hardware store's lighting department. One of the bulbs will automatically turn off after ten minutes; another turns off after thirty minutes. But the third bulb is my favorite —for this reason: The brightness or dimness of a light has no impact on eyesight but it does affect how soon the eye becomes tired. The dimmer the light, the sooner the eye tires. In the third choice, the bulb starts at full brightness but over the next twenty minutes gradually dims until it is only as bright as a four-watt night light. And by that time the child's eyes probably have grown too tired to read any longer.

What Lifetime Readers Liked Best

Our last group of readers are the ones who were so good at it they've made a career of it—librarians and teachers. In the mid-1950s, an English professor named G. Robert Carlsen wondered what made some people readers and others not. Was it something they read or didn't read? Someone in their lives? What were their favorite books? What did they hate about reading? Carlsen decided to ask his students—all of them either librarians or English teachers (or training to be)—to write a short "reading autobiography." For thirty years, he collected them from his students in five states, read them, and filed them away in boxes.

In the 1980s, a doctoral student took an interest in the stacks of boxes and thus was born a fascinating book, *Voices of Readers*.[15] Its hypothesis is simple: If an interest in reading is not a matter of genes but born of experiences, a collection of those experiences should give us clues about how to create lifetime readers.

Before we look at some of the patterns found in their likes and dislikes, keep in mind: These are the recollections of the people who loved reading and books so much they became teachers and librarians. So, if *they* hate something, imagine how much truck drivers, retail clerks, and accountants must hate it.

Some of the common denominators in *Voices of Readers*:

- Being read to was mentioned so often the authors said they could have done an entire book on just those recollections alone.
- Many of the readers had vivid memories of favorite childhood books they wanted read over and over; these memories were almost always associated with warm social experiences with an adult.
- A frequently mentioned early step in learning to read was memorizing a story after hearing it read, then reciting it for appreciative family members.
- A preponderance of the readers began their personal reading with "series" books like Nancy Drew and the Hardy Boys, often reading as though they were addicted to the subject.
- A special subject often caught the readers' attention, provoking them to read everything they could on the subject.
- A large number mentioned comic book reading as being important in their early reading.
- Over and over, readers recalled the interminable boredom they experienced with school readers (like "Dick and Jane").
- Teachers who read aloud to the class frequently were recalled by name, as were the books they read, but as the student moved through school years there were fewer and fewer such recollections.
- The most frequent frustration was being required to read aloud in class from basal readers; the second frustration was being told not to read ahead.

- Bedtime and summer vacations were the favorite time periods for reading.
- Many associated a sudden growth of reading appetite with a periods of forced idleness with no distractions—days or months of being bedridden with an illness, or serving long, boring hours of military duty.
- Sensational magazines like *True Romances* and *Love Story*, as well as notorious bestsellers, frequently took on the attraction of forbidden fruit during adolescence.
- Book reports received consistent abuse from the readers, as did heavy required reading assignments in high school that cut into students' recreational reading.
- Though some readers recalled their high school "classics" with some fondness, most found little or nothing positive to say, and clearly resented the paragraph-by-paragraph dissection.

Listening Level vs. Reading Level

Almost as big a mistake as not reading to children at all is stopping too soon. Remember, the Commission on Reading stated it is "a practice that should continue throughout the grades."[16] In this recommendation the Commission was really asking us to model ourselves on one of the most successful businesses of all time—McDonald's. This fast food chain has been in business for more than thirty years, and never once has it cut its advertising budget. Every year McDonald's spends more money on advertising than it did the previous year, which comes to more than $1 million *per day* just for advertising.

And every time we read aloud to a child or class, we're giving a commercial for the pleasures of reading. But unlike McDonald's, we cut our advertising each year, instead of increasing it. The older the child, the less he is read to—in the home and in the classroom. Typical is a Connecticut school's 1990 survey of its fourth- through sixth-grade students in a middle-class community: only 8 percent of the students had been read to the previous evening.[17] Most teachers confirm similar findings in their assessments of students in middle and upper grades. And *Voices of Readers* (discussed above) confirms how seldom this age group is read to in school.

Parents (and sometimes teachers) say, "He's in the top fourth-grade reading group—why should I read to him? Isn't that why we're sending him to school, so he'll learn how to read by himself?" There are many mistaken assumptions in that question.

Let's say the student is reading on a fourth-grade level. Wonderful. But what level is the child *listening* on? Most people have no idea that one is higher than the other—until they stop and think about it. Here's an easy way to visualize it:

For seven years, the most popular show on American television was *The Cosby Show*, enjoyed by tens of millions each week—including first-graders. Even in reruns it's still one of the most watched shows on TV. What reading level would you estimate the script to have been written on? When a *Cosby* script was submitted to the Harris-Jacobson Wide Range Readability Formula, it came out to approximately fourth-grade level (3.7).[18]

Would those first-graders watching the show be able to read the script of the show? Ninety-nine percent could not. But they could understand it when it is *read to them*—that is, recited by the actors. Until about eighth grade, children listen on a higher level than they read on. Therefore, children can *hear* and *understand* stories that are more complicated and more interesting than anything they could read on their own—which has to be one of God's greatest blessings for first-graders. The last thing you want first-graders thinking is that what they're reading in first grade is as good as books are going to get! First-graders can enjoy books written on a fourth-grade level, and fifth-graders can enjoy books written on a seventh-grade reading level.

In 1990 I was invited to address a community program in Manchester, Massachusetts. Upon arriving at Manchester Memorial School, I was met by the PTO president and escorted toward the auditorium. As we passed the school's classrooms, I couldn't help but notice how the teachers had decorated the bulletin boards outside their classrooms with drawings done by the students—drawings from their *favorite books*. I had a sneaking suspicion this had been done for my personal edification, so I dutifully stopped at each bulletin board and paid my respects. Finally we came to a board that was labeled in large block letters MRS. STASIAK'S CLASS. I noticed that every one of the nearly twenty illustrations was from the same book—*Charlotte's Web*. Turning to the PTO president, I pointed to the bulletin board and asked, "This Mrs. Stasiak's class—what grade level?"

"Oh, that's one of our kindergartens," she said.

My next step was to secretly determine if Mrs. Stasiak was in the audience and I learned she was. So midway into the program, I stopped, reached into my coat pocket, and retrieved a piece of paper. "Excuse me, folks, but I've got a small announcement here," I said. "Is there a Mrs. Stasiak in the audience?" Well, after we gave the poor woman CPR and propped her back into her chair, I apologized for alarming her unnecessarily. "Mrs. Stasiak, I just wanted to congratulate you and your kindergartners on the beautiful bulletin board on *Charlotte's Web* outside your classroom. Also, I must confess my curiosity. How were you able to teach a *kindergarten* class to read a 186-page, fourth-grade novel like *Charlotte's Web*?"

Suddenly, you could feel the temperature in this auditorium of 300 adults make a sudden drop! That is, the parents of the kindergartners who *did not have* Mrs. Stasiak were a little miffed. You could see them sitting there thinking, "Oh, my God! My kid's only been in school four months and already he's four years behind *those* kids."

Meanwhile, Mrs. Stasiak, sensing the unrest, tried to cut it off at the pass. "No, no," she exclaimed, "you misunderstood! My students didn't read *Charlotte's Web*. *I* read it to *them!*"

"But, Mrs. Stasiak, we're talking about fourth-grade, multisyllable vocabulary here," I protested facetiously, picking up a copy of the book and paging through it. "We're talking about words like *nevertheless* and *salutations* and *scruples* and *compunctions*. Why, it must have taken you *forever*, having to write each word on the board and explaining it to the class, right?"

Mrs. Stasiak looked at me and smiled. "Of course not!" Lynne Stasiak understood that kindergarten children listen on a much higher level than they can read on, and that this continues for years to come.

Educators who balk at "wasting time" reading aloud to older students are always ignorant of the research. But even if it didn't affect their literacy skills in such positive ways, reading aloud would still be worth it from the standpoint of what it can accomplish in *advertising* the product the teacher is selling—reading. Few things sell in our culture unless they are promoted. Awareness must come before desire—as proven in the eight-week study of a kindergarten class that had a good classroom library and whose teacher read aloud daily.[19] The library's books consisted of three kinds: *very* familiar (read repeatedly by the teacher); familiar (read once); unfamiliar (unread).

In monitoring which books the kindergartners selected during their free time, it was found they chose the *very* familiar books three times as often, and familiar books twice as often, as the unfamiliar. In addition, these nonreaders more often imitated the teacher and tried to "read" the *very* familiar and familiar books instead of just browsing, as they did with the unfamiliar. The power of advertising!

U.S. children have shown the same response to public television's award-winning series *Reading Rainbow*. In the year before it was read aloud on the PBS show, *Digging Up Dinosaurs*, by Aliki, sold only 2,000 copies. After the show it sold 25,000. According to PBS studies, *Reading Rainbow* is the most used television program in elementary classrooms, with more than 4 million students tuning in regularly. Your local PBS station can provide you with a complete list of *Reading Rainbow* titles, one of the finest children's book lists.

Unbeknownst to most readers-aloud, they can actually accomplish some good by occasionally making a mistake. "Until I was in about third grade," a teacher confided to me, "I was petrified to read in front of my classmates. I wasn't a poor reader but I was extremely shy. With each passing year, I grew more fearful of making mistakes in front of my peers and teacher.

"And then in third grade," she continued, "I had a teacher who read to us daily from big thick books with lots of words and few pictures. To my astonishment, she made mistakes in her reading. She'd occasionally stumble over a word here and there, lose her place once in a while, even mispronounce a word. To my further amazement, she would recover without embarrassment and continue on. It was as though she were saying to each of us, 'Hey, no big deal! *Everybody* makes mistakes.' And that marked the end of my reading terrors and the beginning of my reading passion."

One-on-One Reading

When my children (now thirty and twenty-six) were young, we read the picture books together. But once Elizabeth was ready for novels, I read nearly all of our novels individually—one-on-one. When they're thirty and twenty-six, there is no social or emotional gap between them, but when the same two children were eleven and seven, the gap was sizable. The book that Elizabeth could handle at eleven, Jamie either wasn't ready for or interested in at seven.

Why is this such a difficult concept for parents to understand? And I gather it is, because again and again they say to me, "I have a twelve-year-old, an eight-year-old, and a four-year-old. What one book can I read that will hold all their attentions?" Do they all wear the same size clothes, ride the same size bike, or have the same size friends? Here's a little rule of thumb for parents: If you can't squeeze your kids into the same size underwear, don't try to squeeze them into the same size book! In doing that, you end up watering down the reading material to accommodate the lowest common denominator—the four-year-old—and boring the twelve-year-old. The solution is to read to them individually if there is more than three years' difference in their ages.

And the father in one audience interjected, "Excuse me, but doesn't that take longer?" Yes, it does, sir. But then, parenting is not *supposed* to be a time-saving experience. Parenting is time-*consuming*, time-*investing*—but not time-*saving*.

Beyond the building of attention span and vocabulary, something else is built during these one-on-one hours with a child. When you get to the "heavy stuff" in books, it usually brings to the surface of the child some of his or her "heavy stuff"—his or her deepest hopes and fears. And when that happens—if there is not an obnoxious older sister or younger brother present—children will tell you their secrets. And when they share their secrets, the chemistry that occurs is called "bonding" and that's what *really* holds families together.

Relatively little of what most people do collectively or communally nurtures bonding. Don't tell me the family trip to Disney World is a bonding time. I've stood in the lobby of Disney hotels at nine-thirty at night watched the families come back from a day of "bonding," and it's not a pretty sight. And in all my years of watching families in church on Sundays, I can truthfully say I've seen a lot more pinching, nudging, and whispered threats than bonding.

So when do we bond best with the young? Whenever it's one-on-one: one-on-one walk, one-on-one talk, or one-on-one reading. This appears to be pivotal in language development, as noted by Madden and Kagan earlier in this chapter. And finally, you will discover you have far fewer arguments or problems with a child when you're in a one-on-one situation.

It is far easier to convince a parent to begin reading to an infant than it is to convince a parent or teacher to begin (or continue) reading to older children. So I offer supportive evidence that it is not a waste of time.

The older the child, the more complicated the books become, and the more enjoyable or meaningful they are for the adult reader as well. Some of the novels I read to Jamie and Elizabeth in their middle-grade years were as good as anything I was reading on my own: *A Day No Pigs Would Die*, by Robert Newton Peck; *Slake's Limbo*, by Felice Holman; *Roll of Thunder, Hear My Cry*, by Mildred Taylor; *North to Freedom*, by Anne Holm; *The Foxman*, by Gary Paulsen; and Willie Morris's *Good Old Boy*.

The adult who reads aloud is simultaneously giving a language arts class. There are four language arts: they begin with the art of listening and proceed to the arts of speaking, writing, and reading.

Spoken and Written Language

Discounting sign language and body language, there are two forms of language for most people—spoken and written. While they are intimately related to each other—as close as brother and sister—they are not twins. Written words are far more structured and normally more complicated than are spoken words. Therefore, children who enjoy conversations with adults *and* hear stories are exposed to richer language than is the child who experiences only conversation.

Conversation is imprecise, rambling, often ungrammatical, and less organized than written language. For example, here is the transcript of a public conversation between President George Bush and a high school student after a speech he gave at the University of Tennessee on February 2, 1990:

> STUDENT: *"I loved your State of the Union address on improving education. I was wondering, do you have any plans to get ideas internationally to improve education?"*
>
> PRESIDENT BUSH: *"Well, I'm going to kick that one right into the end zone of the Secretary of Education. But, yes, we have all—he travels a good deal, goes abroad. We have a lot of people in the department that does [sic] that. We're having an international— this is not as much education as dealing with environment—a big international conference coming up. And we get it all the time— exchanges of ideas. But I think we've got—we set out there—and I want to give credit to your Governor McWherter and to your former governor Lamar Alexander—we've gotten great ideas for a national goals program from—in this country—from the governors who were responding to, maybe, the principal of your high school, for heaven's sake."*[20]

Now you know two things: (1) The difference between spoken and written language; and (2) the reason presidents have speechwriters.

In listening to stories being read aloud, a child is learning a second language—the *standard* English of books and the classroom. Most of us speak at *least* two languages—home or family language and standard (or school) language. The language Mario Cuomo used with his immigrant parents in the Bronx was distinctly different from that which he would use at a political convention. Bill Cosby, talking with relatives in Philadelphia, would speak a language distinctly different from that which he used with his doctoral dissertation committee at the University of Massachusetts. Unfortunately, many children never meet this standard language until they arrive at the schoolhouse door. Knowing this language *before* arriving at school jump-starts a child's learning and does it without stress. Witness the case of Betsy Ratzsch, a mother in Grand Rapids, Michigan, and her son Philip.

When Philip was four years old, his favorite book each night was Steven Kellogg's picture book *Paul Bunyan*. And so, night after night, Philip heard this paragraph at the end of the book: "With the passing of the years, Paul has been seen less and less frequently. However, along with his unusual size and strength, he seems to possess an extraordinary longevity. Sometimes his great bursts of laughter can be heard rumbling like distant thunder across the wild Alaskan mountain ranges where he and Babe still roam."

And then came an evening when Philip's mother came to his bedroom door, dreading yet *another* reading of *Paul*. With hope in her heart, she asked, "Well, Philip, what story would you like tonight?"

He thought for a moment, and then declared soberly, "I think—I think I would like a story about 'extraordinary longevity.' "

A year later when Philip showed up for kindergarten, he brought with him two words not in the working vocabularies of most five-year-olds: "extraordinary" and "longevity." He learned them not off flash cards or a vocabulary list, but by hearing them over and over, from an important person in his life, repeated in a meaningful way.

This gift of standard English cannot be overemphasized. Standard English is the primary tongue of the classroom and the business world, yet children who spend 30 percent of their free time watching television learn little of it. Even adults are shocked at the worldwide impact of the English language today. In *The Story of English*,[21] we find what amounts to a "state of the language" report on English:

Of all the world's languages (which now number some 2,700), [English] is arguably the richest in vocabulary. The compendious

Oxford English Dictionary *lists some 500,000 words; and a further half million technical and scientific terms remain uncatalogued. According to traditional estimates, German has a vocabulary of about 185,000 words and French fewer than 100,000. . . . About 350 million people use the English language vocabulary as a mother tongue: about one-tenth of the world's population. . . . Three-quarters of the world's mail, and its telexes and cables, are in English. So are more than half the world's technical and scientific periodicals. It is the language of technology from Silicon Valley to Singapore. English is the medium for 80 percent of the information stored in the world's computers. Nearly half of all business deals in Europe are conducted in English. It is the language of sports and glamour: the official language of the Olympics and the Miss Universe competition. . . . American technology and finance have introduced 20,000 English words into regular use in Japan.*

It is imperative that children learn standard English as a future survival tool. Deprived of the language they need to prosper in the world, children are more apt to commit what Nobel Prize–winner Toni Morrison calls "tongue suicide," referring figuratively to frustrated "children who have bitten their tongues off and use bullets instead to iterate the voice of speechlessness."[22]

A common mistake among teachers is to relegate reading aloud to just the reading or language arts classes. Every teacher should be a role model for the standard language; it's the first tool of the classroom. And when you promote a love of books within students, it affects every part of the curriculum, something not always understood by those who have never taught reading.[23] I am frequently called upon to address a school system's entire faculty—including math, science, art, music, and physical education teachers. My first task is to convince those teachers outside the reading faculty that reading *is* the curriculum and therefore *every* teacher's business. (At this point, the reading teachers nod agreement, but the rest of the faculty is unconvinced.)

Take, for example, vocabulary, spelling, and writing skills—three areas in which English and reading teachers come under constant attack. "Sure," says the history teacher, "I'd love to give more essay questions on exams. But those damn English teachers haven't taught these kids how to write." And the science teacher adds, "Their spelling is even worse, and most have the vocabulary of a squirrel."

Who Spells and Writes Best?

How do we improve vocabulary, spelling, and writing? By reading, reading, reading. Vocabulary and spelling are not learned best by looking words up in the dictionary. You learn the meanings and spellings in the same way teachers learn the names of new students each September: by seeing them again and again, making the connection between the face and the name. Nearly everyone spells by visual memory, not by rules. (There is ample research to indicate that people who have the best recall of graphic or geometric symbols are also the best spellers. This, say the scientists, may have more to do with your memory genetics than with anything else.[24]) Most people, when they doubt the correctness of what they have just spelled, write the word out several different ways and choose the one that looks correct. The more a child meets words and sees how they are used in sentences and paragraphs, the greater the chances he will spell words correctly. Conversely, the less you read, the fewer words you meet and the less certain you are of spelling or meaning.[25]

Writing is a similar story. Becoming a skilled writer requires a process similar to becoming a skilled baseball player. The best players must play a lot of baseball—that's why young players begin in the minor leagues, where they can play more. But baseball players actually spend more of their time *watching* baseball than *playing* it. When they are in the field or in the dugout, only a handful are actually playing; the others are watching how other players throw, hit, and catch the ball. The very same thing is true in writing. Good writers must write a lot, but they read even more—they watch how other people throw words around to catch meaning. The more you read, the better you write—and the National Writing Report Card proves it.[26] The highest-scoring writers were those students who did the most recreational reading, had the most printed materials in their homes, and had regular essay-writing in class.

Reading develops not only writing skill but also writing style—without the student even realizing it. One example of this subliminal copycatting can be found in the experience of popular adult mystery writer Tony Hillerman. Hillerman grew up in Oklahoma, a third-generation German-American, and attended an American Indian boarding school for farm children. After getting a journalism degree from the University of Oklahoma, he worked for years as a wire service reporter and then as an editor with the *Santa Fe New Mexican*. With that varied background, whom did he imitate when he became a novelist? "When my first book

(*The Blessing Way*) was published, a reviewer said it was reminiscent of the *Australian* writer Arthur Upfield. I looked at that and said, 'Aw, yeah! I betcha.' So I went to the library and found some Upfield, and sure enough."

The Upfield connection, it turns out, had been established when Hillerman was a young boy, peddling—and reading—the *Saturday Evening Post*, which often serialized the Australian's novels. In retrospect, Hillerman says, "I went through all my life with these incredible memories from that serial, of the Australian outback and the aboriginal culture. I just loved it."[27]

Read-Aloud Throughout the Curriculum

Of all the qualities a teacher might possess, the most contagious is enthusiasm. Are you enthusiastic about books? Do your students ever see you with something other than a textbook in your hand? Have you shared with your class a book you stayed awake reading until two o'clock in the morning? Have you read a magazine article or newspaper column to your students about something that really interested you? If you're not enthusiastic about reading, you are in the wrong profession.

If you want your science or history class to be alive, wrap the facts and figures, the dates and battles, in flesh-and-blood novels. Read *My Side of the Mountain*, by Jean George, or *Woodsong*, by Gary Paulsen, to your science class. Open your history class with five minutes from *My Brother Sam Is Dead*, by James and Christopher Collier. Art teacher Donalyn Schofield in New Braintree, Massachusetts, used the quiet time during which her students were doing a stitching project to read aloud *The Hobbit*, by J. R. R. Tolkien.

Almost like clockwork, after every speech I give, a worried parent approaches me and asks, "When is it too late? Is there a time when children are too old to be read to?" It is never too late, they are never too old—but it is not going to be as beneficial or as easy as it is when they are two years old or six years old.

Because she has a captive audience, the classroom teacher holds a distinct advantage over the parent who suddenly wants to begin reading to a thirteen-year-old. Regardless of how well intentioned the parent may be, reading aloud to an adolescent at home can be difficult. During this period of social and emotional development, teenagers' out-of-school time is largely spent coping with body changes, sex drive, vocational anxieties, and the need to form an identity apart from that of their families. These kinds of concerns and their attendant schedules don't leave much time for Mom's and Dad's reading aloud.

But the situation is not hopeless. When the child is in early adolescence, from twelve to fourteen, try sharing a small part of a book, a page or two, when you see he is at loose ends. This only has to be several times a week. Mention that you want to share something with him that you've read; downplay any motivational or educational aspects connected with the reading.

The older the child, the more difficult he is to corral. Here, as in early adolescence, you must pick your spots for reading aloud. Don't suggest that your daughter listen to a story when she's sitting down to watch her favorite television show or fuming after a fight with her boyfriend. Along with timing, consider the length of what you read. Keep it short —unless you see an interest for more.

Because so many parents and teachers seemed at loose ends over what to read to this age group, I created an anthology of fifty read-aloud selections for preteens and teens, *Read All About It!* It contains a broad cross section of fiction and nonfiction, short stories, chapters from novels (that will whet the child's appetite for the rest of the book), and newspaper columns from people like Bob Greene and Mike Royko, with biographical sketches of each author.

Secondary students being read to? Certainly. It's the role modeling and sales pitch for the joy of reading that counts here. When my daughter returned from England after a summer studying at Cambridge University, she told me the professors read aloud to literature classes all the time. A year later, I met a Kansas teacher returning from her second straight summer at Oxford University, where she'd been read to regularly. I figure, if it's good enough for Oxford and Cambridge, it's good enough for any junior or senior high school in America.

The older a child is, the easier it is to find nonfiction that can be read aloud. Indeed, if the teachers or parents are active readers themselves, the challenge is to pick from the hundreds of choices. When Jamie and Elizabeth were teens, I was always reading excerpts to them from whatever I was reading myself, be it fiction or nonfiction. I remember reading Ferrol Sams's *Run with the Horseman,* a wonderful Southern novel by a Georgia physician. When I came to an early scene in which a boy has two hilarious incidents with a mule in a field and a rooster in an outhouse, I thought, "Oooh, Jamie will love these!"

So in the morning, I caught up with him. "Hey, Jamie—listen to this!"
Edging to the door, he said, "Sorry, Dad, but I gotta run. I'm supposed
to meet the guys."

"I know, but it will just take a minute—I promise." Rolling his eyes,
he reluctantly sat and I began to read it aloud. And, as I suspected, he
loved it. Several hours later he was back with his buddies in tow, asking
me to read it to them too.

If I had to choose at random right now from my bookshelves, here
are some titles and authors I would read aloud to teens—though they
were written with an adult audience in mind:

- Any of Torey Hayden's powerful books about the psychologically
  damaged children she has worked with through the years: *One
  Child*; *Just Another Kid*; *Murphy's Boy*; *Somebody Else's Kid*; and
  Ghost Girl.

- Jan Brunvand's collections of urban legends, the modern folklore
  tales that keep springing up in America, "Absolutely true, I swear,"
  and always told by a friend-of-a-friend-of-a-friend: *The Vanishing
  Hitchhiker*; *The Choking Doberman*; *The Mexican Pet*; and *Curses!
  Broiled Again*.

- The Pulitzer Prize–winning historian and journalist David McCul-
  lough has a brilliant collection of twenty profiles of exceptional
  men and women from American history entitled *Brave Com-
  panions*.

- Journalist Alex Kotlowitz's award-winning *There Are No Children
  Here*, in which he follows two contemporary children's daily lives
  in one of Chicago's most dangerous public housing projects.

- Doreen Rappaport's *American Women: Their Lives in Their Words*,
  a collection of personal letters, journal entries, and speeches by
  women (some famous, some unknown) that gives a moving view
  of American history that textbooks have ignored.

- Al Silverman used to edit *Sport* magazine, and later he became
  CEO of the Book-of-the-Month Club, so few people know literature and sports the way Silverman does. In *The Twentieth Century
  Treasury of Sports*, he and his son, Brian, offer the reader seventy-
  six classic tales from almost every sport. Here's fiction and nonfiction, tragedy and comedy, from magazine and newspaper articles,
  short stories and novels.

- *Talk That Talk*, edited by Linda Goss and Marian E. Barnes, is a
  fabulous anthology of stories representing the oral tradition in

African-American culture, including sermons, truth tales, poetry, biography, humor, ghost tales, and even rap.

Story as Life's Compass

"But," says a teacher, "these are just stories. I've got a curriculum to cover. I don't have time for *stories!*" Far from suggesting the curriculum be abandoned, I say it is enriched and made meaningful by story. Story does not exist to teach reading skills. Story is the vehicle we use to make sense out of the world—even when we sleep. Dreams are our attempt to make sense out whatever defies logic. Do you know anyone who dreams nonfiction? We dream story.

Some teachers in upper grades are ill at ease with "story." They would prefer information books, nonfiction, instead. Let me address the objections that stories don't build mental muscles. Let's use *The Wizard of Oz* as an example. For almost fifty years, L. Frank Baum's Oz books were frowned upon, often banned, in public and school libraries because teachers and librarians thought they were too imaginative. Since it was believed that children only learned from information, the books were seen as a waste of valuable shelf space and class time.

Time and scientific research now show nothing could have been further from the truth. People do not learn by information—and *The Wizard of Oz* proves it, while showing how we *do* learn.

Listen to a modern wizard and his Oz—Roger C. Schank, former head of the Artificial Intelligence Laboratory at Yale University and now a professor of electrical engineering and computer science, psychology, and education at Northwestern University. In trying to build artificial intelligence in computers, Schank had to reduce human behavior and thinking to its basic formats. And what it often boiled down to was story—the stories each of us make, store, and share. Story, he found, is the basic fabric for intelligence because it determines how we think and behave.[28]

Our brains receive thousands of pieces of information daily, sometimes hourly. Most of it we can't retrieve even minutes later, while other pieces can be easily pulled up years after they entered our memories. The easy pieces had "labels" on them that allowed us to grasp them—that is, stories about the information, the incident, or the person. Abstract concepts are all too quickly lost in the dust of yesterday. In his insightful and entertaining book, *Tell Me a Story: A New Look at Real and Artificial Memory*, Schank notes, "Stories give life to past experiences. Stories make the events in memory memorable to others and to ourselves."

Yes, there was a lot of imagination and story in the *Oz* books (including a mechanical man, fourteen years before the word *robot* was first used). But what Baum wanted to say about technology, about people getting along with each other, about sacrifice, sharing, courage, even greed—all of that is in there too. Not as a long list of abstract human conditions, but buried in story so it could be absorbed by readers, subconsciously labeled, stored, and later retrieved.

It is story that focuses our attention, helps us make sense out of the world around us. The politician or preacher who stands before an audience and says, "That reminds me of a story . . ." has its attention immediately. The biggest moneymaker in CBS history ($1.3 billion in twenty-five years) is the show *60 Minutes*. When Don Hewitt, its producer (and the man who does the final edit of every show), was asked the show's success formula, he replied simply: "Tell me a story."[29]

Studies done with trial juries show jurors remember only 60 percent of the mounds of disconnected evidence and they don't wait until the end of the trial to come to conclusions. Instead, they continually tell stories to themselves, stories that grow and are revised during the trial and in their attempts to make sense of the testimony.[30]

Educating Both the IQ and HQ

Because literature reaches beyond the dispassionate intellect, it can also educate the heart—a curriculum very much on the mind of the nation's business leaders and educators these days. With moral or ethical crises constantly on the nation's front pages and television newscasts, many leading business schools have not only grown weary of seeing their alumni in handcuffs on the five o'clock news, but are also trying to correct the situation.

Educators who find stories to be a waste of valuable instructional time would do well to pay attention to the likes of the Harvard Business School and Brandeis University.[31] Harvard invited the eminent child psychiatrist Robert Coles to teach a course in ethics at the business school. Coles's course syllabus consisted of nothing but literature—stories and novels that grabbed the young business student where it hurts: the heart. Vicariously, through literature, Coles's students explored the gradual slope that leads to compromising one's principles, values, and morality. Quoting William Carlos Williams, Coles states his purpose: "to bring the reader up close, so close that his empathy puts him in the shoes of the characters. You hope when he closes the book his own character is influenced." The Harvard Business School has since launched a $30 million ethics program. Brandeis has been using literature for similar purposes in its business seminars.

If all we're doing in school is teaching students how to answer the calls they'll someday get on their beepers or e-mail, then the curriculum is worthless. The most important calls will not come on beepers; instead they will be the daily calls for love, justice, courage, and compassion. Yes, student scores are important, but *both* scores—the IQ and the HQ (heart quotient). When we begin to focus exclusively on paper scores, we need to be reminded that the most educated nation in two thousand years led the world in math and science in 1930. It also produced the Third Reich. The Holocaust could never have happened if the German *heart* had been as well educated in 1930 as the German *mind*. Science and mathematics are important but they only address the IQ, not the HQ. Have you ever heard of a child crying over the end of a math book? I rest my case.

3

The Stages of Read-Aloud

Few children learn to love books by themselves. Someone has to lure them into the wonderful world of the written word; someone has to show them the way.

Orville Prescott,
A Father Reads to His Children

Staring at the thousands of books in the children's section of the local library, a parent is filled with the same panic that faces the beginning artist with an empty canvas: Where to begin?

I suggest that you first consider the child's age and maturity; then make your decisions accordingly. Let's start with the infant level and work our way upward.

Until a child is six months old, I don't think it matters a great deal what you read, as long as you are reading. What is important up to this stage is that the child becomes accustomed to the rhythmic sound of your reading voice and associates it with a peaceful, secure time of day. Mother Goose, of course, is always appropriate, but my neighbor read Kipling aloud when she was nursing her daughter, who eventually went on to both Princeton and Harvard. Did Kipling have anything to do with that? Not much, compared with her mother's reading to her.

The stumbling block in all this is the awkwardness of reading to a child who doesn't appear to understand what you are doing. Fortunately, the research of recent years gives us a far different view of the child from that of the unaware infant our parents knew. The dubious reader-aloud should consider a few recent discoveries:

- One-day-old babies can be calmed with tape recordings of their own cries and within days are able to distinguish their own cries from those of their peers and older babies.[1]
- Twelve-day-old babies can imitate an adult sticking out a tongue.[2]
- Ten-week-olds with strings attached to slide projectors that change with movement of the wrist will watch the changing slides attentively for an average of fourteen minutes.[3]
- Newborns are very discerning listeners. When exposed to the sounds of real babies crying and then the sounds made by a computer simulating babies crying, newborns cried louder in response to the real babies.[4]
- Can a two-month-old recognize a familiar book? When infants as young as two months old had their ankles connected with ribbons to mobiles above their beds, the babies learned to move the mobile by kicking. If you take the mobile away and reintroduce it a few days later, a two-month-old will recognize it and start kicking again. If it remains away longer than a few days, he will forget it. Do the same experiment with a six-month-old and he can recall it after an absence of as long as two weeks.[5]

Coupling these findings with the fetal research reported in Chapter 2 should ease any awkwardness you might have about reading to infants. While many of these infant abilities are in place at birth, like flowers out of water, they will wilt and be lost if not nurtured over the next two years.

Massaging Baby's Brain with Words

The consensus among scientists is that children are born with a massive number of brain cells and connectors between those cells called synapses—more of them than they will ever need.

A child's brain begins with more cells than it needs, so almost immediately it starts to shed cells, particularly those that are least used. Between six and ten months, there are additional bursts in cell growth within the speech centers of infant brains. Another burst occurs between twelve and eighteen months when they truly discover that words have meaning. The network of nerves that allows this growth, scientists report, is very much affected by how much exercise it receives. However, since infant and toddler children are entirely dependent upon parents and older siblings for their experiences, the fate of a child's brain development—what goes and what grows—rests with a parent. For unstimulated babies who are seldom spoken to and played with, who see only the same dull walls day after day and are left in this condition for too long, there is little chance the child's brain networking ever will develop sufficiently for the child to become a competent student.[6]

The more you talk to children during these critical times, the greater the natural language growth. It's like muscle massage. In fact, a child's brain growth increases with such intensity to meet the challenge of these new words and experiences that between ages four and ten his brain metabolism (the brain's heartbeat) is twice that of an adult's. That's the reason children are able to learn foreign languages and musical instruments so easily during these years—and need naps so often.[7]

With this in mind, your book selections for the next year should be ones that stimulate his sight and hearing—colorful pictures and exciting sounds upon which the child can focus easily. One of the reasons for Mother Goose's success is that she echoes the first sound a child falls in love with—the rhythmic, rhyming "beat-beat-beat" of a mother's heart.

Linguists like MIT's Dr. Steven Pinker (*The Language Instinct*, HarperCollins) point to research that indicates Mother Goose knew what she was doing: Human ears—including babies'—gravitate to rhyming words in the same the way the eyes are attracted to patterns like stripes and plaids. The rhymes appear more "organized" for learning.

Two excellent rhyme collections (blessedly picturing multiethnic children) are: *The Little Dog Laughed and Other Nursery Rhymes from Mother Goose* by Lucy Cousins; and for those who are nervous about the farmer's wife cutting off the blind mice's tails, try Bruce Lansky's delightful *The New Adventures of Mother Goose: Gentle Rhymes for Happy Times.*

Notice how many of the Mother Goose rhymes can be applied to a child's everyday activities: "Hush-a-Bye Baby" (sleeping and waking); "Deedle, Deedle Dumpling" (going to bed); "One, Two, Buckle My Shoe" (getting dressed); "Pat-a-Cake" and "Little Jack Horner" (eating); "Little Bo Peep" (losing toys); "Humpty Dumpty" (falling down); "What Can the Matter Be?" (crying); "Rub-a-Dub-Dub" (bathing).

Many parents find that singing or reciting these rhymes during the appropriate activity further reinforces the relationship between rhyme and activity in the child's mind. Long-playing records, CDs, and tapes of these rhymes are available at your library and local bookstore. An excellent resource for early childhood books and recordings is *Mother Goose Comes First* by Lois Winkel and Sue Kimmel.

Also keep in mind the physical bonding that occurs during the time you are holding the child and reading. To make sure you never convey the message that the book is more important than the child, maintain skin-to-skin contact as often as possible, patting, touching, and hugging while you read.[8] Linked with the normal parent-infant dialogue, this reinforces a feeling of being well-loved.

Infant Book Behavior

Recent interest in early learning has spurred investigations on how infants and their parents react in read-aloud situations, though any reading parent can tell you a child's interest and response to books varies a great deal. But if you are a *new* parent, any apparent lack of interest can be discouraging. Here is a forecast, so you'll not be discouraged or think your child is hopeless.

- At four months of age, since he has limited mobility, a child has little or no choice but to listen and observe, thus making a passive and noncombative audience for the parent, who is probably thinking, "This is easy!"
- Your arms should encircle the child in such a way as to suggest support and bonding, but not imprisonment.
- By six months, however, the child is more interested in grabbing the book to suck on it than listening (which he's also doing). Bypass the problem by giving him a teething toy or other distraction.

- At eight months, he may prefer turning pages to steady listening. Allow him ample opportunity to explore this activity but don't give up the book entirely.
- At twelve months, the child's involvement grows to turning pages for you, pointing to objects you name on the page, even making noises for animals on cue.
- By fifteen months and the onset of walking, his restlessness blossoms fully, and your reading times must be chosen so as not to frustrate his immediate interests.

In nearly all these studies,[9] attention spans during infant reading time averaged only *three minutes* in length, though several daily readings often brought the total as high as thirty minutes a day. There are some one-year-olds who will listen to stories for that long in one sitting, but be assured they are more the exception than the rule.

As babies mature, good parent-readers profit from earlier experiences. They don't force the reading times, they direct attention by pointing to something on the page, and they learn to vary their voices between whispers and excited tones. And they learn that attention spans are not built overnight—they are built minute by minute, page by page, day by day.

Once the child begins to respond to the sight of books and your voice, it is important to begin a book dialogue, *talking* the book instead of just *reading* it, with questions like, "Isn't this a wonderful book, Jennifer?" Or "Would you like a puppy like that someday?" Even though the baby cannot initially respond, your pausing in the appropriate places for answers creates a kind of oral road map the child will soon follow on her own when she starts to talk.[10]

Talking the book requires your reading the pages to yourself ahead of time, or, in the case below, which has a minimum of print, observing the pictures, then having what amounts to a conversation with the child. Here, beside the words from Eric Hill's *Spot's First Walk*, is a transcript of the dialogue between a mother and her twenty-three-month-old.[11]

Notice how the mother gently works in the actual words of the book (italics), something she conveys by a different voice inflection. The give-and-take on the part of reader and child not only builds language skills; it also holds the child's attention to the book. Moreover, it tallies with the Chinese adage: *Tell* me and I forget. *Show* me and I remember. *Involve* me and I understand. The more the child is involved in the reading process, the more he will understand.

BOOK/TEXT	MOTHER/CHILD
What have you found?	CHILD: What's the dog doing? MOM: He's digging in the dirt looking for his bone. Look what he found there. C: Oh. M: *What have you found,* Spot? C: A doggy bone. M: Yes, he's found a doggy bone. He's having fun outside. C: Yeah. M: What is he doing with his feet? C: What's he doing with his feet, Mom? M: He's digging. C: He's digging.
Now for a drink.	M: Look what he's doing next. He's getting a drink. *Now for a drink* of water.
Don't fall in.	C: There's a fish. M: There's a fish saying, *"Don't fall in, don't fall in."*

Children less than eighteen months often find it difficult to understand complicated illustrations that adults recognize easily. Book illustrations consisting of many little figures running here and there may be charming to adults but they are incomprehensible to young children. An adult can recognize instantly a three-dimensional rabbit when it is reduced to one dimension on a page, but a fourteen-month-old child is just beginning this complicated process. To help the child in this task, the picture books you choose now should be uncomplicated—a single image to a page and preferably in color. Plot, if there is any, is secondary to the image. Among the very best for this purpose are those by Dutch author-artist Dick Bruna.

Internationally recognized, the Bruna books are masterpieces of simplicity: simple black outlines, solid colors of red, yellow, blue, and green against plain backgrounds. His subjects are simple enough to border on caricature. Bruna packs language, story, emotion, and color into twelve pages. After *Mother Goose,* among your first books should be Bruna books (see Author-Illustrator Index). Sadly, Dick Bruna books are not currently available in U.S. bookstores. They are, however, available outside the U.S. and are well worth the extra effort to find them. U.S. and Canadian residents can make mail or credit card purchases by contacting any Canadian bookstore; if you know of none, contact The Children's Book Store, 2532 Yonge Street, Toronto, Ontario, Canada M4P 2H7; tel: 416-480-0233; Canadian residents should contact their local bookseller. See *Miffy* in Treasury, page 261.

"Labeling" a Toddler's World

During the toddler stage, an important parental role is serving as a kind of welcoming committee for the child, welcoming him to your world. Just think of yourself as the host of a huge party. Your child is the guest of honor. Naturally, you want to introduce him to all the invited guests in order to make him feel at home.

You do this by helping him learn the names of all the objects that surround him, the things that move, the things that make noises, the things that shine. Picture books are perfect teaching vehicles at this stage. Point to the various items illustrated in the book, call them by name, ask the child to say the name with you, praise him enthusiastically for his efforts. Picture books like *The First Words Picture Book* and *The Early Words Picture Book*, by Bill Gillham, are excellent for this purpose.

The very best picture book at this stage may be the one you make—using photographs taken in your home and of your family. Be sure the images are not smaller than four inches, label each with easy-to-read letters, place the picture on cardboard, and cover it entirely with a piece of self-sealing clear plastic. Metal rings through punch holes will hold it all together as a most durable and personalized "book." The materials can be purchased cheaply wherever office supplies are sold. If the cost is prohibitive, try the method used by the State of Missouri's Parents as Teachers program: Take Polaroid photos or magazine cutouts, paste them on brightly colored pieces of cardboard, put an appropriate alphabet letter at the top of each photo (B for ball; C for cat); insert them into Ziploc sandwich bags. Then tape all the pages together to form a personalized book.

The physical growth of the child also means his moods and needs are growing. To accommodate those needs he develops a vocabulary that is "near-genius"[12] in scope. A two-year-old will use his basic vocabulary to speak a total of 20,000 words a day, as opposed to a fifteen-year-old who uses his to make 23,000.[13] As the principal architect in your child's building years, you should choose reading material that keeps pace with this little "talking machine."

Because of this high-level curiosity and because they haven't yet mastered the idea of story, many young children enjoy nonfiction books as much as fiction at this point. As the "label-the-environment" stage moves into high gear, think of all the things that fascinate children: holes, cars, snow, birds, bugs, stars, trucks, dogs, rain, planes, cats, storms, babies, mommies and daddies. Beginning at around age two, they are interested in everything and have a built-in need to have names for those things. An excellent book to share at this point would be *Three Hundred (300) FIRST WORDS*, by Geoff Dann, containing full-color photographs of the 300 most common objects in a young child's world, along with the words that name them, all stripped of confusing background images, and grouped by subject matter—foods, clothing, et cetera.

Interactive (Touch and Feel) Books

Once the child is calm in the presence of books and more inclined to listen than to rip, introduce "involvement" or "interactive" books. Fifty years ago, Dorothy Kunhardt's *Pat the Bunny* began this genre, but its stereotyped artwork makes it outdated for many of today's families (it's time for Golden Books to offer a new edition). Interactive books allow a child to manipulate a part of the book by lifting a flap or feeling a texture on the page. Three excellent ones are: *I'm a Little Mouse*, by Noelle and David Carter, about a mouse meeting neighbor creatures, printed on heavily textured pages; *Kiss the Boo-Boo*, by Sue Tarsky and Alex Ayliffe, in which the child/reader attaches a bandage to boo-boo spots on the page (via Velcro); and Eric Hill's popular series that begins with *Where's Spot?*, which includes sturdy movable flaps that hide surprise images. Busy babies are most interested in busy books like these.

Since familiarity is important in developing a lasting relationship with books, it's a good idea to purchase your own copies of these "working" infant books. This will give you a good start in building your child's personal library (see Chapter 6). Public libraries find it difficult to keep this kind of book in circulation because the movable parts are easily damaged. Affluent families might keep in mind that it is better to have a limited number of familiar books than numerous titles or a different one all the time. Children under two years of age tend to be confused by a different book every day.

Many publishers are now marketing baby board books, durable volumes printed in nontoxic inks on heavy, laminated pages that are easy for little fingers to turn and can be quickly wiped clean (see Peggy Parish's and Helen Oxenbury's books in the Author-Illustrator Index).

Place the board books in the high chair, the playpen, and the crib. Let your child see books at least as often as he sees toys and television.

Families accustomed to treasuring every book are sometimes afraid to leave a book in the hands of a baby. Dorothy White, in *Books Before Five*, described those early books as the one "fated to suffer every indignity that a child's physically expressed affection could devise—a book not only looked at, but licked, sat on, slept on, and at last torn to shreds." White and her husband wisely decided "that the enjoyment of personal ownership was a fact of life more worth knowing than how to look after this or that. How can one learn to hold, before one has learnt to have?" she asked.[14] The gentle and affectionate way the *parent* treats the book is far more important.

As the child's concept of books begins to evolve, I recommend you start an important but subtle reading lesson: labeling the book. Point to the title of the story each time you read it, and begin to use words like *author, pages, pictures, cover,* and *front* and *back of the book*. Disregard that old third-grade rule about not using your finger when you read. Let your finger occasionally do some "walking and talking" by lightly running it under the text as you read. All these efforts gradually teach the child about the meaning of those black squiggly lines on the page, that reading begins in the front, at the top, and moves left to right. These are essential steps in the act of reading, steps we adults take for granted because they're second nature to us now. But they are not second nature to a child. Given these subtle learning advantages now, he'll have an easier time later on.

If a child is too active to pay attention to a book, try telling some stories about a little boy or girl with the same name as your child. After a week, introduce a character to your stories who is also found in a children's book. For example, have your story-child meet a small puppy named Spot. A week of their adventures should culminate with your introducing Eric Hill's *Where's Spot?* Gradually wean the child from your invented stories to those in books.

Those "Favorite" Books

Frequently the child who is read to regularly can be seen toddling along with his favorite book, looking for someone to read to him. There are two important elements here. One is to keep in mind that as much as anything else, the child is looking for attention; he wants his body cuddled as much as his mind. The other factor is the idea of a "favorite" book. He has already developed literary tastes, and between now and when he is six, he'll have many favorites, books he asks for often, nightly, for months on end. The more frequently you read and the greater the variety of titles, the broader will be the child's appetite. But too frequently, any kind of favoritism by the child for a particular title will irritate parents who are tired of reading the same book.

These rereadings coincide with the way children learn. Like their parents, they are most comfortable with the familiar, and when they are relaxed, they're better able to absorb. The repetition improves their vocabulary, sequencing, and memory skills. Research shows that preschoolers often ask as many questions (and sometimes the *same* questions) after a dozen readings of the same book because they're learning language in increments—not all at once. Each reading often brings an inch or two of new meaning to the story.

Those of us who have seen a movie more than once fully realize how many subtleties escaped us the first time. Even more so with children and books. Because they are learning a very complex language at the adult's speaking pace, there often are misunderstandings that can only be sorted out by repeated readings. Allerton Kilborne, a history teacher in New York City, once told me how, as a child, he used to ask his grandmother "to read the book about the man who got sick," and then hand her Clement Moore's "The Night Before Christmas." The family couldn't figure out why he called it that until one day his grandmother focused on this stanza:

> *"When out on the lawn there arose such a clatter,*
> *I sprang from my bed to see what was the matter.*
> *Away to the window I flew like flash,*
> *Tore open the shutters and* threw up *the sash."*

Although each child may have his own reasons for liking a particular book, there are certain popular reasons. In *Beginning with Books*, librarian Nancy DeSalvo lists nine common reasons why a child becomes attached to a book:

1. Reassurance (family security in *Whose Mouse Are You?*, by Robert Kraus)
2. Identification (toddler behavior in *Sam's Teddy Bear*, by Barbro Lindgren)
3. Humor (*Curious George*, by H. A. Rey)

4. Predictability or repetition (Bill Martin, Jr.'s, *Brown Bear, Brown Bear, What Do You See?*)
5. Artistic distinction (Ezra Jack Keats' *A Snowy Day*)
6. Rhythm (*Madeline* by Ludwig Bemelmans)
7. Happy association (*Blueberries for Sal*, by Robert McCloskey)
8. Gimmick (lift-the-flap books like *Where's Spot?*, by Eric Hill)
9. Special interest (*Big Wheels*, by Anne Rockwell, is a favorite of children fond of trucks and large vehicles)

To Reread or Not to Reread

Psychologist Bruno Bettelheim offers this hope to parents weary of reading the same book: When a child has gotten all he can from the book or when the problems that directed him to it have been outgrown, he'll be ready to move on to something else.[15]

Because visual literacy comes before print literacy, two-thirds of the questions and comments from young children are about the illustrations in the book.[16] The stationary nature of illustrations in books gives them a distinct advantage, allowing a child to "study" the page, unlike film or television, where the images move too quickly for a child to scrutinize.

Parents often are irritated by a child's incessant questions. "My child interrupts the book so often for questions, it ruins the story." First, you need to define the kinds of questions. Are they silly? Are they the result of curiosity or extraneous to the story? Is the child sincerely trying to learn something or just postponing bedtime? You can solve the latter problem if you make a regular habit of talking about the story when you finish, instead of simply closing the book, kissing the child goodnight, and turning off the light.

In the case of intelligent questions, try to respond immediately if the child's question involves background knowledge ("Why did Mr. MacGregor put Peter's father in a pie, Mom? Why couldn't he just hop out?") and thus help the child better understand the story. Extraneous questions can be handled by saying, "Good question! Let's come back to that when we're done." And be sure to live up to that promise. Ultimately one must acknowledge that questions are a child's primary learning tool. Don't destroy that natural curiosity by ignoring it. And finally, a book has many advantages over television, not the least of which is you can put the story on hold while you answer a child's questions, and then come back to the story.

To be candid, many questions are intended to postpone bedtime, a delaying tactic. Put such tactics into the hands of a creative child—a lawyer's child, for example—and you've got a high-powered ploy. A few years ago, the *St. Louis Post-Dispatch Sunday Magazine* did a feature on the books parents hate but young kids love.[17] And there was attorney Marc Braun holding forth on the unworthiness of *The Fire Engine Book*, a little Golden Book with illustrations dating to the 1950s and firemen with pigs' faces.

"But for some reason, my kids fell in love with it—to the point where I had to read it six times in a night! What really did me in, though, was when my son, Jacob, decided that all the firemen had to have names—the same names as the kids in his day-care class. But each night, when we read the book, he would assign different names to the characters, so that the fireman who was Keith one night was someone else the next.

"Pretty soon, a book that should have taken ten minutes at most to read was taking forty-five. I thought I was going to lose my mind," said Braun, sighing. The book itself finally solved the problem when it slowly disintegrated from overuse. If indeed Jacob was less interested in the characters' names than a postponement of bedtime, he's well on his way to a successful law career.

As boring as repeated readings may be for the adult, they can accomplish very important things within a child. To begin with, they learn language by hearing it over and over—this is called immersion. Hearing the same story over and over is definitely a part of that immersion process.

The repeated readings also help build children's self-esteem. First, the reader makes the child feel good by granting his wish for a repeat performance. Second, with each repetition the child is better able to predict what will happen next. Very little in a child's life is completely predictable. They never know what you will give them to wear or to eat, or where you will take them on a given day. And then along comes this book that your repeated readings have made entirely predictable, something at which the young child is suddenly an expert. He can tell you *exactly* what will happen next, word for word, page for page. *Expert*— what a proud merit badge for one so young to wear. The child feels good about himself and associates that good feeling with reading.

For as long as possible, your read-aloud efforts should be balanced by the outside experiences you bring to the child. Barring cases of bedridden children, it is not enough to simply read to the child. The visual literacy I noted earlier applies to life experience as well. The words in the book are just the beginning. What you as a parent or teacher do *after* the reading can turn a mini-lesson into a sizable learning experience. For example, there is a much-loved children's book about a little girl and a department store teddy bear, *Corduroy*, by Don Freeman. The story alone is heartwarming, but the name Corduroy could also be used as a springboard to a discussion and comparison of other common fabrics like denim, wool, cotton, canvas, and felt. And it works in reverse as well: When you find a caterpillar outside, read Eric Carle's *The Very Hungry Caterpillar* inside the house or classroom.

For culturally deprived children, the problem of connecting with what they hear in a story is much more acute. Such children have few positive experiences in the larger world; their lives are often impoverished not just economically, but in terms of activities and adventures as well. Such children were like the three-year-olds living in the shadow of St. Louis's airport who didn't know there were *people* in those planes flying over their homes until their Head Start program took a class trip to the airport. Imagine the difference that made in their understanding of the word "plane." Children who have the opportunity to travel often have higher reading skills.[18]

Just as children are reassured by familiar books, they also are bolstered by predictable routines. Therefore, while allowing for impromptu readings, try to establish a schedule for reading—a time when the child will have few other distractions, a time he can count on, a time as predictable as lunchtime and bathtime.

The time of day my family usually chose was bedtime—both in the afternoon before naps and in the evening. These are the times when the child looks for security, appreciates the physical closeness, and is tired enough to stay in one place. It is an appropriate time to introduce him to "bedtime" books like *Goodnight Moon*, by Margaret Wise Brown (for toddlers), and *No Jumping on the Bed*, by Tedd Arnold (for older children).

For nearly every subject of interest to a child, there is a corresponding book. For example, when last I looked there were more than fifty different books—fiction and nonfiction—published on the subject of snow. (Note the reaction of Erin Hassett on page 33 when she connects the snow outside her window to her book *The Snowman*.)

When you see that your child has developed a fascination for a particular subject, check your neighborhood library for a book on it. The subject listing in the card catalogue will show what the library has on its shelves, and a handy reference guide in all libraries, *Subject Guide to Children's Books in Print*, will show what is available outside the library as well. See also *The Bookfinder*, a two-volume listing of tens of thousands of children's titles under 450 developmental, behavioral, and psychological headings—topics such as adoption, belonging, courage, death, divorce, teachers, and siblings.

Wordless and Predictable Books

When your child is between two and five years of age, his desire to imitate his parent will extend to reading books. In some cases, by the time the child is four, he can recite a book verbatim, page by page. I use "recite" and not "read" because in the majority of cases the child has only memorized what you've been reading to him. He'll boast that he is reading—and that's fine. Reward and encourage his effort by saying how glad you are to see him enjoying himself with a book, but *don't* convey the impression that you like him more because he reads. His self-worth is not predicated upon a performance. If he were learning handicapped, wouldn't you love him just as much?

In continuing these recitations, a child gradually comes closer to the text, and eventually he'll be reading naturally. Two kinds of books are especially helpful in building the confidence, imagination, and vocabulary of prereaders: wordless books and predictable books.

Thirty thousand years ago, in a step toward writing, our ancestors used cave drawings to tell stories—and wordless books follow that tradition. These books convey a story without using words; pictures (interpreted orally by the reader) tell the whole story—books in pantomime, if you will. Children quickly realize the pictures must be followed in sequence for the story to make sense (sequencing skill) and the story is "told" (verbal skills) instead of read. Once the adult has blazed a reading trail through the book, it's relatively easy for the child to pick it up and talk the book to himself or others using the pictures as story clues.

Children with limited English skills find these books immediately accessible and thus gain reading confidence. Writing teachers often ask their students to write the missing text. This has been an increasingly popular genre in recent years; there are now more than one hundred wordless books in print, running from the simple (like *Deep in the Forest*, by Brinton Turkle) to the complex (*The Silver Pony*, by Lynd Ward).[19] (See the Wordless Books listed at the beginning of the Treasury.)

Though the "predictable book" form—i.e., the use of repetition—has been around for ages in folk tale and song, only recently have educators discovered how helpful it is in building readers. Because the story line contains phrases that are repeated over and over ("Then I'll huff and I'll puff and I'll . . ."), the child can easily predict what's coming and often joins in on the reading (which enhances comprehension). For example, in Barbara Seuling's *The Teeny Tiny Woman*, the words "teeny tiny" are repeated fifty times throughout the book's thirteen sentences. In addition, predictable books often contain a cumulative sequence, as in *Henny Penny*: "So Henny Penny, Chicken Licken, Turkey Lurkey and Foxy Loxy went to see the king."

Repeated readings of these books allow children to put the language they already own to immediate use, thus experiencing at least partial success with "memorized reading." It is of critical importance that the child's early experiences with print be successful ones—even if the "success" is only in his own mind.

In classes that have predictable books such as *We're Going on a Bear Hunt*, by Michael Rosen and Helen Oxenbury, beginning readers attempt to read these books twice as often as others during free reading time—largely because they are less intimidating.[20] The same would apply to home libraries as well. The key is: Someone must expose them to the book's pattern through read-aloud. (See Predictable/Cumulative Stories, early in the Treasury.)

Predictable, wordless, and controlled-vocabulary books (like Dr. Seuss's *Cat in the Hat*) build the beginning reader's self-confidence, but beyond a certain point they have limited value as vocabulary builders. Indeed, a continued diet of controlled-vocabulary books is an insult to your child's listening vocabulary. Therefore, don't limit your read-alouds to that genre. After you've familiarized the child with the book, let him read it by himself (that's what it's for) and you introduce him to others, especially books with richer vocabulary and more complex stories.

Educators who work with the children of illiterate and semiliterate adults should make wordless books available to these parents, many of whom desperately wish they could read to their children. Wordless books provide that opportunity: they can "talk" the book by looking at the pictures and interpreting them—in any language, I might add.

In addition to wordless books, most libraries (and bookstores) have hundreds of children's books available on audiocassette, housed with the book in a Ziploc plastic bag. Less than competent readers can sit down and listen to the story side by side with their child, turning the pages when prompted on the tape. Hearing the story more than once helps the adult to memorize the story. They're also sharing their time and themselves with the child. Is someone else's voice better than the parent's? No, but it's a whole lot better than no story at all. Taking the time to listen beside the child—instead of watching TV or talking on the phone—sends a very loud message to the child about the importance the parent places upon books.

Less accomplished readers should be encouraged to begin by reading simple picture books (and not difficult novels). This allows them to gradually build their confidence and reading proficiency as their child grows older.

On the subject of Dr. Seuss, keep in mind that his controlled-vocabulary books are only a small portion of the staggering number he wrote. The very best ones—like *If I Ran the Zoo*—have a story filled with what Seuss called his "logical nonsense"; that is, children find the sights and sounds logical while adults find them nonsensical. The rich vocabulary, verbal gymnastics, and humor permeating these books keep children intrigued and delighted.

Waldo, Pop-ups, and Joke Books

A first cousin to wordless books are pop-up books and visual-puzzle books like the popular *Waldo* series by Martin Handford, which contain minimal plot and text. Can we legitimately call these things books, and what do they have to do with reading?

Yes, "pop-ups" are books—gimmicky, but enormously successful with young and often older readers. If you've seen any of the more elaborate ones, you would find they now include fairly sophisticated text and they are engineering marvels. Moreover, they enable a child to make a "pleasure-connection" with print in a book form, and *that* is always more positive than the "pain-connection" with workbooks and tests in school. Just think of such volumes as books with "training wheels." An unfortunate aspect of pop-up books is their unavailability in libraries. Because the moving parts are so fragile, they have a short "shelf life" and are therefore too risky for most libraries to purchase. Bookstores are practically the sole resource for pop-ups.

The *Waldo* books, which require the reader-viewer to find the peripatetic backpacker amidst thousands of tiny, scurrying figures, hold a similar fascination for young readers, just as crossword puzzles appeal to older readers. But *Waldo* also builds reading skills. In order to find the Waldo character, the child must: (1) focus on the page; (2) recall what he looks like from the first page; and (3) compare and contrast that memory image with each figure on the page. Thus attention span, recall, and visual discrimination are nurtured—three essential skills in reading. Finding Waldo is not terribly far removed from the recall and discrimination necessary to tell the difference between the letters "b" and "d," or the difference between "p" and "q."

Also there are the psychological advantages of *Waldo*: (1) Such books are fun. Never underestimate the power of that three-letter word in attracting and energizing a child's interest; and (2) the *Waldo* books can be "read" or interpreted by children even before they can actually read. Doing so, the child begins to think of himself as a reader (establishing another positive association with books). Numerous "visual discrimination" books (including some for older readers) are now on the market, and a listing can be found under the *Where's Waldo* books in the Treasury.

Even before the child is ready for kindergarten, he can pride himself on having a sense of humor—especially if it has been cultivated with some simple joke and riddle books you've read to him. Start with the books I've listed with *Haunted House Jokes* by Louis Phillips in the Treasury. For beginning readers, put them in handy places like the kitchen table, at the bedside, or in the bathroom, and he'll be reading them, then memorizing and trying them out on family members. Nothing builds self-confidence and esteem like a well-told and well-received joke.[21]

Shared laughter makes everybody feel better. Try these funny picture books: *The Stupids Step Out*, by Harry Allard; *Amelia Bedelia* by Peggy Parish; *Thomas' Snowsuit*, by Robert Munsch; *The Cut-Ups Cut Loose*, by James Marshall; *Not the Piano, Mrs. Medley*, by Evan Levine; and two by Robin Pulver—*Mrs. Toggle's Zipper* and *Nobody's Mother Is in Second Grade*. And here are four humorous novels: *Freckle Juice*, by Judy Blume; *Mr. Popper's Penguins*, by Florence and Richard Atwater; *The Best Christmas Pageant Ever*, by Barbara Robinson; and *Skinnybones*, by Barbara Park.

A Rationale for Fairy Tales

Before most parents realize it, a growing child is ready, in his own mind at least, to go out and challenge the world. In the last two thousand years, nothing has filled this exploratory need as well as the fairy tale.

I know what you may be thinking. "Fairy tales? Is he kidding? Why, those things are positively frightening. Children see enough violence on television—they don't need kids pushing witches into ovens, and evil spells and poisoned apples."

Stop for a minute and remind yourself how long the fairy tale has been with us—in every nation and in every civilization. Surely there must be something important here, an insight so important as to transcend time and geography and cultures to arrive in the twentieth century still intact. There are, for example, nearly seven hundred different versions of *Cinderella* from hundreds of cultures. Nevertheless, they all tell the same story—a truly universal story.

What distinguishes the fairy tale is that it speaks to the very heart and soul of the child. It admits to the child what so many parents and teachers spend hours trying to cover up or avoid. The fairy tale confirms what the child has been thinking all along—that it is a cold, cruel world out there and it's waiting to eat him alive.

Now, if that were *all* the fairy tale said, it would have died out long ago. But it goes one step further. It addresses itself to the child's sense of courage and adventure. The tale advises the child: Take your courage in hand and go out to meet that world head-on. According to Bruno Bettelheim, the fairy tale offers this promise: If you have courage and if you persist, you can overcome any obstacle, conquer any foe. And best of all, you can achieve your heart's desire. G. K. Chesterton even builds a powerful analogy between fairy tales and the essence of Christianity.[22] (Bettelheim's *Uses of Enchantment* is one of the best books to explain the force of story, particularly fairy tales, in shaping children's perceptions of the world. Another excellent source for matching stories with values is *From Wonder to Wisdom: Using Stories to Help Children Grow*, by Charles A. Smith, Ph.D.)

By recognizing the child's daily fears, by appealing to his courage and confidence, and by offering him hope, the fairy tale presents the child with a means by which he can understand his world and himself. And those who would deodorize the tales impose a fearsome lie upon the child. J. R. R. Tolkien cautioned, "It does not pay to leave a dragon out of your calculations if you live near him." Judging from the daily statistics, our land is filled with dragons.

- Advocacy groups receive 3 million child-abuse calls each year, with at least 40 percent substantiated.[23]
- 1,200 children are abused to death each year, and one-half of all abuse victims are under one year of age.[24]
- Every 12 seconds a man batters his wife or ex-wife or girlfriend.[25]

- 14 children are killed by guns each day.[26]
- A theft or violent crime occurs on school grounds once every six seconds.[27]

To send a child into that world unprepared is a crime.

When Dr. Perri Klass, a respected Boston pediatrician and author (and also a parent), pondered the effects on children of emotionally charged movies like *The Lion King,* her response applied to literature as well as film: "If children's entertainment is purged of the powerful, we risk homogenization, predictability and boredom, and we deprive our children of any real understanding of the cathartic and emotional potentials of narrative . . . And when we talk about children made sad by a movie, we are talking about children being moved by things that are not really happening to real people, and that is what art and drama and literature are all about. Those children are recognizing a character and feeling for that character, and that is a giant step toward empathy."[28]

The older the child, the greater the temptation for adults to choose books that will keep the child forever young, books without problems, conflict, or drama. And then all too soon these same parents are asking why their children have lost interest in books. Of all the things we ask our books to be, few are as important as "believable." Fiction, nonfiction, biographies, fantasies—the good ones work because they are believable. A world that is "forever pink," as Natalie Babbitt once put it, doesn't work because children eventually realize its fakery.

The warm and fuzzy world of Beatrix Potter has been popular for almost five generations because it is believable. True, rabbits and squirrels don't talk, but there *are* single parents like Peter's mother who daily warn their children of dire consequences, there *are* lost fathers like Peter's, and there *are* Mr. MacGregors out there. And that's why *The Tale of Peter Rabbit* is the best-selling children's book of all time—not just because the pictures are warm and fuzzy-looking.

As children become more and more aware of the world around them—that it is wider than their own family and their own street—we the readers-aloud can serve by gently holding the child's hand and mind as he or she meets a time and place that is not "forever pink." Representative of children's need for reality is their fascination with "orphanhood." Consider the major pieces of children's literature that have been built on the adventures of orphan children: "Moses in the bulrushes";

Tom Sawyer; *Huck Finn*; *Oliver Twist*; Horatio Alger's novels; *Heidi*; *Tarzan*; *Mowgli*; *The Secret Garden*; *A Little Princess*; *Understood Betsy*; *Anne of Green Gables*; *The Boxcar Children*; *The Wizard of Oz*; *James and the Giant Peach*; and most recently, *Maniac Magee*.

If there is one flaw in the fairy tale, it is that many popular tales are top-heavy with heroes and short on heroines. For balance, readers-aloud will want to try Ethel Johnston Phelps' two collections, *The Maid of the North* and *Tatterhood and Other Tales*, as well as *Wise Women: Folk and Fairy Tales from Around the World*, retold and edited by Suzanne I. Barchers. These are traditional tales about nontraditional, courageous, resourceful, and witty heroines from a variety of ethnic cultures. Try coupling Trina Schart Hyman's excellent version of *Sleeping Beauty* with Jane Yolen's *Sleeping Ugly* and *The Not-So-Wicked Stepmother*, by Lizi Boyd.

Until about seven years of age, children generally won't gravitate on their own to heavy books like anthologies. Therefore, in the Fairy/Folk Tales section of the Treasury I have listed numerous books containing outstanding *individual* tales, as well as anthologies of tales. Recent years also have seen a wave of outstanding fairy-tale anthologies, from the simpler ones, like Anne Rockwell's *The Three Bears and 15 Other Stories* and *Read Me a Story: A Child's Book of Favorite Tales*, by Sophie Windham, to the more complex collections, like *Michael Foreman's World of Fairy Tales* and *The Rainbow Fairy Book*, retold by Andrew Lang. They are excellent for the bedside and to keep in the car in case of emergency (a long wait in the doctor's office and you forgot to bring a book).

From here you can progress gradually in length and complexity as the child's maturity and imagination demand. While I don't recommend *Hansel and Gretel* for three- and four-year-olds, I most heartily recommend it for children of five and older who wonder to themselves: How long could I survive alone out there if nobody loved me? Or my parents died? Books that water down the essence of the tales do an injustice to the book and insult the naturally curious mind.

The very best in contemporary children's books borrow the strong flavor of adventure and quest from fairy tales. Maurice Sendak's *Where the Wild Things Are*, one of the most popular children's books of our time, deals with a child's rage at his parent and his subsequent triumphs in the land of monsters. Ludwig Bemelmans allows his heroine Madeline to enter numerous predicaments, always to emerge devilishly triumphant. In William Steig's *Sylvester and the Magic Pebble* the hero is turned into a stone (talk about predicaments and a cruel world!), but finally emerges triumphant through his own persistence and the unfailing love of his parents.

It is this internal struggle to find out how we feel or who we are that is so central to the idea of reading. More than helping them to read better, more than exposing them to good writing, more than developing their imagination, when we read aloud to children we are helping them to find themselves and to discover some meaning in the scheme of things. When Robert Penn Warren wrote, "We turn to fiction for some slight hint about the story in the life we live," he meant children as much as adults.

Literature and Critical Thinking Skills

Because of the variety involved, children's books offer us an excellent opportunity to introduce children to comparative literature, showing the contrast in viewpoints. It has been said that the most important contribution of the Greeks to the world was this simple turn of phrase: "On the one hand . . ." and "On the other hand . . ."[29] In other words, the Greeks taught us how to think deeply, that deep thoughts require comparisons. So when we invite children to make comparisons, we are teaching them critical thinking skills. The younger people are, the less able they are to think deeply because they have fewer experiences to use in making comparisons. Conversely, the older we get, the more we can compare.

Nonetheless, kindergarten children are capable of making comparisons—not just of objects on the measuring table, but also of ideas. But in order to do so, they must be mature enough to keep more than one thing in their minds at a time—a basis for comparative thinking. If the experiences are interesting and memorable enough, they will relish the opportunity. The key is to keep the story within the developmental range of the child. For example, with three-year-olds you could read two bedtime stories, both using similar patterns: *Goodnight Moon* by Margaret Wise Brown and *Good Night, Gorilla* by Peggy Rathmann, and then discuss the similarities and differences.

You could read different versions of the same fairy tale on successive days: *The Three Bears and Goldilocks*, by Paul Galdone; *Somebody and the Three Blairs*, by Marilyn Tolhurst; and *Deep in the Forest*, by Brinton Turkle. The latter two books reverse the original cast so the bears visit the humans.

With slightly older children, read and invite comparisons of different versions of Little Red Riding Hood: *Little Red Riding Hood*, by Trina Schart Hyman—traditional; *Flossie and the Fox*, by Patricia C. McKissack—African-American; *Ruby*, by Michael Emberley—modern urban; and *Lon Po Po*, by Ed Young—Chinese.

In the Treasury at the back of this book, most main titles include a "related books" listing for similar comparisons. Here are some possible comparisons:

CINDERELLA—FAIRY TALE:
Cinderella, retold by Amy Ehrlich; *Ashpet*, retold by Joanne Compton— an Appalachian version; *The Egyptian Cinderella*, by Shirley Climo; *The Rough-Face Girl*, retold by Rafe Martin—American Indian; *UGH*, by Arthur Yorinks and Richard Egielski—a prehistoric male; *Yeh-Shen*, retold by Ai-Ling Louie—Chinese; and *Princess Furball*, retold by Charlotte Huck

THE SKY IS FALLING—FOLK TALE:
Chicken Little, by Steven Kellogg; and *Foolish Rabbit's Big Mistake*, by Rafe Martin

MAD CHASES:
The Gingerbread Man, by Paul Galdone; *The Bee Tree*, by Patricia Polacco; *Donna O'Neechuck Was Chased by Some Cows*, by Bill Grossman; and *The Elephant and the Bad Baby*, by Elfrida Vipont

TRICKSTER TALES:
Doctor DeSoto, by William Steig; "Brer Fox" stories from *The Tales of Uncle Remus*, retold by Julius Lester; *The Tale of Rabbit and Coyote*, by Tony Johnson—Mexican; *Anansi and the Talking Melon*, retold by Eric Kimmel—African; and *Mule Eggs*, by Cynthia DeFelice— American

BAD GUYS TURNED GOOD:
Burglar Bill, by Janet and Allan Ahlberg; and *The Three Robbers*, by Tomi Ungerer

WOLF-AT-THE-DOOR TALES:
The Three Little Pigs, retold by James Marshall; *The True Story of the Three Little Pigs*, by Jon Scieszka; and *Mr. and Mrs. Pig's Night Out*, by Mary Rayner

OUT OF ONE NEST AND INTO SOMEONE ELSE'S
(OR MOWGLI COMES IN MANY SHAPES):
Stellaluna, by Janell Cannon; *Arnold of the Ducks*, by Mordicai Gerstein; *The Boy Who Lived with the Seals*, retold by Rafe Martin; and *Jumbo the Boy and Arnold the Elephant*, by Dan Greenberg

SECURITY DOLL/BLANKET:
Owen, by Kevin Henkes; *Ira Sleeps Over*, by Bernard Waber; and *Tim and the Blanket Thief*, by John Prater

ENVIRONMENT:
Farewell to Shady Glade, by Bill Peet; *The Lorax*, by Dr. Seuss; and *Just a Dream*, by Chris Van Allsburg

THE POWER OF ART:
The Magic Paintbrush, by Robin Muller; *The Boy Who Drew Cats*, retold by Arthur A. Levine; and *Pumpkin Light*, by David Ray

PETS OUT OF CONTROL:
The Boy Who Was Followed Home, by Margaret Mahy; *The Mysterious Tadpole*, by Steven Kellogg; *Millions of Cats*, by Wanda Gag; and *Poonam's Pets*, by Andrew and Diana Davies

SELF-IMAGES AND TOLERANCE:
Crow Boy, by Taro Yashima; *Oliver Button Is a Sissy*, by Tomie dePaola; and *Company's Coming*, by Arthur Yorinks

IMAGINARY FEARS:
The Bear Under the Stairs, by Helen Cooper; *The Phantom Lunch Wagon*, by Daniel Pinkwater; and *Donovan Scares the Monsters*, by Susan Love Whitlock

GENIE IN THE BOTTLE:
The Secret in the Matchbox, by Val Willis; *Do Not Open*, by Brinton Turkle; and *Aladdin*, retold by Andrew Lang

TAMING THE WILD:

The Biggest Bear, by Lynd Ward; *Cappyboppy*, by Bill Peet; *Honkers*, by Jane Yolen; and *A Snake in the House*, by Faith McNulty

YOUTH AND THE ELDERLY:

When I Am Old with You, by Angela Johnson; *Captain Snap and the Children of Vinegar Lane*, by Roni Schotter; *Now One Foot, Now the Other*, by Tomie dePaola; and *Supergrandpa*, by David M. Schwartz

Humor requires critical thinking skills as well, especially parody or satire, and the exciting fairy-tale parodies of recent years can nurture those skills. Try these: *The Jolly Postman* (the pages of which form envelopes containing letters, postcards, and junk mail from famous fairy-tale characters), *Jeremiah in the Dark Woods* and *Ten in a Bed*, all by Janet and Allan Ahlberg; *The True Story of the Three Little Pigs*, by Jon Scieszka; *The Three Little Wolves and the Big Bad Pig*, by Eugene Trivizas; *The Frog Prince*, by Alix Berenzy; *Jim and the Beanstalk*, by Raymond Briggs; *Jack and the Meanstalk*, by Brian and Rebecca Wildsmith; *The Princess and the Frog*, by A. Vesey; *Beware of Boys*, by Tony Blundell; and *Telling of the Tales: Five Stories*, by William J. Brooke.

Integrating the Curriculum

One of education's recent buzzword phrases is "integrating the curriculum"—incorporating math into reading, reading into social studies, etc. This not only makes sense but has also been a breath of fresh air in many stale classrooms. As you will see in Chapter 8, it can be taken to extremes too. Here are some positive examples of how children's books can be used by both teachers and parents in a holistic fashion for learning and enjoyment.

In the 1989 edition of *The Read-Aloud Handbook*, I mentioned a kindergarten consultant in Hawaii who was concerned about her students' view of the world. "Hawaiian children often have a narrow perspective on the world," she explained. "They think there are only two places: Hawaii and the mainland (which includes everyplace else)." To give her children a sense of geography, the teacher incorporated a large world map into her literature program, on which students placed stickers when she read *The Red Balloon* (France), *Curious George* (Africa), *The Tale of Ferdinand* (Spain), and *The Five Chinese Brothers* (China).

Now most people who read that anecdote might have said, "Nice idea," and left it at that. And then there are people like Janet Moylan of Omaha, Nebraska, a mother of five. "This would be a great tool for our home," she thought as she went out shopping for wall maps of the United States and the world, both of which she promptly hung between the children's bedrooms.

"My four children, Michaela (nine), Amy (eight), Jenny (five), and Daniel (three), were very excited about the maps. On the first night, we located places where *we* had been. We talked about how we would find the locations of the books that we read, and the children were able to name many of our books and locate the cities." They then purchased quarter-inch stickers, numbered them, placed them on the map sites, and entered the numbers and book titles in a spiral notebook.

When they were reading Lois Lowry's Newbery Medal–winning *Number the Stars* (which included incidents from the Danish resistance movement in World War II), they went to the wall map to locate Denmark, Germany, Sweden, Norway, the North Sea, and the cities of Kattegat and Copenhagen. "The map gave us a better sense of location for the setting, and we talked about the size of Germany compared to Denmark," Moylan explained.[30]

Her youngest child, Daniel, became interested in the flags on the edges of the world map and began to associate flags with their countries and the respective books—like China's flag, which he called *Lon Po Po*'s flag (after the Caldecott Medal winner by Ed Young).

At one point she sat with her children and they talked about the map. Among the children's observations were these:

- Author Lois Lowry lives in Boston and her Anastasia books took place in that area.
- Some of the books were about immigrants, and many times they landed in New York—as they did in books like *Papa Like Everyone Else*, by Sydney Taylor; *Watch the Stars Come Out*, by Riki Levinson; and *In the Year of the Boar and Jackie Robinson*, by Bette Bao Lord.
- Maps help you see exactly where a story took place.
- You can see how far people had to travel in the stories—like the route Shirley took from China to New York (*In the Year of the Boar and Jackie Robinson*).

Soon the maps became an inspiration to read about countries where they had no stickers. And finally, consider the skills and subjects the

Moylan family covered with this ongoing activity: reading, geography, history, spatial relationships, cataloguing, and journal-keeping—all for less than twenty dollars, and none of it got in the way of reading.

It is too easy to forget the author's very purpose in writing the book, especially if we add on so many assorted activities they amount to gilding the lily and get in the eyes of the child so he can't see the point of the book. This will be discussed at greater length in Chapter 8. This is not to say activities are *never* appropriate. Proportion and appropriateness—not keeping the class busy—are the key to successful reading activities.

One of the best activities resources I've seen on the market in the last twenty years is the *Story S-T-R-E-T-C-H-E-R-S* series by Shirley C. Raines and Robert J. Canady, two college professors specializing in early-childhood education and language arts. Each volume offers 450 involvement activities that can be used with ninety popular children's books like *Frederick, Millions of Cats, If You Give a Mouse a Cookie, William's Doll,* etc. The activities include circle time, art, music, cooking, drama, dress-up, music and movement, block building, science and nature, listening, and manipulatives. There are three books in the series (*Story S-T-R-E-T-C-H-E-R-S; More Story S-T-R-E-T-C-H-E-R-S;* and *S-T-R-E-T-C-H-E-R-S for the Primary Grades*), with the first two volumes focusing on books for preschool through kindergarten. A similar book is Patricia Buerke Moll's *Children and Books I: African-American Story Books and Activities for All Children.*[31]

More Talk, Higher Grades

Not to be overlooked amidst the activities is this fact: Students from classrooms where there were more book discussions tended to score higher in national reading assessments.[32] Unfortunately, students are seldom invited to participate in the conversations in school. And even when they are, they're not expected to stay very long. Studies reveal most teachers wait only one second or less for answers to their questions. But further research showed if they expanded that to three to five seconds before and after the answer, student responses grew more frequent and more logical, and complex thinking skills improved significantly.[33] When 537 K–6 classrooms were observed by practice teachers in 1992, they found that classroom discussion before or after the story averaged less than five minutes![34] On the other hand, when two teachers stop to discuss a book in the teachers lounge, they'll spend twenty-five minutes discussing it and *never writing about it*. You almost get the feeling the teacher doesn't want to share the spotlight in class.

And things don't get much better as students move up the grade levels. A 1990 study of 15 college classrooms and 331 students showed the students asked only 49 questions in 900 minutes of class time—or 3.3 an hour.[35] Compare that with the nonstop questioning by students in kindergarten classrooms.

Much of the book discussion in the classroom or home will depend initially on your *coaching*. Many children don't know WHAT to listen to, how to separate the important from the unimportant. They also need to be reminded of what to ignore: "Remember, class, part of being a good listener is learning *not* to listen to distractions. For example, when Room 5 across the hall is lining up to go for their recess, we must all try to block those noises from our minds by not concentrating on them."

A good listening coach provides the child or class with a list of "coming attractions" before reading a story, items and ideas to listen for. For example, with Bill Peet's *The Whingdingdilly*, pointing to the book's cover in front of the child or class, you might say: "What do we see here? . . . Does this give us any clues to what the book will be about? What do you think it will be about? . . . The name of the book is *The Whingdingdilly* and it's written by our old friend Bill Peet. That's a pretty long word—Whingdingdilly. Do you know what it means? As we read, let's see if we can discover why author Bill Peet used this title. Last week we talked about the difference between fables and fairy tales and folk tales. Let's see which category this book falls into. And finally, there is someone in this story who reminds me of another character we've read about recently. As we read, see if you can figure out who that might be."

Winners in the classroom, as well as on the field, usually have better coaches. At an important part of the story, stop and ask your audience, "What do you think is going to happen next?" This kind of nonthreatening question solicits children's opinions and nurtures memory and prediction skills. And by involving children in the reading, you enhance understanding.

Educators report the most important critical thinking skill is recognizing the essence of a problem. So, as a problem or conflict develops in the book, stop reading and ask, "What's the problem here?" "What do you think is wrong?" "What would *you* do in this situation?"

With novels, you can begin by asking, "Let's see—where did we leave off yesterday?" "What's happened so far?" and this strengthens memory and sequencing skills. With books that have unnamed chapters, let children take turns naming the chapters at the end of the day's reading. Reading aloud can accomplish many of the same things you do with paper and pencil—depending on how much pleasure you incorporate (or draw from) the experience. Educators will find Dorothy Grant Hennings' brief book, *Beyond the Read-Aloud: Learning to Read Through Listening to and Reflecting on Literature*, to be very helpful in this area.

Stretching the Attention Span

One of the first criteria for lengthening the read-aloud session beyond picture books is the attention span of the child or class. Thanks to our primal need to find out what happens next, read-aloud is a particularly effective tool in stretching children's attention spans. Just keep in mind that endurance in readers—like runners—is not built overnight; start slowly and build.

If I had a primary class (or child) that had never been read to (like the ones who spent all of kindergarten filling in blanks and circling letters), I'd start the year with the repetition of *Tikki Tikki Tembo*, by Arlene Mosel; the poignancy of *The Biggest Bear*, by Lynd Ward; the mystery of *The Island of the Skog*, by Steven Kellogg; the humor of *Foolish Rabbit's Big Mistake*, by Rafe Martin; and the suspense of Paul Zelinsky's retelling of *Rumpelstiltskin*. The following week would be called "A Walk in the Woods," focusing on children's adventures in the woods—starting with Trina Schart Hyman's *Little Red Riding Hood* and followed by books chosen from the titles listed with it in the Treasury.

Moving to books with more words, I'd schedule Bill Peet Week. Then I would choose a week's worth of reading from his more than thirty books (enough to even have a Bill Peet *month*). On the day I read *Kermit the Hermit* (a stingy hermit crab), I'd introduce it with the "Hector the Collector" from Shel Silverstein's poetry collection *Where the Sidewalk Ends*. From then on I'd begin or end the reading with a poem—not necessarily connected to the reading—and gradually sprinkle poetry throughout the day: waiting for the bell in the morning, between classes, et cetera.

I'd culminate Bill Peet Week (or month) by sharing parts of *Bill Peet: An Autobiography*, his 190-page Caldecott Honor Book that explores the roots of his life and books—with pictures on every page. Then I'd move on to something a little more complex—like Carol and Donald

Carrick's eight-book series (listed with *Sleep Out* in the Treasury) that follows a child's maturing and heartwarming struggles with sleeping out, the death of his dog, and being lost on a class trip. Eight books, eight days, all linked by the common thread of one family and their concern for one another.

Introducing Chapter Books

Once you have built a child's or class's attention span, it's an easy jump to "chapter books"—either long picture books or short novels of sixty to one hundred pages. These are books that don't have to end with Monday—that can be stretched into Tuesday and Wednesday. Even pre-schoolers can enjoy chapter books. Given the opportunity, they'll respond enthusiastically to picture books divided into chapters, like *Mr. Hacker*, by James Stevenson; *Grandaddy's Place*, by Helen Griffith; *Emily's Own Elephant*, by Philippa Pearce; *Wagon Wheels*, by Barbara Brenner; and *The Josefina Story Quilt*, by Eleanor Coerr. Then I'd do a collection of stories in one volume about one family. Two of my favorites are *The Big Alfie and Annie Rose Storybook*, by Shirley Hughes, and *My Naughty Little Sister*, by Dorothy Edwards.

Sometimes you'll encounter a picture book that may be too long for one sitting. Solve the problem by dividing it into chapters yourself. That works especially well with Rumer Godden's classic Christmas book, *The Story of Holly and Ivy* (you've got to love a book that opens on Christmas Eve in an orphanage). Excellent starters for short novels are *The Courage of Sarah Noble*, by Alice Dalgliesh, and William McCleery's *Wolf Story*. And don't miss *The Iron Giant*, by Ted Hughes (a terrific science fiction tale for primary grades), and *Lafcadio, the Lion Who Shot Back*, a slapstick novel by the popular Shel Silverstein.

I am firmly convinced that some of the blame for children's short attention spans must be placed on the shoulders of parents and teachers who continually underestimate these capacities. "That story would be too long. They'd never sit still that long," says the teacher, forgetting the fact that the children sit still for three hours of television every day. They have no trouble enjoying and understanding the movie *The Lion King* and they'll have no difficulty appreciating lengthy books—if they are exciting and meaningful.

Underestimating children is a common mistake, especially when it comes to literature, as Dr. Gayle Frame discovered early in her career. Frame is director of curriculum and instruction for the Howard-Suamico

School District in Green Bay, Wisconsin. "I spent the first five years of my teaching career with the fourth through sixth grades. Four of those years had been in a school with gifted kids who were intellectually much older. Each year, I read many of my favorite books to them—including my all-time favorite, *The Lion, the Witch, and the Wardrobe*." (For the uninitiated, this is a series that can be read with equal success as a children's adventure story or as an allegory of the life of Christ, written by one of the most noted Christian apologists of this century, C. S. Lewis.)

Frame went on to explain:

Year six found me teaching first grade in a school on the fringes of the inner city in St. Louis. I wasn't certain about reading [the books] to this group. After all, aside from the fact that they were considerably younger, the language experience of most of the kids was far different from that of my previous students. But I decided to tackle it anyway. If nothing else, I'd enjoy it!

As I neared the end of Chapter 14 (the one where Aslan [the lion-hero who is the Christ figure] is killed), one chunky little boy named Andrew headed back to the cloakroom for his coat—his standard procedure when he was mad at me. He would put his coat on backwards and pull the hood up over his face. He seemed to reason that my inability to see his face would somehow punish me. I quickly realized, however, that this time was different. Andrew was crying inside the hood of his jacket.

I finished the chapter, reading and saying, ". . . despair and die. The children did not see the actual moment of the killing. They couldn't bear to look and had covered their eyes."

I then said to the class, "And that, boys and girls, is the end of Chapter 14. We'll have to wait until tomorrow to see what happens." And then, from inside the hood, a voice sobbed, "They've killed that lion! You might as well quit. This story isn't worth reading any more."

I knew then that I couldn't let the story hang! After all, I was afraid Andrew wouldn't come back. So I said to the class, "Perhaps we can take time to read just a little more," and began the next chapter—which described how Aslan's dead face began to change, the Stone Table was broken, and Aslan was returning to life. As I continued to read the chapter, the hood inched its way down, re-

vealing those watery brown eyes. Although I couldn't see Andrew's
mouth yet, his eyes revealed that a big smile was replacing the tears.
And then he yelled, "It's like Jesus!"

It was almost twenty years later that Dr. Frame related the incident to
me, but the moment was as fresh as yesterday in her memory. "That
day I learned the power of a good story to transcend age, race, background experiences, or any other factor that adults often perceive as
hindrances."

Picture Books for Upper Grades

Teachers and parents often ask me, "When do you stop the picture
books and start the novels?" Although I understand their impatience to
get on with the business of growing up, I wince whenever I hear them
phrase it that way.

First of all, there is no such time as "a time to stop the picture books."
I know nursery school teachers who read Judith Viorst's *Alexander and
the Terrible, Horrible, No Good, Very Bad Day* to their classes, and I
know a high school English teacher who reads it to his sophomores
twice a year—once in September and, by popular demand, again in
June.

Shouldn't those fifteen-year-olds have outgrown a picture book like
Alexander? Not by my standards. A good story is a good story. Beautiful
and stirring pictures can move fifteen-year-olds as well as five-year-olds.
A picture book should be someplace on the reading list of every class
at every grade level.

I might also add, most U.S. high school students were not read to
regularly in primary grades and have done little or no reading on their
own. I remember talking with a remedial class of ninth-graders in California one day: of the twenty-one students, not one had ever heard of
the Pied Piper, none had heard of the Wright brothers, only two had
heard of David and Goliath, and none could remember the last time
they went to a movie theater. Their cultural references were a bit shallow
and ripe for planting. In sharing an occasional picture book you would
give teens a chance at what they missed in primary years—*The Pied
Piper of Hamelin*, retold by Barbara Bartos-Hoppner, and *Sleeping
Beauty* and *The Story of Ferdinand* (Munro Leaf's little book that
pushed *Gone With the Wind* out of the number-one spot on the bestseller list half a century ago). Many of our students are at the doorstep

of parenthood. In New York City alone, there are twelve thousand kindergarten children with teenage mothers; nationwide, *every day* forty teenage girls give birth to their *third* child.[36] If they and their friends are ignorant of childhood's stories, how can they share them with their children?

Writing in *The Journal of Reading*, William Coughlin, Jr., of the University of Massachusetts–Lowell explained the difficulties he encountered in trying to teach literary form (plot, setting, character) to secondary-school students.[37] The complexity and subtlety of the text he was using, Herman Melville's *Moby-Dick*, appeared to overwhelm the class. Coughlin began to wonder if the mistake was in trying to teach a simple idea with a complex book. Why not introduce the concepts of plot and point of view through a simple book and then apply them to a complex work?

Coughlin chose to work with Leo Lionni's *Frederick*, a picture book he describes as "a story of less than six hundred words, but the beautifully structured craftsmanship with which its elements of form interrelated exhibited perfectly what I wanted to my students to see when they read." The response by his class was immediate and the results positive. In the same article, coauthor Brendan Desilets explained how picture books were used in a similar manner at Bedford (Massachusetts) High School. Both authors agree that to "ignore children's literature in the high school classroom is to overlook a valuable resource for teaching advanced reading skills."

When we go back as adults to the books we enjoyed as children, we often bring to those books a perspective that was missing earlier and discover new dimensions. The weight of *The Velveteen Rabbit* by Margery Williams is in direct proportion to our age—the older we are, the more it means to us. Recent years have seen a wave of picture books containing themes sometimes better appreciated by older students than younger, themes that could serve as springboards to deeper classroom discussion with adolescents: aging—*Wilfred Gordon McDonald Partridge*, by Mem Fox, and *Old Henry*, by Joan Blos; war and peace—*The Butter Battle Book*, by Dr. Seuss; *Pink and Say*, by Patricia Polacco; and *Hiroshima No Pika*, by Toshi Maruki; selflessness—*Good Griselle*, by Jane Yolen; racism and imperialism—*Encounter*, by Jane Yolen; drugs and addiction—*The House That Crack Built*, by Clark Taylor; television—*The Wretched Stone*, by Chris Van Allsburg; loneliness—*Somebody Loves You, Mr. Hatch*, by Eileen Spinelli; death and grief—*When I Die, Will I Get Better?*, by Joeri and Piet Breebaart. Many upper-grade teachers are now familiar with Jon Scieszka's clever twist on an old story, *The True Story of the Three Little Pigs*, as told by the wolf. If my freshman English prof had had that book, we could have knocked off "point of view" in an afternoon instead of belaboring it for a week.

What Makes a Good Read-Aloud Novel?

The difference between short novels and full-length novels (I've chosen approximately 100 pages as a demarcation point) is sometimes found in the amount of description, the shorter ones having much less detail, the longer requiring more imagination and concentration on the part of the listener/reader. Children whose imaginations have been atrophying in front of a television for years are not comfortable with long descriptive passages. But the more you read to them, the less trouble they have in constructing mental images. Indeed, research shows us that listening to stories stimulates the imagination significantly more than television or film.[38]

In approaching longer books, consider my earlier statement—that all books are not meant to be read aloud and that some books aren't even worth reading to yourself, never mind boring a family or class with them. Some books are written in a convoluted or elliptical style that can be read silently but not aloud. Even adults find this difficult listening. For example, Sven Birkerts, a writer, critic, and Harvard writing teacher, found he could enjoy Saul Bellow's reading of *Herzog* on tape as long as there was description or narrative. When Bellow got to philosophical passages, he lost Birkerts' attention.[39] That kind of writing needs to be read silently to oneself, pondered, and then reread for clarification.

Ideal for reading aloud is the style alluded to by the great Canadian adult novelist Robertson Davies in the preface to a volume of his speeches. He asked readers to remember they were reading *speeches*, not essays: "What is meant to be heard is necessarily more direct in expression, and perhaps more boldly coloured, than what is meant for the reader."[40] This is a fact missed by many speakers, preachers, professors who write their speeches as if the audience were going to read them instead of listen to them.

Consider this one-sentence example of Edgar Allan Poe's prose that makes for distinguished silent reading but horrendous reading aloud: "It was this deficiency, I considered, while running over in thought the perfect keeping of the character of the premises with the accredited character of the people, and while speculating upon the possible influence which the one, in the long lapse of centuries, might have exercised upon the other—it was this deficiency, perhaps, of collateral issue, and the consequent undeviating transmission, from sire to son, of the patrimony with the name, which had, at length, so identified the two as to merge the original title of the estate in the quaint and equivocal appellation of the 'House of Usher'—an appellation which seemed to include, in the minds of the peasantry who used it, both the family and the family mansion."[41] How would you like to diagram *that* baby?

When will you know if children are ready for a full-length novel? Does the child ask you each night to keep reading? What kinds of questions does he ask about the stories you read: insightful or perplexed? Are the descriptions or characters confusing to him?

The first novel I read to Jamie would be my first choice a thousand times over, for almost any child or class—*James and the Giant Peach*. I know a kindergarten teacher who ends her year with this book and I know a sixth-grade teacher who started her September class with it for twenty years. Any book that can hold the attention span and lift the imaginations of six-year-olds as well as eleven-year-olds has to have magic in it. And *James and the Giant Peach* has that.

Once a child or class has reached the novel stage, it is increasingly important for the adult to preview the book before reading it aloud. The length of such books allows them to treat subject matter that can be very sensitive, far more so than a picture book could. As the reader, you should first familiarize yourself with the subject and the author's approach. Ask yourself as you read it through, "Can my child or class handle not only the vocabulary and the complexity of this story, but its emotions as well? Is there anything here that will do more harm than good to my child or class? Anything that might embarrass someone?"

Along with enabling you to avoid this kind of damaging situation, reading the book ahead of time will enable you to read it the second time to the class or child with more confidence, accenting important passages, leaving out dull ones (I mark these lightly in pencil in the margins), and providing sound effects to dramatize the story line (I'm always ready to knock on a table or wall where the story calls for a "knock at the door").

Celebrating the Author

Earlier in this chapter I mentioned having a Bill Peet Week author celebration. I don't know of a single lifetime reader who doesn't have favorite authors. It's a truism whether they read fiction, nonfiction, newspapers, or magazines. Until the arrival of literature-based instruction in the last decade, schools had pretty much ignored authors in favor of "Class, turn to page 52 in your reader . . ."

Once children discover that books are written by people—*special* people called authors—they develop favorites as specific as ice cream flavors. Master teacher Doris Winslow of Mount Washington Elementary in Baltimore, Maryland, has an author-of-the-month program, complete with cupcakes. Author celebrations in preschool and primary grades usually involve the teacher sharing personal information about the author each day and then reading one or more of the author's books. Some even go so far as to schedule author teleconferences via the phone. I recall listening to a marvelous tape recording of a teleconference between twenty-five students in Merry Kahn's school library in Maquoketa, Iowa, and the late Roald Dahl, sitting at home in Great Missenden, Buckinghamshire, England.

Before doing an author study or celebration with a class, write to the children's marketing department at the author's publisher and ask for any author bios, posters, or photos they might have; check *Something About the Author* in the library; and look in the *Reader's Guide to Periodic Literature* for any author profiles that may have been done. Many publishers offer inexpensive video visits with authors and illustrators, often filmed in their homes and studios. Also look for author interviews on audiocassette offered by school book clubs. I've yet to hear a bad one. And by all means consider a teleconference if you are seriously pursuing an author celebration.

Be sure to honor current authors as well as older ones. When author-illustrator Keith Baker visited an elementary school a few years ago, one student asked, "Have you been dead?" When the question-and-answer period was over, Baker quietly asked the child, "Why did you ask me if I had been dead?" To which the boy replied, "Well—whenever we talk about authors, they're dead!"[42]

Among the people who haven't quite caught on to the celebration of authors are—believe it or not—publishers. My work has brought me into contact with hundreds of authors and I've met few who didn't have an anecdote worth sharing with readers. So what do we get at the back of the book or on the dust jacket? "She is the author of many children's novels and lives with her husband and their two dogs in New Jersey."

I recently looked at the hardcover dust jacket and end pages of *Charlotte's Web* and found not a *single* biographical sentence about E. B.

White, though there are six empty pages at the start or end of the book. For all intents and purposes, the book might have been written by a machine! The fifth-bestselling middle-grade novel of the last twenty-five years is *Where the Red Fern Grows* by Wilson Rawls. But ten years later, the paperback edition of *Red Fern* is still running the same twenty-year-old paragraph about Rawls that has him living in Idaho Falls, Idaho. The publisher changed the cover art in 1989 but never updated the biography, though Rawls died in 1984.

Such failings have always bothered me, and when I edited my two anthologies of read-aloud stories (*Hey! Listen to This* [for K–4] and *Read All About It!* [for preteens and teens]), I wrote biographies for each author, most of the time using the common reference resources of my local public library, which led me to other resources and even to the author himself. The single best resource for author information is *Something About the Author* and its smaller partner, the *Author Autobiography* series.

Here are a handful of facts I uncovered—all of which ought to appear in back-of-the-book profiles but never do:

- *The kids and faculty from Louis Sachar's* Sideways Stories from Wayside School *were based upon the students and teachers he met as a teacher's aide while in college.*
- *It took Robert McCloskey one year to write the 1,152 words in* Make Way for Ducklings. *As his models he used real ducklings, which he bought at the local market and fed red wine so they'd slow down enough for him to draw them in his apartment.*
- *Florence and Richard Atwater coauthored* Mr. Popper's Penguins *without exchanging a single word between them. Richard had been left mute and immobile by a stroke, so his wife took his old story, which had been rejected by publishers, and successfully rewrote it.*
- The Tales of Uncle Remus *was the childhood inspiration of Beatrix Potter, while Potter's books became the childhood inspiration of C. S. Lewis.*
- *Hans Christian Andersen dropped out of elementary school at age ten, returned at age seventeen, and barely graduated at age twenty-three.*
- *Wilson Rawls' first manuscript for* Where the Red Fern Grows *was so filled with poor grammar and misspellings and was so lacking in punctuation that the author's shame provoked him to burn the entire manuscript after working on it for twenty-five years.*

✔ *L. Frank Baum found the name for the land of Oz while staring at the label on the bottom drawer of his filing cabinet: O–Z.*

✔ *The Secret Garden was written by an English immigrant to Knoxville, Tennessee, who sent her first short story to an American magazine, only to have the editors reject it on the grounds it was too good and too British to be written by a seventeen-year-old in Tennessee.*

✔ *Jerry Spinelli, author of* Maniac Magee, *spent sixteen years' worth of lunch hours writing unpublished novels before his first book was accepted.*

✔ *Harper Lee never wrote another book after* To Kill a Mockingbird, *but she did help her childhood friend write one of his. The childhood friend—the real-life model for Dill in her book—was Truman Capote.*

✔ *The award-winning Cynthia Rylant grew up in rural West Virginia in a home that had no books, in a community that had neither a library nor a bookstore, but did have a drugstore— which sold comic books that Cynthia devoured by the hundreds (especially* Archie*).*

✔ *Allan Eckert, author of* Incident at Hawk's Hill, *received 1,147 rejection notices before selling his first story.*

✔ *Rudyard Kipling wrote* The Jungle Book *not in India or England but in Brattleboro, Vermont, before fleeing America after a bitter fight with his brother-in-law.*

✔ *Ernest Lawrence Thayer, the author of "Casey at the Bat," was a straight-A philosophy major at Harvard and during his lifetime earned only $5 from his famous poem; Robert W. Service, the author of "The Cremation of Sam Magee," was expelled from eighth grade for harassing the gym teacher, later was inspired by "Casey at the Bat," and during his lifetime became rich and world famous for his Klondike poetry.*

✔ *The teenage boy whom George Burns used to smuggle into his radio show every week, the one who used to badger him with awful scripts that Burns pretended to read, was Ray Bradbury.*

✔ *Frederick Douglass learned to read by using table scraps to bribe literate white street kids to teach him.*

✔ *Because of a writing disability, the novelist Avi once flunked out of high school and even now must rewrite all of his works at least twenty times.*

✔ *The novelist Gary Paulsen was raised by abusive parents, never*

spent more than five months in any one school during his child-
hood, and was always the worst student in his class—yet wrote
more than one hundred books by the time he was fifty-five.

Teen Tips

Many of the guidelines suggested for reading to younger students also apply to older ones. Just because they are older doesn't mean they have longer attention spans or that they've been read to previously. Tailor your initial readings to the class situation, win their confidence, and then broaden the scope and introduce them to times and places other than their own.

Where time constraints make a novel impossible, or for a change of pace, read a poem from *Where the Sidewalk Ends*, then try reading from Paul Harvey's *The Rest of the Story*. The latter book (and its two sequels) contains nearly one hundred historic and contemporary true stories originally read aloud on Harvey's national radio program of the same name. Written by his son, Paul Aurandt (Paul Harvey, Jr.), the stories are only four minutes in length and each is highlighted by an O. Henry–type ending. These readings also can serve as conditioning exercises for short attention spans.

In choosing novels at elementary and secondary levels, avoid falling into the old book report trap of "thicker is better." There are thousands of children every day who report to the media center and tell the librarian: "My teacher said this book doesn't count for a book report—it's gotta be at least 125 pages." And that's how you kill a reader! There is no connection between thickness and goodness. Remember: the Gettysburg Address was only two and a half minutes long, 272 words.

Read-aloud selections don't even have to be books. In your leisure reading, if you find a magazine article your class would enjoy, read it to them. Reading aloud a newspaper column may turn a student into a daily newspaper reader. You'll know you're on the right track when a student stops you between classes and asks, "Did you read Bob Greene's column last night? Wasn't it great?" And if you are looking for a fast-moving novel that will grab even the most reluctant audience, try Avi's *Wolf Rider*! When you look up the phrase "page-turner" in the dictionary, there ought be a picture of *Wolf Rider*.

A parent can use read-aloud to challenge a child's mind and take care of his emotional needs in other ways. But classroom teachers are limited in the ways they can reach and touch children. Education critics who say teachers should restrict themselves to teaching only the basic learning skills and curriculum are professing their ignorance of life beyond their narrow neighborhood. Each day millions of children arrive in American classrooms in search of something more than reading and math skills. They come to school looking for a light in the darkness of their lives, a Good Samaritan who will stop and bandage a bruised heart or ego. We fail to help them with the daily curriculum often enough that one thousand teenagers attempt suicide every day, and one succeeds every ninety minutes. Bibliotherapy can be extremely effective.

Diary of a Middle-School Reader-Aloud

Nothing I could say or write about reading to adolescents would equal the true-life adventures of Jeff Smoker, veteran teacher in both public and private schools. Here is an excerpt from his journal during a new assignment at an inner-city middle school.[43] Smoker had seen the impact of reading aloud upon his own three sons and thought its ability to focus children and enrich their vocabularies and interests would work with adolescents as well:

> *Initially, I started out slowly with my read-aloud program by only reading 5–10 minutes at a stretch. I recall how frustrated I felt as I began reading aloud, for students would squirm in their desks, whisper to classmates, and attempt to pass notes back and forth. I was absolutely committed to my read-aloud program, however, so I firmly but gently impressed upon them, "When I'm reading aloud, you may lay your head on your desk or draw pictures, but you may not talk to anyone else or pass notes." I sincerely wanted this read-aloud time to be a pleasurable experience for my students and not something they associated with pain and suffering. It was important, however, that my students understand that I needed their co-operation during the read-aloud time. Those first few weeks of my read-aloud program were turbulent ones, riddled with numerous student disruptions, yet I pursued it with unrelenting enthusiasm, confident that eventually my students would catch the infectious read-aloud spirit.*
>
> *I began with* Call It Courage, *by Armstrong Sperry, because I had read this book with seventh-graders previously, and they loved this short adventure novel. The chapters were fairly short, the action sustaining, and I was familiar enough with the story so I could*

comfortably share it with my students. I began by reading aloud 5–10-minute segments, but as the weeks progressed, I gradually increased the read-aloud time to 15–20 minutes.

I concluded the novel by having students illustrate any memorable scene from the novel. I was impressed with their ability to render artistically significant events from the novel and I proudly displayed their artwork in my classroom. The final art project made my walls come alive with student work and poignantly advertised a positive read-aloud experience. Furthermore, the various illustrated scenes gave me tangible evidence of students' increased listening comprehension. I felt my students were making tremendous progress in their listening skills, and they were demonstrating a sustained interest in the read-aloud story.

The Sign of the Beaver, *by Elizabeth George Speare, was another book my previous seventh-graders had read and enjoyed. Additionally, these eighth-graders were studying the westward expansion in their history class. In an attempt to integrate the curriculum, I figured an action-packed story about a young boy struggling to survive on his own in a newly settled Maine territory would be well suited for a read-aloud.*

Recent research indicates that student learning is increased when different modalities are used; therefore, I tried to plan class activities in conjunction with the novel that would involve active student participation. Matt, the main character in The Sign of the Beaver, *solved my desire to involve the student in an activity. Matt, through the aid of a helpful Indian, learned how to construct a bow and then fashion the arrows to shoot from the bow. I figured if the main character needed to struggle with a bow and arrow, then my students could attempt a similar challenge.*

My students could hardly believe it when one day I brought a bow and a quiver full of arrows into class. During a quick in-class demonstration of how a person would shoot a bow and arrow, several students queried, "Can we try it?" To their astonishment I said, "Yes, let's go." And within minutes we were on our way outside to give each student an opportunity to shoot a bow and arrow. Days after that bow-and-arrow experience, during my reading of The Sign of the Beaver, *my students could identify how masterful Attean, the Indian who helped Matt, must have been in order to be able to bring down a duck in flight with a single arrow fired from his bow. I know students would not have identified with this section of the novel unless they had had direct hands-on experience shooting the bow and arrow.*

Once I concluded The Sign of the Beaver, *I felt the students were ready for still another adventure story, so I launched into* Hatchet *by Gary Paulsen. This is a modern-day survival story set in the north woods. I wanted to capture my students' immediate attention, so I introduced it in a unique way.*

At the beginning of class on January 3, I reached for the sunglasses in my book bag and placed the glasses over my eyes. I received numerous "oohs" and "ahs" as they said things like "Wow, look at him. What kind of car do you drive, Mr. Smoker?" "I have better sunglasses than yours." I ignored their comments and I continued to set up my work area, placing several sections of newspaper upon my desk. Then I walked over to a prominently displayed cardboard box and removed one of the oak logs contained inside. In addition to the oak log, I picked up a hatchet and carried both items over to my desk. After dropping the log on the desk, I raised the hatchet high in the air, and began to strike wildly on the log.

As the wood chips flew, students seated in the front row vacated their desks and hurried to the rear of the classroom. Students were somewhat concerned about being injured by the flying wood chips, but ignoring their frantic urgings to stop, I continued to pound away with considerable gusto. I could tell by their comments and reactions that they thought I had gone mad. As a side note, I must point out that on this day I didn't need to raise my voice to get the class under control; my pounding on the log attracted their immediate and complete attention.

After several minutes of pounding, I stopped chopping, turned to the students, raised the hatchet high into the air, and asked them, "What is this?" Some responses included: ax, hammer, hatchet, roofing hammer.

Without speaking, I retrieved an ax that I had brought into the room, and lifting both the ax and hatchet into the air asked them to identify the two items. After they correctly identified the hatchet, I asked them another question: "Why would I bring this hatchet to class?" Most students responded with either a dazed look or a "Don't know." Several students, however, looked in the direction of the chalkboard, where I always have the daily agenda written, and saw that I was beginning a new read-aloud book that day. Therefore, the next comment was, "It must have something to do with the story you are going to read aloud."

I responded by throwing out another question: "What would the hatchet have to do with the story?" Responses included "Maybe a character murders people with a hatchet." Several variations on that theme continued, with one reference made to the movie Texas Chainsaw Massacre. Other responses included "Maybe a character in the story uses a hatchet to survive." After a brief discussion in which they shared their interpretations as to why I brought the hatchet into class, I revealed the book Hatchet, which had previously been hidden. Holding up the book, I asked them, "What is the title of this book?" In a surprised sort of way, most of them said the word "hatchet" aloud. Immediately, I opened the book and began reading Chapter 1.

I knew that I had hooked students from day one with this novel for several reasons. Within the first week of reading the story aloud, several of my reluctant readers went to the library to check out Hatchet. One of the more memorable of those reluctant students was a Latino boy named Jesus. Daily, he would swagger into the classroom, plunk himself down in a chair toward the back of the room, and proceed to do absolutely nothing for the duration of class. He was resistant to all my attempts to involve him in class discussions or writing activities related to the stories. Several days after I began reading Hatchet to the class, however, I happened to meet Jesus in the library and this exchange occurred:

JEFF: (warmly greeting him) "Jesus, how are you doing?"

JESUS: "Hey, Mr. Smoker, where's the hatchet?"

JEFF: "Oh, it's back in the classroom in my desk drawer." (After my initial hatchet-chopping introduction to the novel, I had returned the hatchet to my desk drawer.)

JESUS: "No, I mean Hatchet—the book." (His body language indicated he had been searching for the book on the shelves and was unsuccessful in his attempt.)

JEFF: "Come here." I excitedly motioned for him to follow me to the librarian's back room. I knew the librarian had stacked several copies of Hatchet on the reserve shelves. Fortunately, Hatchet was being considered that year for the California Young Reader Medal, so the library had several copies available for immediate checkout. Jesus wasn't quite sure what I was doing leading him back to the office, but nevertheless he followed along. When I produced a copy of Hatchet, he nodded, signifying that was the book he wanted. I *patted him on the back and exclaimed, "Here's your own copy, check it out."*

From that point forward, each day as I began reading Hatchet *aloud, Jesus would perk up and his eyes would light up as if to say, "I know what's going to happen in this part of the story." His effort to check the book out of the library and then independently read the story was a significant affirmation that my read-aloud program motivated reluctant readers.*

In addition to inspiring reluctant readers, I could tell that students were developing their listening comprehension. One day just prior to reading aloud Chapter 15, I developed a small group project designed to investigate the problems the main character had encountered thus far in the novel. I asked students to brainstorm in small groups and identify some of the problems Brian, the main character, had faced up to this point. From my personal reading, I knew that Brian was about to undergo a series of particularly stressful circumstances. I wanted to see what students remembered about the story before I launched into the next major section of the novel. I was amazed by the comprehensive catalog of conflicts the groups assembled. One particular group of boys in my second-period class managed to tally 34 separate conflicts Brian had faced thus far. This group project clearly demonstrated to me that students had the ability to recall numerous facts related to the story.

After I finished reading Hatchet, *many students were asking, "What book are you going to read next?" The fact that students demonstrated interest in the next book affirmed their enjoyment of the read-aloud experience.*

The central theme running through all of my read-aloud pieces with these students has been one of survival. I think the theme of survival is critical in the lives of adolescents today. In order to be productive, contributing members of society, this generation will have to overcome many obstacles. The odds against them seem overwhelming, but I think I can bolster their ability to survive by sharing survivor success stories. A critical quote I shared with my students, excerpted from Hatchet, *deals with the spirit within a person that makes him a survivor. At a certain moment in the novel Brian, the main character in* Hatchet, *makes a critical realization about himself, remembering an English teacher (wouldn't you know it) who used to tell him, "You are your most valuable asset. Don't forget that. You are the best thing you have." I want my students to realize*

*that they have a powerful resource lodged inside their skull. They
need to regularly exercise their mind to make it even more powerful
and productive. I hope my message of encouragement voiced
through the pieces of literature I selected to read aloud strongly
influences my students to flourish and blossom into life-sustaining
human beings.*

When I last talked with Jeff Smoker, he had become a parochial
school principal in Northern California, was still reading to his three
sons, and was still advocating reading aloud to students at every grade
level.

What's Right or Wrong with Poetry

If "lobster" were an important subject in the curriculum, we would
have lobster classes for twelve straight years: where to find them, how
they live, and, of course, how to catch, prepare, cook, and eat them.
But if, after graduating from school, the end result was a lifelong loss of
appetite for lobster, there would be a general reassessment of the lobster
curriculum. And this is precisely what has happened to poetry in the
United States—except no one is reassessing the poetry curriculum.

The contrast between how children respond to poetry and how adults
do is seen most strikingly in two facts:

1. Until *The Road Less Traveled* surpassed it, Shel Silverstein's collection
    of children's poetry, *A Light in the Attic*, held *The New York Times*
    record for the longest time on its bestseller list (186 weeks).
2. The worst-selling department in bookstores is adult poetry; it sells
    so poorly, many stores no longer even stock it.[44]

Poetry dies for most people on graduation day. The thickest coat of
dust in a public library can be found in its poetry section. Considering
how much time is spent in secondary classrooms dissecting poetry, one
would expect graduates to be ravenous poetry consumers. Wrong. Why
is this so?

One of poetry's strengths is its brevity. A poem is not a novel or a
short story, yet it can be very revealing in its smallness—like one of
those see-through Easter eggs. A poem should add up to something, a
slice of life. One expert put it this way: "Unless a poem says something
to a child, tells him a story, titillates his ego, strikes up a happy recol-

lection, bumps his funny bone—in other words, delights him—he will not be attracted to poetry regardless of the language it uses."[45]

Therefore the choice of poets and poems will have everything to do with how children react to poetry. But the American approach ignores those factors. It is more interested in "covering the core curriculum" than creating lifetime interest. The higher the grade level, the more obscure and symbolic and less humorous and understandable the poetry becomes. Because all the poetry is obscure, every poem must be dissected like some kind of frog in biology class, and we end up making poetry appear so unnecessarily complicated, people like children's author Jean Little decide not to stop the next time they come to the "woods on a snowy evening."[46]

This attitude of the secondary faculty may be a result of the Segal Syndrome (in honor of Erich Segal, the Yale classics professor and author of *Love Story*). Usually associated with college faculties, but often spilling down to high school English departments, the Segal Syndrome works like this: A professor's esteem on the faculty is in inverse proportion to his or her public popularity; that is, if a professor writes a book, the more copies it sells, the lower he sinks with his peers; the fewer it sells, the higher the peer rating. "After all, if the public understands and enjoys him," the faculty reasons, "how deep can the guy be?" Extended to poetry, if anyone can understand it—or, God forbid!, someone laughs over it—how deep can it be?

The Segal Syndrome affects even elementary grade poetry. Shel Silverstein, Judith Viorst, and Jack Prelutsky are three of the most popular children's poets of the last twenty-five years, yet none of them has collected any of the major poetry awards from the academicians. (How good can they be if the kids like them?) If teachers or parents are sincerely interested in turning children on to poetry, they need to look first at which books actually work with children and then at why they work.

To begin with, all three poets can be serious but, more often, they make young people laugh. And laughter is a dirty word with some educators. As Garrison Keillor once noted in an interview with Larry King, humor may be one of the things missing in the American poetry picture. King mentioned that Keillor was going to a poetry reading that evening at Georgetown University, a reading with Rowland Flint, whom Keillor described as "the only very good poet in America who is really funny. In American poetry, there's an excess of symbol and a dearth of humor," Keillor noted.[47] Any high school student in America would have agreed with him.

In an effort to find the poetry pulse of middle-grade students, Karen Kutiper exposed 375 Texas seventh-, eight- and ninth-graders to 100 poems (10 a day for 10 days, from a variety of forms), and surveyed their preferences. In a listing of their top 25, there were tongue-twisters, limericks, nonsense poems, and two poems each by both Shel Silverstein and Jack Prelutsky. Nearly all their favorite poems were narrative (with an emphasis on humor), all but one rhymed, and only two could be considered serious. The ninth-graders, however, showed a slightly higher preference for serious poetry, a sign of maturity and perhaps a signal to teachers that serious poetry can be taught if you keep in mind that readers are first interested in story or narrative.[48]

If secondary schools included more narrative and more humor in the poetry curriculum, there might be more interest in complex poetry as adults. In any case, the old prescription hasn't worked, so why keep prescribing it?

Where the Sidewalk Ends, by Shel Silverstein, is so popular with children, librarians and teachers insist it is the book most frequently stolen from their schools and libraries. Over the last eight years I've asked eighty thousand teachers if they know *Where the Sidewalk Ends* (two million copies in print), and three-quarters of the teachers raise their hands. "Wonderful!" I say. "Now, who has enough copies of this book for every child in your room?" Nobody raises a hand. In eight years, only eighteen teachers out of eighty thousand had enough copies in their rooms for every child.

I continue, "Do each of you know the books in your classroom no child would ever consider stealing?" They nod in recognition. "Do you have enough copies of *those* books for every child in the room?" Reluctantly, they nod agreement. Here we've got a book kids love to read so much they'll steal it right and left and we haven't got enough copies; but every year we've got twenty-eight copies of a book they hate.

If we wish children to believe poetry is important, the *worst* way to teach it is to develop a two-week poetry block, teach it, and then forget it—because that's what children will do with it. The *best* way is to incorporate meaningful poetry throughout the day. The question of which poems to read has already been answered for you by the anthologists included in the poetry section of the Treasury, who pored through tens of thousands of children's poems to come up with children's favorites.

4

The Dos and Don'ts of Read-Aloud

> Writing begins long before the marriage of pencil and paper. It begins with sounds, that is to say with words and simple clusters of words that are taken in by small children until they find themselves living in a world of vocables. If that world is rich and exciting, the transition to handling it in a new medium—writing—is made smoother. The first and conceivably the most important instructor in composition is the teacher, parent, or older sibling who reads aloud to the small child.
>
> —Clifton Fadiman,
> *Empty Pages: A Search for Writing Competence in School and Society*

Dos

- Begin reading to children as soon as possible. The younger you start them, the easier and better it is.
- Use Mother Goose rhymes and songs to stimulate an infant's language and listening. Simple black-and-white illustrations at first, and then boldly colored picture books, arouse children's curiosity and visual sense.
- With infants through toddlers and preschoolers it is critically important to read and reread books that are predictable and contain repetitions.
- During repeat readings of a predictable book, occasionally stop at one of the key words or phrases and allow the listener to provide the word.

- Read as often as you and the child or students have time for.
- Set aside at least one traditional time each day for a story.
- Remember: The art of listening is an acquired one. It must be taught and cultivated gradually—it doesn't appear overnight.
- Start with picture books, and build to storybooks and novels.
- Vary the length and subject matter of your readings.
- To encourage involvement, invite the child to turn pages for you when it is time.
- If a child is too active to pay attention to a book, try telling some stories about a little boy or girl with the same name as your child. After a week, introduce a character to your stories who is also found in a children's book like Eric Hill's *Where's Spot?* Gradually wean the child from your invented stories to those in books.
- Before you begin to read, always announce the name of the book and the author and illustrator—no matter how many times you have read the book.
- The first time you read a book, discuss the illustration on the cover. "What do you think this is going to be about?"
- As you read, keep listeners involved by occasionally asking, "What do you think is going to happen next?"
- Follow through with your reading. If you start a book, it is your responsibility to continue it—unless it turns out to be a bad book. Don't leave the child or students hanging for three or four days between chapters and expect interest to be sustained.
- Occasionally read above children's intellectual level and challenge their minds.
- Picture books can be read easily to a family of children widely separated in age. Novels, however, pose a challenge. If there are more than three years (and thus social and emotional differences) between the children, each child would benefit greatly if you read to him or her individually. This requires more effort on the part of the parents, but it will reap rewards in direct proportion to the effort expended. You will reinforce the specialness of each child.
- Avoid long descriptive passages until the child's imagination and attention span are capable of handling them. There is nothing wrong with shortening or eliminating them. Prereading helps to locate such passages, and they can then be marked with pencil in the margin.
- If the chapters are long or if you don't have enough time each day to finish an entire chapter, find a suspenseful spot at which to

stop. Leave the audience hanging; they'll be counting the minutes until the next reading.

- Allow your listeners a few minutes to settle down and adjust their feet and minds to the story. If it's a novel, begin by asking what happened when you left off yesterday. Mood is an important factor in listening. An authoritarian "Now stop that and settle down! Sit up straight. Pay attention!" is not conducive to a receptive audience.

- If you are reading a picture book, make sure the children can see the pictures easily. In school, with the children in a semicircle around you, seat yourself just slightly above them so that the children in the back row can see the pictures above the heads of the others.

- In reading a novel, position yourself where both you and the children are comfortable. In the classroom, whether you are sitting on the edge of your desk or standing, your head should be above the heads of your listeners for your voice to carry to the far side of the room. Do not read or stand in front of brightly lit windows. Backlighting strains the eyes of your audience.

- Remember that even sixth-grade students love a good picture book.

- Allow time for class and home discussion after reading a story. Thoughts, hopes, fears, and discoveries are aroused by a book. Allow them to surface and help the child to deal with them through verbal, written, or artistic expression if the child is so inclined. Do not turn discussions into quizzes or insist upon prying story interpretations from the child.

- Remember that reading aloud comes naturally to very few people. To do it successfully and with ease you must practice.

- Use plenty of expression when reading. If possible, change your tone of voice to fit the dialogue.

- Adjust your pace to fit the story. During a suspenseful part, slow down, and lower your voice. A lowered voice in the right place moves an audience to the edge of its chairs.

- The most common mistake in reading aloud—whether the reader is a seven-year-old or a forty-year-old—is reading too fast. Read slowly enough for the child to build mental pictures of what he just heard you read. Slow down enough for the children to see the pictures in the book without feeling hurried. Reading quickly allows no time for the reader to use vocal expression.

- Preview the book by reading it to yourself ahead of time. Such advance reading allows you to spot material you may wish to shorten, eliminate, or elaborate on.
- Bring the author, as well as his book, to life. Consult *Something About the Author* at the library, and read the information on your book's dust jacket. Either before or during the reading, tell your audience something about the author. Let them know that books are written by people, not by machines. You also can accomplish this by encouraging individual children (not the class collectively —authors hate assembly correspondence) to write and share feelings about the book with the author. *Something About the Author* will provide an address, or you can write care of the publisher. It is important to enclose a self-addressed, stamped envelope *just in case* the author has time to respond. The child should understand from the start that the letter's purpose is not to receive a response.
- Add a third dimension to the book whenever possible. For example: Have a bowl of blueberries ready to be eaten during or after the reading of Robert McCloskey's *Blueberries for Sal*; bring a harmonica and a lemon to class before reading McCloskey's *Lentil*; buy a plastic cowboy and Indian for when you read *The Indian in the Cupboard*, by Lynn Reid Banks.
- Every once in a while, when a child asks a question involving the text, make a point of looking up the answer in a reference book with the child. This greatly expands a child's knowledge base and nurtures library skills.
- Create a wall chart or back-of-the-bedroom-door book chart so the child or class can see how much has been read; images of caterpillars, snakes, worms, and trains work well for this purpose, with each link representing a book. Similarly, post a world or U.S. wall map on which small stickers can be attached to locations where your books have been set.
- When children are old enough to distinguish between library books and their own, start reading with a pencil in hand. When you and the child encounter a passage worth remembering, put a small mark—maybe a star—in the margin. Readers should interact with books, and one way is to acknowledge beautiful writing.
- Encourage relatives living far away to record stories on audiocassettes that can be mailed to the child.
- Reluctant readers or unusually active children frequently find it difficult to just sit and listen. Paper, crayons, and pencils allow

them to keep their hands busy while listening. (You doodle while talking on the telephone, don't you?)

- Follow the suggestion of Dr. Caroline Bauer and post a reminder sign by your door: "Don't Forget Your *Flood* Book." Analogous to emergency rations in case of natural disasters, these books should be taken along in the car, or even stored like spares in the trunk. A few chapters from "flood" books can be squeezed in during traffic jams on the way to the beach or long waits at the dentist's office.

- Always have a supply of books for the babysitter to share with the child and make it understood that "reading aloud" comes with the job.

- Fathers should make an extra effort to read to their children. Because 88 percent of primary-school teachers are women, young boys often associate reading with women and schoolwork. And, just as unfortunately, too many fathers would rather be seen playing catch in the driveway with their sons than taking them to the library. It is not by chance that most of the students in U.S. remedial-reading classes are boys. A father's early involvement with books and reading can do much to elevate books to at least the same status as sports in a boy's estimation.

- Arrange for time each day—in the classroom or in the home—for the child to read by himself (even if "read" only means turning pages and looking at the pictures). All your read-aloud motivation goes for naught if the time is not available to put it into practice.

- Lead by example. Make sure your children see you reading for pleasure other than at read-aloud time. Share with them your enthusiasm for whatever you are reading.

- When children wish to read to you, it is better for the book to be too easy than too hard, just as it is better that a beginner's bicycle be too small than too big.

- Encourage older children to read to younger ones, but make this a *part-time*, not a full-time, substitution for you. Remember: The adult should be the ultimate role model.

- Regulate the amount of time children spend in front of the television. Research shows that after about eleven TV hours a week, a child's school scores begin to drop. Excessive television viewing is habit-forming and damaging to a child's development.

- When children are watching television, closed-captioning should be activated along with sound. But for older children who know how to read but are lazy about it, turn the volume off and captioning on.

Don'ts

- Don't read stories that you don't enjoy yourself. Your dislike will show in the reading, and that defeats your purpose.
- Don't continue reading a book once it is obvious that it was a poor choice. Admit the mistake and choose another. Make sure, however, that you've given the book a fair chance to get rolling; some, like *Tuck Everlasting*, start slower than others. (You can avoid the problem by prereading at least part of the book yourself.)
- If you are a teacher, don't feel you have to tie every book to class work. Don't confine the broad spectrum of literature to the narrow limits of the curriculum.
- Don't overwhelm your listener. Consider the intellectual, social, and emotional level of your audience in making a read-aloud selection. Never read above a child's emotional level.
- Don't select a book that many of the children already have heard or seen on television. Once a novel's plot is known, much of their interest is lost. You can, however, read a book and view the video afterward. That's a good way for children to see how much more can be portrayed in print than on film.
- In choosing novels for reading aloud, avoid books that are heavy with dialogue; they are difficult reading aloud *and* listening. All those indented paragraphs and quotations make for easy *silent* reading. The reader sees the quotation marks and knows it is a new voice, a different person speaking—but the listener doesn't. And if the writer fails to include a notation at the end of the dialogue, like "said Mrs. Murphy," the audience has no idea who said what.
- Don't be fooled by awards. Just because a book won an award doesn't guarantee that it will make a good read-aloud. In most cases, a book award is given for the quality of the writing, not for its read-aloud qualities.
- Don't start reading if you are not going to have enough time to do it justice. Having to stop after one or two pages only serves to frustrate, rather than stimulate, the child's interest in reading.

- Don't get too comfortable while reading. A reclining or slouching position is most apt to bring on drowsiness.
- Don't be unnerved by questions during the reading, particularly from very young children. Answer their questions patiently. Don't put them off. Don't rush your answers. There is no time limit for reading a book, but there is a time limit on a child's inquisitiveness. Foster that curiosity with patient answers—then resume your reading.
- Don't impose interpretations of a story upon your audience. A story can be just plain enjoyable, no reason necessary. But encourage conversation about the reading. Only 7 minutes out of 150 instructional minutes in the school day are spent on discussions between teacher and student.
- Don't confuse quantity with quality. Reading to your child for ten minutes, given your full attention and enthusiasm, may very well last longer in the child's mind than two hours of solitary television viewing.
- Don't use the book as a threat—"If you don't pick up your room, no story tonight!" As soon as your child or class sees that you've turned the book into a weapon, they'll change their attitude about books from positive to negative.
- Don't try to compete with television. If you say, "Which do you want, a story or TV?" they will usually choose the latter. That is like saying to a nine-year-old, "Which do you want, vegetables or a doughnut?" Since *you* are the adult, *you* choose. "The television goes off at eight-thirty in this house. If you want a story before bed, that's fine. If not, that's fine, too. But no television after eight-thirty." But don't let books appear to be responsible for depriving the children of viewing time.

5

Read-Aloud
Success Stories

You see things: and you say, "Why?" But I dream things that never were; and I say, "Why not?"

—George Bernard Shaw

In 1989, Arthur Tannenbaum was just a few years away from retirement when he brought new meaning to the term "power lunch." Working in New York City as an executive with CHF Industries, a leading home textiles supplier, and married to an employee of the New York City Board of Education, Tannenbaum was surrounded by extremes. On his walk to work he passed adults who came from the finest colleges in the nation, and children who came from the homes most at risk. "What can I do about it?" he wondered.

And then one day he picked up the 1989 edition of the book you are holding in your hand, and within a few chapters an idea began to form. "I could do this!" he said to his wife, Phyllis. "If I had someone to read to—I could do this." And then he thought of Public School 116 down the avenue from his office. "I wonder if they could pair me up with a student?" But why do it alone? he thought next. "I wonder if anyone else in the CHF offices would be interested." After consulting with school officials, Tannenbaum and five other CHF volunteers were paired with city students once a week for lunch and a book. Neither the student nor the adult lost any "work time," since everything was accomplished during the lunch hour.

"The results were positive immediately," Tannenbaum explains today. "It was a case where *everybody wins:* the students meet good books with good people who care about them individually, and the volunteer readers feel as though they're making a difference." And so was born the name of the program: Everybody Wins. What began with a handful of people quickly expanded as each volunteer told others in the textile industry, who in turn spread the word throughout Manhattan.

In 1991, Tannenbaum retired from CHF to form the nonprofit Everybody Wins Foundation. Hunter College came on board with education students who combined their lunchtime readings with course work for credit. In 1992, the New York Police Department began to participate, seeing the program as a means to heal the often troubled relationship between young people and police. That same year, a satellite program began in Torrington, Connecticut, where the Tannenbaums have a second home.

By 1994, major funding grants began to come in, along with more than six hundred volunteers from major corporations like MasterCard International, *The New York Times,* and McGraw-Hill. MasterCard International alone had 125 volunteers each week, including a senior vice president. In Torrington and northern Connecticut, the partnership had spread to six area schools.[1] And it all began with one reader dreaming of what didn't exist and wondering, in George Bernard Shaw's words, "Why not?"

Social research has shown word of mouth to be the most important influence in women's shopping choices—over advertising, sales, and coupons.[2] Human nature is such that when we discover an otherwise unknown medicine, detergent, movie, or recipe, we feel compelled to share it with as many friends as possible. They, in turn, trust the message because it came from a friend. If reading is to survive as a meaningful part of this culture, it will need this same endorsement. Plato addressed this thousands of years ago when he said it is the responsibility of people who carry torches to pass them on. The death of a culture is imminent when the torchbearers stop passing their torches.

This chapter, therefore, is about the torchbearers, the men and women who have taken the torch of literacy and passed it with such passion and ingenuity, it is imperative that everyone see and learn from their examples.

Not everyone, of course, has the sphere of influence that Arthur Tannenbaum had. So let us start small—what one teacher or school community might do to create an environment that nurtures reading.

Books for Birthdays

I know parents who give their children a day off from school on their birthday (tell me what that says to the child). I would suggest a more positive approach, like the one used at the Waldorf School in Lexington, Massachusetts, where parents are encouraged to purchase a book for the school library on the occasion of their child's birthday. The program, which has brought hundreds of books to the school, is sponsored by the parents and faculty, with the librarian providing a list of recommended titles. Couldn't your PTA sponsor a similar program, with teachers or the school librarian supplying a "wish list"?

Teachers in Dana Point, California, used a similar approach to defuse a classroom-birthday "competition" among parents: "We will no longer accept cupcakes or pizzas for your child's birthday but you may donate a book to our school library in his or her name." Taking a hint from the school's policy, the El Camino Real Junior Women's Club in Dana Point began donating a book to the library of the mother's choice every time one of its members had a baby.

Reading Sleep-overs

Anything you can do as a parent or educator to heighten public awareness of reading is a plus—be it in large ways or small. In Sergeant Bluff, Iowa, principal George Holland and fifty parents planned an overnight read-in that took place in the school's multipurpose room and hosted 194 (K–4) children with sleeping bags. Between 7:00 P.M. Friday and 7:00 A.M. Saturday, there was silent reading, storytelling, exercise, a snack, writing time, read-aloud, creative dramatic presentations by high school students, a closed-caption movie, lights out, breakfast (cooked by parent volunteers), and more reading. The event proved so popular that succeeding ones focused on certain age groups and were attended by nearly half the school. When Holland's school celebrated the American Library Association's Night of 1,000 Stars (in which local celebrities are invited to read aloud in libraries across the nation), they had thirty-six people doing readings through the evening in the school's multi-purpose room. The layout there included six living-room setups. Several politicians, unable to attend, had videotapes made of themselves reading aloud and sent them to be played on TVs set up in the various living rooms.

Following the lead of people like George Holland, many districts have begun to use reading sleep-overs. But for inner-city schools, such programs can be difficult. If that is what keeps your school from attempting it, try emulating the Bruce-Monroe Elementary School's overnight read-in/sleep-over. Located in Washington, D.C., the school worked closely with local businesses like the Howard Inn Hotel, which donated its elegant ballroom to the student sleep-over. Other local businesses contributed dinner pizzas, fortune cookies, and bedtime snacks. And community volunteers and parents—including Washington's delegate to Congress, Walter E. Fauntroy—shared their enthusiasm by dropping in to read aloud. The hotel donated the next morning's breakfast to the seventy children—many of whom had never been in a hotel before, according to reading specialist Marlene Piscitelli.

But sleep-overs don't have to be as elaborate as those. When my friend Anne Marie Russo of Holy Cross School in Springfield, Massachusetts, saw how fascinated her kindergartners were with the book *My Teacher Sleeps at School* by Leatie Weiss, she scheduled a classroom "sleep-over." On the appointed day, students came to school equipped with bathrobes, slippers, teddy bears, toothbrushes, and sleeping bags. Then they went through the usual sleep-over ritual—movie, snacks, a read-aloud book (*Ira Sleeps Over*), prayers, toothbrushing, and sleep before the buses arrived to end the day.

Athletes Score for Reading

If we can find the wherewithal to work out intricate bus and class schedules to allow our student athletes to compete all over the state, we should also be able to devise a way to put the athletes' influence to classroom use—as they did in Lynden, Washington, a picture-postcard Dutch community (complete with windmills) four miles from the Canadian border. Lynden's dynamic reading specialist at Fisher Elementary, Cindy Visser, saw an opportunity to get some extra mileage out of Lynden's athletes. She got an enthusiastic response from the high school coach/physical education teacher—who himself had had reading problems as a child—and he agreed to recruit varsity athletes. And so was born Lynden's High School Readers program, in which student athletes arrive monthly (in a bus driven by their coach and wearing their team jerseys) to read to the elementary students. Elementary teachers choose the books to be read (mostly picture books) and place them in a box that is delivered to the high school. The athletes choose a book and take it home to practice reading it aloud. (Early in the year they are given instructions on how to read to classes.) The athletes average about twenty minutes with a class, reading, talking about the book, and answering some sports questions.[3] In 1991, the football team played for the state championship on the weekend, then went right to the elementary school on Monday morning to read aloud to classes. Suppose that were the reading climate for the entire country. Could it change the atmosphere and emphasis in some communities, where the scorecard is more important than the report card?

There is no reason to stop such athletic efforts at the high school level. Why can't college communities follow the lead of Rutgers, the state university of New Jersey? Since 1990, Rutgers has required its 700 student athletes to perform two hours of public service each semester—ranging from visiting hospitals to helping at the Special Olympics. But the most popular and widely known of the series has been R.U. RAP (Rutgers University Read-Aloud Program), in which hundreds of male and female student athletes read to students in local schools, from preschool through sixth grade. Some of the athletes opt to return to their own hometowns to read in classrooms there. Johnson & Johnson's corporate headquarters is located nearby and has become the corporate sponsor for the program, helping with the cost of books that are read and then left with each class, and local bookstores have also contributed books.

Buddy Readers

Upon completing his exhaustive study of American education (*A Place Called School*), John Goodlad commented: "One of the blind spots in American schooling is our almost complete failure to use peer teaching. In British schools you see children helping each other. The teacher has twenty-five assistants, so when a child comes in, a couple of other children take that child over, just as older brothers and sisters in big families do."[4] Indeed, in forty-five of fifty-two studies, students who were tutored by older students outperformed those in comparison groups, with significant improvement in student attitudes.[5]

What we're talking about here is resurrecting what was best about the one-room schoolhouse—the chance for younger children to model themselves on older, achieving ones. Since Goodlad's report, "buddy reading" has become increasingly popular throughout the country. One of the very first, and still my favorite, is the PAC-Readers program (PAC-Reader stands for Pittston-Area-Capable-Reader), founded in 1983 by the Pittston Area Schools in Pennsylvania. Fifth- and sixth-grade student volunteers read aloud to first- and second-grade classrooms during the pre-school breakfast time. After being trained in reading aloud, discussing an appropriate book choice with a teacher, and rehearsing the book (with a teacher or aide), the PAC-Reader introduces himself to the class, says a few words about the author, and begins reading aloud.

"The response was unbelievable," explained principal Ross Scarantino. "We initially thought the sixth-grade boys might feel too sophisticated to go into the lower grades, but were we ever wrong! Boys volunteer as often as girls," he noted. Listener reaction has been just as positive. "The appearance of that excited fifth-grader with a book in hand says more to that first-grade beginning reader than the teacher could say in an entire week." The volunteer visits are biweekly, thus allowing adequate preparation time. When I visited the community, parents told me their first-grade beginning readers could often be heard in their bedrooms, imitating their PAC-Readers: "Good morning," they would say to a teddy bear or sibling, "my name is Bobby Snyder and I'm your PAC-Reader and today I'm going to read . . ."

Parents can practice the Pittston idea by encouraging older siblings to read to younger ones when they are busy. Reading aloud should also be included among the tasks of every babysitter. (Make sure you provide the books.) Why not get your money's worth from the sitter? Babysitting today is too expensive to settle for TV watching—on the part of kids *or* sitter!

Story Lunch

Just as Pittston couldn't abide wasting that peer influence, media specialist Louise Sherman hated to waste five lunch hours a week at Anna Scott School (K–4) in Leonia, New Jersey. So she sent notes home to parents advising them a thirty-minute storytime would be offered to all interested children during lunch. Since then, volunteer readers (parents, teachers, principal, superintendent) read novels four times a week to one hundred and fifty students who listen and eat lunch.[6]

The program covers about ten novels a year, has significantly increased library circulation, and generates enthusiasm like this from the mother of a fourth-grade reluctant reader: "At first he didn't want to be in it. Now he can't wait to find out what's going to happen each day." Two special education teachers were inspired enough to begin a similar project with multiply handicapped students.

Guest Readers as Motivators

In attempting to combat students' stereotypical view that all readers are women or teachers, some school systems (and individual teachers) sponsor guest-reader programs in which community leaders, parents, and other volunteers visit classes to read aloud and demonstrate that reading is for everyone, of every age, of every color, and from every walk of life. Here are two examples:

In my home city, Springfield, Massachusetts, an urban community of 160,000, the 12,000 (K–5) students are read to three times between September and November by 550 guest readers, with readings provided in either English, Spanish, or Russian. Because the project has generated so much support from educators and readers since its beginning in 1986, Westvaco Envelope Division has contributed $7,000 each year to fund promotion and coordination efforts, and the school system adds the remaining funds so that each of the more than 2,000 books can be given to the class by its guest reader. A guide to the program is available by sending a self-addressed, stamped (for eight ounces), 9-by-12-inch envelope to: Springfield Read-Aloud Project, School Volunteers Office, Springfield Public Schools, 195 State Street, Springfield, MA 01103.

The timing was perfect in 1990 when Alachua County (Gainesville, Florida) kindergarten teachers made a special request of their school volunteers office. They'd noticed an alarming increase in kindergartners testing below grade level in language development and wondered if the office could round up some volunteers to read one-on-one with Head Start and kindergartners. Simultaneously, the state was giving education grants to districts that made innovative use of senior citizens. Thus was born Rockin' Readers, which today includes more than 150 volunteers and has spread beyond just senior citizens. "Many of the University of Florida students participate, going into schools and lap-reading with the same child each week," explains volunteers director Marge Baker. "It has been the most highly rated program we've ever done. Teachers found dramatic gains in the students' self-esteem and vocabulary development." The Women's Club of neighboring Hawthorne liked it enough to adopt a Head Start class each year since 1991, each member teamed with a child for the year. To obtain a copy of their camera-ready, generic training materials, send $5.00 to Rockin' Readers, Attn: Marge Baker, 3700 NE 53rd Avenue, Gainesville, FL 32609.

Of all the guest-reader programs in the country, it would be hard to beat Overbrook School's for pure celebrity appeal. The program was the brainchild of Antonia (Toni) Carter, mother of four, who was inspired by the examples she had found in this chapter of previous editions of *The Read-Aloud Handbook* and created an event she called Leaders Are Readers. The program brings nineteen different community leaders to the Nashville, Tennessee, Catholic school's classes (from preschool through eight grade), but the roster and its book choices are what make the program unique. Let's see if another school in the country can match this:

- A Holocaust survivor reading from *Anne Frank: The Diary of a Young Girl*;
- Students from the Tennessee School for the Blind reading Braille;
- An Olympic air-pistol champion reading from a history of the Olympics;
- Vanderbilt University's football coach reading *Oh, the Places You'll Go!* by Dr. Seuss;
- A heart-lung transplant surgeon reading from Ben Carson's *Gifted Hands*;
- An American Airlines pilot reading of Lindbergh's journey in *Flight* by Robert Burleigh;
- A former U.S. ambassador to France reading from *The Red Balloon*, by Albert Lamerisse;
- A local country-club chef reading Tomie dePaola's *PANCAKES, PANCAKES*;
- The dean of Vanderbilt University School of Nursing reading from Joanna Cole's *The Magic School Bus Inside the Human Body*;
- The general manager of the Nashville Sounds minor-league baseball team reading "Casey at the Bat" and "Casey's Revenge";
- The Vanderbilt football team's placekicker reading from *The Dallas Titans Get Dressed* by Karla Kuskin;

- The county sheriff reading from *Encyclopedia Brown*, by Donald Sobol;
- A Marine captain reading from Eve Bunting's *The Wall*;
- A local veterinarian reading a James Herriott short story;
- And Nashville's senior FBI agent reading "The Hitchhiker," by Roald Dahl.

Needless to say, if you are going to organize a guest-reader program, it is essential to ensure the reader's book is matched to the right grade level. Therefore it is usually best for organizers to be involved in book choices right from the very start. In one community I visited, they were still talking about the time the principal showed up for his guest appearance, only to pass out ditto sheets and read about the state seal and symbols from the Wisconsin Blue Book. How's that for creating future readers?

But some principals do great work to encourage reading, especially those who have a reading background themselves. For example:

- In 1988, Dave Ivnik and his faculty chose pages and miles instead of minutes in challenging the 330 students at Maercker School (grades 3 through 5) in Westmont, Illinois, "to read to the moon and back!" That meant they, as a group, would have to read at least 480,000 pages outside school. Motivated by the two fifteen-minute read-aloud and SSR periods scheduled daily, students finished the year with 750,000 pages (2,200 pages per child). In addition, 142 families participated in a family reading program, discipline problems and remedial-reading referrals were down in spite of increasing enrollment, and the school's reading scores are all above average, with most at the highest level. Ivnik read aloud to every class, and the faculty's lunch conversations were often about children's books.
- Boulder Elementary School library (450 students) in Montgomery, Illinois, circulates eighty books a day. The reason can be found in the directive principal Jerald Tollefson gives to his teachers each fall: "I believe children need to be read to every day and given time to practice whole reading (SSR). These two things should take place every day without fail. Yes, even if it means a basal reading story hasn't been done, vocabulary words not finished, and a workbook page must be skipped." Willing to lead by example, Tollefson spends sixty hours a year reading aloud to his students,

beginning the year with daily readings to the fifth grade from *The Cay* by Theodore Taylor. Completing that, he shifts to the fourth grade and begins another novel with them. In addition, his librarian reads an average of six novels a year to her "lunchtime listeners."

There was no guest-reader program in Abington, Pennsylvania, but that didn't stop Alexander Randall IV. A Princeton graduate, the seventy-four-year-old Randall invited himself, after running out of grandchildren to read to. He already had one foot in the school door, however, so getting the second one in was not too difficult. You see, Alexander Randall is Dr. Randall—community pediatrician and physician to the Abington School District.

Dr. Randall's devotion to reading aloud goes back to before his own children were born, to when he met his wife, Nina, during his internship. He read to her in his deep baritone voice during quiet times at the hospital.

Thus, forty-five years later, each Wednesday afternoon finds Dr. Randall reading a novel to a sixth-grade class for thirty minutes. Then he moves to two more sixth grades, each for thirty minutes. He's been doing it for five years and chose sixth grade because "they're a challenge. Anybody can read to kindergartners—but sixth-graders think they're too old to be read to. And they end up loving it."

"He does it like we're the audience, and he's the play," explained one sixth-grade boy. Dr. Randall is not one to take his audience or his performance for granted, and Tuesday evenings are often spent rehearsing aloud the next day's chapters.

A few years ago, before reading the riveting novel *Weasel*, by Cynthia DeFelice, Dr. Randall announced, "There's something very special about this book and its author, but I'm not going to tell you what it is until we've completed the book." In the end, his listeners rated this pioneer adventure tale as their favorite of the year. And then he told them the secret: When Cynthia DeFelice was a child, her name was Cynthia Carter. And she was a patient of his. "I gave her immunization shots and checkups—just like I give some of you. Not only that," he went on, "but she went to THIS school. Sat in this room." And with the students' eyes widening, he added, "She might even have sat in the very seat you're in right now!"

Dr. Randall's devotion to reading is not restricted to those ninety minutes and three classes a week. The state of Pennsylvania requires all fifth-grade students to have a physical examination before entering sixth grade, so many of the community's children show up in Randall's office. But Dr. Randall gives out an unusual prescription—he asks each student to read a book before sixth grade, and he recommends titles as well. Ah, if only we could clone this good doctor and spread him throughout America!

As this chapter demonstrates, ideas are like the concentric ripples in a pond—you never know how far they will eventually travel. Back in the 1980s, Sallie Barker, librarian and wife of the headmaster at Salisbury School (Maryland), heard me speak on the importance of reading aloud. Sallie, in turn, told her mother, Cynthia Prince, about the program and recommended she go to hear me if I was ever in the area. As luck would have it, shortly thereafter I was presenting for the Duval County Reading Council in Jacksonville. And there in the audience, unbeknownst to me, was Cynthia Prince.

As a point of explanation, Cynthia Prince is one of these compelling, dynamic senior citizens who make the rest of us look like we're sleep-walking. A former administrative head at Potomac School and then dean of girls at Madeira School (both in Washington, D.C.), Prince was living in retirement in Ponte Vedra, Florida. Although she and her husband resided in a rather well-heeled corner of the community (Vicar's Land-ing), the local public schools included a cross section of children from every social stratum. Upon hearing the read-aloud message, Mrs. Prince set to work.

First she corraled dozens of senior-citizen volunteers from Vicar's Landing, most of them people with good educational backgrounds who needed an outlet for their intellectual energies. As one of them told me later, "There is no way you can turn this woman down once she sets her sights on something!" Within a year (1988), Prince had founded "Readers Aloud," and by 1994 it had grown to seventy volunteers (not just senior citizens) reading one day a week for thirty minutes in seventy classrooms, kindergarten through fifth grade. In addition, St. Augustine's public schools had adopted her program for four of its schools, and the Junior League of Jacksonville adopted it for a school there as well.

Prince's efforts were felt not only at the elementary grade level, but on the next level as well, when teachers and administrators at Landrum Middle School (grades 6 through 8) voted to extend the school day for thirty-five minutes (with no increase in pay) in order to add reading aloud and sustained silent reading. The offshoot of that was a 75 percent increase in the school library circulation.

Books for Newborns

Until recently, programs to promote reading among new parents have largely been left to libraries. But now many state and local councils of the International Reading Association are joining that effort. The ultimate model for such efforts can be found in Beginning with Books, a prevention-oriented literacy program affiliated with the Carnegie Library in Pittsburgh, Pennsylvania, and focused on bringing good books and children together, while simultaneously educating parents to the benefits of both reading aloud to their children and the library. With subsidies from the Pennsylvania Department of Education, the Carnegie Library, and individuals, the program annually distributes 5,000 packets of books (containing three paperbacks). They also offer a manual called "How to Start a Gift Book Program" for those wishing to start similar programs elsewhere. The program was begun in 1984 by Drs. Joan Friedberg and Elizabeth Segel.[7]

But what about someone who doesn't have the underpinning of a Carnegie Library? Take the case of Joy Sakai, a hospital pharmacist in Visalia, California, part of Tulare County, which has more children living in poverty than any of the state's other fifty-six counties.

Sakai grew up in a home of voracious readers. For her own children, bookshelves were as much a part of the house as the bread box. "But when my children got to school," she explained to me, "I discovered that California had the nation's worst record for school library support. My children were in a K–3 school without a library. So I worked with the principal to get a grant to create one. And while I was working with them—this was back in 1989—I came across a flyer announcing that Jim Trelease would be giving an all-day teacher workshop in Fresno.

"And I remember at one point you said, 'The schools are doing a better job than they used to, but it's not enough. It's not SOON enough. We have to start earlier. How about if each of you teachers went home and talked to your pediatricians?' You reminded us how parents put their pediatricians on pedestals, believing everything they said. 'Get the pediatricians to tell parents they should be reading to their children every day.'

"And I thought, This is perfect for me. I work in a hospital, I have connections to both the health community and schoolteachers. So I got together with five other women and we founded a family-based literacy program for the county and called it Read for Life."

At first they worked with just the Tulare Reading Council (teachers) and Visalia Community Hospital, giving children's books to new parents. In the intervening years, their approach and goals have broadened. "For one thing," says Sakai, "we no longer bother the new moms immediately after they have the baby. We discovered they had too many higher priorities at that point. Now we reach them in the birthing classes at the local hospitals and county health facilities *before* they have the baby."

Read for Life next connected with Reading Is Fundamental in Washington, D.C. and obtained a grant that allowed them to set up mini-libraries in a women's shelter, a health clinic, an Indian reservation, and the teen parenting program. Tulare County has a heavy Southeast Asian immigrant population, and through the local school district, Read for Life reached out to those who were taking English as a Second Language classes. They give each parent-student a book they can read to their children; then, once a month, they host a small party for the parents and their children, celebrating what they have accomplished in their classes and bringing small gifts to the children.

Six years after they began as a committee of six, they have grown to twenty (eighteen women, two men) and are funded by a cross section of the community: United Way; Tulare County Reading Council; the local Rotary chapter; local hospitals. To date they have personally reached almost 6,000 families. In addition, Sakai and the preschool teacher from the original committee have been elected to the community school board, where they dare to dream of a better world for all children.[8]

Three State Programs

Great things so often begin not with a mass movement but with one dedicated individual who dares to stand and lead. Here are my favorite examples:

Read-Aloud Delaware is a statewide program founded by State Representative Kevin W. Free in 1984 shortly after reading the first edition of *The Read-Aloud Handbook* during a plane flight. A native of New Zealand, Free remembered the achievements of that country's Plunkett Society, a health maintenance organization working with parents to meet the physical needs of young children. He wondered if the same principles couldn't be applied to the intellectual needs of the child. Why not start a kind of Plunkett Society for the minds of young children in the state of Delaware?

He also reasoned that the best start for the mind is to be read to. Within months of conceiving the idea, he founded Read-Aloud Delaware

(RAD), a nonprofit corporation to ensure that every preschool child in the state has someone to read to him or her. Today RAD has two full-time and six part-time staff members to coordinate activities throughout the state, with half of its nearly $200,000 budget coming from the state. In a given year its 250 volunteers read 14,000 times, one-on-one, to 5,800 children in day-care centers serving low-income families, clinic waiting rooms, hospitals, shelters, and sites where teen mothers and fathers attend high school or literacy classes. In addition, they distribute 10,000 books to parents and newborns.[9]

Recruiting from local libraries, day-care centers, Scout groups, and Red Cross classes, the organization has collected hundreds of volunteers willing to read to children who otherwise might not have a reader within the family. They do this in neighborhood health clinics where parent and child are waiting for pediatric help, demonstrating the interaction between reader, child, and book—pointing to pictures, turning pages, asking and answering questions.

The largest statewide program to date is Read-Aloud West Virginia (RAWV), founded in 1986 by Mary Kay Bond and thirty community women (mostly mothers like Mary Kay). RAWV was initially modeled on Delaware's program, but with illiteracy woes far surpassing Delaware's, and a much larger state, the West Virginia group began with just a few counties. It provides books and material to new families, supplies speakers for prenatal classes, PTAs, and civic groups, and sends regular guest readers to fifty schools.

Each year, the thirty moms, working without the government leverage of Delaware's program, nonetheless expanded RAWV into more and more counties. Then, early in the 1990s, it was absorbed by the West Virginia Education Fund, the nation's first statewide education fund— created to involve the private sector in the quality of the state's schools. Thanks to a $300,000 grant from the Benedum Foundation, RAWV now has a full-time director, and is linked through its training and 5,000 volunteers to more than fifty of the state's counties. How crucial is a program like this? West Virginia ranks fourth in the nation in the number of children living in poverty, and forty-ninth in per capita income of its adults (only Mississippi is lower); it has the lowest national percentage of college degrees and second highest percentage of eighth-grade (or below) educations. Read-Aloud West Virginia's volunteers work in areas so rural and isolated, it is estimated that seven counties don't have a single traffic light. By 1994, RAWV volunteers were reading to more than 65,000 children—the single largest read-aloud effort of any volunteer organization in America. Not bad for something that started out with a couple of dozen dedicated moms.[10]

The most inclusive state plan to date has been Hawaii's Read to Me program. Few mainlanders know the extent of literacy problems in the fiftieth state, but its First Lady Lynn Waihee was a former high school English teacher and understood it firsthand. And she knew what would solve the problem best—early intervention by parents and relatives who read to a child while it was "still in the nest." Thus was established Hawaii's Governor's Council for Literacy. But government offices seldom effect change unless they broaden their base. So in 1992, the Council joined hands with Rotary Clubs of Hawaii. Rotary International—composed of community business leaders—has long been the epitome of volunteerism and community leadership throughout the world, and Hawaii's clubs were no exception.

One of Rotary's Sunrise members worked for advertising agency Starr-Seigle-McCombs, which knew a thing or two about campaigns and set to work developing a theme that would catch the attention of both children and adults. In the meantime, the Governor's Council continued to make its support base as diverse as possible, bringing aboard the State Library, KHET (the state's PBS station), Hawaii Pizza Hut, Inc., McDonald's, and the prestigious Bishop Estate/Kamehameha Schools. The advertising agency's campaign consisted of print, radio, and television ads, with the TV ads aimed at children and the radio and print focusing on adults. The message was that children should be read to for at least ten minutes a day. The TV and radio ads were built around themes, like one that portrayed children as little mynah birds that need to be fed books by parents, the big birds in their lives. These ads also featured a "Read to Me" song that quickly became a statewide hit. Radio, television, and newspapers throughout the state quickly picked up on the campaign's importance and began donating free space and airtime for the ads. Because of Hawaii's cultural diversity, the ads appeared in several different languages and reminded adults that reading to children in any language is important.

In 1993, when Consolidated Theaters/Pacific Theaters began showing the Read to Me commercial prior to its feature, audiences spontaneously joined in on the theme song they had all come to love. An offshoot of this has been a renovation project launched by Consolidated Theaters to rebuild school libraries, and just recently Pizza Hut began a similar project. Hawaii was the seedbed for the national POG craze (cardboard bottle-cap covers that are traded and collected like baseball cards), and

Rotary soon produced 25,000 sets of Read to Me caps. Not to be out-done, the Girl Scouts of Hawaii developed a Read to Me merit badge. Mrs. Waihee's and Rotary's political influence, combined with the natural power of their idea, soon spread to the mainland, and by 1994 the Rotary chapters and First Ladies of two more states—Colorado and Wyoming—launched their own Read to Me campaigns based on Hawaii's.[11]

Businesses That Bank on Books

As noted previously, national corporations like Pizza Hut, Inc., and McDonald's have outstanding records in their support of children and reading—much the way Kellogg's has supported secondary education so splendidly through the last fifty years. But smaller local businesses should not be discouraged from doing their share. Look at what Hills Bank and Trust Company has done in Iowa City, Iowa.

In 1988 the development office of the University of Iowa approached local businesses, looking for $500 contributions toward university events. By the time they approached Hills Bank Senior Vice President Tom Cilek, the only event without sponsorship was a reception for a children's literature program. He agreed to sponsor it, but in the ensuing weeks he also decided to meet with a group of local school librarians —Jean van Deusen, Victoria Walton, Suzanne Bork, Barb Stein, and Paula Brandt from the University of Iowa education department. "What can we do to make this more than just a reception?" he asked them.

Their brainstorming created an event called Children's Reading Month that subsequently broadened into a Community Reading Month that has swept Iowa City and neighboring communities. Along with publishing a month's calendar of books that adults can and should read to children, the program helps sponsor a "author-in-residence" event in which fa-mous authors like Jerry Spinelli, Ashley Bryan, Janice Lee Smith, and Brian Jacques visit local schools; book-talk luncheons in which local celebrities read from and talk about their favorite adult books; a com-munity read-in that promotes the idea of everyone stopping work for fifteen minutes at 10:00 A.M. on a designated day and reading something for pleasure; and a campaign to get families to turn off the television set for one hour on a preordained evening. Newspapers publish company ads in which employees write about their favorite book. In 1994, the celebrity readers included the Catholic bishop of Davenport, Iowa; the president of the University of Iowa; and the university's head basketball coach.

In the space of eight years, the campaign has turned the month of November into reading month for its schools, families, and citizenry. And if business owners wonder what it did for Hills Bank and Trust: In 1988, Hills Bank ranked second among the three banks in Iowa City, $17 million smaller than its largest competitor. By 1994, with no appreciable interest rate difference between them, Hills Bank was the largest bank by $41 million. A major difference appears to be a reading campaign that touches tens of thousands each year and creates a corporate identity associated with community improvement. What a difference it would make if every community were filled with businesses as civic-minded as Hills Bank.

Since bookstores and newspapers have a vested interest in developing future readers, it amazes me more bookstores and newspapers don't adopt programs like that of Davis-Kidd Booksellers in Tennessee and the *Chadron Record* in Chadron, Nebraska. Davis-Kidd Booksellers in Memphis, an outstanding general bookstore, worked with First United Methodist Church to establish a homeless children's library in their city. Each book donated by the public was matched by Davis-Kidd, and the family donations could consist of books their children had outgrown— so they didn't even have to go out and buy new books. The little *Chadron Record* sponsors a Share-A-Book This Christmas program. Readers wishing to donate new or "gently used" children's books can drop them off at the newspaper's editorial offices for distribution by the local public schools, community outreach services, Head Start, and VISTA volunteers.

Reading Behind Bars

Dr. Frank Boyden, the legendary headmaster of Deerfield Academy of Massachusetts, once explained why he refused, if possible, to give one of his boys bad news at night: "Darkness and a troubled mind are a poor combination."[12] Most people would agree, recalling events that seemed so staggering to us in the dark but smaller in the light of the next morning.

Betty Frandsen never knew Dr. Boyden, but his night-time sentiments were hers too. Frandsen often found it difficult to fall asleep at the end of a day. The day's events—worries about her children and her job as an advertising executive in San Francisco—all seemed to collide in her head and keep her awake. Finally she took to using one of those tiny radio earplugs, and it helped. Listening to talk radio at night shifted her focus and she drifted off to sleep.

Ten miles away in Martinez, though, there were no earplugs, no Boyden-like sentiments, and the boys weren't preppy. The night came every twenty-four hours, and it was the worst part of the day for many of the 140 boys and girls locked in the Contra Costa Juvenile Hall, a holding pen for juveniles ranging in age from eight to eighteen. Each had been arrested for committing an adult crime, most were already veterans of the criminal justice system, many came from homes where they were badly abused, and most—though not all—were raised in extreme poverty. There were murderers, rapists, thieves, drug dealers—you name it, they were there.

Betty Frandsen, however, was unaware they existed until the day she saw the newspaper photo (three boys in a cell, two on cots and one sleeping on the floor) that accompanied a story on the institution's crowded conditions. Her own two children were on their own now and she was looking for something to do with her spare time. "Maybe they could use me there as a volunteer," she thought. And they did, assigning her to the "special needs" unit, the residents who were too dangerous to have roommates, who often mutilated even themselves. All she would have to do is play games with them, maybe some cards, talk.

And before she knew it, they were telling her about the nights, how they hated those most of all, lying in bed in the dark alone, wondering why their parents never came to visit, why they wouldn't even accept their collect calls, thinking about the dreadful things they'd done to someone, and listening to the night noises that come with jails—the cries, the embittered curses, the moans, the pounding of someone's head on the wall.

And that's when Frandsen began to wonder "If—maybe—bedtime stories might help. What if someone read bedtime stories through the intercom?" It sounded so simple, so childish even, yet so workable. "Here would be something that could help them get through the night, could make them end the day on a happy note, and they might even learn something in the process," she thought.

The authorities agreed to at least give it a try and Frandsen rounded up some volunteer readers—a lawyer, a hypnotherapist, an energy consultant, a construction worker—for what they decided to call "The Late Show." The young-adult librarian at the county library offered to choose some titles that would appeal to this specialized audience.

For some, it was the first time they had ever been read to, and for most it was the first at bedtime. And it worked. Officials reported the nights became calmer, and the residents were often overheard bragging to newcomers, "And you know what we got here—every night? 'The Late Show.' They read stories, novels and stuff, over the speakers." Several of the "graduates" doing time at the California Youth Authority wanted to know why they couldn't have the show there too. Fresno's Juvenile Hall has picked up on it and now has its own version.

The fifteen volunteers read three nights a week, each having an audience of forty in the Hall's individual units. Rick Kozen, one of the Juvenile Hall's probation managers, calls the program remarkably successful in easing the stress at a critical time of day, and even provoking some of the residents to read. "In the U.S., this is being looked at as an *innovative* program. Which is shocking. It manifests where we're at in this country—that reading bedtime stories to children is *innovative!*"[13]

The next logical step would be to bring the importance of reading into the adult prison population, where school dropouts make up 82 percent of the population—and that's what Nancye Gaj did. After fifteen years working in adult education, Nancye Gaj had seen that one of the top three reasons given by adults for learning to read is the desire to read to their children or grandchildren. Why not tap into that built-in motivation and build a program around it? But when Gaj tried to convince North Carolina state authorities to fund parent education, they saw no sense in it. And that's when she hit upon the idea of combining the state's needs with her own: Where is the state's highest concentration of illiterate mothers? In state prison.

If those women could be reached through a literacy program, the chances of their returning to prison were slimmer, as were the chances of their children growing up illiterate. And most of these women had the same parenting concerns that other mothers have—except they are magnified if the parent is in prison.

That argument worked with state officials and they funded the start of MOTHEREAD at North Carolina Correctional Institute for Women. "We thought at first that it would be for one year, as a kind of experiment. As it turned out," recalls Gaj, "the impact was so great—upon the women, the prison staff, and the VISTA volunteers—it couldn't be discontinued. What we'd stumbled on was that when you combine the power of the heart with the power of a book, you've got something very powerful. Here were people who will do for their children what they wouldn't otherwise do for themselves—learn to read." Many of these women had been through remedial reading programs while they were in school but the lessons failed to stick. "The 'self' was usually lost in their classes and in their readings," explains Gaj. "It had nothing to do with them as a person—until a child was added to the picture."

Today more than four hundred women inmates a year come through MOTHEREAD, and two more North Carolina penal institutions are using the program. In addition, it has spread outside prisons to cities and towns where annually another five hundred parents (there is now a FATHEREAD) are coached not only in literacy but also in reading with expression and involving a child in the reading by asking the right questions or soliciting opinions. They have also trained volunteers presently working in South-Central Los Angeles, Boston, Fairbanks, as well as Minneapolis and St. Paul.[14]

Undergraduates as Volunteer Readers

Sometimes great ideas are staring us in the face and we cannot see them for the distractions around us. Think of the thousands of colleges and universities in America offering or requiring children's literature programs. Most often the main focus of the student and curriculum is the textbook and grades. But should that be the ultimate objective or focus?

Dr. Hazel Fisher teaches children's literature at Bucks County Community College in Newtown, Pennsylvania. A requirement for education majors, the course calls for seventy-five books to be read during the semester. But Fisher wanted those books to impact on more than her students and with that in mind, developed Rent-a-Kid Storytime, which requires each of the course's students to find a child—any child—to whom they can read each week. Students must select age-appropriate books for these readings, keep a before-and-after journal about the readings, and give a semester-end oral and written report to the class about their read-aloud experiences.

"I cannot begin to tell you all the wonderful accomplishments of my students with the Rent-a-Kid program," Fisher tells anyone who will listen. "Several dedicated students read weekly to deaf children, patiently reading and 'signing' each book. Another young woman read to a visually impaired child, a Down syndrome child, as well as her own hearing-impaired child. Another student, a social studies teacher, began reading to her skeptical seventh-grade parochial school students, starting with *Life* magazine and moving on to Edgar Allan Poe's short stories after she discovered their favorite author was Stephen King. She also began SSR time in her class, which led to the entire school adopting it.

"Another student helped her sister through a time of grief by reading aloud books that dealt with the subject. Another read aloud *The Ugly Duckling* in Spanish and soon her young listener was bringing home fiction written in Spanish for their read-aloud sessions. Some students began the semester with one Rent-a-Kid only to find their numbers increasing as friends and neighbors joined the weekly sessions. In fact, some of my students read aloud as often as seven times a week, depending on their home or work situation." The semester totals averaged 2,000 books read aloud to more than 350 children.[15]

As the above examples demonstrate, there are places that thrive on books and the excitement of reading. If yours is not one of those schools or communities, ask yourself, Why not? I've personally met most of the people noted in the above examples and I assure you, only one or two of them would I label "genius." These are average people—until you look at their extraordinary dedication, leadership ability, and willingness to pursue dreams that others label "impossible" before they even try.

Most of the aforementioned programs began with one person's idea. So begin yourself. If you are a classroom teacher, consider this approach: Since most parents will not have read *The Read-Aloud Handbook* or any other book on children's literature, you are their principal resource for information and enthusiasm. Share it by compiling short read-aloud book lists (long lists frighten working parents) that can be given to parents at parent conferences, before school vacations, and for holiday shopping guides. Research shows us 58 percent of parents rarely or never receive such tips on how they can be more involved in the learning process.[16] And you can be sure, the ones who most need them seldom get them.

In compiling the recommended-book lists, be sure to make the distinction between those books read *by* the child and those intended for reading *to* the child, explaining briefly the difference between listening levels and reading levels—something few parents consider until it is brought to their attention. (Use *The Cosby Show* example on page 46.) When you have students mesmerized by a book, you can be sure they are talking about it at home too. Capitalize on that by letting parents know about other books by that author or related books (as I do in the Treasury). Such communications are all the more important as parent-teacher conferences grow rarer with both parents working.

Generally speaking, parents like Mary Kay Bond and her mom-colleagues who founded Read-Aloud West Virginia are rare. Most parents are very reluctant to pass along unsolicited suggestions to teachers, and this is unfortunate. Good teachers are not threatened by such well-intentioned ideas but are honored by parental involvement. Conversely, the teacher who responds negatively to parents' suggestions is probably a bad teacher, and therefore your involvement is even more necessary to encourage your child during the school year. Three-fourths of my children's elementary teachers did *not* read aloud. Therefore it behooved me to continue reading—and be more involved at the school.

If it becomes apparent that your child's teacher is not reading aloud daily, you might consider either scheduling a conference or writing a note describing the benefits of your home read-aloud program, even listing some of your child's favorite titles. Suggest that a similar program might be a good idea for the classroom, that it develops listening comprehension, vocabulary, and positive attitudes toward the pleasures of reading and not just the skills of reading. And for documentation, obtain a copy of *Becoming a Nation of Readers* from the library and photocopy the title page, the commission members on page iii, and pages 23 and 51, which state that reading aloud is the best activity in school or out to create readers. Emphasize that your note is not intended to interfere with the curriculum but to reinforce it. Unlike parents who are writing notes to teachers requesting permission to take a child out of school for vacations, shopping trips, and sports tournaments, you are writing to add something to learning instead of subtracting from it. Or devote one of the school's monthly PTA meetings to the topic of read-aloud, and there you can clarify the need for it.

A Tale of Two Families

I have saved for last two of my favorite stories. They summarize everything I have tried to say both in this chapter and in this book. Here we will meet two families, separated by color, by thirty-four years, and by several income levels. In spite of those differences, they eventually were united by a simple act of intelligence and one newspaper.

On a vacation morning, while my wife and I were having breakfast in a hotel dining room, I overheard the conversation at the next table. There a mother, father, two children, and grandfather—all handsomely dressed in the latest yuppie leisure styles—were also having breakfast. One child was eight months old and the other was twenty-three months, so one wouldn't expect them to add much to the conversation. But for me, they were the most interesting part.

The mother kept up a steady stream of small talk with the eight-month-old, while the father worked at keeping the older child's interest at his own table instead of neighboring ones. He accomplished this by using the morning's *New York Times*. With the business pages spread in front of the child, he would ask him to find the story about Nike. The boy responded by pointing to the Nike logo buried in the company news briefs. He then asked for the Pepsi logo and others on the page. The child scrutinized the page and found each one. In effect, the father had succeeded in turning *The New York Times* business section into *Where's Waldo*. Then, picking up the breakfast menu, the father requested the child find the "100% Colombian Coffee." And each time the child found the assigned logo, he was rewarded with praise from around the table. The mother even held the youngest one's hands and mimicked applause.

Such simple lessons cost as little as the morning newspaper or the breakfast menu, and alone would hardly add up to much in the way of education. But taken collectively, day after day, meal after meal, vacation after vacation, they add up to a child who slips into the world of print confidently, without trauma and with a strong sense of excitement. I didn't know that child or family, so we'll never know what eventually will come of their breakfast conversations, though I can imagine.

For a look at the second family in this tale we must go back thirty-four years—to the Marriott family, living in a black neighborhood in Louisville, Kentucky, in the summer of 1960. They are poor but not deprived. The father, Louis, is a custodian at a local factory, always working overtime and often two jobs in order to make ends meet. They never have enough money to take a family vacation—except for one automobile trip to visit relatives in Philadelphia—but they're not so poor that they cannot afford a daily newspaper.

A high school graduate, the father hoped to go to college but gradually those dreams faded. He settled for self-education, buying and reading books on philosophy, art, and literature, then proudly quoting from them to his family.

The mother, Glenda, the daughter of a hotel doorman, was also a high school graduate and part of the first integrated class at the University of Louisville. Then she met a handsome army lieutenant named Louis, who swept her off her feet. She left college and convinced him to do the same with the army and settle down to raise a family.

On a particular summer evening in 1960, Mrs. Marriott and her five-and-a-half-year-old son Michel are sitting on the living room sofa. Spread before the boy are pieces of clear plastic, shaped like parts of the human body. On the table beside them is an empty box labeled "The Visible Man," a gift from last Christmas.

The boy chooses a piece from the table and hands it to his mother. She, in turn, examines it, consults the small booklet in her hand, returns the piece to the boy, and begins to read aloud from the booklet while her son assembles what eventually becomes a foot-tall human body, the skeleton and organs showing through the clear plastic. The booklet she is reading came with the kit and amounts to an anatomy booklet, describing organ functions like how many fluid ounces of blood are pumped by the heart or the capacity of the lungs. While she reads, she marvels at the quickness with which her son makes his connections. Perhaps she is dreaming that someday he will be a doctor. If she harbors such fantasies, they are hers in private, never shared.

Meanwhile, the boy is enchanted by the specialness of it all. His mother had read to him before—fairy tales and things—but this, he sensed, was different. For one thing, his mother was using a different voice, filled with an earnestness that wasn't there for other stories. Partly because of this, he looks forward to this shared ritual each evening. Neither of them can possibly know how truly special these moments would become, how they would change Michel's life forever—beginning in just a few weeks. They could not have known that any more than the couple in the hotel coffee shop could know the outcome of their morning lessons with *The New York Times*. But the hindsight of thirty-four years reveals the results of Mrs. Marriott's reading, and Michel remembers it this way:

"All of this was happening in the weeks before I was to begin school for the first time [Virginia Avenue Elementary—an all-black school, part of de facto segregation]. When I began school—first grade—one of the first things they wanted you to do was show 'n' tell. But while other kids brought in things like toys, I brought in The Visible Man. And lo and behold, I'm standing in front of the class and go into this spiel as though I was at medical school. Not only am I holding up the various organs and describing their functions just the way my mother read them to me, but I'm also *assembling* the thing. My first-grade teacher was amazed! In fact, she decided this was too good for just this one class. She immediately takes me on a tour of all the school's first-grade classes, and then the upper grades too.

"It gave me immediate gratification. It stripped away any of the intimidation that school might have had for me, going to school for the first time. There was all this praise, people making a big deal over me. Suddenly I had a reputation as some kind of little professor. It had nothing to do with how I looked or how I dressed. It only had to do with what I could *do*. And from that point on, school was fun for me. I wanted to get that kind of reaction from *everything* I did. And reading was really the key to it. From the very beginning, I realized the power of words. Words and reading brought immediate feedback and response from people—even little kids made a big thing out of it."

Such a simple thing—reading aloud from an anatomy booklet to a five-and-a-half-year-old. Yet its ripple effect would be profound, almost immediately. By fifth grade, Michel's teachers convinced him to join the Optimists, a club aimed at promoting and developing public-speaking techniques. "After three years," he recalls, "I found I enjoyed writing the speeches even more than delivering them." Soon he was a freshman in high school and the first test in his history class was an essay. As fate would have it, the history teacher was also advisor to the school newspaper. And he was so impressed with the freshman's essay, he suggested Michel join the paper's staff, a privilege normally reserved for sophomores.

Two years later, convinced of Michel's writing talents, the advisor suggested he enter the journalism contest promoted by *The Louisville Courier-Journal*. His prize was an all-expenses paid summer at the journalism school at Northwestern University. Standing on the sprawling Evanston, Illinois, campus, "I swore that someday, somehow, I would come back here. I didn't know how, but I'd do it," Marriott told me. First, though, there would be four years at Morehead State University. There his 3.7 average earned him a Scripps-Howard scholarship and Ford Foundation fellowship back to Northwestern for a master's degree. His first job was with the *Marion* (Indiana) *Chronicle Tribune*, from which he was successively recruited by *The Louisville Courier-Journal, The Washington Post, The Philadelphia Daily News*, and then *The New York Times*—the same newspaper the couple was using in the coffee shop that Saturday morning.

Two families who would have been worlds apart less than two generations ago are united today by education, an education that began with a mother's simple act of reading aloud and thereby gave her son the tools he would need not only to survive but also to flourish.[17]

Perhaps nothing better demonstrates the inspiring nature of education than the evening a few years ago when Michel Marriott returned home as a guest speaker for a journalism seminar at the Brown Hotel, Louis-ville's swankiest hotel. His mother brought her retired father to hear the speech and afterward they visited with Michel in his hotel room.

"My grandfather was a very gregarious man, but that night I couldn't figure out why he was so quiet," Marriott recalled. "Just standing there by the window, looking down at the street. And then it dawned on me: He was looking down on his old spot—the corner of Fourth and Broadway—the spot he'd worked as a doorman. He'd worked in the Brown from the age of sixteen until he retired at sixty-seven. For most of that time, it was a segregated hotel. This was the first time he'd ever been in one of the hotel's rooms."

In *The Disappearance of Childhood*, author Neil Postman offers this powerful metaphor of childhood: "Children are the living messages we send to a time we will never see." One cannot begin to estimate the powerful messages sent by the people in this chapter to a time they will never see. We easily can count, like the seeds in an apple, the number of books read by one child. But only God can count the number of apples that will come from a single seed or the number of readers who will eventually follow from one lifetime reader.

6

Home, School, and Public Libraries

In a large metropolitan Israeli school district during the 1980s, researchers found kindergartens where year after year children read poorly (most located in economically poor neighborhoods) and then found other kindergartens where the children read well (in affluent neighborhoods). Fifty-one families were identified in each category.

Teams of researchers then visited each home and interviewed the parents. It was found that 96 percent of the "achieving" kindergartners were read to daily, including 45 percent who were read to for at least 30 minutes daily. Fifty percent had parents who reported reading regularly to the child before the age of two. Conversely, 60 percent of the "underachieving" kindergartners were never read to.

And then the researchers asked to see any books owned by the child.

Among the less affluent families, half the children owned no books at all, and others produced books that appeared to actually belong to older siblings. Nonetheless, these children managed to produce 243 books. The affluent families—the ones who read almost daily to their children—owned 2,774 volumes. In other words, the achieving children came from homes where they were not only read to but had ten times as many books as did children who struggled with schoolwork.[1]

Readers raise readers because they do the raising in a home environment that nurtures it, in the same way athletes tend to raise athletes. Look at all the balls, bats, and gloves in the closet of your star high school athlete. In this chapter I will share some of the latest research about home, school, and public libraries, along with how any family or school—regardless of income—can create a successful library.

We begin by repeating the premise of earlier chapters: The more you read, the better you get at it. The reader-aloud provides the motivation for *wanting* to read, but this must be supported by easy access to a variety of books.

So let's look again at the study *How in the World Do Students Read?*,[2] which assessed 210,000 children from thirty-two different countries. The highest scores were achieved in countries where students had access to the most books:

- The larger the school library, the higher the scores; the ten highest-scoring countries have libraries twice as large as lower-scoring countries.
- The larger the classroom library, the higher the scores (even in the poorest of countries).

What the Finns Read

Finland was the nation with the highest citizen literacy rate (99 percent) and it also has the highest library usage. Looking closely at the patterns in Finnish students' homes and classrooms reveals[3]:

- At least 75 percent of students had 50 or more books in their home (with 25 percent reporting more than 200).
- 30 percent of students visit the library at least once a week.
- 44 percent of students watched no more than 2 hours of TV daily.[4]
- Less than 12 percent of students had a father and/or mother who graduated from college.

Among the Finnish nine-year-olds:

- 8 percent read BOOKS for pleasure almost every day.
- 59 percent read COMIC books almost every day (highest in any of thirty-two nations).
- 35 percent read a NEWSPAPER almost every day.

The Home Library

With all of this in mind, one can safely say that long before children are introduced to their neighborhood public library, books should be a part of their home lives. Begin a home library as soon as the child is born. If you can provide shelving in the child's room for such books, all the better. The sooner children become accustomed to the sight of the covers, bindings, and pages of books, the sooner they will begin to develop the concept that books are a part of daily life.

Admittedly, we were late in starting our home library for Elizabeth, our first child. Public library books were heavily relied upon until she was about four years old—the time when her younger brother, Jamie, was born. Since we had begun to see the positive effects of reading aloud to Elizabeth, my wife and I decided at that point to begin the children's home library. We had no idea, of course, that this library would eventually serve not only the children but their parents as well. Within a few years of Jamie's birth, Susan took a teaching degree in elementary education and used the books every day in her classes. It was the reaction of my own children and of those in my wife's classes that first inspired me to write this handbook.

In beginning a home library, particularly if you have children under the age of four, divide your books into two categories: expensive and inexpensive. The higher-priced or fragile books should be placed up on shelves out of the reach of sticky fingers, dribbles, and errant crayons. While out of reach, they should still be within sight—as a kind of goal. On lower shelves and within easy reach should be the less expensive and, if possible, more durable books. If the replacement price is low enough, you'll have fewer qualms about the child "playing" with the books. This playing is an important factor in a child's attachment to books. He must have ample opportunity to feel them, taste them, and see them.

Your home (and classroom) library should contain not only books the child will immediately relate to, but also those he or she will grow into—like encyclopedias. Someone had told me of a young osteopath, Dr. Charles Allen Holt, who preached the doctrine of read-aloud to the undereducated, poor parents he met during his internship at Cardinal Glennon Memorial Hospital for Children in St. Louis. Curious about his background, I finally found him living in Indianapolis and asked if he could spare a minute to tell me how he came to be a reader and proponent of reading aloud.

He told me that during his childhood in Jefferson City, Missouri, his parents read to him all the time, that television viewing was controlled in his home, and that books were available even before he could read. Dr. Holt also explained, "I remember my [schoolteacher] mother placing a *World Book Encyclopedia* on the floor in front of me to peruse in my leisure hours. By the time I was in kindergarten, I could find something within one minute in the encyclopedia on any topic you could suggest."

Reading that sentence set off bells in my memory bank as I recalled sitting through long hours of my own childhood in the 1940s with volumes of our encyclopedia curled in my lap. Since visual literacy comes before print literacy, I could locate the volume with photos from World War II, the pages with pictures of leopards and panthers, and the anatomy pages long before I could read. My father would make a point of looking up answers to my questions using the encyclopedia. Moreover, those volumes helped me feel comfortable with books, letting me overcome any negative feelings brought on later by workbooks and watered-down texts.

While an encyclopedia is an excellent family investment, at $1,000 or more it is not inexpensive. But just because you cannot afford one doesn't mean you can't own reference books. Consider as a short-term and immediate substitute the picture reference volumes listed in the Treasury on page 233. Taken individually or collectively, these books will give a child thousands of hours' worth of stimulation, information, and entertainment both before and after he learns to read and at one-tenth the cost of a full set of encyclopedias. For example, *The Kids' Question & Answer Book* (now expanded to three separate volumes) contains more than one hundred questions and answers commonly asked by children.

Never before in publishing history have so many nonfiction books been published for children, and never with such magnificent illustrations. (The illustrations often entice children into a subject they might otherwise have ignored.) Typical of the diversity is the Eyewitness Books series. Produced as individual volumes, each sixty-plus-page book is devoted to a single subject. To date the series has covered nearly fifty subjects, and the striking combination of detailed photographs and text makes each book a minimuseum. Another example of unique picture reference books is Stephen Biesty and Richard Platt's *Incredible Cross Sections* (Knopf). Using illustrations that feature painstakingly detailed cutaway cross sections of objects like a castle, observatory, subway train, helicopter, space shuttle, car factory, submarine (all parts of which are explained and labeled), the creators offer parent and child a classroom that is unparalleled in the history of publishing. Here is nonfiction's answer to *Where's Waldo*, by Martin Handford.

As I noted earlier, until your child is about two years old, his reading interest is usually better served by a few books that he sees and hears regularly than by dozens and dozens with which he never develops a working familiarity. However, as his attention span and interests grow, that home library should expand if your family budget permits.

The Classroom Library

The same principles that apply to home libraries also apply to school or classroom libraries. Having easy access to books makes it easier to read them, especially if they are right in the classroom and one doesn't have to get a hall pass to go down to the library. One study found that children in schools with in-class libraries read up to 50 percent more books.[5] In a separate study of 183 elementary classrooms, more than half had no classroom library (though 75 percent of the kindergartens did). The higher the grade level, the less chance of a classroom library. And since reading interest and achievement decline as one ascends the grade levels, one can only wonder at the coincidence.[6] Professor Richard Anderson's classroom research prompted him to call for a "virtual book flood"—that is, a thoughtfully constructed classroom library of paperback trade books introduced by an interested and motivated teacher—if we sincerely wish to raise a nation of readers.[7] A classroom without a library is like a gymnasium without a basketball hoop, a home economics class without a stove.

A living example of this approach to reading was my friend Kathy Nozzolillo's room when she taught at White Street School in Springfield, Massachusetts. Working each year with the bottom fourth-grade reading group, Kathy saw her immediate goal as dismantling the frightening barriers these urban children have erected between themselves and books—to turn books into friends, not enemies.

Kathy reasoned that her classroom was like an orchestra—it can't function without a conductor. As such, she read aloud three times a day (picture books and novels), drawing from the 450 volumes in the classroom library. Reading enthusiasm began with her and spread to the students. She knew her books as well as her class and quickly connected the right book with the right child. SSR was offered every day.

Yes, she had to use the basal text and a certain number of skill sheets (as required by the supervisor)—but they were limited to supporting trade books, not the other way around. Each May she borrowed two hundred of my best picture books for her students to read during the last month of school—no basals, no skill sheets. (She could also borrow from the library.) They just talked books, kept journals, and compared authors and illustrators. And by year's end, despite the IQ differences, her "bottom" reading group's scores were as high as those of the school's top group.

What prevents that from happening in all classrooms? Generally speaking, it's not money or equipment; it is ignorance on the part of educators who don't read the research.

Here are some ideas for building a home or school/classroom library that might be useful for those who, like me as a young parent, are operating on a limited book budget.

Twenty years ago, most of the books in my family library were bought secondhand at garage sales, the Salvation Army thrift shop, and used-book stores. As a result, I think my children were nearly ten years old before they realized not all books came with scribble marks and strange names crayoned inside the covers. Given the choice, I guess we all prefer the qualities of a brand-new book—its bright, crisp pages, its fresh smell. But struggling young families and teachers don't always have the money. If it's any consolation, "used" reads as well as "new," but "used" costs one-tenth as much.

In justifying the money you spend on books, compare inflation within the book industry with the rise in price for a movie or dinner. Moreover, the day after that movie or dinner, all you have left is the memory. With a book, you have both the memory and the book in hand—which can be enjoyed again and again at no extra cost. And the paperback revolution in publishing provides a further savings for home libraries. Unlike a decade ago when a handful of publishers controlled the children's paperback industry and only the sure sellers (and relatively few picture books) made it into paperback, today nearly all the hardcover publishers are producing softcover editions at less than half the cover price of hardcovers. That, in turn, allows bookstores to stock more children's titles and greatly improves the quality of choices.

Most schools today subscribe to one of several young people's paperback book clubs. These clubs offer nearly forty monthly selections at half price. The paperback your child pays $2.50 for in class will cost $4.95 in the bookstore and $12.95 in hardcover. Encourage your child's school to belong to one of these clubs and look over the selection sheets each month. By adding your choices for the family library to the child's selections, you'll be saving a considerable amount as well as showing the child your interest in books.

The question of durability frequently arises in discussing paperbacks. If the book is to be used only as a read-aloud by a teacher or parent, this is not a problem. But if it is going to be handled by a family of children or circulated through a classroom, its durability becomes important. My own solution, and one that has had considerable testing, is to protect the paperbacks with clear plastic self-sticking shelf paper, which can be bought in your local supermarket or discount department store.

Measure the cover beforehand to allow an overlap of several inches, cut the laminate, and adhere it to the cover of the paperback in the same way you would cover schoolbooks. For good measure, cut a pair of two-inch-wide strips for where the cover and pages meet at the spine (inside front and back). For classroom or home, these procedures lengthen the life of the book, and they also protect the cover from peanut butter and cocoa stains.

Another way for parents, teachers, and school librarians to cut costs is to compile a wish list of books you would like to have. In families, this is given to grandparents or other relatives who prefer to give long-lasting gifts like books but need title suggestions. And schools should make their wish lists available to parents several times a year through the principal's newsletter, PTA meetings, and open-house programs.

Magazines are frequently found in the homes of successful child readers. The International Reading Association offers a comprehensive guide to children's magazines and their subjects: Magazines for Children (U.S. $5.25) from IRA, Order Department, P.O. Box 8139, Newark, DE 19714-8139. Search out a magazine that will interest your child and subscribe. If you're looking for excellent stories and literature, my three favorite children's magazines are: *Ladybug* (ages two to six); *Spider* (six to nine); and *Cricket* (nine to twelve). Subscription information can be obtained at your local library.

The School Library

Americans pay wonderful lip service to libraries, yet few use them with any regularity. Any increase in circulation during the last decade can largely be attributed to the circulation of free videos and compact disks. School libraries in many states are always among the first targets when it comes to cutbacks—much sooner than sports.

There is no state that cares more about education or works harder to produce good students than California. But it ranks fiftieth in school library support. In 1990 Richard K. Moore, a high school librarian in Garden Grove, California, reported the following to the *Los Angeles Times*: Based on the number of librarians available to juvenile offenders in California correctional institutions and the number of librarians working in the state's K–12 schools, a convicted felon has a better chance of meeting a librarian than does the average California student (1 in 700 vs. 1 in 4,000).[8] In California, which has led the nation with demands for more trade books and literature in the classroom, officials have closed one-half of all school libraries in the last ten years due to budget constraints. By 1993, the national average was one librarian for every 722 students, versus California's 1 librarian to 6,400 students.[9]

Community and education decision-makers, like those in California, who cut or eliminate libraries are demonstrating how little they know about reading—and doing it publicly. For example, nearly everyone agrees that reading is the most important subject in school, since nearly all other subjects rest upon it. And the research that opened this chapter shows that the best readers in thirty-two nations came from the schools and classrooms with the most library books. But the powers-that-be don't know this because they don't read professionally. So they cut the library budget or eliminate it entirely—and still expect the scores to rise. That's like digging up the airport runways and expecting safe landings.

Many communities are strapped for funds, and something must be trimmed. If not the library, what? Cut the sports program. That's neither as bad nor as drastic as it sounds. Here's what happens. As soon as you cut school sports, there is a community uproar (anybody ever notice that the higher the community's sports scores, the lower the reading scores?). The end result is usually a grand rescue plan in which booster clubs, businesses, and parents find a way to raise funds to save sports —bake sales, dances, raffles, etc. And it works. But it doesn't work the *other* way. Cut the library and there are complaints—but nobody holds a bake sale or a fund-raiser.

subject of books and money leads me directly into school book
. There are two possible purposes to a book fair: (1) to deliver
oks into the hands of children who might not otherwise have them;
⅟r (2) to raise money for the school. The latter reason is shameless and
deserves immediate censure. Far too often the national book fair companies that offer schools the most profit also offer the worst collection
of titles posing as books. Shame on both your houses. If the ultimate
purpose is to raise money, don't hide behind books and pretend you're
doing something educational. Sell magazine subscriptions or candy. At
least that way people will know your true purpose. If your purpose in
the book fair is to enlarge children's contact with books, form a committee of parents, librarians, and teachers to review what the company
will offer and limit sales to what is approved—just as you do in choosing
a new textbook series.

Boys and Sports Reading

Social commentator Fran Lebowitz once wrote that magazines most
often lead to books and therefore should be regarded by the prudent
as the heavy petting of literature. In that regard, I recall the mother who
said to me, "I just don't know what to do with my thirteen-year-old. He
hates to read."

When I asked what his interests were, she replied, "Sports." But when
I suggested a subscription to a sports magazine, she said, "Oh, he already gets *Sports Illustrated*. He reads it cover to cover."

"Excuse me, but I thought you said he hates to read?" I inquired. The
woman looked puzzled for a moment and responded, "Well, I didn't
think *Sports Illustrated* counted." I quickly explained to her that it did
count, that I had read (and saved) every issue of *Sports Illustrated* from
the time I was thirteen until I was eighteen and that was where I first
encountered Faulkner, Hemingway, and J. P. Marquand.

For those educators inclined to look down their noses at magazine
reading as being less than complex, I refer you to a paragraph pulled
at random out of old clippings in a file drawer, and I confidently declare that most, if not *all*, textbook publishers would reject it as too
complex for American high school students. The magazine was *Sports
Illustrated;* the subject was the former Yale president Bart Giamatti, soon
to become baseball commissioner and too soon thereafter to die; the
author was Frank Deford:

"So it was, this April Fool's Day, that the man who stood with God at the helm at Yale became the man who stands with the child in all our selves on behalf of baseball. *Quo vadis?* Giamatti, in his new book, quotes an apocryphal memo he supposedly wrote and released to 'an absent and indifferent' university community upon assuming the presidency at Yale: 'In order to repair what Milton called the ruin of our grandparents, I wish to announce that henceforth, as a matter of University policy, evil is abolished and paradise is restored.' "[10]

Look at those literary allusions, the figurative writing, the vocabulary, the complex and compound sentences. Please don't tell me those wouldn't challenge college-bound readers or any adolescent with a brain.

American sport became the campgrounds for dumbbells partly because intellectuals abandoned it to beer-guzzling couch potatoes. What we need at this juncture is for teachers and parents to go back and reclaim some of that ground by putting "brains" back into sport. There is a rich American heritage in which our greatest writers have written about sport. Since the most learning takes place at the point of interest —and most kids are interested in sports—I suggest middle and high school teachers chase down a copy of a textbook—yes, textbook—built entirely around a sports theme, and created by a high school English supervisor, Bruce Emra. He reasoned that everything accomplished with traditional texts could also be done with *Sports in Literature*, which includes poetry, essays, biographies, short stories, and even a teacher's manual. Of course, if you *don't* want the students interested, avoid this textbook.[11]

If you are a parent or teacher looking to build a collection of sports books in the home or classroom, here are five authors who may have turned more boys on to reading than all the textbooks combined. Take their names to the library or bookstore:

- Matt Christopher, the most popular sports author for grades 1–4;
- Alfred Slote, grades 5–7;
- Thomas J. Dygard, grades 7–10;
- John R. Tunis, a writer from the thirties through the sixties, whose stories still hold up, grades 5–10;
- And keep an eye on a rising young star in psychological sports fiction named Carl Deuker, for grades 8–12.

Great Guides to Children's Books

What children read is less important than the fact *that* they read, but most adults want the best for their money. Therefore, how should you decide which books to buy? This handbook, with its list of read-alouds in the treasury, should solve at least part of that problem. If your child's teacher reads aloud, she probably has a long list of choices she can't possibly get to in the course of the year. At your next parent-teacher conference, ask her for some recommendations. She may even have one she thinks is particularly suitable for your child.

If you are fortunate enough to have a bookstore that specializes in children's books in your community (or a general bookstore that gives more than cursory attention to children), by all means tap them as a resource. Many have free newsletters to keep you abreast of new titles in children's books.

Most libraries have a variety of outstanding resource books on children's literature that can be tapped for inspiration and titles, books by respected children's literature experts like Charlotte Huck and Bernice Cullinan that contain comprehensive lists of outstanding children's books.

In addition, your neighborhood library subscribes to several journals that regularly review new children's books, including *The Horn Book*, *Kirkus Reviews*, *Booklist*, and *School Library Journal*. These will give you an idea of what's new, good and bad, in children's publishing. The latest arrival on the scene, though, may just be the most accessible: *Book Links*, published bimonthly by the American Library Association. This slim magazine is aimed at teachers and librarians, but devoted read-aloud parents will love it too. Each issue's six or seven articles include author profiles and interviews, as well as reviews of groups of books on certain subjects or themes, for a variety of grade levels. For a mouse theme, they included mini book talks on seven famous mouse books (like Arnold Lobel's *Mouse Tales* and Beatrix Potter's *The Tailor of Gloucester*), and then an annotated bibliography of twenty other mouse titles. The Mother Goose theme included not only a comprehensive bibliography but news of how various schools incorporate her rhymes into the entire curriculum, throughout the grades.[12]

Additionally, here are some inexpensive resources for finding the newest and best children's books:

- Published each fall, winter, and spring, *T'N'T* (*Tips and Titles of Books for Grades K–6*) is a newsletter for busy parents and teachers, covering more than a hundred books each year. Written by Jan Lieberman, a librarian and former elementary teacher who truly understands children and their reading appetites, each issue covers a cross section of literature with creative tips on related activities. Subscribers are free to make copies for faculties and PTA groups at no extra charge. Send three self-addressed, stamped envelopes (legal size) with $1.00 in cash or stamps to: Jan Lieberman, T'N'T, 121 Buckingham, Apt. 57, Santa Clara, CA 95051.

- Call your local Public Broadcasting Service (PBS) TV affiliate and tell them you want a copy of *Reading Rainbow*'s complete booklist—one of the best you'll find anywhere. For 101 of the show's best titles, see *Reading Rainbow Guide to Children's Books*, by Twila C. Leggett and Cynthia Mayer Benfield.

- Largely unknown to parents and teachers, but among my favorite resources for new titles (books and audiocassettes), are the fall and spring Children's Book issues of *Publishers Weekly* magazine, which can be purchased individually without subscription. Each season's titles are listed with plot synopses, along with more than 150 pages of advertising from the major publishers promoting their top authors. In addition, there's a sneak preview of what's coming next season. The issues must be requested separately each spring or fall by sending a check or money order for $10.00 (total cost, including shipping and handling) to: *Publishers Weekly*, P.O. Box 7820, Torrance, CA 90504. Be sure to indicate fall or spring issue, since it comes out twice a year, and specify adult or children's issue.

- Several year-end lists of the best of each year's children's books are also available. "Children's Books [year]" is published by the Library of Congress and covers preschool through junior high. It is available for $1.00 from the Superintendent of Documents, U.S. Government Printing Office, Washington, D.C. 20402 (Library of Congress Catalog Card Number: 65-60015).

- The American Library Association's "Notable Children's Books [year]" is available for fifty cents (and a self-addressed, stamped envelope) from: American Library Association, ALSC, 50 East Huron Street, Chicago, IL 60611.

- The Cooperative Children's Book Center at the University of Wisconsin: "CCBC Choices [year]." Priced around $5.00 (write to them for the latest price), it is a sixty-page guide to the year's best in children's literature, compiled by some of the most respected librarians and professors in children's literature (CCBC, 4290 Helen C. White Hall, 600 N. Park St., Madison, WI 53706). It also provides special emphasis on multicultural literature and a unique yearly overview on trends in children's publishing.

The IRA Choice awards, in conjunction with the Children's Book Council, consists of three separate annual lists:

✔ *Children's Choices (chosen by elementary-graders)*
✔ *Young Adult Choices (chosen by teens)*
✔ *Teachers' Choices (chosen by the teachers themselves)*

Each list includes more than thirty outstanding fiction and nonfiction titles and is available in two formats: full 8-by-11-inch pages (with annotations about story line) or in bookmark form (no annotations, just titles and author-illustrators). There are three ways of obtaining these lists:

1. For the annotated list of Children's Choices or Teachers' Choices for a given year, look for a copy (at your library or through subscription) of the October and November issues, respectively, of *The Reading Teacher.* The Young Adult (teens) list is reprinted in each November's issue of *The Journal of Reading.* (Both are IRA publications.)

2. You can also obtain the annotated list by sending a check for $1.00 to Dept. EG, International Reading Association, 800 Barksdale Road, P.O. Box 8139, Newark, DE 19714-8139, USA—ATTN: Children's Choices [year]; Teacher's Choices [year]; or Young Adult Choices [year]. Each list is $1.00.

3. Single copies of the bookmarks are available at no charge by sending a self-addressed, stamped business envelope with first-class postage for one ounce to International Reading Association, P.O. Box 8139, Newark, DE 19714-8139: ATTN: Bookmarks (state the year and "Choices" you wish). All three for one year will fit into a one-ounce envelope.

• *Children's Books of the Year*, [year] *Edition*, an annotated listing of 600 books published by the Child Study Children's Book Committee at Bank Street College, 610 West 112th Street, New York, NY 10025 (the cost is presently $6.00, but write for details).

The Important Role of Junk or Series

In building any library for children, try to resist an elitist approach in which you offer only the best. One of the patterns that continues to surface in research is the important role that "junk" fiction plays in forming lifetime readers. By junk I mean formula fiction like Nancy Drew and comic books (see Chapter 8 for comics). As noted in Chapter 2, Carlsen and Sherrill's massive study of lifetime readers (*Voices of Readers*) showed a preponderance of such books in these college students' childhoods. For forty years the literary and library gatekeepers attempted to ban "series" as "worthless, sordid, sensational, trashy and harmful" and "*the* menace to good reading."[13] The H. W. Wilson Company even refused to print catalog cards for series books, hoping to ignore them out of existence.

But as hard as the adults resisted Nancy Drew, the Hardy Boys, the Bobbsey Twins, the Five Little Peppers, the international Twins series, and the Oz books, children took them to their hearts. Initially, the reason may have just been pure contrariness on the part of children, but eventually, as they went from book to book in a series, the reason was more profound. The book was filling a need for nonthreatening, immediately accessible reading.

And what effect did all of this have on generations of readers? In the 1993–94 school year, I asked 850 *teachers* (90 percent women and most of them with at least 10 years' experience) to select their favorite childhood book. I told them I was not interested in the quality of their choice as much as the affection with which they held the book as a child. Here are the top 31 choices, along with the number of votes each received.

1. *Little Women (45)*
2. *Heidi (44)*
3. *Little House in the Big Woods* series *(35)*
4. *Nancy Drew* series *(33)*
5. *Charlotte's Web (28)*
6. *The Boxcar Children* series *(23)*
7. *Black Beauty (22)*
8. *Anne of Green Gables* series *(15)*
9. *The Secret Garden (14)*
10. *Little Black Sambo (12)*
11. *The Bobbsey Twins* series *(11)*
12. *The Little Engine That Could (8)*
13. *The Poky Little Puppy (8)*
14. *The Black Stallion* series *(7)*
15. *Pippi Longstocking* series *(7)*
16. *Bambi (6)*
17. *Cinderella (6)*
18. *The Five Chinese Brothers (6)*
19. *Andersen's Fairy Tales (6)*
20. *Mr. Popper's Penguins (6)*
21. *The Velveteen Rabbit (6)*
22. *Where the Red Fern Grows (6)*
23. *Winnie-the-Pooh (6)*
24. *Big Red (5)*
25. *Caddie Woodlawn (5)*
26. *Curious George* series *(5)*
27. *Follow My Leader (5)*
28. *Madeline* series *(5)*
29. *Make Way for Ducklings (5)*
30. *Mary Poppins* series *(5)*
31. *The Tale of Peter Rabbit (5)*

It is worth noting that almost one-third of the titles were associated with a series. From 850 possible votes, the top 31 books received 395 votes, leaving the remaining 455 votes spread through an additional 311 titles, each averaging less than two votes each. This diversity certainly speaks to the need for a broad selection in what you read aloud and in the home or classroom library. Also keep in mind, these were the votes of teachers. If the general public had been surveyed, the listing most likely would have been even *more* diverse.

I wish you could have seen these teachers' expressions as they recalled their childhood favorites. From my own experience as well as thousands of conversations with adult readers, I can declare this early bond with a book is one of the most powerful forces in becoming a lifetime reader. I cannot begin to estimate the number of people who have told me, eyes brimming, voices cracking, about their long-lost childhood favorite book. Used-book stores throughout the country do a sizable business routinely searching for such volumes, as do libraries.

Searching for a Childhood Favorite Book

If you are earnestly searching for a childhood favorite, you will need the name of either the book or the author. "It was about either a gray or a black kitten that slept in an abandoned car" isn't enough information for a book search. Next, check the reference *Books in Print* to see if it is still available. Sometimes a bookstore will carry this; otherwise, telephone your local library reference room. If the book's out of print (OP), used-book stores will often place a national advertisement for just a few dollars. If you just want to read it (and not own it), ask your library to do a computer search. If this comes up empty, they can check the Online Computer Library Catalog (known as OCLC), which has computer connections to national libraries, some of which house collections upwards of 300,000 books.

When I was a first-grader at St. Michael's School in Union, New Jersey, back in the 1940s, our classroom teacher, Sister Elizabeth Frances, read aloud every day after lunch from a small novel about a guardian angel. It was, to be candid, the best part of school for the ninety children in the room (yes, that's correct!). I never forgot the experience of that book, but in the intervening forty-five years I somehow forgot the title. And Sister Elizabeth Frances could not remember it either. But one month ago I described it to my friend Chris de Vinck and he said it sounded like a book called *Wopsy: The Adventures of a Guardian Angel.* Yes, I declared, that was it.

So after writing the above paragraph, I put America's library services to the test, and OCLC uncovered five libraries still holding copies of *Wopsy* by Gerard F. Scriven, along with its three sequels (all OP).

But even if a search does produce your childhood favorite, it is unlikely you could equal the adventure of Stanley Woodworth. Growing up in Massachusetts during the Depression, Woodworth spent long hours devouring childhood classics like *The Merry Adventures of Robin Hood* and *Treasure Island,* but none had the emotional hold on him of *Porto Bello Gold* by Arthur D. Howden Smith—an obscure volume of pirate tales.

Somewhere between childhood and adulthood, Woodworth and his beloved book parted company. Perhaps it was lost, maybe worn out— he never knew. But he did remember it fondly and often found himself searching for his old friend on the dusty shelves of used-book stores— but to no avail. For forty years Woodworth taught ancient and foreign languages, English, and philosophy at the Cate School in Carpinteria, California, living on the school grounds and becoming a beloved campus figure. All the while, he built his personal library.

And then one day he was browsing the shelves of Bart's Books, a legendary used-book store in nearby Ojai, and there it was—*Porto Bello Gold,* for just $2.50. "I was so excited," he said later, "I would have paid $250 for it." And yet, when he got it home, he was afraid to open it, never mind read it, for fear it would be too much of a disappointment after sixty years. But finally he did and what he found was beyond even his wildest expectations. There, following the title page, was a child's scribbled signature—*Stanley Woodworth.*

What he had found was the original volume from his childhood shelf. The boy and his book finally had been reunited.[14]

Supermarket Principles in the Library

Let's look at the libraries that haven't been closed—school or public. What could be done to make them work better? The first step is to visit your neighborhood supermarket. A major portion of a supermarket's sales is attributed to "impulse" shopping—items the customer did not have on a list but chose after seeing them on a shelf. That's the reason they always put the dairy section in the deepest reaches of the store— so the customer must pass the largest number of other items en route to it. Now notice how items are shelved—with the *cover* or *label* facing out, not with the side of the box facing out. Next, look at the "dump bins" at checkout counters. They seldom contain essentials, nor are they there for customer convenience. They are positioned to catch the eye of customers in line and to sell things you might easily forget.

Bookstore purchases and library circulations are built around the same principles. Most people do not come to the store or library with a book already in mind, and most leave with at least one "impulse" book in hand. Fifty years ago paperback publishers discovered the "supermarket" formula—that the book cover sells the book—and bookstores began displaying paperbacks with the cover facing out.

With that in mind, school, classroom, and home libraries should be arranged accordingly. If you don't have room to turn large numbers of books cover-out, you have too many books. Do some weeding, delete the outdated stuff, store others in boxes. Then display dozens and dozens with the cover facing out. Watch—those will be the first ones read. Displaying books by the spine is space efficient but *not* cost efficient, reading efficient, or customer efficient. The reason you bought the book was to have it read. Since no one reads with their head tilted at a 45- or 90-degree angle (as one must do to read the spine), spine-out books are harder to select. And since there is no illustration on the spine, it is harder to determine the subject matter of the book.

The majority of public and school libraries I see in my travels are clueless when it comes to these principles. Many don't have a single book shelved cover-out. If you need further proof, consider the research of Miriam Martinez and William H. Teale of the University of Texas–San Antonio. When they observed a kindergarten classroom library for one week, 90 percent of the books that children chose had been shelved *with the covers facing out.*[15] (I once spoke at a southwest Kansas school where the principal boasted of how they'd remove the dust jackets on their library books. "The kids just rip 'em anyway. This way we don't have to put those plastic covers on them." The only word that came into my mind was "pathetic.")

Speaking of merchandising techniques: Do you have students who won't come to the library? At Lakewood Middle School in Pompton Lakes, New Jersey, librarian Villy Gandhi went to them instead. She filled a bright red wheelbarrow with paperbacks and pushed it into classrooms. The students then exchanged their book for one in the barrow. "They love to exchange things at that age," she reasoned, "clothes, sandwiches, anything. So why not swapping books?"

From Feast to Famine

Before you take umbrage at the statement I made a few paragraphs ago—that you possibly can have too many books in the library—give some thought to the experience of my friend Jim Jacobs. In 1991, Jacobs took a sabbatical from his job as associate professor of elementary education and children's literature at Brigham Young University. "My teaching credentials were in secondary education, but most of my college students were elementary majors. So I decided to get my elementary credentials and prove to myself that *I* could do what I tell *them* to do," Jacobs says. So he secured a fourth-grade teaching job in Germany with the Department of Defense DODDS program. It took him an entire year to build a classroom library of trade books, but by the start of year two, his scrounging and personal investments had created a collection of 1,500 titles for his incoming fourth-graders.

"I thought, 'These kids are going to walk in here the first day of school, take one look at this magnificent collection of books, and say, "Wow! This Mr. Jacobs is great!" ' But it didn't happen," Jacobs told me. "These weren't book readers to begin with. I knew that, but compared to the previous year when the class was so book poor, I believed just having access to the books would make all the difference. Wrong. Without a book background, fifteen hundred titles were overwhelming, not exciting—even with reading aloud and SSR every day."

Six weeks into the year, he added a daily routine of book talks. Selecting 20 to 25 titles out of the 1,500, he gave brief talks about them through the course of the day. "What I learned is that we [teachers] don't have a clue as to what will turn a kid on to a book or which book will reach them. There was a girl in the class, very giddy, and the very last student I would expect to be interested in a biography of Hitler. And what happened? She devoured it, every page!

"If I had it to do over again, I'd cover all the bookcases with brown wrapping paper for the start of the year. And then each day, I'd uncover fifteen books, giving book talks on each. And gradually build the interest through the year. And that way," Jacobs noted, "they wouldn't be overwhelmed by the choices and numbers."

The other extreme, of course, is the school where they don't have *enough* books. And in such cases, a little leadership goes a long way. For example, back in the late 1980s, Rebecca L. Menti was a school librarian in Arlington, Texas. When she heard children complaining about local branch libraries being "out of books," her investigations proved the students correct. Even with five-book limits, there were still shortages of books in two of the branches.

With some trepidation, Menti asked to address the city council—telling them how grateful she was that they did not cut the library's book budget but citing the critical shortage during summer months when children had no school libraries. Her plea was personal enough to win an additional $30,000 in children's book money for the two branches in question.

Inspired by that success, Menti then turned to the affluent students at her own school and asked them if they would consider donating the books they had "outgrown" at home. The resulting 1,000 volumes were used to supply the two branches and a local women's shelter, as well as an overnight shelter. For several years, Menti arranged for first-grade students at her school (Key Elementary) to donate books to the public library instead of exchanging Christmas presents with each other, thus garnering almost $300 in books each year. *That's* leadership.

South Gate's Four-Star Library

If you want an exemplary school library, visit South Gate, California. In 1992, the skies to the south, west, and north of South Gate were bleak with smoke and fire. South-Central Los Angeles was burning, its stores looted, its citizens terrorized. But in nearby South Gate, there were no fires, looting, or terror. Having visited there and having met its faculty, students and parents, I think some of its peace had to do with South Gate Junior High School, enrollment 4,000, one of the largest junior highs in the United States, 99 percent Hispanic, one-third speaking no English at all.

I believe much of the school's civility springs from its library, where two librarians, Ruby Ling-Louie and Dale Buboltz, have lifted its book circulation from 300 a month to nearly 5,000. When Buboltz took over in 1985, there were few books in Spanish and little contact between library and faculty. Here's what they accomplished in the next six years:

- Raised funds to renovate the library.
- Raised funds to buy more books (Spanish and English).
- Created a "reading road show" to visit classes and motivate students by reading aloud.
- Recruited parents to sign contracts agreeing to set aside time for reading at home.

- Raised funds to purchase a weather dish and satellite dish that would bring in educational broadcasts from around the world.
- Distributed 12,000 free books to families.
- And, just for the fun of it, arranged the school's 4,000 students in a parking lot, spelling out "READ," and had a low-flying aerial photographer capture it on film.

It should come as no surprise that in 1992, Ling-Louie and Buboltz were recognized with Reader's Digest's Heroes in Education award, thus earning $10,000 for their library. In places where children and parents think the sun rises and sets on the library, the sunrises and sunsets are brighter with hope, and there is less despair.

Public Libraries: Where the Gold Is Buried

As important and convenient as home libraries and school libraries may be, they cannot replace a public library. They should act as appetizers, stimulating a child's taste for the vast riches offered by the public library. It is a town's or city's most important cultural and intellectual asset, yet less than 10 percent of the American people are regular patrons. No wonder, in this age of declining literacy and skyrocketing inflation, libraries often face life-threatening times.

America leads the world in library access. Yet, the last five years have seen state after state, community after community curtail library support. In one year alone, California closed twenty-five public libraries; Massachusetts, the cradle of learning, closed twenty-seven branches in four years. Americans seem to be saying, "Libraries are nice—as long as they don't cost me anything." Of course, what you don't use, you don't value—or miss when it's gone. It is widely agreed by professionals that only 30 percent of adults own library cards.[16]

Since its beginnings in 1731 under Benjamin Franklin, the public library has been one of our principal sources of culture. Today it can truly be called "the people's free university," as it daily welcomes rich and poor alike, lawyers and doctors, homemakers and the homeless. True, it is the most marvelous of resources for the student doing research, but it is most important for the poor and the immigrant—who cannot afford to *buy* their books, who often lack the funds for or information about magazine or newspaper subscriptions. Jim Fish, director of the San Jose (CA) Public Library, recently told me they had just finished a library study that showed 55 percent of their Asian collection is in constant circulation. This coincides with one of the findings in a study by The Center for the Book at the Library of Congress during the early 1980s. Of all ethnic groups in America, only the Jewish immigrants at the beginning of this century appear to rival the current Asian-Americans in grasping the role a library plays in personal success. Both groups understood that all the information gold in America is buried in the library.

Libraries offer our kindest and smartest helping hand to newcomers, teaching them everything from English and tax laws to cooking and parenting. In one year alone, the Queens Borough Public Library in New York City will teach English to three thousand immigrants from more than eighty nations and speaking fifty languages.[17]

Therefore, if we expect to increase the nation's overall literacy, if we truly wish to bridge the "us" and "them" gap between native-born and immigrant, we must *stop* saying no to tax increases or bond issues that support libraries.

Aside from the cultural advantages, the public library is still the biggest "dollar for dollar" bargain in America—any book or magazine or recording you want (they run and get it for you) for *free*. Yet I can't begin to estimate the number of times I've heard parents (rich and poor) say they'd like to bring their children to the library more often but there just isn't time. And to each of them I reply, "Would you estimate that you've taken your child to the shopping mall ten times more often than to the library or one hundred times more often to the video store than the library?" What does this say to your child about your priorities?

It also helps when the library doesn't wait for others to discover it— the good ones know how to promote themselves. And they live the philosophy that "the early bird catches the worm." In outstanding library systems (large and small) like Orlando, Florida; Harrisburg and Pittsburgh, Pennsylvania; Cuyahoga County, Ohio; and Decatur, Illinois, extraordinary efforts are made to reach new parents. With gift books, brochures, parent-education programs, and even videos, these programs are all aimed at promoting both library usage and community spirit. One of the best examples I've found is "Babies & Books: A Joyous Beginning," an outstanding parent/infant guide developed by the Baby Talk division of the Decatur Public Library under a Title I grant and the Illinois State Library. Copies are available for $7.00 (prepaid) from: Rolling Prairie Library System, 345 West Eldorado Street, Decatur, IL 62522.

The early intervention theme is also seen in the increasing number of toddler story hours sponsored by public libraries, including some that schedule them on Friday evenings, when fathers can bring the child to the "bedtime" story hour.

Innovative libraries provide registration tables at nursery and elementary schools in the first week of school to distribute library information and register parents and children for cards.

Help Needed from Clergy and Pediatricians

Two potentially valuable links in the family-reading–library connection are churches and pediatricians. Churches have a proud history of support for family reading. Unfortunately, it is largely *ancient* history: In Colonial America church elders regularly inspected homes and businesses to ensure that children and servants were being taught to read. Since church theology held that only those who read the Bible could be saved, those who impeded that opportunity would be held accountable.[18]

In a strange turn of events, today's reading connection with churches seems to be more negative than positive, with churches often focused on the banning of books. Indeed, organized religion could be doing a whole lot more for literacy. Family is still the centerpiece in most congregations, and since few experiences tighten family ties and strengthen the minds of future generations the way reading does, why is the subject addressed so seldom in the nation's pulpits? In much the same way that black churches are stepping in to try and heal the damage to black family life in the wake of desertions, teenage parenthood, and economic despair, so too can clergy attempt to repair the ravages of illiteracy and aliteracy.

Librarians and educators must work together to provide materials and reminders for the clergy to disseminate—so that a year doesn't pass without clergy reminding parents of the importance of reading aloud within the family, the ease of obtaining a library card, and the dangers of over-viewing television. My lecture travels often find me attending weekend worship service someplace other than in my home parish, and not once in more than fifteen years have I ever heard a sermon given on this subject.

Urban clergy might also remind their parishioners that in the midst of drug abuse and moral perversion, the library can be a physical as well as an intellectual haven. In that respect, things haven't changed a great deal since writer Pete Hamill grew up in a working-class section of Brooklyn during the forties, surrounded by mobster hit men, youth gangs, homeless rummies, deranged vets still fighting old wars, cops on the take, and brawling dockworkers. "As a boy," he recalls, "I was afraid of them, a condition that went beyond the normal fears of childhood. But I knew one thing: none of them ever came to the library. So, in one important way, the library was a fortified oasis." Impoverished parishioners should be read parts of Hamill's essay that describe being one of seven children in a poor family: "The library allowed me to borrow the first beautiful things I ever took home. When I was not reading them, I would place them on tables, on the mantelpiece, against a window, just to be able to see them, to turn from dinner and glance at them in the next room. I hated to bring them back, and often borrowed some books three or four times a year, just to have them around."[19] (See page 168 for the role Hamill's mother played in this.)

With the deterioration of the extended American family, pediatricians (along with the churches) are a prime resource for teaching the business of parenting, providing the common sense formerly passed along by grandparents. Almost everyone eventually brings a child to a pediatrician. As new parents, my wife and I didn't see the pediatrician's words as suggestions or even recommendations. As far as we were concerned, his words were carved in stone and handed down from the mountain. In the eyes of new parents, a pediatrician is the closest thing to God on Earth. Imagine, therefore, the impact they could have on a nation's literacy if their message reinforced that of clergy, educator, and librarian: that is, the need for parents to read to their child and control family television viewing. Pediatricians tell me they are never approached by teachers or librarians to work in concert. And then there are those like Dr. Alexander Randall IV, who don't wait to be asked (page 122).

What effect could pediatricians have if they incorporated a literacy message into their office visits with families? Dr. Robert Needlman (a devoted reader and the son of an early childhood teacher), along with Kathleen Fitzgerald and colleagues at Boston City Hospital's Pediatric Primary Care Clinic, created a program called ROAR (Reach Out and Read) that would attempt to encourage at-risk inner-city parents to read with and to their children.

ROAR was organized around three simple activities:

1. Volunteers would read aloud to children in the waiting room of the clinic.
2. A pediatrician would counsel the parents on the importance of reading to the child at home.

3. A child would be given a free book by the doctor with each visit to the clinic.

The third activity was incorporated into the program only after it was noticed that any books left in the waiting area disappeared with patients. Approximately 50 percent of the families reported reading to the child at home following the visit. But in the program's evaluation study, the single most important factor proved to be the "gift" book.[20] Those who received a book were four times more likely to have read to the child at home afterward. Just as important, the poorest families (receiving Aid for Dependent Child [AFDC]) were eight times more likely to have read the book. AFDC families are among the most at risk for reading failure when the child enters school.

"It may be that for the poorest children, the lack of books poses the greatest barrier to literacy-promoting experiences," Needlman reports. "By supplying books in those homes, we may have been not only communicating the importance of book sharing to parents but also providing them with the means to act on the information. Informal discussions with parents indicate that the books often provided a vehicle for the child to secure parental attention. 'He's always bringing me a book to read to him.' The fact that the books were given by a pediatrician or nurse practitioner was meaningful to some parents: 'Every time I brought her to the clinic, the doctor gave us a book, so I figured he must want me to *do* something with them.' "

ROAR reinforces the need for libraries and school districts to make a concerted effort to work in concert with physicians, dentists, and health clinics. If you have to lead them by the hand, then do it. With more and more of these professionals using VCRs to entertain patients and families in their reception areas, they offer yet a new possibility for reaching the American family. Librarians and teachers should be developing video-cassettes to be used in these areas, including demonstration cassettes of an adult reading to a child. These would instruct parents on the importance and pleasure of reading aloud while at the same time holding the attention of the patients.

7

Television

> *I believe television is going to be the test of the modern world, and that in this new opportunity to see beyond the range of our vision we shall discover either a new and unbearable disturbance of the general peace or a saving radiance in the sky. We shall stand or fall by television—of that I am quite sure.*
>
> —E. B. White,
> "Removal from Town," *Harper's* (October 1938)

———

Modern technology, if we use it instead of abuse it, can actually help us create lifetime readers. This chapter will cover both the positive and negative aspects of the technology—from television to video, from Channel One's school broadcasts to books on audiocassette. What helps and what hurts? I'll also describe some electronic devices that take the policing duties out of your hands and *automatically* limit your child's viewing.

Nothing exemplifies my entire thesis better than the following story.

It begins with a woman named Sonya Carson, trying to raise two sons in inner-city Detroit as a single parent. One of twenty-four children, Mrs. Carson had only a third-grade education. A hard-working, driven woman, she worked as a domestic or child-care provider for wealthy families—sometimes working two or three jobs at a time to support her sons. Sometimes she worked so hard that she had to "get away to her relatives for a rest." Only years later did her sons discover that she was checking herself into a mental institution for professional help for depression.

Her sons, on the other hand, were not working *themselves* into any kind of frenzy. Both were on a slow ship to nowhere in the classroom. Bennie, the younger, was the worst student in his fifth-grade class. The two brothers had done fine previously in the church school in Boston, but the change to Detroit public schools revealed the low standards of the earlier institution. As if raising two sons in one of the most dangerous cities in America were not enough, Mrs. Carson now had a new challenge—the boy's grades. She met it head-on. "Bennie—you're smarter than this report card," she declared, pointing to his math score. "First thing, you're going to learn your times tables—every one of them!"

"Mom, do you know how many there are? It would take me a whole year!" he replied.

"I only went through the third grade and I know them all the way through my twelves," his mother answered. "And furthermore, you are not to go outside tomorrow until you learn them."

Her son pointed to the columns in his math book and cried, "Look at these things! How can anyone learn them?"

His mother simply tightened her jaw, looked him calmly in the eye, and declared, "You can't go out until you learn your times tables."

Bennie learned his times tables—and his math scores began to climb. His mother's next goal was to get the rest of his grades up. Her intuition pointed to the television that never seemed to be off when the boys were home. "From now on, you can only watch three television programs a week!" A week! (What Sonya Carson lacked in book sense she made up for with common sense—that would be vindicated nearly thirty years later when major research studies showed a powerful connection between "over-viewing" and "underachievement.")

She next looked for a way to fill the free time created by the television vacuum. She said, "You boys are going to the library and check out two books. At the end of each week you'll write me a report on what you've read." (Only years later did the boys discover she couldn't read well enough to understand any of the reports.)

They didn't like it, of course, but they didn't dare refuse. And in reading two books a week, then talking about them to his mother, Bennie did raise his reading scores. And because the entire curriculum is tied to reading, the rest of the report card began to improve. Each semester, each year, the scores rose. And by the time he was a senior in high school he was third in his class, scoring in the 90th percentile of the nation.

With colleges like West Point and Stanford waving scholarships in his face but only $10 in his pocket for application fees, he decided to choose whichever school won the *College Bowl* television quiz that year (Yale). He spent four years majoring in psychology at Yale, then went on to the medical schools of the University of Michigan and Johns Hopkins— where he is today. At age forty-five, Dr. Ben Carson is one of the world's premier pediatric brain surgeons. When Johns Hopkins named him head of pediatric neurosurgery at age thirty-three, he was the youngest in the nation.

Ask Dr. Carson to explain how you get from a fatherless inner-city home and a mother with a third-grade education, from being the worst student in your fifth-grade class to being a world-famous brain surgeon with a brother who's an engineer. Again and again, Ben Carson points to two things: his religion (Seventh-Day Adventist) and the pivotal moment when his mother turned off the television set and ordered him to start reading.

I meet people in my audiences with three times the education of that young Mrs. Carson and ten times her income—but not half her commonsense when it comes to raising children. They can't bring themselves to "raise" children—they can only "watch them grow up," and most of the "watching" occurs from the couch in front of a television set.

True, television is powerful enough to help topple the Berlin Wall and Iron Curtain, something a half century of American soldiers and diplomacy were unable to do. But history also shows that "power corrupts," and if left unchecked in the home, so too does television. My question to you is: Do you have the courage and common sense of Sonya Carson? For the complete story, read *Gifted Hands: The Ben Carson Story* by Ben Carson. For an audiocassette of Dr. Carson's interview on *The Larry King Show*, send $4.95 (postage and handling included) to: Lion Recording Services, P.O. Box 962, Washington, DC 20044; be sure to request Larry King–Ben Carson (2/13/92).[1]

Television as Liberator

While this chapter is largely a documented plea to control the amount of television viewed within the home and classroom, it is not a petition

to eliminate the medium. There is little evidence to support the elimi-
nation of television. There is even some research to support the premise
that children who have *no* television in their homes do no better than
do those who watch a moderate amount. The American Academy of
Pediatrics recommends a *maximum* limit of two hours of TV a day for
children. But academic research shows that after ten hours a week,
school grades begin to dip.

In other words, the culprit is not television itself but the *over-viewing*
of it. The addition of cable TV, Nintendo, and a VCR only magnifies the
problem. My goal is to work toward a national consciousness in which
people understand television's potential, its minuses as well as its pluses.

Television as Addiction

If you use television exclusively to entertain instead of inform, its
cumulative effect is highly detrimental.

The A. C. Nielsen Company reports the average television set ran for
four hours, thirty-five minutes each day in 1950; by 1987, the daily total
had risen to seven hours.[2] (Adding daily VCR use to that figure would
bring it to at least seven hours, thirty minutes.)

Don't misunderstand—there is nothing wrong with entertainment. To
my way of thinking, we all need a daily dose of entertainment to break
the routine in our lives. It's like dessert, something to look forward to.
The danger comes when you allow it to become the main course. And
over the last thirty years, entertainment, which is television, has become
the main course in children's and families' intellectual lives. Both children and adults average nearly four hours a day, passively letting someone else do all the thinking, speaking, imagining, and exploring. The
result has been an unprecedented negative impact on American reading
and thinking habits.

If parents and educators are to buy into the premise of limiting TV
viewing, they must first recognize its full power on a child. We'll first
look at its addictive nature, then examine why it must become increasingly violent, why it interferes with learning, and what effect heavy viewing has on children's school scores and on family life in general.

Two decades ago, when author Marie Winn called TV the "plug-in
drug," it was not without reason. Its psychological control of humans
was already demanding and extensive. For those who doubt the addictive nature of television, consider this: For more than a decade, a group
of psychologists conducted television studies with hundreds of people

of all ages, from many countries, and from different walks of life. The purpose was to determine what people actually got out of their television viewing. Were they happier? What, exactly, was their purpose in watching?

The subjects in the studies were equipped with beepers and were signaled seven times a day, at which time they had to report on their emotional and mental states. The beeps occurred when they were eating, working, driving, viewing, and sleeping. The studies were unique of their kind. The researchers found:

- "Most viewing involves less concentration and alertness—and is experienced more passively—than just about any other daily activity. These very basic findings held up for people from ages 10 to 82."
- The main benefit of TV viewing is relaxation. And the more relaxed the viewer became, the less inclined he or she was to turn off the set and the more he or she watched.
- A kind of psychological and physical inertia develops, and one's body stays on the couch—or, as Newton put it, "A body at rest tends to remain at rest."
- "The habit is readily formed but difficult to break."
- People who watched the most television reported lower levels of personal happiness than did those who watched less television.[3]

This study reinforces the connection between heavy television viewing and poor school grades. As viewing increases, the time for reading (or anything else) decreases. Or, "The mind at rest tends to remain at rest."

Parents who proudly announce their children only watch children's channels like Nickelodeon are only kidding themselves. They might have second thoughts after hearing the president of Nickelodeon describe why the network was going to spend $30 million to create preschool programs for the first time: Acknowledging the advertising and marketing aspects of the younger audience, Geraldine Laybourne said, "We recognize that if we start getting kids to watch us at this age, we have them for life. That's exactly the reason we're doing it." In other words, they will become addicted.[4] Everything I have experienced myself and heard from teachers leads me to state unequivocally that computer games like Nintendo are just as addictive and time-consuming as television, if not more so.

To give you an idea of its compulsive nature, prison officials at the maximum security prison in Erie County, New York, found the most effective threat against even the most incorrigible inmates was to deny them television privileges. In 1986, the inmates voted unanimously to give up their right to receive packages from outside the prison (the prime source of drugs) in exchange for the option to buy personal televisions for their cells.[5] Similarly, parents—either because of their *own* need for television or in recognition of their children's addiction—are increasingly reluctant to withhold TV privileges in the home. In 1962, 38 percent of parents used TV privileges as form of discipline; in 1992 only 15 percent did.[6]

As the writer Pete Hamill pointed out when he saw American family viewing had reached seven hours a day, "This has never happened before in history. No people has ever been entertained for seven hours a *day*. The Elizabethans didn't go to the theater seven hours a day. The pre-TV generation didn't go to the movies seven hours a day," he wrote in building a powerful connection between the addictive nature of television and a generation that cannot say no to either cocaine or television.[7]

Hamill grew up in a poor Brooklyn, New York, neighborhood. His mother landed in New York from Belfast, Northern Ireland, on the day the stock market crashed in 1929, and she lived for years as an indentured servant. Eventually she married, began a family, and worked as a movie-theater cashier. Among her rules was one similar to Sonya Carson's: Hamill's children were not allowed into the theater until each had a library card and could read. Was it difficult to raise children during the Great Depression? Was it easy for her to say no to them in such times? But parenting is not about what's "easy." It's often about what's difficult. Today, Anne Hamill's children include an engineer, an editor for navy publications, a photographer, a television producer, and three professional writers.

Social critic Marie Winn recently looked back nostalgically on the sixties, seventies, and eighties—when there were actually periods in the day when there was nothing suitable for young children on television. So what did parents do? They parented. They connected their children to games and toys and other children. As parents, they supervised, cautioned, participated, ruled, entertained, and enjoyed their children.

"Then," says Winn, "along came the VCR. In recent conversations with dozens of parents throughout the country, it became apparent that the very parents who once carefully controlled their children's TV consumption are now using well-chosen video programs to buy peace and quiet from the kids. . . . These parents make it clear that they don't turn on the VCR because what it has to offer is so wonderful; they turn it on because it is a swift and effective child sedative."

Winn recalled that during the nineteenth century there was a common patent medicine (now outlawed) called Mother's Helper, used to calm unruly children. "Its main ingredient," notes Winn, "was laudanum, an opium derivative." That palliative now appears to have been replaced by another addictive mother's helper—the VCR attached to a television set.

There are, of course, legitimate medications that are both helpful and addictive. And for the latter reason, the dosage is monitored. Therefore an important step toward teaching children to cope with television is to put the same controls on your television that you already have on your medicine cabinet. Television will largely determine what children will wear and won't wear, what they eat and won't eat, what they play and won't play, what they read and won't read. If there were a medicine that had as much influence on child behavior, it would be strictly monitored, would it not? Yet 37 percent of parents do not set any limit on children's television viewing or hours.[8]

Research shows children one to two years of age watch about two hours of television a day; but between age two and five that balloons to four hours a day.[9] The dosage increases with age to the point where almost 50 percent of children between ages six and seventeen have a television set in their bedroom, compared with only 29 percent with telephones.[10] One in four nine-year-olds spends six hours or more a day watching TV.[11] And families with the most children do the most television viewing.[12]

Several children's books have dealt with the addictive nature of television. Three of my favorites are *Fix-It!* by David McPhail; *The Problem with Pulficer*, by Florence Parry Heide; and *The Wretched Stone*, by Chris Van Allsburg.

Television and School Scores

A 1990 NAEP study showed 69 percent of fourth-graders, 71 percent of eighth-graders, and 48 percent of twelfth-graders averaged well over three hours of television a day. If the bulk of your free time is spent watching other people do things and little or no time is spent doing things yourself, it is impossible to grow smarter.[13]

Until recently unearthed statistics on the SAT class of 1941 (which became the national standard of "average" for the next fifty years), some of us were quick to connect the decline in SAT scores with television viewing. We now know the average high school student in 1941 was no more intelligent than today's (see Appendix). The real problem is that student knowledge has not kept pace with the growing complexity of the world. Social scientists, educators, and psychologists point to television as a prime suspect. In and of itself, television probably hasn't made American schoolchildren less intelligent, but its time-consuming nature may have prevented them from becoming *more* intelligent by interrupting the largest and most instructive class in childhood: life experience.

Paul Copperman, author of *The Literacy Hoax*, saw the interruption in these terms: "Consider what a child misses during the 15,000 hours [from birth to age seventeen] he spends in front of the TV screen. He is not working in the garage with his father, or in the garden with his mother. He is not doing homework, or reading, or collecting stamps. He is not cleaning his room, washing the supper dishes, or cutting the lawn. He is not listening to a discussion about community politics among his parents and their friends. He is not playing baseball or going fishing or painting pictures. Exactly what does television offer that is so valuable it can replace these activities that transform an impulsive, self-absorbed child into a critically thinking adult?"[14]

Statisticians calculate that the average child will view 1,300 hours of television and video this year, and 20,000 hours by age eighteen. Those are hard figures to interpret. A better way to understand them would be to say that 1,300 hours is the equivalent of watching *Gone With the Wind* 336 times in a year. Television has become an electronic pacifier for entire families, putting them into states of semi-wakefulness.

Is there any hard evidence connecting TV viewing with student scores?

- In 1991, when thirteen-year-olds from fifteen different nations were tested in science and mathematics, students who watched the most television had the lowest scores.[15]
- When similar tests were given for math in 1990 to eighth-graders in thirty-seven U.S. states and territories, the same pattern persisted: The more they watched, the lower the scores.[16]

The same research found that reading helps with the entire curriculum. Students who read the most outside school had significantly higher math scores. And the more types of reading material found in the home, the higher the student's math scores.

Further research provides the following facts:

- In 1980 California's Department of Education administered a standard achievement exam and survey to all the state's sixth- and twelfth-graders (half a million students), with these results: the more time in front of TV, the lower the scores; the less time, the higher the scores. The statistics proved true regardless of the child's IQ, social background, or study practices.[17]
- The 1992 National Writing Report Card (on 30,000 fourth-, eighth-, and twelfth-graders) showed the lowest scores were achieved by children who watched the most TV and/or read the fewest pages outside school.[18]
- When Tannis Macbeth Williams of the University of British Columbia studied three Canadian towns, two with television and one without, she found that the children in the community without television had higher reading scores. As soon as TV was introduced, the scores declined.[19]
- The relationship between television and reading scores is further reinforced along social class lines. Economically depressed communities watch more and score lower than do the advantaged. For example, African-American students' verbal (reading) SAT scores, though making the largest gain of any ethnic group (including whites) in recent years, were still 91 points lower than white scores in 1993. And for the same period, the Census Bureau reported that black families had the lowest average income base of any U.S. ethnic group (50 percent less than whites).[20] Black households that year were averaging 73.6 hours of TV each week, while white ones averaged 50.2 hours, almost 50 percent less.[21]

Television versus Reading

Television fails most of the time as a positive educator because of the following:

1. *Television is the direct opposite of reading*. In breaking its programs into eight-minute segments (shorter for shows like *Sesame*

Street), it requires and fosters a short attention span. Reading, on the other hand, requires and encourages longer attention spans. Good children's books are written to hold children's attention, not interrupt it. Because of the need to hold viewers until the next commercial message, the content of television shows is almost constant action. Reading also offers action but not nearly as much, and books fill the spaces between action scenes with subtle character development. Television is relentless; no time is allowed to ponder characters' thoughts or to recall their words because the dialogue and images move too quickly. The need to scrutinize is a critical need among young children, and it is constantly ignored by television. Books, however, encourage the reader to move at his own pace as opposed to that of the director or sponsor. The reader can stop to ponder the character's next move, the feathers in his hat, or the meaning of a sentence. Having done so, he can resume where he left off without having missed any part of the story.

The arrival of remote control is only exacerbating the attention-span problem: the average family "zaps" once every three minutes, twenty-six seconds, versus those who have no remote (once every five minutes, fifteen seconds); and higher-income families zap three times more often than poorer families.[22]

2. *For young children television is an antisocial experience, while reading is a social experience.* The three-year-old sits passively in front of the screen, oblivious to what is going on around him. Conversation during the program is seldom if ever encouraged by the child or by the parents. On the other hand, the three-year-old with a book must be read to by another person—parent, sibling, or grandparent. The child is a participant as well as a receiver when he engages in discussion during and after the story.

3. *Television deprives the child of his most important learning tool: questions.* Children learn the most by questioning. For the thirty hours a week that the average five-year-old spends in front of the set, he can neither ask a question nor receive an answer.

4. *Television interrupts the child's most important language lesson: family conversation.* Studies show the average kindergarten graduate has already seen nearly 6,000 hours of television and videos before entering first grade, hours in which he engaged in little or no conversation. And with 30 percent of all adults watching TV during dinner and 50 percent of preteens and teenagers owning their own sets (and presumably watching alone in their rooms), the description of TV as "the great conversation stopper" has never been more appropriate.

5. *Much of young children's television viewing is mindless watching, requiring little or no thinking.* When two dozen three- to five-year-olds were shown a *Scooby Doo* cartoon, the sound track of which had been replaced by the sound track from a *Fangface* cartoon, only three of the twenty-four children realized the sound track did not match the pictures.[23]

Nor does the mindless viewing stop at kindergarten. With upwards of 100 cable channels to chose from, including all-news stations broadcasting round the clock, one would expect today's young adults to be among the most informed citizens in our history. They are not. A major 1990 survey of 4,890 adults concluded that "young Americans, aged 18 to 30, know less and care less about news and public affairs than any other generation of Americans in the past 50 years." What the X generation absorbs is seldom remembered unless it is titillating. For example, during the Panama invasion, 60 percent said they followed the war closely but only 12 percent were able to identify General Colin Powell. Conversely, 37 percent could identify Donald Trump's alleged mistress, Marla Maples.[24]

6. *Television encourages deceptive thinking.* In *Teaching as a Conserving Activity*, Professor Neil Postman pointed out that implicit in every one of television's commercials is the notion that there is no problem that cannot be solved by simple artificial means.[25] Whether the problem is anxiety or common diarrhea, nervous tension or the common cold, a simple tablet or spray solves the problem. Seldom is mention made of headaches being a sign of more serious illness, nor is the suggestion offered that elbow grease and hard work are viable alternatives to stains and boredom. Instead of making us think through our problems, television promotes the easy way. The cumulative effect of such thinking is enormous when you consider that between ages one and seventeen the average child is exposed to 350,000 commercials (four hundred a week), promoting the idea that solutions to life's problems can be purchased.

7. *Television has a negative effect on children's vital knowledge after age ten, according to the Schramm study of 6,000 schoolchildren.*[26] It does help, the report goes on to say, in building vocabulary for younger children, but this stops by age ten. This finding is supported

by the fact that today's kindergartners have the highest reading-readiness scores ever achieved at that level and yet these same students tail off dismally by fourth and fifth grades. Since television scripts consist largely of conversations that contain the same vocabulary words these students already know, few gains are made.

As I mentioned earlier, shows like *Cosby* are written on a fourth-grade reading level, hardly an enriching vocabulary for anyone older than eight. Moreover, a study of the scripts from eight programs favored by teenagers showed sentences averaging only seven words (versus eighteen words in my local newspaper).[27] Thus we have the following contrast:

- 72 percent of the scripts consisted of simple sentences or fragments.
- In *Make Way for Ducklings*, by Robert McCloskey, only 33 percent of the text is simple sentences;
- In *The Tale of Peter Rabbit*, by Beatrix Potter, only 21 percent of the text is simple sentences.

Thus one can safely say that even good children's *picture* books contain language that is twice as complex as television's. Imagine how much more complex and enriching the novels are.

8. *Television stifles the imagination.* A study of 192 children from Los Angeles County showed children *hearing* a story produced more-imaginative responses than did those *seeing* the same story on film.[28]

9. *Television's conception of childhood, rather than being progressive, is regressive—a throwback, in fact, to the Middle Ages.* Postman points to Philippe Ariès's research, which shows that until the 1600s children over the age of five were treated and governed as though they were adults.[29] After the seventeenth century, society developed a concept of childhood which insulated children from the shock of instant adulthood until they were mature enough to meet it. "Television," Postman declares, "all by itself, may bring an end to childhood." I offer these prime examples of that thesis:

    ✓ *In 1991, when children in the Hartford, Connecticut, area saw a network rerun of* Peter Pan, *they also saw a commercial for an upcoming* Hard Copy *show about a serial rapist-killer. Repeated incidents like that prompt critics like the*

Hartford Courant's Jim Endrest to say, "Leaving a child in front of the TV without a parent present is like leaving your kid in the middle of the mall, walking away and hoping he'll find a safe ride home."[30]

✔ *The last five years has seen daytime and prime-time television become video encyclopedias for deviant behavior.* USA Today *columnist Joe Urschel kept notes on one week's representative viewing on such shows. Keep in mind, what you are about to read is only* one *week's shows, and it was a presidential election week (November 1993). The shows featured: "Aphrodisiacs; Women Who Love Unconditionally; Women Who Killed Their Abusive Husbands; Runaways in Hollywood Who Turn to Prostitution; Possessive Former Lovers; Older Women Who Love Younger Men; Thin Wives, Obese Husbands; Divorcees and Dating; Oft-Married People in Their 20s; Wives and Girlfriends of Mama's Boys; Egotistical Men; Men's Reproductive Rights; The Woman Who Cut Off Her Husband's Penis; Compulsive Gamblers; Pre-Menstrual Syndrome; Haunted Houses; Encounters with the Dead; People Who Have Had Encounters with Aliens; Teens Who Kill; Girls in Gangs; Battered Women; Women Who Hate Their Daughters; Murdering Newlyweds; Former Lovers Who Reunite; People Who Stole Their Best Friend's Lover; and Mothers Who Stole Their Daughter's Man."*[31] *Need I remind you that these shows often were being watched by both parent and child or by a latchkey child alone?*

10. *Television overpowers and desensitizes a child's sense of sympathy for suffering.* Extensive research in the past twenty years clearly shows that television bombardment of the child with continual acts of violence makes the child insensitive to violence and its victims.[32] Any classroom teacher or pediatrician will tell you of the connection between children's viewing of violent films and classroom behavior. From the American Medical Association, June 1994: "Over the past two decades a growing body of scientific research has documented the relationship between the mass media and violent behavior . . . namely, that programming shown by the mass media contributes significantly to the aggressive behavior and, in particular, to aggression-related attitudes by many children, adolescents, and adults."[33]

TV Violence and Crime

Though literature could never be labeled a nonviolent medium, it cannot begin to approach television's extreme. The AMA report says children who watch up to four hours of television a day will see 8,000 killings and 100,000 other violent acts by age eighteen, a experience that "can have lifelong consequences."[34]

In 1992 and again in 1994, the Center for Media and Public Affairs monitored television violence through one eighteen-hour viewing day on ten channels. The reports were commissioned by *TV Guide* and the Guggenheim Foundation, respectively. On the given day, the movie channels did not show any unusually violent films like *Rambo* or *Scarface*, yet the ten channels collectively produced (1994 figures in parentheses):

- 1,846 (2,605) individual acts of violence at a rate of 103 (145) an hour
- 389 (726) scenes of serious assaults
- 362 (526) scenes of gunplay
- 673 (805) scenes of punching, slapping, or other physically abusive acts

Dramas or movies produced an average of ten violent scenes per hour, per station, with cartoons proving to be most violent of all in both studies. The 1994 study, coming on the heels of the networks' promise to Congress that they would curtail violence, showed violence increased by 41 percent. Prime-time fiction shows had no significant rise in violence, but nonfiction—news and "reality" shows—increased by 244 percent, confirming the latest adage in TV news: "If it bleeds, it leads."[35]

Why do programs become increasingly violent? Wally Bowen, who teaches media literacy at the University of North Carolina's Principal's Executive Program, quotes advertising executives in saying that "people don't watch television like they're taking notes for an exam. They're half conscious most of the time when they're watching television." Realizing this, the advertisers encourage a steady dose of violence to wake up the audience. Most stories are built around a hero, and Bowen points to the increasing level at which television and film heroes solve their problems violently. The role model of the violent hero, in turn, is absorbed by the children who watch him daily, and as the viewers grow older, they become more immune to the violence and therefore the dosage must be increased to hold their attention.[36]

But does all that violence *really* provoke a child to imitation? After all, you as an adult see those films and are not moved to violence. The difference is maturity. The adult's value system is already in place, you know right from wrong, but not only are the child's values still forming, they are in ferment. If you need more evidence, perhaps these findings by writer Carl M. Cannon[37] will convince you:

> *Two doctors, Leonard Eron and Rowell Huesmann, followed the viewing habits of a group of children for twenty-two years. They found watching violence on television is the single best predictor of violent or aggressive behavior later in life, ahead of such commonly accepted factors as parents' behavior, poverty, and race.*
>
> *Fascinated by an explosion of murder rates in the United States and Canada that began in 1955, after a generation of North Americans had come of age on television violence, University of Washington professor Brandon Centerwell decided to see if the same phenomenon could be observed in South Africa, where the Afrikaner-dominated regime had banned television until 1975.*
>
> *He found that eight years after TV was introduced—showing mostly Hollywood-produced fare—South Africa's murder rate skyrocketed. His most telling finding was that the crime rate increased first in the white communities. This mirrors U.S. crime statistics in the 1950s and especially points the finger at television, because whites were the first to get it in both countries.*

Simply put, if television can inspire a viewer to buy a certain brand of lipstick or sneaker or cereal or car, it also can inspire a child to solve problems violently.

When an entire country spends forty years being entertained for most of its leisure hours, its citizens begin to see everything in terms of amusement. For example:

1. In June of 1994, O. J. Simpson was accused of murdering two innocent people, and while he fled his police pursuers thousands of adult spectators stood on California freeways and roadsides, cheering on the suspect; within two days of a witness's testimony on national television that he had sold the alleged assailant a stiletto, major supply houses were sold out of that model of knife.[38]

2. That same month, the driver of a Mister Softee ice cream truck in Philadelphia was fatally shot by a teenager in a robbery attempt, and as this father of three lay bleeding, neighborhood teenagers surrounded him, laughing and making up songs of ridicule about him while he died before their eyes.[39]

My Family's TV Diet

Bob Keeshan, "Captain Kangaroo," places the prime responsibility for television's negative influence upon the parent. "Television is the great national babysitter," Keeshan says. "It's not the disease in itself, but a symptom of a greater disease that exists between parent and child. A parent today simply doesn't have time for the child, and the child is a very low priority item, and there's this magic box that flickers pictures all day long, and it's a convenient babysitter. I'm busy, go watch television. . . . The most direct answer to all our problems with television and children is the parent, because if the parent is an effective parent, we're not going to have it."[40]

It's easier to call for parental control of the television set than exercise that control, as any parent can tell you. I know firsthand.

My family's restricted viewing began in 1974, at about the time I'd begun to notice a growing television addiction in my fourth-grader daughter and kindergarten-age son. (They are now thirty and twenty-six.) Even our long-standing read-aloud time each night had begun to deteriorate because, in their words, it "took too much time away from the TV."

One evening while visiting Marty and Joan Wood of Longmeadow, Massachusetts, I noticed that their four teenage children went right to their homework after excusing themselves from the dinner table.

I asked the parents, "Your television broken?"

"No," replied Marty. "Why?"

"Well, it's only six forty-five and the kids are already doing homework."

Joan explained, "Oh, we don't allow television on school nights."

"That's a noble philosophy—but how in the world do you enforce it?" I asked.

"It is a house *law*," stated Marty. And for the next hour and a half, husband and wife detailed for me the positive changes that had occurred in their family and home since they put that "law" into effect.

That evening was a turning point for my family. After hearing the details of the plan, my wife, Susan, agreed wholeheartedly to back it. "On one condition," she added.

"What's that?" I asked.

"*You* be the one to tell them," she said.

After supper the next night, we brought the children into our bedroom, surrounded them with pillows and quilts, and I calmly began, "Jamie . . . Elizabeth . . . Mom and I have decided that there will be no more television on school nights in this house—forever."

Their reaction was predictable: they started to cry. What came as a shock to us was that they cried for four solid months. Every night, despite explanations on our part, they cried. We tried to impress upon them that the rule was not meant as a punishment; we listed all the positive reasons for such a rule. They cried louder.

The peer group pressure was enormous, particularly on Elizabeth, who said there was nothing for her to talk about during lunch at school since she hadn't seen any of the shows her friends were discussing. There was even peer pressure on Susan and me from neighbors and friends who thought the rule was needlessly harsh.

As difficult as it was at first, we persevered and resisted the pressure on both fronts. We lived with the tears, the pleadings, the conniving. And after three months we began to see things happen that the Woods had predicted. Suddenly we had the time each night as a family to read aloud, to read to ourselves, to do homework at an unhurried pace, to learn how to play chess and checkers and Scrabble, to make plastic models that had been collecting dust in the closet for two years, to bake cakes and cookies, to write thank-you notes to aunts and uncles, to do household chores and take baths and showers without World War II breaking out, to play on all the parish sports teams, to draw and paint and color, and—best of all—to talk to one another, ask questions and answer questions.

Our children's imaginations were coming back to life again.

For the first year, the decision was a heavy one, but with time it grew lighter. Jamie, being younger, had never developed the acute taste for television that Elizabeth had over the years, and he lost the habit fairly easily. It took Elizabeth longer to adjust.

Over the years the plan was modified until it worked like this:

1. The television is turned off at suppertime and not turned on again until the children are in bed, Monday through Thursday.

2. Each child is allowed to watch one school-night show a week (subject to parents' approval). Homework, chores, et cetera must be finished beforehand.

3. Weekend television is limited to any two of the three nights. The remaining night is reserved for homework and other activities. The children make their selections separately.

We structured the diet to allow the family to control the television and not the other way around. Perhaps this particular diet won't work for your family, but any kind of control is better than none.

TV Control Devices

How can today's working parents control their children's viewing? Until recently their only option was to play video cop and incur the wrath of their children, something few had the courage (or wisdom) to endure. At some point, almost every parent has exclaimed, "If only there were some way to put a lock on that thing!" And now, thanks to the same technical wizardry that gives us fifty channels on a single cable, we can limit our children's television "dosage" each week—with less household strife.

One device, the simplest and cheapest, is a lock that blocks the flow of electricity to the television. And since you hold the key, nothing is watched without your approval. Two companies make this device for approximately $30: TV LockOut, Recoton, Lake Mary, FL 32746; tel: 800-732-6866; The Switch, AJ Marketing, Inc., 267 Walker Avenue, Clarendon Hills, IL 60514; tel: 800-535-5845.

At least three video "dosage" devices are now available (with more in the development stages). Although they operate in different ways, all three computerized devices limit the amount of time each child (or the entire family) spends watching television or videos or playing Nintendo. The television is plugged into the device, and the device into the wall. Using the device, parents assign a password or number to each child and then enter the number of weekly TV hours for that child.

From that point on, the child must punch in the password or number in order to activate the television. The dosage device's inner clock immediately begins to keep track of the time used. When the assigned limit is reached, the set darkens, and the child is unable to activate it for the rest of the day or week. Several of the devices even allow parents to block out certain hours of the day or night when children are unable to *ever* activate the set.

Reports to date on experiences with these devices indicate that children: (1) watch less television; (2) become more discriminating in how they spend their television allowance; and (3) seldom leave the room with the set still on.

Each of the dosage devices is priced around $100. You can call for literature from the three companies: TimeSlot (tel: 800-653-5911); SuperVision (tel: 800-845-1911); TV Allowance (tel: 800-231-4410).

These devices may not win any popularity points with kids, but they do eliminate the role of "video cop" from a parent's job list while simultaneously preventing the child's mind from atrophying in front of a plastic box for thirty hours a week.[41]

Captioned TV and Reading

A fourth device is free and has come with every television set sold in the United States since July 1993, thanks to a federal law signed by President George Bush. All televisions now are equipped with a computer chip allowing closed captioning (subtitles) to appear at the bottom of the screen. Initially invented to make television and film accessible for the hearing-impaired, the captions reach all but the blind. Because of its newness, research is just beginning with captioned TV, but there are enough data to indicate significant gains in comprehension and vocabulary development (especially among bilingual students) when receiving instruction with educational television that is captioned.[42] Since we know children easily learn to read words from pages or product labels when they see the words and simultaneously hear the parent say the words, it appears that reasonable doses of captioned television can do no harm and most likely help with reading.

Research among nine-year-olds in Finland appears to confirm this. These children are the highest-scoring young readers in the world, but they also spend more time watching TV than reading. "However, there is a special feature in Finnish TV programs and also those of other Nordic countries," reports Pirjo Linnakylä, a Finnish national research coordinator. "Many programs have subtitles, and watching these programs seems to motivate and enhance reading among young students." In fact, almost 50 percent of Finnish television consists of foreign TV programs and movies that must be read—and read quickly—in order to be understood. Finnish nine-year-olds want to learn to read in order to understand TV and therefore watch a moderately heavy amount. By age fourteen, however, the situation reverses itself and Finnish children who watch a light amount of TV outscore the heavy viewers.[43]

And a final aspect of captions you might wish to consider: For children who already are competent but lazy readers and prefer watching television to reading, turn the sound off and the captioning on; this requires children to *read* their shows instead of just watching them. With the sound off, there are no vocabulary gains, but with achieving readers, that's not your goal: It is to keep the child's mind from turning to mush and discourage TV overdosing. Reading the captions prevents *mindless* viewing.

TV Turn-Off Campaign

If you are going to require your children to curtail their TV viewing, thus creating a three-hour void in their daily lives, then *you* must make a commitment to fill that void. *You* have to produce the crayons and paper, *you* have to teach them how to play checkers, *you* have to help with the cookie mix. And most important, *you* must pick up those books—books to read to the child, books to be read by the child, books to be read to yourself—even when you have a headache, even when you're tired, even when you're worried about your checkbook. You'll be surprised. Just as that book will take your child's mind off television, it also will take your mind off the headache or the checkbook.

If we are ever going to dilute the negative impact of television, we will have to do it by educating the public with campaigns not only to make families aware of how addicted they are to TV but also to suggest alternative activities.

By far the most extensive, successful, and famous example to date was the Farmington Turn-Off, a month-long campaign staged by the Farmington (CT) Public Library in 1984 through 1988 and copied by hundreds of towns throughout North America, as well as the entire nation of New Zealand in 1992. It also demonstrates the impact one person can have in his or her community—and beyond. Under the direction of children's librarian Nancy DeSalvo, the campaign was intended to make families aware (through temporary withdrawal) of television's addictive nature and to give them alternative activities to pursue instead of mindless viewing. The latter requires involvement by as many agencies as possible—libraries, schools, churches, and park and recreation departments—which, in turn, heightens a sense of community among families.

The campaign generated extraordinary attention in the media. Farmington's coverage was worldwide, including features in *The New York Times* and *The Wall Street Journal*, a spot on *Entertainment Tonight*, and a week of on-the-air calls from David Letterman to DeSalvo in which he promised her nearly three thousand dollars in prizes if she'd break her TV fast and turn on his show. (She declined.)

If you are considering a TV turn-off project, I suggest two excellent resources:

- For schools and libraries, order the $7.50 Farmington TV Turn-Off Kit from the Farmington Public Library, 6 Monteith Drive, Farmington, Connecticut 06032.
- The best family handbook for handling television woes is *Kick the TV Habit* by Steve and Ruth Bennett, parents of two, who are familiar with all the pitfalls and benefits of controlling television within family and community. Their ideas for family activities minus TV are outstanding.

It would be naive, however, to assume that even half of parents will avail themselves of such programs. Thus one of our best hopes for changing America's television habits rests with the classroom teacher who is educating tomorrow's parents. We're spending a great deal of time and money educating children to the dangers of alcohol and drug abuse, teenage pregnancy, and AIDS, but so far we've done *nothing* to teach them how to cope with television.

Teaching Critical Viewing Skills

As long as Americans spend more time watching than reading, educators must address the need for critical *viewing* as well as critical *reading*. If readers are trained to read interpretively, so too must viewers be taught to look critically at TV. And if we succeed with this teaching, we can alter the present pattern, in which 70 percent of what Americans hear in a political campaign is thirty- and sixty-second commercials that consist largely of half-truths and innuendo. The whole country benefits if we teach the next generation to know when the TV evangelist is talking about the almighty God and when he's talking about the almighty dollar.

Drs. Jerome and Dorothy Singer of Yale University are two of America's leading experts on child development and its relationship to electronic media. Few congressional hearings on violence and children have not sought the testimony of these two authorities. No one better understands the power of television—its power to harm children and its power to inform and enlighten. If that power can be harnessed, much of the damage can be prevented or defused. So rather than wait for government intervention, the Singers founded the Family Television Research Center at Yale University, and were among the first to develop media literacy programs for children, carefully constructed lesson plans and videos that teach children how to watch television critically. No, the lessons do not take an entire semester, nor will any part of the curriculum be sacrificed. Instead, they can be easily integrated into the curriculum.

One of their most successful programs is "Getting the Most Out of TV," which includes seven twelve-minute videos aimed at grades three, four, and five. Another course, "Creating Critical Viewers," consists of ten lessons and is aimed at middle and high school students. The Singers are also the authors of *Use TV to Your Child's Advantage: A Parent's Guide* (Acropolis). For further information, contact: Family Television Research Center, c/o Psychology Department, Yale University, P.O. Box 208205, New Haven, CT 06520-8285; tel: 203-432-4565.

I also highly recommend the book *How to Watch TV News*, by Neil Postman and Steve Powers, to any school using television news in the classroom.

You might ask, "What about *Sesame Street*? How about *Mr. Rogers*?" I am happy to report that not all television is mindless or violent. Parent-fans of PBS can take heart from a two-year study of 326 five- and seven-year-olds that showed viewing of educational television has a positive effect on children's reading while noninformative shows (situation comedies) have a detrimental effect.[44] Therefore a distinction should be made as to the *kinds* of television program children watch, though even educational programs hurt when they become substitutes for play or socializing or when viewed to excess—more than ten hours a week. That same long-term project concluded that the biggest influence on children's reading development and skills was parent attitudes about reading and the availability of books in their homes. On the subject of educational TV, it is my opinion (one shared by many) that *Mr. Rogers*, with its civil, value-oriented focus on children through conversation, is the finest programming for young children today and proves you can hold their attention without car chases or violent robotics.

Reading Rainbow, the award-winning PBS series on children's books, shows what can be accomplished when the industry sets its mind to educate *and* entertain. It is presently the most used television program in elementary classrooms, with more than 4 million students tuning in regularly. Your local PBS station can provide you with a complete list of *Reading Rainbow* book titles, one of the best children's book lists available. Once a book is spotlighted on the show, libraries and bookstores report immediate interest among children and their parents. It is not unusual for a book that normally sells 1,200 copies to sell 20,000 after being featured on *Reading Rainbow.*

Although television and video are easily abused in the classroom setting, video can be used effectively to increase "visual background knowledge." An inner-city child may not have the visual inventory of the far north that a child in Minnesota does. So if you are reading *Call of the Wild*, by Jack London, a partial showing of the recent *White Fang* video would improve that. Showing the entire video is usually a waste of valuable class time and an insult to the teacher's salary scale (and to the taxpayer's pocketbook). Television screens usually are too small for an entire class to view comfortably for more than fifteen minutes, so partial showings work much better. But be sure to move the class close enough to the set to see the images clearly.

Videos also are an excellent vehicle for teaching the difference between the art forms of film and book. Occasionally, *after* (never before) reading a book, show the video and compare the differences, noting how much was left out and why. A few of the titles and films worth comparing are *Stone Fox*; *Where the Red Fern Grows*; *Anne of Green Gables*; *Sarah, Plain and Tall*; *Charlotte's Web*; *The Lion, the Witch, and the Wardrobe*; *The Hobbit*; and *Pinocchio.*

ATTENTION, SCHOOL BOARD MEMBERS—If you wish to prevent mindless viewing in your schools and the abuse of VCRs, then emblazon this rule on the front of every school's televisions: No videos may be shown unless a set of questions has been presented to the class beforehand. That is, the teacher explains the purpose of the video and directs the class to find answers to a set of questions. Without such, as soon as the room lights dim, many in the class will slump into a mindless stupor. If you doubt this, switch on the lights after thirty minutes and notice how many heads are on the desks.

Looking for an excellent free resource for educational videos? Call PBS video at 800-344-3337 and ask for their latest video catalog. It's nearly 300 pages thick and contains many of the best shows from PBS's history. The choices are so varied, there is almost no lesson you could teach that could not be augmented by a portion of a video. When you've selected the video you want, check your local library to see if it's in their collection. If not, have them get it through interlibrary loan.

Channel One

One of the most startling events since the last edition of this book was the birth of Channel One in the American secondary classroom. It was remarkable not for its programming (which research shows to be largely forgettable) but because its acceptance flies in the face of research connecting increased viewing to declining scores. Nonetheless, Whittle Communications was able to convince an initial 10,000 communities, and another 2,000 schools one year later, that today's teenager needs *more* television. In return for showing Channel One's ten minutes of news features and two and a half minutes of commercials daily, each school district received $50,000 in TV, video, and broadcast equipment.[45]

With six "news" stories squeezed into 10 minutes, the result is 96 seconds per story. How deep can one go in 96 seconds? With flash-by maps, sound bites, film, and breathless narration, nearly all of the program ends up unintelligible and therefore useless as a learning tool. And research proves it. In the two years following start-up, Channel One commissioned studies[46] to evaluate its impact. The first study showed the Channel One audience scored only 3.3 percent higher than those who did not watch it, something the report called "statistically significant but educationally unimportant." Advanced students scored higher than did the poorer ones, but most students chatted with classmates or did homework instead of watching the show (which is not mandatory viewing). The second study found that in the rare instances where Channel One audiences showed knowledge gains, it was being shown not in homeroom periods but in extended classroom periods, and teachers were incorporating it into the class's discussion and writing activities. Suffice it to say, simply showing Channel One in homeroom periods is completely ineffective.

Just as damaging was a 1993 report from the University of Massachusetts showing schools with high concentrations of low-income students were twice as likely to offer Channel One's program as were schools with a more diverse student population. Channel One, said the report, "is more often shown to the students who are probably least able to afford to buy all the products they see advertised," and thus increases the students' alienation and frustration.[47]

The accumulation of 12.5 minutes a day, 180 days a school year, amounts to 8 school days a year. With public cries for a longer school year and more student "time on task," how can any school district allow its students to sit and watch television for eight full days? Some school districts—like Chadron, Nebraska—begin Channel One as early as fifth grade, which means those fifth-graders end up watching forty days' worth of TV by the time they graduate—one-fifth of an entire school year. "And our well-trained, professional teachers will have spent forty days, with pay, waiting for the show to get over," editorialized the *Chadron Record.*[48]

Educators who signed on with Channel One would have less reason to be ashamed if there were any evidence connecting increased viewing to higher scores. Not only is the opposite case firmly established in the national and international research listed in this chapter, but a 1990 study of American eighteen- to twenty-nine-year-olds found they "knew less, cared less, voted less" than any young adults in the last fifty years—despite the fact they watched more television than any previous generations.[49] Feeding more television to this generation is like taking diabetics to a candy store.

On the one hand, educators worry about shrinking attention spans, and on the other hand, they sign up for Channel One's 96-second news niblets. If there is a shrinking attention span, surely television is the main culprit. For example, when analysts compared network newscasts from 280 weekdays of the 1968 presidential election (Nixon vs. Humphrey) with the campaign in 1988 (Bush vs. Dukakis), they found a dramatic difference in the length of the candidates' on-screen, uninterrupted speech ("sound bites").

- In 1968, sound bites averaged 42.3 seconds.
- In 1988, sound bites averaged 9.8 seconds, a 75 percent decrease.
- In 1968, 21 percent of the telecasts carried candidates' speeches of at least one minute without interruption.
- In 1988, *no* network telecasts contained campaign speeches of one minute or longer.[50]

Books on Audiotape

As the above examples demonstrate, technology can be used or abused; it very much depends on the people in charge. The same formula applies to audiocassettes. Young parents are forever asking me,

"What about all those stories on tape? Are those okay for my child?" Used as a full-time substitute for a literate parent, no, they're not okay. But used to supplement your readings or used by children whose parents are illiterate or unavailable, they are excellent!

As Americans spend more and more time in their cars (average commute time is now forty-five minutes), audio recordings have become a growing segment of the publishing industry, with 1,139 publishers producing more than 55,000 audio titles each year.[51]

Salespeople are driving the breadth of the land listening to classics they never got around to reading; family car trips have grown noticeably calmer with children's stories in the tape deck. All are examples of how technology can be used to make us a more literate nation.

For family or classroom use, audiocassettes are a big plus. And while it lacks the immediacy of a live person who can hug and answer a child's questions, a story on tape can fill an important gap when the adult is not available. Even when the cassette is used as background noise while a child is playing, its verbal contents are still enriching his vocabulary more than television would with its abbreviated sentences. So by all means begin your cassette library with songs, rhymes, and stories. Community libraries and bookstores now have a wide assortment for all ages. Better still, record the stories yourself.

For the traveling parent (or absentee grandparent), the tape recorder is an excellent surrogate storyteller. When illustrator Steve Bjorkman's work takes him away from home, he still manages to read to his children. He purchases a children's book, reads it aloud into a tape recorder (complete with a water glass–and–spoon chime to signal when it's time to turn the page), and then uses overnight mail to ship the book and tape home to California and his three children. Joe Kane, of Somers, Connecticut, works for a utility company during the day and at Federal Express four nights a week but he still manages to read aloud to his children each evening (including son Bobby, age ten) by taping chapters before leaving for work. The night job puts extra money in the bank but the extra effort with his children puts something in their heads even more valuable than money, to say nothing of the bond he builds with them.

Do you remember the excitement you felt as a child when you saw one of your teachers in the supermarket or waiting in line at the movies? It was like seeing a movie star on the street. What children would most love to do is bring their teacher *home* with them—so their family could meet her and see how terrific she is. In one-room schoolhouses, when teachers boarded in the homes of students, that was possible, but not today. Or is it? Couldn't that be done vicariously through taped stories sent home with the child in a plastic Ziploc bag that also contained a paperback of the story? Hearing the teacher reading in his own home would inspire more than just the child; it might also reach siblings and the illiterate or semiliterate parent.

While a story on tape is almost never as good as having someone read it aloud in person, it *is* better than nothing at all. At Santa Clara (CA) Public Library, whoever does Saturday morning duty in the children's room also records a story to be used on the library's telephone story-line. In the course of a week, they receive between 120 to 175 calls on this line. Asian-Americans who have not mastered English sometimes record the story off the phone and then borrow the book from the library so their child can hear *and* see the book. But for other children, like Sarah, that story on the telephone is much more. Here is ten-year-old Sarah's letter (complete with her invented spellings) to librarian Jan Lieberman:

> *Dear Mrs. Leaberman:*
> *I moved to Santa Clara when I was 5, and I lessend to the storys of the library over and over again. But when I herd your storys it was different. More sarcasem and exprechon! I'm having problems at home because my dad just died so sometimes I need something to help me get to sleep at night so I push 241-1611 and hug my teady bear and lessen!*
>
> *Thanks,*
> *Sarah*

One of the early, and sometimes current, fears is that the audio book will make readers "print lazy." This is similar to the fear the Greeks had about writing—that it would shrivel the memory muscles.

Since the full text of books requires so much tape and time, most of the recording industry centers on abridged versions of books (*Reader's Digest* for the ears?). These abbreviated versions can often leave much to be desired in the way of substance. On the other hand, some writers could use a better editor, and the tape serves as that editor. But when it comes to good books, what can possibly be served by shrinking eight cassettes to two? Yes, people are in a hurry today, but two companies —Books-on-Tape, Inc., and Recorded Books, Inc.—have found enough nationwide interest to build their entire inventories around the rentals of unabridged books on tape. The tapes also are available for sale, but most of the 100,000 subscribers prefer to rent because of the high cost.

If you're wondering about the folks who have the time to listen to an unabridged novel, Helen Aron of Union College (NJ) did a random survey of 1,000 audio book renters, and the results were quite revealing.[52] Renters proved to be among the most educated, literate, affluent citizens in America. The average respondee rented 11 audio books a year while personally reading an average of 12 books. Other findings included:

- Men outnumbered women, 55 percent to 45 percent.
- The majority of renters were in their forties and fifties.
- 47 percent also borrow tapes from their local library.
- 75 percent were college graduates.
- 41 percent had postgraduate degrees.
- 80 percent had an annual family income of $51,000 or higher.
- 86 percent read at least one newspaper daily.
- 95 percent read at least one magazine monthly.
- 21 percent read at least 25 books a year.
- 80 percent usually listened while driving, only 7 percent while exercising.

For adults who are poor readers themselves, audio books can serve several purposes:

- They provide a common ground upon which you and your family or class can listen to literature.
- Since the readers are professional performers, they offer excellent role models for how to read aloud with the right expression and pace.
- For families embarking on long car trips, audio books can serve as peacekeepers as well as entertainers.

Your local library may be your cheapest resource for audio books and will often search area libraries for titles it doesn't have. You can also send for the catalogs of the major companies. Here are some of the juvenile novels offered by the two unabridged companies. As you will see, there is a great diversity in the offerings.

FROM RECORDED BOOKS
(TEL: 800-638-1304)
The True Confessions of Charlotte Doyle; *Wolf Rider*, by Avi
Tuck Everlasting, by Natalie Babbitt
The Wizard of Oz; *The Land of Oz*, by L. Frank Baum
The House with a Clock in Its Walls; *The Lamp from the Warlock's Tomb*, by John Bellairs
The Secret Garden, by Frances Hodgson Burnett
Nightjohn, by Gary Paulsen
Black Beauty, by Anna Sewell
The Hobbit; *The Lord of the Rings*, by J. R. R. Tolkien
The War of the Worlds, by H. G. Wells
Dear Mr. Henshaw; *Strider*, by Beverly Cleary
Pinocchio, by Carlo Collodi
The Monster's Ring, by Bruce Coville
The Ghost in the Noonday Sun; *The Whipping Boy*, by Sid Fleischman
Old Yeller, by Fred Gibson
The Jungle Books I & II; *Just So Stories*, by Rudyard Kipling
The Call of the Wild; *White Fang*, by Jack London

FROM BOOKS ON TAPE
(TEL: 800-626-3333)
The Adventures of Huckleberry Finn; *The Adventures of Tom Sawyer*, by Mark Twain
Aesop's Fables, by Aesop
Call It Courage, by Armstrong Sperry
The Count of Monte Cristo, by Alexandre Dumas
Kim, by Rudyard Kipling
King Solomon's Mines, by H. Rider Haggard
The Merry Adventures of Robin Hood, by Howard Pyle
My Friend Flicka, by Mary O'Hara
Peter Pan, by J. M. Barrie
The Adventures of Sherlock Holmes, by Sir Arthur Conan Doyle
Swiss Family Robinson, by Johann David Wyss
Tanglewood Tales, by Nathaniel Hawthorne
Tarzan of the Apes, by Edgar Rice Burroughs
Treasure Island, by Robert Louis Stevenson
20,000 Leagues Under the Sea, by Jules Verne
The Wind in the Willows, by Kenneth Grahame

The largest producer of children's audio novels is Listening Library (800-243-4504), with excellent recordings, mostly of shorter books, for purchase only—no rentals.

Is your favorite book on audiocassette? Your library should have R. R. Bowker's *On Cassette*, listing more than 44,000 titles and their data.

Another example of the power of technology can be seen in a Springfield, Virginia, company that saw the growing market for books on tape and thought: "What if we took this idea to the college lecture hall?" Thus was born The Teaching Company, which rounds up top college professors and puts their lectures on both video and audio tape. The same courses university students pay thousands of dollars to take on campus are available now to anyone with a tape deck or VCR. This allows an individual, a family, or a class to eavesdrop on some of the great minds in America today. The costs vary between video and audio but remain very reasonable. Call 800-832-2412 for a free sample audiotape featuring superstar college teachers.

The old-time radio shows could be considered the predecessors of books on tape. Radio drama may have died on the airwaves but it is very much alive in libraries, bookstores, and mail-order services through audiocassettes of shows like *Superman*, *The Green Hornet*, *The Lone Ranger*, *Sergeant Preston of the Yukon*, and *Inner Sanctum*. These shows not only condition a child's listening skills for the longer audio books, but they are also excellent stimulants of the mind—requiring the listener to imagine what the people in the dramas look like, what they're wearing, what they're doing, and to picture the landscape or setting. Such imagining is a long way from the passive nature of television viewing.

I have found two excellent resources for cassettes of these old family radio programs. Both companies have very reasonable prices (less than $10 for two shows) and extensive catalogs:

- Radio Spirits, Inc., P.O. Box 2141, Schiller Park, IL 60176; tel: 800-729-4587;
- Carl Froelich, Jr., 2 Heritage Farm Drive, New Freedom, PA 17349.

8

Sustained Silent Reading: Reading-Aloud's Natural Partner

> . . . *Those who do not develop the pleasure reading habit simply don't have a chance—they will have a very difficult time reading and writing at a level high enough to deal with the demands of today's world.*
>
> —Stephen Krashen,
> *The Power of Reading*

Among the prime purposes of reading aloud is to motivate the child to read independently for pleasure. In academic terms such reading is called SSR—Sustained Silent Reading. Take a book, a newspaper, or a magazine and enjoy it! No interruptions for questions, assessments, or reports; just read for pleasure. The concept operates under a variety of pseudonyms, including DEAR time (Drop Everything And Read); DIRT (Daily Individual Reading Time); SQUIRT (Sustained Quiet Un-Interrupted Reading Time); and FVR (Free Voluntary Reading).

This chapter will be devoted to SSR in school as well as at home. I'll also examine a variety of topics associated with silent reading: reading incentive programs; Hooked on Phonics; censorship; teachers' reading habits; classics; the "dumber in the summer" syndrome; and the role of comics books and "series" fiction.

SSR is based upon a single simple principle: Reading is a skill. And as with all skills, the more you use it, the better you get at it. Conversely, the less you use it, the more difficult it is. As with swimming, once you learn it, you never forget it. But in order to get better at either reading or swimming, you must jump into the book or the water and do it over and over.

How effective is SSR? When the International Association for the Evaluation of Educational Achievement (IEA) compared the reading skills of 210,000 students from 32 different countries,[1] it found the highest scores (regardless of income level) among children:

- who were read to by their teachers daily;
- who read the most pages for pleasure daily.

Moreover, the frequency of SSR had a marked impact on scores: Children who had it daily scored much higher than those who had it only once a week. American NAEP assessments have found an identical pattern for the nearly twenty-five years NAEP has been testing millions of U.S. students.[2] The evidence for reading aloud to children *and* SSR is overwhelming—yet most children are neither read to nor experience SSR in the course of a school day.

During one week in April 1994, I personally surveyed 300 teachers in four states: Does their school have a time set aside for SSR? Only 28 of the 300 teachers said yes. This is supported by the 1992 NAEP report showing that more than half of all students have no SSR. Simply put, it defies logic. It also helps explain why test scores have stagnated for twenty years and why we have so few lifetime readers.

It is only natural that student tests would show reading aloud and SSR to be common denominators among highly skilled readers. After all, there is a causal relationship between them. Most children who are read to, who are given a taste of the magic called reading, eventually want to work the magic themselves. With the sounds and desire already planted, they learn more easily and willingly, enjoy it more, and end up reading more. And the more they read, the better they get at it. Nothing complicated about it.

How Much Do Students Read?

Students don't read very much, a fact conceded by most teachers and unknown to most parents. Even worse, they don't read much when they grow up either, as you'll see later in this chapter. Two comprehensive investigations of how 155 capable fifth-grade students spent their after-school time showed that 90 percent of those students devoted only 1 percent of their free time to reading and 30 percent to watching televi-sion. Indeed, 50 percent read for an average of four minutes or less a day, 30 percent read two minutes a day, and 10 percent read nothing at all.[3] (More on these studies later in the chapter.)

"Well," says the parent, "they may not be reading much outside school but they certainly must be reading during the five hours they're in school!" Nice thought, but not true. The most comprehensive look at the American classroom is John Goodlad's seven-year study, *A Place Called School*, in which he reports that only 6 percent of class time is occupied by the act of reading in the elementary school, 3 percent in the middle school, and 2 percent in the high school.[4] (Yes, there are exceptions to these averages. If your child or school is the exception, consider yourself fortunate.)

Clearly, students are not reading much and therefore not getting much better at it. The important question is: *Why* are they not reading? The only logical answers are because they don't like it or because they don't have the time. There are no other major reasons. Eliminate those two factors and you've solved the American literacy dilemma. Reading aloud goes to work on the first factor and SSR attacks the second.

Originally proposed in the early 1960s by Lyman C. Hunt, Jr., of the University of Vermont, SSR received some of its most important support from the research of reading experts Robert and Marlene McCracken.[5] Experimenting with a variety of techniques and schools, the McCrackens recommend the following structures for SSR programs:

1. Children should read to themselves for a *limited* amount of time. Teachers and parents should adapt this to their individual class or family and adjust it with increasing maturity. Ten or fifteen minutes is a common choice for the classroom.
2. Each student should select his own book, magazine, or newspaper. No changing during the period is permitted. All materials must be chosen before the SSR period begins.
3. The teacher or parent must read also, setting an example. This cannot be stressed too strongly.
4. No reports are required of the student. No records are kept.

Krashen's *Power of Reading*

The single most interesting and comprehensive study ever done on SSR is Stephen Krashen's compact 100-page volume, *The Power of Reading*.[6] It is inconceivable that anyone could read this book and *not* resolve to incorporate SSR into the school day.

Krashen is one of the most accessible, stimulating, intelligent, and entertaining researchers in language and reading—certainly the *only* one who incorporates all of those characteristics. If I could require that one professional book be read by all teachers and librarians, *The Power of Reading* would be my choice. Krashen incorporates all the language-acquisition and reading research he has done over the last twenty years, along with hundreds of studies by others, building an indisputable case for SSR—which he calls FVR (free voluntary reading). It was so stimulating a read, my copy looks like the Dead Sea Scrolls from all the annotations I put in the margins when I was reading. It also caused my wife to finally move off the beach and back to the hotel because I kept interrupting her novel by reading aloud select passages.

In examining forty-one comparison studies that have been done between SSR students and traditional language-arts students, Krashen found that 93 percent of the SSR students did as well as or better than students having no SSR time. His examination of recreational reading's impact on spelling, writing, and language skills may provoke many educators to reassess previous positions.

The Benefits of SSR

SSR allows the child to read long enough and far enough so the act of reading becomes automatic. If one must stop to concentrate on each word—sounding it out and searching for meaning—then fluency is lost along with meaning. It is also fatiguing. Being able to do it automatically is the goal.[7] To achieve this, the Commission on Reading (*Becoming a Nation of Readers*) recommended two hours a week of independent reading and less time on skill sheets and workbooks.[8]

SSR also provides students with a new perspective on reading—as a form of recreation. Judging from the number of people (graduates of our schools) who come home from work at night and think they can relax only by watching television, there is a critical need for such early lessons.

On the secondary level, SSR may not cause a change in student skills, but there are positive changes in attitude concerning the library, voluntary reading, assigned reading, and the importance of reading. This affects the amount students read and thus their facility with the process.[9]

Younger readers, however, show significant improvement in both attitude and skills with SSR.[10] "Poor readers," points out Professor Richard Allington of the State University of New York, "when given ten minutes a day to read, initially will achieve five hundred words and quickly increase that amount in the same period as proficiency grows."

Administrators worried over the ungraded, free-form nature of students reading library books, paperbacks, magazines, or newspapers should not consider SSR a departure from the curriculum just because no textbook is involved. By third grade, SSR can be the student's most important vocabulary builder, more so than basal textbooks or even daily oral language. The Commission on Reading noted: "Basal readers and textbooks do not offer the same richness of vocabulary, sentence structure, or literary form as do trade books. Analyses comparing stories in basal readers with trade books show that the ones in primary-grade basals have fewer plot complications, involve less conflict among and within characters, and offer less insights into characters' goals, motives, and feelings. . . . A diet consisting only of basal stories probably will not prepare children well to deal with real literature."[11] Indeed, about half of the 3,000 most commonly used words are not even included in K–6 basals.[12]

Here are the results of a study[13] done of vocabulary words—familiar and unfamiliar—as encountered in conversation, television, children's books, comic books, and newspapers. Notice that most conversation (95.6 percent) consists of common words we already know. Then note that we are more likely to meet rare (or newer) words in reading than in conversation. (Rare words were defined as those not appearing among the most commonly used 10,000 words.)

	Percent of text from most common 5,000 words	No. of rare words per 1,000
Adult talking to child	95.6%	9.9 words
Prime time TV/adult	94.0%	22.7 words
Children's book	92.3%	30.9 words
Comic book	88.6%	53.5 words
Newspaper	84.3%	65.7 words

As you see, in reading aloud to a child or during SSR, we introduce three times as many rare words as we do in conversation, while simultaneously reinforcing common words. Also notice the reference to comic books—I'll be dealing with that later.

Another aspect of SSR that Krashen noted in his research is the work of educational psychologist Mihaly Csikszentmihalyi.[14] The latter shows that when people (children or adults) enjoy what they are doing—find it interesting and challenging—they slip into a state of "flow," a feeling so intense that the world hardly seems to exist. It is in "flow" states that great scientists make their discoveries, athletes set records, and musicians create scores. The object of SSR, therefore, is to allow the student to build the skills and attitude for a reading "flow." Needless to say, it is difficult to slip into a "flow" if you are being badgered with questions every two minutes.

Csikszentmihalyi cautions that it is impossible for "flow" to occur in reading if the task (book) is either too easy or too difficult. Thus it is important for SSR classrooms to have a broad variety of books that will meet the range of reading levels and interests in one classroom. "Flow" research shows that libraries or teachers who refuse to allow children to read above a prescribed level ("Those are for the fourth-graders. You stay here in the third-grade section") are hindering instead of helping.

Addressing these issues, the McCrackens report that most of the instances where SSR fails are due to:

- Teachers (or aides) who are supervising instead of reading
- Classrooms that lack enough SSR reading materials

The McCrackens call attention to the overwhelming part the teacher plays as a role model in SSR, reporting widespread imitation by students of the teacher's reading habits.[15]

Students in one class noticed the teacher interrupting her reading to look up a word in the dictionary and began doing the same. When a junior high teacher began to read the daily newspaper each day, the class began doing the same.

When teachers talk about what they are reading or describe a spine-tingling section of their book, students are quick to follow suit and share their reaction. By doing this, the McCrackens note, "they are teaching attitudes and skills; they are teaching children that reading is communication with an author, an assimilation of and reaction to an author's ideas."

Mary Griscom, a first-grade teacher at Christ the King School in St. Louis, told me how one day she noticed that she read with her left shoe off during her class's SSR period. Shortly thereafter she discovered seven of her students minus their left shoes during SSR. Incidentally, her first-graders don't call it SSR; they call it "reading in your head."

SSR Classroom Samples

Martha Efta offers a special example of SSR's worth. Efta taught a primary-level class of educable mentally retarded children in Westlake, Ohio. The children, ranging in age from seven to ten, were frequently hyperactive and nonreaders. When she heard of the SSR procedure in a graduate course, she was cautious about the idea despite the professor's wholehearted support for it. After all, she thought, the experts were talking about normal children, not the retarded.

With some trepidation, she explained the procedures to her students and reshaped the rules to fit her classroom. Because of their short attention spans, she allowed each student to choose as many as three books or magazines for the period. Students were allowed to sit any way and in any place they chose in the room. Ms. Efta initially kept the program to three minutes in length, then gradually increased it to thirteen minutes over a period of weeks. This was the class's limit.

"From the onset [of SSR]," Ms. Efta explained, "the students have demonstrated some exciting and favorable behavior changes—such as independent decision making, self-discipline, sharing . . . and broadened reading interests. The enthusiastic rush to select their day's reading materials following noon recess is indicative of the children's interest and eagerness for SSR. The children seem to delight in the adult-like responsibility of selecting their own reading matter."[16] Efta, who was in my audience a year ago, told me she still does SSR with her students, as well as reading aloud chapter and picture books to them each day. Ruth Stiles Gannett's series, beginning with *My Father's Dragon*, is a particular favorite of her students.

Since it doesn't entail any grades or paperwork, SSR sometimes has to be explained to parents. At St. Louis King of France school in Metarie Park, Louisiana, the principal explained the purpose of daily SSR in his newsletter: "It is a serious effort to raise the student's awareness of reading. All in the school participate. Please do not call or come to school during that fifteen-minute span."

You say there isn't enough time in the curriculum for SSR? Then do what they did at the Alice B. Landrum Middle School in Ponte Vedra, Florida—they extended the school day by thirty-five minutes to allow for SSR and read-aloud. (And the teachers believed in it so strongly, they did it without pay!) If you have time for gym, art, music, recess, assemblies, and field trips to the zoo, then you better find the time for reading real books. If you can't find the time in school, students won't find it outside either.

Time posed a problem for the folks at E. R. Dickson Elementary School in Mobile, Alabama, when Milbra Galbraith instituted SSR throughout the school. The problem was students were missing their buses because they didn't want to stop reading. Would that every school had such problems!

Stan Chapman told me his students at Sing Lum School in Bakersfield, California, held special SSR sessions during which they took bedsheets, draped them over their desks, and read under them with flashlights during DEAR time. (This is a nifty idea but, for obvious reasons, I suggest you not try it above fifth grade.)

I've been in classrooms that had reading lofts and even piles of pillows, but nothing I've seen can rival Sandra Odom's sixth-grade classroom at Northwest Laurens Elementary in Dudley, Georgia, where students begin each period with ten minutes of SSR in her fifteen rocking chairs, amidst her 2,200 books! Noticing how much her son enjoyed rocking while reading, Odom talked a manufacturer into donating the rockers if she paid the freight. Besides the obvious comfort factor, Odom claims the rockers are an excellent discipline-deterrent for hyperactive students and a calming agent for students who stutter while reading aloud.

I sometimes wonder if SSR could solve the "school prayer" dilemma. As I write this, there is a renewed debate over school prayer, particularly whether "a minute of quiet reflection" violates the spirit of the Supreme Court ruling. School prayer advocates propose these minutes of quiet reflection would, if nothing else, have a civilizing and calming effect on the atmosphere of school.[17] Wouldn't sustained silent reading fill the same bill and please both sides of the prayer issue? It is silent, it requires reflection on the part of the student, and since it is private, it could be as religious or secular as the text the student chooses to read. I know of no school that forbids a child from reading the Bible or the Koran during SSR.

"Lite" Reading in Series Books

A critical part of the formula is the *kind* of reading done during SSR. Some schools (and parents) are overly concerned that only the finest of materials be read by children. Parents are always complaining to me, "How do I get my son out of science fiction?" "How do I get my daughter out of romance novels?" Exposing them to a broader variety of literature by reading it to them aloud will help mightily, but Carlsen and Sherrill's massive study of college students' childhood reading shows a preponderance of series books and comics.[18] Series books would be formula fiction like Nancy Drew, Hardy Boys, or today's Sweet Valley High books.

Why do so many lifetime readers cut their reading teeth on series? For beginning readers there appears to be a need for the familiar—characters, text, and situations that are predictable enough to be nonthreatening, inviting, and mindless enough to allow a young reader to become proficient and fluent, and to meet lots of words without having to contend with subplots and character development. In other words, comic books without pictures.

Since series books work so well with the young reader, why not try them with adults for whom English is a second language (ESL)? Stephen Krashen and Kyung-Sook Cho (professor and graduate student at the University of Southern California–Los Angeles) decided to give it a try.[19]

They selected four immigrant women, three Korean and one Hispanic, whose ages were thirty, twenty-three, thirty-five, and twenty-one. Their average residency in the U.S. was 6.5 years. The oldest of the four was a thirty-five-year-old Korean who had majored in English in college and had taught it for three years in a high school. None of them, however, felt confident enough with English to speak it unless it was required and most did little or no recreational reading in English.

Wishing to combine the women's low reading levels with interesting text, they chose the grade-2 level of the Sweet Valley High series, called Sweet Valley Kids (70 pages). After being given some background information about the series and characters, the women were simply asked to read the books during their free time for several months. Occasional discussions took place between one of the researchers and the women, to answer any questions they might have had, but for the most part they were comprehending what they read.

The response was just as anticipated. All four women became enthusiastic readers. Mi-ae reported she read eight Sweet Valley Kids books during one month, Su-jin read eighteen volumes in two months, Jin-hee (the English major) read twenty-three in a little less than one month, and Alma (the Hispanic woman) read ten volumes over a two-week period. Two of the women read as many words per month as would a native-born student in the same amount of time.

All became very fond of the series. "This is the first experience in which I wanted to read a book in English continuously," said one woman. The one who had taught English in high school said, "I read the Sweet Valley series with interest and without the headache that I got when reading *Time* magazine in Korea. Most interestingly, I enjoyed reading the psychological descriptions of each character." She went on to read thirty Kids volumes, along with seven of the Twins series and eight of the Sweet Valley High books. All of the women reported an involvement with the characters in the books that served to bring them back for more.

All displayed greater proficiency not only in their reading but in spoken English as well. And all demonstrated increased vocabulary development.

Krashen and Cho noted: "Our brief study with these four women also supports the value of 'narrow' reading—reading texts in only one genre or by only one author—for promoting literacy development. Narrow reading allows the reader to take full advantage of the knowledge gained in previously read text."

This study is one of many that demonstrate the powerful role that recreational "lite" reading—series books and comic books—plays in developing good and lifetime readers. Is it classic literature? Of course not. Does it have a better chance of creating fluent readers than the classics would? Definitely. And can it eventually lead to the classics? Yes, and certainly sooner than would *The Red Badge of Courage*.

I should also add that Krashen and Cho's work was inspired by the SSR research done by Elley and Mangubhai with ESL fourth-graders in the Fiji Islands who were given SSR and "floods" of trade books and reduced English instruction.[20] The Fiji SSR students doubled the gains of their control group.

And how would the lords of academe respond to such procedures? Some would consider it blasphemy, but not all. Jacques Barzun had this to say about so-called junk reading by children: "Let me say at once that all books are good and that consequently a child should be allowed to read everything he lays his hands on. Trash is excellent; great works . . .

admirable. . . . The ravenous appetite will digest stones unharmed. Never mind the need to discriminate; it comes in its own time."[21]

Susan Ohanian is my favorite education writer. No one else even comes close. (Read *Who's in Charge?* to see why.) Before her career as a journalist, she taught a class of "forty disaffected students" in an alternative high school. Having determined that her students "could" read but "wouldn't," she set about creating an atmosphere to reverse the tide. Her classroom was filled with newspapers, magazines, and paperbacks of every stripe: bestsellers, thrillers, mysteries, romances, joke books, science fiction, sports, biographies, how-to books.

She then announced one of her classroom ground rules: Everyone had to read for half an hour a day. "They were all expert at faking reading. How I got them reading is a rather involved story, but it wasn't by ordering forty copies of *The Old Man and the Sea.* Once a student got hooked on a book—be it *Flowers for Algernon, The Outsiders, Temple of Gold, Richie Rich*, or something else—other students noticed and demanded, 'Let me see.'

"I kept tabs on things but didn't interrogate those students about their understanding of plot, theme, rising action, and so forth. I judged a book a success when a student closed the last page and asked, 'Do you have any more?' On their own, about three-fourths of the students began stretching the obligatory half-hour into an hour a day. And more. Even those who stuck to the half-hour reading were amazed. They told me they'd read more in the three months in my classroom than they had read in eleven years in regular school. In traditional classrooms, kids are too busy answering questions to do much reading."[22]

The Comic Book Factor

As I mentioned earlier, comic books are a frequent childhood choice of people who grow up to become fluent readers. The reasons for their popularity and success are the same as for series. And anyone questioning their success in creating readers should consider this: In the IEA assessment of 210,000 children in thirty-two countries, Finnish children achieved the highest reading scores. And what is the most common choice for recreational reading among Finnish nine-year-olds? Fifty-nine percent read a comic almost every day.[23]

I am not recommending comic books as a steady diet for reading aloud but as an introduction to the comic format. Young children must be shown how a comic "works": the sequence of the panels; the way to tell when a character is thinking and when he is speaking; the meaning of stars, question marks, and exclamation points. A comic can be viewed as a sequential diagram of conversation—a language blueprint. Once the blueprint is understood, the child will be ready and willing to follow it on his own without your reading it aloud.

Adults who provide a wide variety of reading materials for the child need not fear that the child or class will develop a "comic-book mentality." A number of studies show that more top students (nearly 100 percent) in all grades read comics or comic books than did lower-ranking students.[24]

In recent years, comic books have experienced a revival and revolution, to the point where many communities now have whole stores devoted exclusively to comics. Unfortunately, the revolution has included new lines of comics with heavy strains of sex and violence. (Need I say this is not peculiar to comics—books and film have similar woes.) So the days of giving a young child the money for a comic and sending him or her off to the store are a thing of the past. As with television, videos, and books, parents must stay aware and awake. The old favorite "entry level" comics like *Richie Rich*, *Little Audrey*, *Wendy*, *Little Lulu*, and *Casper the Friendly Ghost* are still around and sold under the trade label Harvey Classics. Consult your yellow pages for "comic stores" to locate them in your neighborhood. The same places probably also sell the more advanced *Archie*, *Batman*, *Superman*, and *Spider-Man* comics.

In *The Power of Reading*, Krashen gives an extensive overview of the research on children and comic book reading, including a chart of readability levels for nineteen of the most popular comics. What do you think the difference in reading level is between the following comic books: *Archie*, *Batman*, and *Spider-Man*?[25] He also shows the positive effect on library traffic and noncomic library circulation when comics are included in a school noncirculating library collection.

On the basis of my personal experiences and the research available, I would go so far as to say, if you have a child who is struggling with reading, connect him or her with comics. If an interest develops, feed it with more comics.

In reading novelist John Updike's memoirs, I was struck by how closely one area resembled my own. Recalling his Pennsylvania childhood and the early experiences with print that eventually lead him to Harvard, Updike wrote the following: "I loved comic strips. I copied their characters onto sheet after sheet of blank paper; I traced my copies onto plywood and cut them out with a coping saw and set them in rows on the shelf in my bedroom; I cut my favorite strips out of the newspaper and bound them in long books with covers of white cardboard, lettered by me in India ink and crayon. . . . On Saturdays, as I grew older, I was permitted to take the trolley and roam downtown. . . . In the five-and-ten cent stores along Penn Square—Kresge's, Woolworth's, McCrory's—a counter toward the back would hold Big Little Books: chunky volumes, costing a dime, assembled from comic strips. . . . I collected these, and traded them with my friends."

What we see here is an early connection to print that was so pleasurable Updike wanted to make it a permanent part of his life—in scrapbooks. Gradually the strip comics would lead to successively higher levels of humor and print in magazines, then Harvard, but all of it began with his appetite for comics.

There is, of course, the old saw that comic books will corrupt or weaken a child's moral fiber. Heated congressional hearings were devoted to this back in the early 1950s, when people were convinced that eliminating comics would eradicate juvenile delinquency. In response to such folderol, I offer this reflection from Nobel Peace Prize winner Bishop Desmond Tutu: "My father was the headmaster of a Methodist primary school. Like most fathers in those days, he was very patriarchal, very concerned that we did well in school. But one of the things I am very grateful to him for is that, contrary to conventional educational principles, he allowed me to read comics. I think that is how I developed my love for English and for reading."[26]

All right, you say, but these are freak situations—Updike and Tutu were coming from cultured, literate homes, and the positive influence of their parents outweighed the comic books. Suppose, then, we take an extreme situation: A child raised in a shack amidst squalor and rats, who grew up in a South African ghetto where people combed garbage dumps to find food, where human atrocities were committed daily and nightly, a boy whose father was a common laborer who hated education and burned the boy's schoolbooks and beat the child's illiterate mother for encouraging him to stay in school, who went to poor tribal schools in South Africa where English was outlawed from the curriculum; a boy who was so overwhelmed by the deprivation around him, he contemplated suicide at age ten. Such was the childhood of Mark Mathabane, the author of *Kaffir Boy*, a bestselling indictment of South Africa's apartheid.[27]

How was Mathabane able to grow up in such circumstances and become the author of an American bestseller? The initial springboard was the collection of used comic books (*Batman and Robin*, *Richie Rich*, *Dennis the Menace*, *The Justice League of America*) that a white family gave to his grandmother.

He recalls: "Having never owned a comic book in my life, I tirelessly read them over and over again, the parts I could understand. Such voracious reading was like an anesthesia, numbing me to the harsh life around me. Soon comic books became the joy of my life, and everywhere I went I took one with me: to the river, to a soccer game, to the lavatory, to sleep, to the store and to school.

"Midway through my eleventh year, Granny started bringing home strange-looking books and toys. The books, which she said were Mrs. Smith's son's schoolbooks, bore no resemblance whatsoever to the ones we used at my school. Their names were as strange to me as their contents: *Pinocchio*, *Aesop's Fables*, and the fairy tales of the brothers Grimm. At this point, because of reading comic books, my English had improved to a level where I could read simple sentences. I found the books enthralling." His reading and schoolwork began to soar.

My argument here is twofold:

- First, Mathabane's experience shows precisely how and why comics (or "junk" fiction) are successful with children, leading to higher levels of reading if they are available. Comics' enticing visual cues and simple sentences give the struggling young reader "training wheels" while the student develops proficiency.
- And second, if comics could be so successful in South Africa's squalor, why wouldn't they work with the urban and rural poor in America? Have we found anything as inexpensive that works better? Why aren't comics in Chapter I and remedial classes?

Tintin, the Comic Classic

If you are looking to challenge a child's mind and vocabulary with comics, then I'd choose *The Adventures of Tintin*. If you looked closely at the bedtime story Dustin Hoffman was reading to his son in *Kramer vs. Kramer*, you would have seen that it was *Tintin*. Or if you read the list of favorite read-alouds offered by historian Arthur Schlesinger, Jr., in *The New York Times Book Review*, you would have found Hergé's *Tintin* between *Huckleberry Finn* and the Greek myths.[28]

Begun as a comic strip in Belgium in 1929, *Tintin* now reaches, in comic-book form, thirty countries in twenty-two languages and is sold only in quality bookstores. The subject is a seventeen-year-old reporter (Tintin), who along with his dog and a cast of colorful and zany characters travels the globe in pursuit of mad scientists, spies, and saboteurs.

Two years were spent researching and drawing the seven hundred illustrations in each issue. These pictures vary in size, shape, and perspective, and run as many as fifteen panels to a page. This layout, with its minute detail and run-on dialogue, inhibits the child from understanding the book by merely looking at the pictures. To be understood, *Tintin* must be read—and that is the key for parents and teachers who care about reading. Each issue contains 8,000 words. The beautiful part of it is that children are unaware they are reading 8,000 words—which means you don't tell them either. They are reading for the fun of it. I might add, when Tintin's creator died, it was news enough for *The Washington Post* to run his obituary on page 1.

While on the subject of *The Post*, one could argue that it has one of America's more sophisticated readerships. In 1991, when it solicited reader opinions on its comic pages, 15,000 phone calls and 2,000 letters poured in, passionate declarations of affection for one strip or another.[29] The *Post* estimates that 73 percent of its subscribers read at least one comic strip daily. If comic pages are challenging enough for those Washington lawyers and lobbyists, they should be adequate fare for reading classes.

"Dumber in the Summer" Syndrome

Further proof of SSR's benefits is found in the "summer gap." Many parents, especially parents whose children are having difficulty with school, see summertime as a school vacation and take it literally. "Everyone needs a vacation, for goodness' sake. He needs to get away from school stuff and relax. Next year will be a new start." That attitude can be extremely detrimental to the child.

There is an old axiom in education: "You get dumber in the summer." A two-year study of 3,000 students in Atlanta, Georgia, attempted to see if it was true. They found that *everyone*—top students and poor students—learns more slowly in the summer. Some, though, do worse than slow down; they actually go into reverse.[30]

Top students' scores rise between the end of one school year and the beginning of the next. Conversely, the bottom 25 percent (largely urban poor) lose most of what they gained the previous school year. Average students (middle 50 percent) make no gains during the summer but lose nothing either—except in the widening gap between themselves and the top students.

Another study, which examined first-graders from a broad socioeconomic base, all of whom were academically equal, found they progressed at the same rate while in school but as soon as summer vacation arrived, a knowledge gap appeared and continued to widen *each year.* (The evidence suggests the average gap between white and black students' verbal scores can be attributed largely to annual losses during the summer months, when many of the latter students did little or no reading.) Such findings are reinforced by the higher reading scores of students enrolled in year-round schools.[31]

How to prevent the gap? The research gives no support to summer schools, but a great deal to summer reading—reading *to* the child and reading *by* the child. Most libraries have summer reading incentive programs; make sure your child is enrolled and participates. And take your child on field trips—even if you just visit local places like a fire station, the museum, or the zoo, and talk and listen. In that regard, one peculiar piece of information appeared in the "summer gap" research that is worth noting. Among those who suffered little or no summer loss, a prevalent factor was the availability of a bicycle.[32] Although the research does not expand upon this, I have two immediate reactions:

1. Many libraries would be inaccessible to certain children without a bicycle.
2. In evaluating adults who are unable to read on at least an eighth-grade level, teachers at community-learning centers point to a lack of decoding skills and sight vocabulary, and also to a shallow knowledge of the world around them. They know only what they have experienced. In other words, they haven't traveled much. There may be a strong connection between children who have the opportunity (via a bicycle) to move beyond the narrowness of their own family or community and the acquisition of new vocabulary and background knowledge.

SSR's World Champion

The most dramatic example of learning by simply reading—and maybe the Guinness world record for SSR—is found in Robert Allen.[33] Fatherless at birth in 1949 and abandoned by his mother at age six, Allen was raised by his grandfather, three great-aunts, and a great-uncle living in a farmhouse without plumbing in the hills of west Tennessee. And there Robert Allen stayed for the next twenty-six years, never attending school or riding a bicycle or going to a movie theater or having a single playmate his own age.

When he was seven, one of his aunts began reading to him and soon taught him to read for himself. His grandfather then taught him to write. He began reading the Bible to his blind aunt. Since his relatives were so elderly, one of them was always bedridden, and young Robert's duty was to take care of them. Looking to fill the vacant hours, at age twelve he picked up an old copy of Shakespeare's plays and read it through in one sitting. Soon he was scavenging yard sales for old books, magazines, and comics. Books became his playmates, his escape from the loving but grim reality of where he was.

He read anything and everything until he discovered the county library. There the world's classics awaited him and he waded into them, even teaching himself to read Greek and French, until he had read every book in the library. Not surprisingly, the librarian encouraged him to pursue a college education, and in 1981, at age thirty-two, he showed up at Bethel College, a small Presbyterian college just fifteen miles from his farmhouse. His placement test showed he knew more than almost every faculty member, and they had him skip the freshman year.

Graduating summa cum laude in three years (only typing kept him from straight A's in his senior year), he went on to Vanderbilt University, where he earned *simultaneous* master's and doctoral degrees in English. For a guy who came from the Tennessee backwoods, where they weren't exactly speaking the King's English, who missed all those childhood spelling quizzes, vocabulary tests, book reports, and the fifteen questions at the end of every chapter, who did no seat work except SSR for twenty-five straight years, and, by my calculations, missed at least 8,000 worksheets, he certainly did all right for himself.

Among the things Robert Allen's situation might prove, none is stronger than the case it makes for pure, unadulterated, uninterrupted, random, and purposeful reading.

Grading the Classics: "F"

Now that I've made such a strong case for "lite" reading, some may be wondering, "What ever happened to the classics? Where do they fit into this?" Well, an interesting thing happened to the classics. About the only people in this country who read them are teenagers—and only because they are required to.

Don't misunderstand me: I am awed by great minds and great writing. I read and revere the classics. But everything I have seen in the last thirty years indicates we are misusing them in schools, to the point that we are undoing much of the good they were created to accomplish. We've got ninth-graders reading books like *The Great Gatsby* before they're old enough to bring a frame of reference to them. And to make things worse, when the best of books are *compulsory reading* and endlessly dissected, they inevitably lose their appeal.

When I took the eleven most frequently used works of literature in American junior and senior high schools,[34] their average age came to 222 years. Even subtracting the four plays by Shakespeare, the remaining seven averaged sixty-eight years of age. (Oddly, four of those are among the most contested by "book banners": *Huckleberry Finn; To Kill a Mockingbird; Of Mice and Men;* and *Anne Frank: Diary of a Young Girl.*) To my mind, there is nothing wrong with those four or any of the remaining seven—they include some of my favorite books—but their age does prompt me to wonder: Has anyone on the faculty read anything *new* in the last sixty-eight years? It's also worth noting, almost every one of the core books was originally written for an adult audience. (So no wonder the faculty likes them.)

Education reporter Susan Ohanian once interviewed then Secretary of Education William Bennett, a man who is especially fond of lists, particularly lists of classic books that should be read by children. Knowing this predilection, Ohanian asked if he would be so kind as to recommend a single book that had been published in this century, or at least since *Heidi.* Bennett paused, and then confessed he could not.[35]

By almost every gauge available, the teaching of the classics or serious literature in American schools has been a gigantic failure. The most comprehensive evaluation of U.S. adult reading habits is found in *Who Reads Literature?* by Nicholas Zill and Marianne Winglee and is based upon 1982 and 1985 national surveys sponsored by the National Endowment for the Arts and conducted by the U.S. Census Bureau with 30,929 people.

In terms of general novel reading, that is, books never included in the secondary curriculum (mysteries, romances, thrillers, etc.), 30 percent of the adult population can be described as regular readers. Serious contemporary literature (authors like William Styron, John Updike, and Alice Walker) is read by only 11 percent of the population; classics are read by only 7 percent. (Serious and classic book sales account for only 1 percent of bookstore sales.) Only 4 percent of adults read poetry. (Poetry magazines and journals have circulations in the low thousands and often only in the hundreds.) And only 3 percent report reading a play in the last year.[36]

In other words, about 80 percent of the adult population never reads what they were taught to read in high school. Isn't there something wrong here? If we spent twelve years teaching children to brush their teeth and then 80 percent of them grew up and never brushed their teeth, wouldn't it be logical to conclude that we were doing something wrong?

One of the oldest and most prestigious universities in the world is Harvard. There is no greater plum for the guidance department of any school than to land a student at Harvard. It is the ghost of Harvard— and its brother/sister Ivies—that looms largest in high school advanced-placement classes, justifying the stacks of classics and the student papers about them in the sophomore, junior, and senior years of high school.

But what price Harvard admission? What is the cumulative effect of all those papers on the classics? Critic Sven Birkerts had taught six years of expository writing at Harvard when he wrote the following for the *Harvard Book Review*: "Almost none of my students read independently." On the first day of class Birkerts asked them to write a reading autobiography—what do they read, how much, when, where. "The responses are heartbreaking. Nearly every student admits—some of them sheepishly, others not—that reading is a problem. 'Too busy!' 'I wish I had the time.' 'I've always had a hard time with books that are supposed to be good for me.' And then, proudly, 'If I have time, I like to relax with Stephen King.' I can't tell you how many of my best and brightest have written that sentence."[37]

If Harvard students are inept in their writing and nearly comatose in their recreational reading, what can be expected of the average or below-average student? If a three- to four-year diet of high school classics and paperwork creates high scores but turned-off readers and poor writers, shouldn't we reevaluate the process?

At some point, it might be helpful for secondary English department heads to define the goal of their curriculum: Is it to create future English professors or future readers? Most junior high and high school English classes are structured with future English professors in mind, yet the last thing 99 percent of their graduates would like to be is an English professor.

Grade 'Em by the Pound

While I'm on the subject of English departments and classics: A writer for *School Library Journal* surveyed the English departments at Ivy League and Seven Sisters colleges (like Harvard, Yale, Radcliffe, and Smith) in 1984, seeking a list of books high school librarians should have on the shelf.[38] Some responded with lists, but no one title made all lists.

Professor Arthur Gold, then chair of the English department at Wellesley, came the closest to the "lite" reading proposition I offer in this chapter. He preferred that teachers and librarians simply encourage wide reading and not bother themselves with specific titles. "I'd have secondary school teachers weigh books on a scale and award letter grades for reading done by the pound," Gold declared. "My general sense is that memory needs to be stored at an early age," he argued, "that people need a good supply of anecdote, gossip, and emotional experience, and that the appropriate time for sorting things out comes after we have acquired a stock of information. Helter-skelter, chaos, putting first things last and last things first, not worrying whether one hasn't read what everyone should have read—these seem to me the appropriate terms and principles for a secondary-school approach to reading."

Gold argued *against* including Shakespeare, Greek mythology, modernist poetry, and Robert Frost, and says, "High school's the time for Thomas Wolfe, Vachel Lindsay, Jack London, Kipling, Robert Service, Vonnegut, and whatever's in fashion on the national scene."

Gold sounded iconoclastic, but at least rational. Since the old formula of lumbering classics has not turned high school students into either generations of future English teachers or even lukewarm readers, why stick with a formula that doesn't work? Why not Gold's "by the pound" formula? SSR by the pound? Could we be worse off than we are right now?

The ultimate purpose of the book you are holding is to create lifetime readers—not English teachers. If we read aloud to children—early and often, if we do not stop when they learn to read for themselves, if we create atmospheres in the home and classroom that nurture readers instead of torturing them, we will create a nation of lifetime readers. And those readers will come to the classics at an appropriate age and with an avidness the books deserve.

SSR in the Home

SSR works as well in the home as in the classroom. Indeed, considering that by the end of eighth grade, a child has spent only 9,000 hours in school compared to 95,000 outside school, it behooves parents to involve themselves in home SSR before they challenge a teacher on "why Jesse isn't doing better in reading this year."

The same SSR rules should apply in the home; that is, don't tell your child to go read for fifteen minutes while *you* watch television. You can, of course, tailor SSR to fit your family. For children who are not used to reading for more than brief periods of time it is important at first to limit SSR to ten or fifteen minutes. Later, when they are used to reading in this manner and are more involved in books, the period can be extended—often at the child's request. As in the classroom, it is important to have a variety of available material—magazines, newspapers, novels, picture books. A weekly trip to the library can do much to fill this need.

I should also note that the "Three B's" (Books, Bookbaskets, and Bed Lamps) I mentioned on page 42 are invaluable to the success of family SSR.

The time selected for family SSR is also important. Involve everyone in the decision, if possible. Bedtime seems to be the most popular time, perhaps because the child does not have to give up any activity for it except sleeping—and most children gladly surrender that.

If you're curious as to how most schoolchildren spend their free time, consider what researchers found in conducting the most comprehensive study ever done on how children spend their time outside school.[39] They selected 155 fifth-graders and monitored what they did during out-of-school time and how much time was devoted to each activity—from eating and reading to watching television, playing games, listening to music, talking on the phone, doing chores, etc. They also compared the children's reading scores from when they were in second grade with their scores in fifth grade. The report found:

- Students who read the most also had the most success in reading between second grade and fifth grade.
- Students who spent more time eating with their families had higher reading achievement.
- Students who read the most came from classrooms where the teachers most frequently:

   ✔ read aloud to the class
   ✔ made a wide assortment of books available to the class
   ✔ used incentives to motivate students
   ✔ scheduled sustained silent reading during the school day

- 90 percent of the 155 students spent 30 percent of their free time watching television and only 1 percent of their time reading.
- Up to 10 hours of television a week did no apparent harm to the student's reading achievement, but after that scores dropped sharply.

How Many Books in Twenty Minutes a Day?

When people first look at the small amount of time required for most SSR programs (about fifteen to twenty minutes), they often discount it as insignificant. But who says only longer periods of reading count? It reminds me of all the parents and teachers who sheepishly confess to me, "I know I should read more. But there just isn't enough time!" Really? Exactly how much time is necessary to read something? It's not as though you need to set up a camper or fill the hibachi with charcoal in order to do this. Suppose you set aside just twenty minutes every day, at a time least open to interruptions. Let's see how much a teenager, a parent, or a teacher could read with a regimen of twenty minutes a day.

USA Today's Dennis Kelly calculated that reading twenty minutes a day, six days a week, the average reader would accumulate 104 hours in a year and 3,000 pages. The 3,000 pages are the equal of Dickens' *Bleak House, Little Dorrit, Great Expectations,* and *Our Mutual Friend*; or five novels by Judith Krantz; or twenty-one John D. Macdonald mysteries.[40] On the other hand, if you convert the 104 hours to television shows, it comes out to about eight seasons of *Roseanne*.

How Much Do Teachers Read?

Throughout this book I have offered research showing the impact of parent role models on children's reading habits. Though they have less impact than parents, teachers can and should be effective reading role models—especially for those children whose parents cannot or will not do the job. The trouble, however, is that *most* teachers are seldom seen reading for pleasure. Reading for work, from the text, from lesson plans, yes. But sitting back and savoring a book for its own sake? Talking about a book they read last night? Seldom.

Research with teachers shows that in schools where their administrators talk about books and professional journals, the teachers read more on their own.[41] So why wouldn't the same be true for students if *their* instructional leaders talked more about books? In other words, if the teacher stood before the class and gave daily mini book talks based on the classroom library.

The fly in this ointment is that book talks work best only when the person talking has actually read the book—and most teachers don't read much. That is not a speculative comment but based on both research[42] and personal experience. One study of 224 teachers pursuing graduate degrees showed the teachers read few or no professional journals that included research. (Suppose your doctor only read *Prevention* magazine?) More than half said they had read only one or two professional books in the previous year, and an additional 20 percent said they had read nothing in the last six months or one year. What did they read beyond professional material?

- 22 percent read a newspaper only once a week.
- 75 percent were only light book readers—one or two a year.
- 25 percent were heavy readers (three to four books a month). This means that teachers don't read any more often than adults in the general population.[43]

Although this teacher reading study was done in 1977, nothing I have seen in 1,000 school districts in the last ten years leads me to believe much has changed. Are there districts where teachers are practicing what they preach? Yes, but they are still in the minority. Simply put, children cannot catch the fever of reading from nonreading teachers any more than they can catch a cold from someone who doesn't have one.

There is, however, a hopeful sign on the horizon. It took the Association of American Publishers (AAP) to come up with an antidote for teacher aliteracy. Beginning with New York City public schools, in association with Columbia University's Teachers College, AAP reasoned that reading is a social experience—readers need others with whom they can share their responses to a book. Teaching is often an isolated experience, with teachers separated from each other by walls and hundreds of children. Suppose a book discussion group were funded within schools so teachers could meet with each other to talk books. No grades, no required attendance, no papers; just read a book and sit with friends to discuss it. What began with fifty teachers in a few schools soon spread to more than 125 different schools throughout the New York metropolitan area.

On the basis of its New York experience, AAP founded Teachers As Readers (TAR) and, recently, Administrators As Readers (AAR), with a Parents As Readers slated for the future. To date, there are more than 600 TAR sites operating throughout the United States. Monthly meetings are used to discuss one professional book and one children's or young adult book that all participants have read prior to the meeting. For information, contact Teachers As Readers, AAP Reading Initiative, Association of American Publishers, 71 Fifth Avenue, New York, NY 10003-3004 (tel. 212-255-0200, ext. 229).

Strange Reading Messages

If you look at the things we do in many classrooms, it's a wonder anyone reads. For example, Jeanne Jacobson of Western Michigan University, Kalamazoo, tells of working with a functionally illiterate man in his mid-twenties whose *only* experience with reading had been reading *out loud*. Every teacher he ever had required him to read out loud. Thus, when his family was busy, he thought he couldn't practice reading because there was no one to listen to him. Among his many teachers and tutors, no one had ever modeled any other kind of reading to him. He saw no one in his home reading silently, no one at work.[44]

Many schools have a strange capacity for insulting their own curriculum, as when they establish programs like Reading Is Fun Week, in which class time is devoted to silent reading and reading aloud to children. And the following week, everyone returns to the workbook treadmill. Reading is not supposed to be fun for a *week*. Indeed, if reading isn't fun *every day*, there's something wrong with the curriculum. Doesn't anyone ever wonder why they don't need to schedule Recess Is Fun Week or Lunch Is Fun Week?

Writing: The Latest Weapon of Choice

An integral part of reading and language arts is the writing connection. For more than thirty years, American classrooms, obsessed with worksheets, suffered from writing neglect. But beginning in the 1980s, that changed. The whole-language movement made writing a major focus;

schools hired writing consultants who taught teachers how to write and then how to teach writing to children. Good so far.

Writing became the new buzzword in most schools. Students began to spend more time writing. When some teachers read the research that showed worksheets had no impact on children's reading skills, they began to look at writing as the new "crowd control" device. It would cover language arts, keep the class busy and focused, and give the teachers something they could put grades on. Writing became the new weapon of choice.

And then some people began to wonder: Isn't all this writing taking an awful lot of time away from reading? The writing process brings fresh air into stale classrooms, but one of the pitfalls is we'll attach so many writing activities to a book, we'll obscure its original purpose. Witness this letter I received a few years ago from Mary W. Williams, a North Carolina elementary school librarian. See if this doesn't give you pause:

"We did literature across the curriculum activities every class, every day. We speculated, counted, sequenced, matched, discriminated, imagined, listened, listed, and wrote, wrote, wrote. And I came to wonder . . .

"In the middle of one of the worst days ever—the rain was unrelenting, equipment broke and had to be repaired *now,* my aide was 'borrowed,' Kathy threw up, I missed lunch, Richard ate the last red crayon—in walked one of my best classes ever. They obediently seated themselves in the story corner and I enthusiastically introduced the book I would read to them. And Rusty—sunny, charming, cooperative Rusty —raised his hand and asked, 'Do we have to do something with this, or can we just enjoy it?'

"Revelation.

"Just for Rusty, we enjoyed that book, and the next, and the next . . . We spent forty minutes enjoying books that they knew and loved, books they would come to love. I was besieged by eager children thrusting books at me, eyes shining as they pleaded, 'Read this, read this . . .'

"I do not believe that using literature throughout the curriculum is a bad idea. But I believe even more firmly that we too often lose our way in attempting to improve our students' test scores; we forget there is nothing wrong in simply enjoying the sound, the thrill, the magic of a good story."[45]

Associating every book with various activities often amounts to gilding the lily, and the gilding can blind the child to the purpose of the book. What we need are more Rustys out there to wake us up.

Certainly writing is important, but is it as important as some schools are making it? Of the four language arts (the art of listening, the art of speaking, the art of reading, and the art of writing), the art of writing is the one least used in the workday of an average adult.

I am *not* saying writing is unimportant or that we shouldn't have writing experiences connected to reading. And I see the importance of children's wanting to read their own words before those of others. I grant you the importance of writing as an exercise in mental discipline that requires us to collect our thoughts in a coherent fashion—unlike the randomness of conversation. And I recognize how writing gives the individual a rare sense of inner focus, an opportunity for self-examination. In that respect, there is research to show writing makes the writer more intelligent.[46] So for all of those reasons, writing should never be ignored to the degree it was in the fifties, sixties, and seventies.

Having conceded that, I must still conclude that *writing is not as important as reading*. And when students spend more time writing than reading—or think they have to write every time they read—the end result will be they hate *both* reading and writing.

Writing does not build vocabulary as effectively as reading,[47] nor does it teach grammar, spelling, or reading skills as well. It doesn't offer the writer as much knowledge or information as reading, and it doesn't even teach writing as well as reading does. And research (as well as common sense) clearly confirms *each* of these points.[48]

Reading Incentive Programs

One form of SSR has been both successful and hotly debated: "incentive" programs like Pizza Hut's Book It! program. Begun in the 1985–86 school year, it is now used in 51,000 schools with 812,000 students. Well over half the students in America regularly obtain coupons for free pizzas—depending on how many books they've read. And though the program costs Pizza Hut more than $100 million in free pizzas each year, the company says, "We believe a child's potential is not just everybody's business. It is everybody's future." What could we accomplish if every corporation in America had the same philosophy?

For all its popularity, such incentive programs disturb education purists who are uncomfortable with the idea of offering prizes to children for reading.

Proponents, on the other hand, argue that our capitalist society successfully uses incentives with adults, so why not with children? Most ballplayers' contracts contain a clause guaranteeing them more money if they win the home-run title. Companies provide lucrative bonuses to their sales staff for exceeding a yearly quota, and many have policies that reward employees with time off for x number of days without being late or ill. Indeed, the entire frequent-flyer concept is built upon the cumulative reward system. If incentives really don't work, how come they haven't told all the coaches and school booster clubs? Why haven't they called for the dismantling of all the trophy cases in the school lobbies? Have they bothered to tell anyone that the kids don't really care about those team jackets? Isn't the report card really nothing more than a paper pizza reward?

Research on the subject is mixed. Both points of view can be substantiated,[49] which makes for an interesting debate. One reading of the data would lead you to believe that math and science students find enough reward in the challenge of the work, while students in the arts (art, music, theater, literature) need outside incentives—some kind of applause, if you will.[50] One thing worth reflecting on is that for a struggling beginning reader, reading is far from the easy thing we adults are now doing; it's labor-intensive. To complicate matters, much of what we ask a beginning reader to find an intrinsic reward in is just plain boring—especially if it's from a traditional basal reader.

Three of the better national reading incentive programs worth examining are:

- Pizza Hut's Book It! Program, P.O. Box 2999, Wichita, KS 67201.
- The Accelerated Reader, Advantage Learning Systems, Inc., 2610 Industrial Street, P.O. Box 36, Wisconsin Rapids, WI 54495-0036 (tel: 800-338-4204).
- Books and Beyond, Solano Beach School District, 309 North Rios, Solano Beach, CA 92075 (619-755-8000).

Hooked on Phonics

One of the saddest facts of the last ten years has been the incredible numbers of parents who think the product Hooked on Phonics will be an incentive to their child. First of all, if quick-cure programs like Hooked on Phonics really worked, we'd be using them in what is simultaneously one of the most expensive ($150 a day), most dangerous, and most illiterate places in America: the federal prison system, where

60 percent of the inmates are illiterate and 82 percent lack a high school diploma.

Promises of overnight cures are unfair and cruel to both the parent and the child. The suggestion is often made that these commercial programs are so simple they can be used by the child all by himself. This holds special appeal for the parent who either has reading problems himself or is "too busy" to work with the child one-on-one. When the reading product weighs in at seventeen pounds and consists of thirteen audiocassettes, 400 flash cards, and seven workbooks, it's more than unrealistic to expect that a struggling reader—or four-year-old—will be able to float it alone. And how many parents will be willing or able to put in a hundred hours sounding out all those vowels and consonants, endings and blendings? (How much is seventeen pounds? The user's manuals for my Macintosh computer [400 pages], Microsoft Word [800 pages], and Microsoft Works [500 pages], and the Osborne complete guide to the Internet [800 pages] only come to eleven pounds!)

In 1991, the International Reading Association, the largest international organization of reading educators, asked leaders in the field (including phonics experts) to review Hooked on Phonics and its claims. The reviews were unfavorable.[51] Subsequently the company made some adjustments but no evaluation has been done since. In 1994, however, the IRA board issued guidelines for parents and teachers in choosing commercial reading programs like Hooked on Phonics, citing four pitfalls:[52]

1. Do promotional materials promise quick fixes with no independent research to support their claims?
2. Does the product profess to be self-teaching?
3. Does the product include minimal or no opportunities for whole stories or informational text?
4. Does the product approach reading as a collection of skills to be practiced apart from meaningful text?

On all four counts, Hooked on Phonics fails the IRA product evaluation. It also failed the candor test with the National Advertising Division of the Council of Better Business Bureaus, which accused its parent company, Gateway Educational Products, of misleading customers.[53] In December 1994, the Federal Trade Commission charged that Hooked on Phonics was unable to scientifically substantiate its product claims and issued a cease-and-desist order, requiring advance FTC approval for Hooked on Phonics advertisements for approximately one year.[54]

School districts that are pestered by parents to add such commercial products to the classroom should not only provide the IRA guidelines to parents, but should also purchase for the district an inexpensive video entitled "What Is Reading?" Created and produced by Professor Pamela Perkins, director of the Reading Center at Chapman University in Orange, California. It is an enlightening demonstration of a child reading aloud for her teacher. The film's audience watches and listens to the child for nineteen minutes, while periodically throughout being asked to evaluate her performance. When the reading is completed and the evaluations are in, the child is interviewed about her reading. The results are surprising and instructive enough to make many reassess their thinking about what reading is.[55]

Hooked on Censorship

More and more teachers are looking over their shoulders during read-aloud or SSR periods, worrying that someone in the community will take offense at some book. Such fears are becoming so widespread that I sometimes wonder whether this is America or Iraq.

Though I'm a strong First Amendment advocate, I confess to "censoring" everything I read—newspapers, books, billboards, junk mail, what I read to myself and what I read aloud. Another word for it would be "editing." If I'm bored with something I'm reading for pleasure, I usually skip over it, as most people do. (Incidentally, Charles Dickens, whose publisher paid him by the word, edited out the extra adjectives and adverbs when he read his works aloud during lecture tours.) If there is something in the text that will detract from the book's impact or disturb the class or child, skip it or change it. *You're* running the program, not the person who wrote the book, who has no idea what the problems are in your classroom or home. I am not suggesting, as one author-friend feared, that you rewrite the book to the tastes of the reader. Reason is called for, not revisionism. The business of plodding along word for word, never missing a line, said Clifton Fadiman, is "chronic reverence," something that may be good manners, but also a "confounded waste of time."

Insignificant editing is a long way, however, from the extremes to which some would take us. Typical is the yearly ranting over Katherine Paterson's *Bridge to Terabithia*. Number seven on *The New York Times* children's bestseller list nearly twenty years after it was published, *Ter-*

abithia was the third most frequently contested book in America by religious extremists in the 1992–93 school year.[56]

Traditionally read by fourth through sixth grades, this Newbery winner describes the friendship between a ten-year-old boy and girl and the subsequent accidental drowning of the girl. The author is the daughter of two Christian missionaries to China and married to a Christian minister. The book is widely regarded as one of the most beautiful books on friendship and childhood published in the last quarter century. Nonetheless, extremists have pressured to have it banned because: (1) Several four-letter words ("hell" and "damn") appear; and (2) one of the children professes to her Christian friends that, impressed as she is with the story of Christ, she is a nonbeliever.

The offending two words are not strewn throughout the text. They are uttered in a nonprofane, almost solemn manner by a father after the death of his son's best friend. Nor are they earthshaking. Normal people don't expect the characters in children's books to behave like sadists or serial killers, but they don't expect them to behave like saints, either. If everyone in children's books must act like Mother Teresa, we're going to have to stop reading those Old Testament stories to children.

As for the objections to *Terabithia* because of the young girl's agnosticism, what law says we must all wear the same spiritual uniform? Christians can't even agree whether Christ's mother was a virgin, whether He had brothers and sisters, or whether the Communion host is real, symbolic, or hocus-pocus. If we're going to eliminate nonbelievers or doubters from books, will we start by erasing the disciple Thomas?

In so many of these book protests, there is the explicit suggestion that the books will corrupt not only the souls of children but the fabric of American society as well. If such were true, we'd be able to trace a pattern between reading "trashy" children's books and criminal behavior. Our prisons would be populated by the grown-up readers of banned books, right? In fact, the opposite is true. With 85 percent of juvenile inmates experiencing literacy problems, the majority of inmates couldn't read *any* children's novels, never mind "trashy" ones.

It's ironic that while religious extremists expend so much energy in book bannings, America's largest Christian publisher, Zondervan Publishing House, publishes an excellent guide to teenage literature for Christian families (*Read for Your Life* by Gladys Hunt and Barbara Hampton) that includes praise for some of the same books others are protesting: *Bridge to Terabithia; The Goats,* by Brock Cole; *A Day No*

Pigs Would Die, by Robert Newton Peck; *The Dark Is Rising,* by Susan Cooper; and *A Wrinkle in Time,* by Madeleine L'Engle.[57]

And then there are the modern-day witch-hunts in which extremist parents push to remove all books with references to witches in them. Their premise is that such books—even Halloween books!—promote Satanism. I am sure they are sincere in their beliefs, but that doesn't mean the majority believes as they do. I wonder if it would help to remind them that the bestselling witch book of all time—*The Lion, the Witch, and the Wardrobe*—was written by one of the most famous Christian apologists of this century, C. S. Lewis. Are there any Satan worshippers who list that book as their childhood inspiration?

You will find numerous instances throughout the course of this book where I call upon parents to be involved in what is read by their children. That is a parent's right and responsibility. Where I draw the line is in their imposing their own family's views or restrictions on *other* people's children. Instead of declaring this idea or that book un-American or un-Christian, we should remember the meaning of the phrase on the Great Seal of the United States, *E pluribus unum*—one out of many. We are creating one nation out of many beliefs, cultures, religions, philosophies, theories, colors, languages, and dialects. It is our diversity that strengthens us. Anything that diminishes that diversity goes against the grain of the Constitution and reeks of a church state.

The book banners might also consider the effect of forbidden fruit on human behavior. Seldom is the book successfully banned; sales and circulation almost always increase. This is as true with children as with adults. When editor Michael Dirda of the *Washington Post Book World* declared the film *Jurassic Park* to be too frightening and therefore off-limits to his nine-year-old son, he failed to take into consideration the powerful lure of forbidden fruit. That attraction, combined with the television commercials, was enough to provoke the boy to go to the original source. Painstakingly but with great motivation, the nine-year-old read the entire 399-page book that summer. This, in turn, provoked his editor father to wonder if maybe this isn't the key to turning on all those reluctant readers: Make movies of our great books, and then forbid children to see them.[58]

9

How to Use the Treasury

> The success we have in helping children become readers will depend not so much on our technical skills but upon the spirit we transmit of ourselves as readers. Next in importance comes the breadth and depth of our knowledge of the books we offer. Only out of such a ready catalogue can we match child and book with the sort of spontaneous accuracy that is wanted time and again during a working day.
>
> —Aidan Chambers,
> "Talking About Reading," *The Horn Book* (October 1977)

An essential element in reading aloud is *what* you choose to read aloud. Not all books are worth reading aloud. (Some aren't even worth reading to yourself, if you want to be candid about it.)

The style of writing—if it's convoluted or if the sentence structure is too complex for the tongue or ear—can make your read-aloud choice unsuccessful. And reading aloud a boring book induces the same results as reading it silently. Boring is boring. Therefore, the aim of the Treasury is to list books whose subject matter, style, and structure make successful read-alouds.

There are two ways to use the Treasury. One way offers more than three hundred and fifty titles and synopses; the second, however, will triple the number of titles. For example, when you look up *The House on East 88th Street*, by Bernard Waber, in the picture book section, you will find more than just a synopsis of that book; reading beyond the synopsis reveals the six other books in the Lyle series, an additional book by the author, and five related titles, including cross-references to other books, *Amos: The Story of an Old Dog and His Couch* (p), and *The Whingdingdilly* (p), where more books are listed.

In the reference (p), the letter in parenthesis refers to one of the categories into which the Treasury is divided: Picture Books (p); Short Novels (s); Novels (n); Poetry (po); Anthologies (a); and Fairy/Folk Tales (fa). All books in the respective categories are listed alphabetically by title. The Author/Illustrator Index to the Treasury will also help you locate books.

In the synopses, I have indicated wherever I thought certain books needed special attention from the reader-aloud. For example, Harry Mazer's *Snow-Bound* is a compelling novel about two teenagers fighting for their lives in a snowstorm. Many of my public-school teacher friends read it to their middle-school classes each year and skip over the occasional four-letter words in the text. The story is one of the children's favorites and it would be a shame to deprive them of its excitement and values because of a dozen strong words. Nevertheless, the reader-aloud should be alerted to the situation.

I have noted "for experienced listeners" to indicate those books I feel would be poor choices for children just beginning the listening experience. These books should be read aloud only after the children's attention and listening spans have been developed with shorter books and stories.

The number of pages noted for each book should indicate to the reader the number of sittings the book requires. A children's book of thirty-two pages can be completed easily in one session.

What is the difference between those titles given main entries and those listed after the synopsis? Most of the time there is only a fine distinction, sometimes none. The problem in compiling the Treasury is there isn't enough room to give every book a main entry and synopsis.

Of the more than 4,000 books published each year, about 60 percent could be categorized as fast food for the mind, and of minimal lasting value. Only about 10 percent of the year's crop could be rated Grade A.

This is not to say that fast-food books are worthless. On the contrary, they serve as hors d'oeuvres and build appetites (to say nothing of reading skills) for more nourishing books later. As I pointed out in Chapter 8, they also serve as valuable transition steps between textbook reading and leisure reading.

The reader-aloud, however, offers an alternative for the child, allowing him to sample the Grade A books which may be beyond either his reading skills or his surface appetites. Therefore, in reading aloud we should concern ourselves primarily (though not exclusively) with books that will stimulate children's emotions, minds, and imaginations, stories that will stay with them for years to come, literature that will serve as a harbor light toward which a child can navigate.

Few parents and teachers have the time or opportunity to wade through the vast numbers of newly published books, not to mention the previous year's volumes. Librarians and booksellers can help in this chore, especially when they know the patron's needs and preferences. But not everyone has access to such professional services before they visit a bookstore, and it is my hope the Treasury will help in that regard.

I fully recognize the danger in compiling any book list. There will always be those who see it as exclusive ("If it's not mentioned in *The Read-Aloud Handbook*'s Treasury, it can't be that good!"). As well-intentioned as such thinking may be, it is wrong, wrong, wrong. If Harvard and Stanford can't agree on which classics constitute the core curriculum, how could I come up with the ultimate list? And with more than 4,000 new children's books being issued this year, the best of those will already be missing from this revision and must wait for the revision four years from now. If you find someone using the list exclusively, please call this paragraph to their attention.

I make no boast of the Treasury being a comprehensive list. It is intended only as a starter and time-saver. (I'd be willing to wager, in fact, that I've left your all-time favorite off the list.) One thing to keep in mind as you look through the list is that these are *read-aloud* titles, which eliminates some titles that are difficult to read aloud or, because of the subject matter, are best read silently to oneself—like Robert Cormier's *The Chocolate War* (subject) or Mark Twain's *Tom Sawyer* (dialect).

I have tried to make the collection as balanced as possible between classical, traditional, and contemporary titles. When *The New York Times* ran its bestseller list of children's books in the spring of 1994, the average publication date for picture books was 1966, making each book an average of twenty-eight years old. The chapter books (including *The Secret Garden* (1911) and *Charlotte's Web* (1952) averaged twenty years of age. The picture books included oldies but goodies like *Goodnight*

Moon (1947), *Pat the Bunny* (1940), *The Runaway Bunny* (1942), *The Velveteen Rabbit* (1922), and *The Tale of Peter Rabbit* (1902 in the U.S.). In the world of children's books, once a favorite has been settled upon, it sinks deep roots into traditional family life. Grandmothers and aunts walk into a bookstore, don't recognize the new titles, and opt to shop on the safe side, with the old favorites.

The drawback in such a pattern is that wonderful new books—like *Owen* by Kevin Henkes—will not sell enough copies to stay in the bookstore or in print. So my hope is that the Treasury will do at least two things: (1) introduce the standard titles to new parents and teachers; and (2) introduce new titles to experienced parents and teachers. Maybe it will help also to keep good books in print longer.

Some of the choices are entirely subjective. If I want a listing of Christmas books, which titles do I choose and which one as the main listing? In this edition, I picked *Santa Calls* by William Joyce as the main listing, not because it is better than Chris Van Allsburg's *The Polar Express* or David McPhail's *Santa's Book of Names*—though they all have much in common. I chose *Santa Calls* because it was so extraordinarily good *and* unusual, and because it was newer and therefore fewer people would know about it. Other Christmas picture-book titles would be listed as related books beneath it.

I must also confess to being the beneficiary of a network of parents, teachers, and librarians whom I meet in my travels and who give me tips on titles. ("Jim, you missed a wonderful book in your last edition, one I think you should know about. It's called . . .") I immediately think of two books that came to my attention this way: *Sideways Stories from Wayside School* by Louis Sachar (many teachers and librarians recommended it) and *The Girl with the Silver Eyes* by Willo Davis Roberts (from a Florida mother who said her daughter "would prefer listening to that book to going to Disney World").

In making my selections, I use the following criteria:

1. I must have read the book. (After all these years of reading aloud, I can tell almost immediately if it works "aloud.")
2. The book must have a proven track record as a read-aloud with children. Teachers, librarians, and other parents assist in such evaluations.
3. The book must be interesting enough to inspire children to want to read another one like it, or even the same book again.

Nearly all the books listed are strong on narrative. By and large, they have a story to tell in which there is a conflict, some drama, and a conclusion. Nothing consistently holds the attention of a classroom of children with divergent interests quite like fiction.

Below the main entry for each book, you will find the names of the author and illustrator, along with recommended grade level, the number of pages, and the publisher and year of publication.

The grade recommendations for each book refer to the "listening level" of the book; in other words, Gr. 1–3 means this book can be understood when read aloud to most children in grades one through three. There will be many first-graders who couldn't read it on their own but could certainly comprehend it when it is read to them. But I must emphasize that these grade recommendations are meant to be flexible guidelines, not rules. In addition to the numbered grade levels, the following codes are included where appropriate:

Tod.—Infants and toddlers, up to three-year-olds

PreS.—from three-year-olds to five-year-olds

K—kindergartners

In listing the publishers, it is impossible to stay abreast of the changes in the publishing industry as one publisher absorbs another, or as a book goes into or out of paperback. So I have just listed the original hardcover publisher (or paperback if that is the only form in which it is available). As this book goes to my editor, everything is still in print—but changes occur monthly.

Let's say you find a book in the Treasury that you are interested in purchasing, like *Not the Piano, Mrs. Medley*, by Evan Levine and S. D. Schindler. When you approach your local bookseller, it may not be in stock. When they check their computer listing it may or may not be listed with their wholesaler. If they tell you it's not listed with their wholesaler, this does not mean it is out of print. It just means you have to be assertive. The *easy* way for a bookstore to get a book is through its wholesaler. The longer and harder way is for it to order directly from the publisher. Check either at the bookstore or at your library to ensure the book is still in print, using *Books in Print* as a reference. You can do this by phone with your library reference room. If it's still in print and you want the book, tell the bookstore you want them to order it from the publisher. Most will do this willingly. If they balk—think seriously about taking your book business elsewhere.

10

Treasury of Read-Alouds

WORDLESS BOOKS

(These books contain no words; the story is told entirely with pictures arranged in sequence. Wordless books can be "read" not only by pre- and beginning readers, but also by illiterate or semiliterate adults who want to "read" to children. They "tell" the book, using the pictures for clues to the emerging plot. Books marked with an * are described at length in the Picture Book section of the Treasury.)

Ah-Choo!, by Mercer Mayer (Dial, 1976)
Amanda and the Mysterious Carpet, by Fernando Krahn (Houghton Mifflin, 1985)
Amanda's Butterfly, by Nick Butterworth (Delacorte, 1991)
The Angel and the Soldier Boy, by Peter Collington (Knopf, 1987)
The Bear and the Fly, by Paula Winter (Crown, 1976)

Ben's Dream, by Chris Van Allsburg (Houghton Mifflin, 1982)

A Boy, a Dog, and a Frog, by Mercer Mayer (Dial, 1967)

Bubble, Bubble, by Mercer Mayer (Simon & Schuster, 1973)

Changes, Changes, by Pat Hutchins (Simon & Schuster, 1971)

The Christmas Gift, by Emily McCully (HarperCollins, 1988)

*Deep in the Forest, by Brinton Turkle (Dutton, 1976)

Do You Want to Be My Friend?, by Eric Carle (Putnam, 1971)

Don't Forget Me, Santa Claus, by Virginia Mayo (Barron's, 1993)

Dreams, by Peter Spier (Doubleday, 1986)

Ernest & Celestine's Patchwork Quilt, by Gabrielle Vincent (Greenwillow, 1982)

Frog Goes to Dinner, by Mercer Mayer (Dial, 1974)

Frog on His Own, by Mercer Mayer (Dial, 1973)

Frog, Where Are You?, by Mercer Mayer (Dial, 1969)

The Garden of Abdul Gasazi, by Chris Van Allsburg (Houghton Mifflin, 1979)

The Gift, by John Prater (Viking, 1985)

Good Dog Carl, by Alexandra Day (Green Tiger, 1985)

The Grey Lady and the Strawberry Snatcher, by Molly Bang (Simon & Schuster, 1980)

The Hunter and the Animals, by Tomie dePaola (Holiday, 1981)

I Can't Sleep, by Philippe Dupasquier (Orchard, 1990)

Little Red Riding Hood, by John Goodall (Atheneum, 1988)

The Midnight Circus, by Peter Collington (Knopf, 1993)

Moonlight, by Jan Ormerod (Morrow, 1982)

Noah's Ark, by Peter Spier (Doubleday, 1977)

One Frog Too Many, by Mercer Mayer (Dial, 1975)

The Other Bone, by Ed Young (HarperCollins, 1984)

Pancakes for Breakfast, by Tomie dePaola (Harcourt, Brace, 1978)

Peter Spier's Christmas, by Peter Spier (Doubleday, 1982)

Peter Spier's Rain, by Peter Spier (Doubleday, 1982)

Puss in Boots, by John S. Goodall (Simon & Schuster, 1990)

Rainy Day Dream, by Michael Chesworth (Farrar, Straus and Giroux, 1992)

Rosie's Walk, by Pat Hutchins (Macmillan, 1968)

*The Silver Pony, by Lynd Ward (Houghton Mifflin, 1973)

The Snowman, by Raymond Briggs (Random House, 1978)

Sunshine, by Jan Ormerod (Morrow, 1981)

Time Flies, by Eric Rohmann (Crown, 1994)

*Tuesday, by David Wiesner (Clarion, 1991)

Up a Tree, by Ed Young (HarperCollins, 1983)
Up and Up, by Shirley Hughes (Morrow, 1986)
Where's My Monkey?, by Dieter Schubert (Dial, 1987)

PREDICTABLE/CUMULATIVE BOOKS

(These picture books contain word or sentence patterns that are repeated often enough to enable children to predict their appearance and thus begin to join in on the reading. Books marked with an * are described at length in the Picture Book section of the Treasury.)

All Join In, by Quentin Blake (Little, Brown, 1991)
Are You My Mother?, by P. D. Eastman (Random House, 1960)
Ask Mr. Bear, by Marjorie Flack (Macmillan, 1986)
The Big Sneeze, by Ruth Brown (Lothrop, 1985)
Brown Bear, Brown Bear, What Do You See?, by Bill Martin Jr. (Holt, 1983)
Bye-Bye Baby, by Janet Ahlberg (Little, Brown, 1990)
The Cake That Mack Ate, by Rose Robart (Little, Brown, 1986)
Cat Came Back, illustrated, retold by Bill Slavin (Whitman, 1992)
The Cat Sat on the Mat, by Alice Cameron (Houghton Mifflin, 1994)
Chicka Chicka Boom Boom, by Bill Martin Jr. and John Archambault (Simon & Schuster, 1989)
Chicken Soup with Rice, by Maurice Sendak (HarperCollins, 1962)
Cock-A-Doodle-Doo!, by Jill Runcie (Simon & Schuster, 1991)
Cockatoos, by Quentin Blake (Little, Brown, 1992)
Do You Want to Be My Friend?, by Eric Carle (Putnam, 1971)
Drummer Hoff, by Barbara Emberly (Simon & Schuster, 1967)
The Elephant and the Bad Baby, by Elfrida Vipont (Putnam, 1986)
Froggy Gets Dressed, by Jonathan London (Viking, 1992)
The Gingerbread Boy, by Paul Galdone (Clarion, 1975)
Good Night, Gorilla, by Peggy Rathmann (Putnam, 1994)
*_Goodnight Moon_, by Margaret Wise Brown (HarperCollins, 1947)
The Gunnywolf, by A. Delaney (HarperCollins, 1988)
Hattie and the Fox, by Mem Fox (Simon & Schuster, 1987)
Henny Penny, by Paul Galdone (Clarion, 1968)
The House That Crack Built, by Clark Taylor (Chronicle, 1992)
The House That Jack Built, by Jenny Stow (Dial, 1992)
*_If You Give a Mouse a Cookie_, by Laura Numeroff (HarperCollins, 1985)
If You Give a Moose a Muffin, by Laura Numeroff (HarperCollins, 1991)

The Important Book, by Margaret Wise Brown (HarperCollins, 1949)

Is It Time?, by Marilyn Janovitz (North-South, 1994)

It Looked Like Split Milk, by Charles Shaw (HarperCollins, 1947)

Just Like Everyone Else, by Karla Kuskin (HarperCollins, 1959)

Knick Knack Paddywack, by Marissa Moss (Houghton Mifflin, 1992)

Knock, Knock, Teremock, by Katya Arnold (North-South, 1994)

Let's Go Home, Little Bear, by Martin Waddell (Candlewick, 1993)

The Little Old Lady Who Was Not Afraid of Anything, by Linda Williams (HarperCollins, 1986)

The Little Red House, by Norma Jean Sawicki (HarperCollins, 1989)

Matthew and the Midnight Towtruck, by Allen Morgan (Annick, 1984)

The Matzah That Papa Brought Home, by Fran Manushkin (Scholastic, 1995)

Millions of Cats, by Wanda Gag (Putnam, 1977)

The Napping House, by Audrey Wood (Harcourt, Brace, 1984)

No Jumping on the Bed, by Tedd Arnold (Dial, 1987)

Old Black Fly, by Jim Aylesworth (Holt, 1992)

Old MacDonald Had a Farm, illustrated by Lorinda Bryan Cauley (Putnam, 1989)

Over in the Meadow, by Olive Wadsworth (Viking, 1985)

Owl Babies, by Martin Waddell (Candlewick, 1992)

Papa's Bedtime Story, by Mary Lee Donovan (Knopf, 1993)

Pierre: A Cautionary Tale, by Maurice Sendak (HarperCollins, 1962)

The Pig in the Pond, by Martin Waddell (Candlewick, 1992)

Polar Bear, Polar Bear, What Do You Hear?, by Bill Martin Jr. (Holt, 1991)

She'll Be Coming 'Round the Mountain, adapted by Tom and Debbie Holsclaw Birdseye (Holiday, 1994)

Simpkin, by Quentin Blake (Viking, 1994)

Sitting in My Box, by Dee Lillegard (Dutton, 1992)

The Teeny Tiny Woman, by Barbara Seuling (Puffin, 1978)

That's Good! That's Bad!, by Margery Cuyler (Holt, 1993)

This Is the Bear, by Sarah Hayes (Candlewick, 1993)

This Is the Bread I Baked for Ned, by Crescent Dragonwagon (Simon & Schuster, 1989)

Three Blind Mice, by John Ivimey (Clarion, 1987)

The Three Little Pigs, by Paul Galdone (Clarion, 1970)

Tikki Tikki Tembo, by Arlene Mosel (Holt, 1968)

The Tree in the Wood, adapted by Christopher Manson (North-South, 1993)

The Very Hungry Caterpillar, by Eric Carle (Philomel, 1969)

We're Going on a Bear Hunt, by Michael Rosen (Atheneum)

The Wheels on the Bus, by Maryann Kovalski (Little, Brown, 1987)

Where's Spot?, by Eric Hill (Putnam, 1980)

Who Is Tapping at My Window?, by A. G. Deming (Puffin, 1994)

PICTURE REFERENCE BOOKS

Do Animals Dream? by Joyce Pope

Viking, 1986   K-5   96 pages

Information, illustrations, and charts to answer the nearly 100 questions children ask most often at the American Museum of Natural History, New York. Related books: *Why Did The Dinosaurs Disappear?* and *Why Do Volcanoes Erupt? Questions About Our Planet*, both by Dr. Philip Whitfield.

Extraordinary Origins of Everyday Things

See page 338 in Anthologies

The Kids' Question & Answer Book(s)
by the editors of OWL Magazine

Grosset, 1988   K-6   77 pages

Questions and answers on 100 topics—from dinosaurs and dizziness to sneezes and hiccups—and handsomely illustrated. Also in the series: *The Kids' Question and Answer Book Two*; *The Kids' Question and Answer Book Three*. An equally good series, all in paperback, comes from the distinguished science editor of *Highlights* magazine, Dr. Jack Myers, with twenty-five years' worth of readers' questions: *Can Birds Get Lost?*; *Do Cats Really Have Nine Lives?*; *What Makes Popcorn Pop?*; and *How Do We Dream?*

Know It All! by Ed Zotti

Ballantine, 1993   Gr. 5 and up   211 pages

On a more sophisticated level than *The Kids' Question and Answer Books*, the author gives you the "how" and "why" answers to common questions—from why the moon is larger on the horizon than overhead and why yawns are contagious, to how the telephone company chose specific area code numbers and why electrical plugs have one prong larger than the other. This is an excellent short read-aloud book for science classes or to keep in the glove compartment for family trips.

Also by the author: *The Straight Dope*; *More of the Straight Dope*. Related books: *Ever Wonder Why?*, by Douglas B. Smith; and *Mistakes That Worked*, by Charlotte Foltz Jones.

Life Through the Ages by Giovanni Caselli
Dorling Kindersley, 1992   Gr. 3–8   64 pages

In hundreds of color illustrations, the great ideas and moments in history (from Stone Age to Space Age) are chronicled. Related book: *How Children Lived*, by Chris and Melanie Rice.

The Random House Children's Encyclopedia
Random House, 1991   K–5   640 pages

A lavishly illustrated A to Z reference guide for young readers, this is the most comprehensive single volume of its kind. The maps, photos, and cutaway illustrations of cars, castles, computers, ships, and the human body are breathtaking.

PICTURE BOOKS

Aesop and Company
prepared by Barbara Bader ✶ Illustrated by Arthur Geisert
Orchard, 1989   Gr. 2–5   64 pages

Aesop's fables offer us not only wisdom but also an introduction to characters, ideas, and images that turn up again and again in stories in the European tradition. Along with twenty of his most famous tales, this volume provides us with a unique view of Aesop's legendary life and the history of fables. Other Aesops: the largest, most economical collection is *Aesop's Fables*, selected and adapted by Jack Zipes; smaller collections of fables: *Aesop's Fables*, compiled by Russell Ash and Bernard Higton; *Anno's Aesop: A Book of Fables by Aesop*, by Mitsumasa Anno. Other fable collections: *Fables* (contemporary), by Arnold Lobel; *Frederick's Fables*, by Leo Lionni; and *The Tales of Uncle Remus* (a).

Aladdin
retold by Andrew Lang ✶ Illustrated by Errol Le Cain
Viking, 1981   Gr. 2 and up   30 pages

This is the world-famous tale about the magic lamp that brings the poor Persian boy his heart's desire—but only after great trials. Related books: *The Arabian Nights Entertainments*, by Andrew Lang; *Catkin*, by

Antonia Barber; *Do Not Open*, by Brinton Turkle; *The Wish Giver* (n); *The Secret in the Matchbox* (series), by Val Willis.

Alexander and the Terrible, Horrible, No Good, Very Bad Day
by Judith Viorst ✯ Illustrated by Ray Cruz
Atheneum, 1972   K and up   34 pages

Everyone has a bad day once in a while, but little Alexander has the worst of all. Follow him from a cereal box without a prize to a burned-out night-light. A modern classic for all ages. Sequel: *Alexander Who Used to Be Rich Last Sunday*. Also by the author: see listing with *If I Were in Charge of the World and Other Worries* (po).

The Amazing Voyage of Jackie Grace
by Matt Faulkner
Scholastic, 1987   Pre-S.-1   38 pages

Once he climbs into the bathtub, Jackie's imagination carries him away to the high seas, where he battles pirates and a fierce sea storm in a book that does for bathtubs what *Where the Wild Things Are* does for bedrooms. Related books: *And to Think That I Saw It on Mulberry Street*, by Dr. Seuss; *The Beast in the Bathtub*, by Kathleen Stevens; and *Burt Dow, Deep-Water Man*, by Robert McCloskey; see also listing with *Captain Abdul's Pirate School* (p).

Amelia Bedelia
by Peggy Parish ✯ Illustrated by Fritz Seibel
HarperCollins, 1963   K-4   24 pages

America's most lovable maid since Hazel, Amelia is a walking disaster—thanks to her insistence on taking directions literally, causing her to: "dust the furniture" with dusting powder; "dress the turkey" in shorts; and "put the lights out" on the clothesline. She makes for a hilarious exploration of homonyms and idioms. Sequels: *Amelia Bedelia and the Baby*; *Amelia Bedelia and the Surprise Shower*; *Amelia Bedelia's Family Album*; *Amelia Bedelia Goes Camping*; *Come Back, Amelia Bedelia*; *Good Work, Amelia Bedelia*; *Play Ball, Amelia Bedelia*; *Teach Us, Amelia Bedelia*; *Thank You, Amelia Bedelia*. Related books: *All of Our Noses Are Here and Other Noodle Tales*, retold by Alvin Schwartz; *The King Who Rained*, by Fred Gwynne; and Harry Allard's zany Stupids series: *The Stupids Step Out*; *The Stupids Die*; *The Stupids Have a Ball*; and *The Stupids Take Off*.

Amos: The Story of an Old Dog and His Couch
by Susan Seligson ✭ Illustrated by Howie Schneider

Little, Brown, 1987   Pre-S.-2   32 pages

In this the first in the series, Amos, a lazy "couch potato" of an Irish setter, discovers his couch can be driven—just like a car. So as soon as his masters depart, "Varooooom!"—off he goes, driving all over town. Because of the small but expressive pictures, this is a book best done with a small audience. Sequels: *The Amazing Amos and the Greatest Couch on Earth*; *Amos Ahoy!*; and *Amos Camps Out*. Other books about humanlike animals: *Dinosaur Bob and His Adventures with the Family Lazardo* (p); *The Giraffe and the Pelly and Me*, by Roald Dahl; *The House on East 88th Street* (p); *Jumbo the Boy and Arnold the Elephant* (p); *Maxi, the Hero*, by Debra and Sal Barracca; *Mrs. Dunphy's Dog*, by Catharine O'Neill; and *The New Creatures*, by Mordicai Gerstein.

Anatole by Eve Titus

Bantam, 1990   Gr. 1-3   32 pages

Very popular when first published, *Anatole*, the chivalrous mouse, is back in print (paperback), continuing his hair-raising adventures in and under Paris. For experienced listeners. Other books in the series include: *Anatole and the Cat*; *Anatole over Paris*; *Anatole and the Piano*; *Anatole and the Thirty Thieves*; *Anatole and the Toy Shop*. Other mouse books: *Broderick*, by Edward Ormondroyd; *Dear Brother*, by Frank Asch and Vladimir Vagin; *Doctor DeSoto*, by William Steig; *Chester's Way* (p); *The Farmhouse Mouse*, by Cynthia Rogers Erkel; *Frederick* (p); *If You Give a Mouse a Cookie* (p); *The Island of the Skog* (p); *Little Mouse's Painting*, by Diane Wolkstein and Maryjane Begin; *Loud-Mouse*, by Richard Wilbur; *The Marvelous Blue Mouse*, by Christopher Manson; *Mouse Tales*, by Arnold Lobel; *Mouse's Birthday*, by Jane Yolen; *Norman the Doorman*, by Don Freeman; and the novel *Stuart Little*, by E. B. White.

Angus and the Ducks by Marjorie Flack

Doubleday, 1930   Pre-S.-K   32 pages

Angus, the Scotch terrier, represents all inquisitive young children exploring and confronting their surroundings. Created more than sixty years ago, this tale and the two sequels—*Angus and the Cat*, and *Angus Lost*—are timeless. Also by the author: *The Story About Ping* and *Ask Mr. Bear*.

Arnold of the Ducks by Mordicai Gerstein

HarperCollins, 1983   Pre-S.-2   54 pages

A contemporary Mowgli, little Arnold disappears from his backyard wading pool one day and finds himself not only adopted by a family of ducks, but also thinking and acting like a duck. He even learns to fly. All goes well until the "call of home" drowns out the "call of the wild." Related books: *Avocado Baby*, by John Burningham; *The Boy Who Lived with the Seals* (p); *Pumpkin Time*, by Jan Andrews; *Shorty Takes Off* (p); and *Stellaluna* (p).

Arthur's Chicken Pox by Marc Brown

Little, Brown, 1994   Pre-S.-1   28 pages

By the time you read this, there will be more than twenty *Arthur* adventures, a series of wildly popular stories about an aardvark family's warm and often hilarious adventures at home, at school, and in the neighborhood. In this adventure, he's got a case of that childhood staple, chicken pox, along with all its lifestyle complications for the entire family. Also in the series: *Arthur Babysits*; *Arthur's Family Vacation*; *Arthur's New Puppy*; *Arthur's Pet Business*; *Arthur Meets the President*; and *Arthur's Baby*.

The Biggest Bear by Lynd Ward

Houghton Mifflin, 1952   K-3   80 pages

Johnny adopts a bear cub fresh out of the woods and its growth presents problem after problem—the crises we invite when we tame what is meant to be wild. Also by the author: *The Silver Pony* (p). Related books: *Backyard Bear*, by Jim Murphy; *Bear*, by John Schoenherr; *The Carp in the Bathtub*, by Barbara Cohen; *Cappyboppy*, by Bill Peet; *Daisy Rothschild*, by Betty Leslie-Melville; *Emily's Own Elephant*, by Philippa Pearce; *Faithful Elephants*, by Yukio Tsuchiya; *Honkers*, by Jane Yolen; *The Josefina Story Quilt*, by Eleanor Coerr; *Old Bet and the Start of the American Circus*, by Robert McClung; and *Two Travelers*, by Christopher Manson.

The Boy Who Lived with the Seals
retold by Rafe Martin ✵ Illustrated by David Shannon

Putnam, 1993   Gr. 1-4   32 pages

This Chinook legend from the American Indians of the Northwest is comparable to the Scottish selkie tales or Kipling's Mowgli stories. The illustrations are powerfully haunting and, when combined with the simple story, make for a dramatic book. Also by the author: *Foolish Rabbit's Big Mistake*; *The Rough Face Girl*; and *Will's Mammoth*. Related books: *Greyling* (p); *The Jungle Books*, by Rudyard Kipling; see also the listing with *Ladder to the Sky* (p).

Brave Irene by William Steig
Farrar, Straus and Giroux, 1986   K-5   28 pages

When Irene's dressmaker mother falls ill and cannot deliver the duchess's gown for the ball, Irene shoulders the huge box and battles a winter storm to make the delivery. For other books by this great artist/storyteller, see *Sylvester and the Magic Pebble* (p). Related books: *Deer in the Hollow*, by Efner Tudor Holmes; for other books on courage, see *The Courage of Sarah Noble* (s).

Brown Bear, Brown Bear, What Do You See?
by Bill Martin, Jr. ☆ Illustrated by Eric Carle
Holt, 1983   Tod.-K   24 pages

This classic predictable book follows the question through various animals and colors. Sequel: *Polar Bear, Polar Bear, What Do You Hear?* Also by the author: *Barn Dance*; *Chicka Chicka Boom Boom*; *The Ghost-Eye Tree*; and *Knots on a Counting Rope*. For other predictable books, see listing on page 231.

By the Dawn's Early Light: The Story of
the Star-Spangled Banner
by Steven Kroll ☆ Illustrated by Dan Andreasen
Scholastic, 1994   Gr. 3-8   34 pages

In this book about the origin of the U.S. National Anthem, we see how a picture book can be used to explain complicated or little-known historical moments, and can be used across grade levels. Other examples of outstanding historical picture books: *But No Candy*, by Gloria Houston; *Christmas in the Big House, Christmas in the Quarters*, by Patricia and Fredrick McKissack; *Daniel's Duck*, by Clyde Robert Bulla; *Dear Benjamin Banneker*, by Andrea Davis Pinkney; *Encounter*, by Jane Yolen; *Errata: A Book of Historical Errors*, by A. J. Wood; *Flight*, by Robert Burleigh; *Follow the Drinking Gourd*, by Jeanette Winter; *George Washington: A Picture Book Biography* (p); *Going West*, by Martin Waddell; *The Heroine of the Titanic*, by Joan W. Blos; *The House on Maple Street*, by Bonnie Pryor; *If You Traveled West in a Covered Wagon*, by

Ellen Levine; *The Josefina Story Quilt*, by Eleanor Coerr; *The Land of the Gray Wolf*, by Thomas Locker.

Also: *The Last Princess: The Story of Princess Ka'iulani of Hawai'i* (p); *Lewis and Clark: Explorers of the American West*, by Steven Kroll; *The Librarian Who Measured the World*, by Kathryn Lasky; *My Prairie Christmas*, by Brett Harvey; *Obadiah the Bold* and *Thy Friend Obadiah*, both by Brinton Turkle; *Old Bet and the Start of the American Circus*, by Robert McClung; *Peppe the Lamplighter*, by Elisa Bartone; *Pink and Say* (p); *Polar, the Titanic Bear*, by Daisy Spedden; *The Sign Painter's Dream* (p); *Thomas Jefferson: A Picture Book Biography*, by James Giblin; *Wagon Wheels* (p); and *Watch the Stars Come Out*, by Riki Levinson.

Captain Abdul's Pirate School
by Colin McNaughton
Candlewick, 1994   Gr. 1-5   32 pages

Hoping to toughen up their children, parents send them off to pirate school—something like a contemporary military or prep school. With great tongue-in-cheek humor (some of it scoundrel-crude), the kids shape up and then turn against the pirates. Other pirate books: *The Amazing Voyage of Jackie Grace* (p); *Andy's Pirate Ship*, by Philippe Dupasquier; *The Babies of Cockle Bay*, by Angela McAllister; *Maggie and the Pirate*, by Ezra Jack Keats; *Mary Mary*, by Sarah Hayes; *Maury and the Nightpirates*, by Dieter Wiesmuller; and *Pirate's Promise*, a short novel by Clyde Robert Bulla.

Captain Snap and the Children of Vinegar Lane
by Roni Schotter ✮ Illustrated by Marcia Sewall
Orchard, 1989   K-2   28 pages

Captain Snap is the frightening object of neighborhood children's curiosity and pranks. But when he suddenly falls ill, it is the children, led by the smallest and bravest of them, who come to his rescue. And it is then they discover that Captain Snap is really a gentle artist who creates art out of pieces of scrap. For related books on the elderly, see listing with *Old Mother Witch* (p).

A Chair for My Mother by Vera B. Williams
Greenwillow, 1982   K-3   30 pages

This is the first book in a trilogy of tender picture books about a family of three women: Grandma, Mama, and daughter Rosa (all written in the first person by the child). In this book, they struggle to save their loose change (in a glass jar) in order to buy a chair for the child's mother— something she can collapse into after her waitressing job. In *Something Special for Me*, the glass jar's contents are to be spent on the child's birthday present. What an important decision for a little girl to make! After much soul-searching, she settles on a used accordion. In *Music, Music for Everyone*, the jar is empty again. With all the loose change going for Grandma's medical expenses now, little Rosa searches for a way to make money and cheer up her grandma. Also by the author: *More, More, Said the Baby*; and *Stringbean's Trip to the Shining Sea*.

Related books with a gift theme: *The Best Present*, by Holly Keller; *The Country Bunny and the Little Gold Shoes*, by Du Bose Heyward; *Elijah's Angel: A Story for Chanukah and Christmas*, by Michael J. Rosen; *A Gift for Tia Rosa* (p); *The Lemon Drop Jar*, by Christine Widman; *The Magic Purse*, retold by Yoshiko Uchida; *Mr. Rabbit and the Lovely Present*, by Charlotte Zolotow; *The Polar Express*, by Chris Van Allsburg; *Santa Calls* (p); *What Goes Around Comes Around*, by Sally G. War; for older students: *A Gift for Mama*, a short novel by Esther Hautzig; and the story collection *The Witch of Fourth Street*, by Myron Levoy.

Charlie Drives the Stage
by Eric A. Kimmel ✿ Illustrated by Glen Rounds
Holiday, 1989   K–4   28 pages

When blustering Senator McCorkle can't find anyone willing to drive the stagecoach to his train station and risk the avalanches, bandits, Indians, and floodwaters, Charlie calmly takes the reins and saves the day. Only at the end do we discover that "Charlie" is short for Charlene! Also by the author: *Anansi and the Moss-Covered Rock*; *Anansi Goes Fishing*; *Asher and the Capmakers: A Hanukkah Story*; *Baba Yaga*; *The Chanukkah Guest*; *The Chanukkah Tree*; *Four Dollars and Fifty Cents*; *Hershel and the Hanukka Goblins*; *Nanny Goat and the Seven Little Kids*; *The Three Princes*; and *Three Sacks of Truth*.

Related books about heroines: *Airmail to the Moon*, by Tom Birdseye; *Annie & Co.*, by David McPhail; *The Crab Prince*, retold by Christopher Manson; *The Heroine of the Titanic*, by Joan W. Blos; *The Hunter*, by Paul Geraghty; *The Journey of Meng*, by Doreen Rappaport; *The Lighthouse Keeper's Daughter*, by Arielle North Olson; *The Little Jewel Box* (p); *Little Kit*, by Emily Arnold McCully; *Maggie and the Pirate*, by Ezra Jack Keats; *Matt's Mitt and Fleet-Footed Florence* (p); *My Great-Aunt Arizona*, by Gloria Houston; *Nice Little Girls*, by Elizabeth Levy; *Ride on the Red Mare's Back*, by Ursula K. Le Guin; *Rosie and the Rustlers*, by Roy Gerrard; *Ruth Law Thrills a Nation*, by Dob Brown; *The Samurai's Daughter* (p); *Swamp Angel*, by Anne Isaacs; *The Wild Swans*, retold by Deborah Hautzig; *Zerlada's Ogre*, by Tomi Ungerer; see also the listing with *The Maid of the North: Feminist Folk Tales from Around the World* (fa).

Chester's Way by Kevin Henkes

Greenwillow, 1988   Pre-S.-1   28 pages

In this celebration of childhood friendships, we meet two child-mice, Chester and Wilson, best friends who are exactly alike in everything they do. Then the irrepressible Lilly moves into the neighborhood. Chester and Wilson shun her—after all, she is not a *he!* But when she comes to their rescue, their chauvinistic ways begin to dissolve. Also by the author: *Owen* (p). Other books about mice: see listing with *Anatole* (p).

Cloudy with a Chance of Meatballs
by Judith Barrett ☆ Illustrated by Ron Barrett

Atheneum, 1978   Pre-S.-5   28 pages

In the fantasy land of Chewandswallow, the weather changes three times a day, supplying all the residents with food out of the sky. But suddenly the weather takes a turn for the worse; instead of normal size meatballs, it rains meatballs the size of basketballs; pancakes and syrup smother the streets. Something must be done! Also by the author: *Animals Should Definitely Not Act Like People*; *Animals Should Definitely Not Wear Clothing*; and *Benjamin's 365 Birthdays*. Related books: *Well, I Never!*, by Susan Pearson; see also listing with *Never Take a Pig to Lunch and Other Poems About the Fun of Food* (po).

The Complete Adventures of Peter Rabbit
by Beatrix Potter

Warne, 1982   Tod.-1   96 pages

Here in one volume are the four original tales involving one of the most famous animals of all time—Peter Rabbit. In a vicarious way children identify with his naughty sense of adventure, and then thrill at his narrow escape from the clutches of Mr. MacGregor. All twenty-three of the Potter books come in a small format (recently republished by Warne from the original artwork) that I think is ideal because young children feel more comfortable holding that size (3 inches by 5 inches). This larger volume is the most *economic* choice, while still retaining the Potter illustrations. For author profiles, see: *Hey! Listen to This* (a); the children's biography, *Beatrix Potter: The Story of the Creator of Peter Rabbit*, by Elizabeth Buchan; and Margaret Lane's excellent adult biography, *The Tale of Beatrix Potter*. Related book: *Rabbit Hill*, by Robert Lawson.

Corduroy by Don Freeman
Viking, 1968   Tod.-2   32 pages

The story of a teddy bear's search through a department store for a friend. His quest ends when a little girl buys him with her piggybank savings. Also by the author: *A Pocket for Corduroy*; *Beady Bear*; *Bearymore*; *Dandelion*; *Mop Top*; and *Norman the Doorman*. Related books: for other teddy bear or doll books, see *Ira Sleeps Over* (p).

Curious George by H. A. Rey
Houghton Mifflin, 1941   Pre-S.-1   48 pages

One of the classic figures in children's books, George is the funny little monkey whose curiosity gets the better of him and wins the hearts of his millions of fans. Among the more than twenty books in the series: *Curious George and the Dump Truck*; *Curious George Flies a Kite*; *Curious George Goes to a Restaurant*; *Curious George Goes to the Hospital*; *Curious George Learns the Alphabet*; *Curious George Plays Baseball*; and *Curious George Rides a Bike*. Also by the author: *Cecily G. and the Nine Monkeys*.

The Cut-Ups Cut Loose by James Marshall
Viking, 1987   K-2   30 pages

Armed with rubber snakes, spitballs, and stink bombs, Spud and Joe are the quintessential neighborhood and school cut-ups and every reader/listener will love their antics in battling Mr. Spurgle—who not only lives in their neighborhood but is their school principal too. Also in the series: *The Cut-Ups*; *The Cut-Ups at Camp Custer*; *The Cut-Ups Carry On*; *The Cut-Ups Crack Up*. Also by the author: *George and Martha* (series); *Space Case*; and these books written with Harry Allard: *Miss Nelson Is Missing* (p); *The Stupids Step Out*; *The Stupids Die*; *The Stupids Have a Ball*; and *The Stupids Take Off*.

Deep in the Forest by Brinton Turkle
Dutton, 1976   Pre-S.-2   30 pages

A wordless book reversing the conventional Goldilocks/Three Bears tale. This time the bear cub visits Goldilocks's family cabin, with hilarious and plausible results. Also by the author: *Thy Friend, Obadiah*; *Do Not Open*. For a list of other wordless books, see the list on page 229. Related books: *The Three Bears*, by Paul Galdone; *Goldilocks and the Three Bears*, by James Marshall; *Somebody and the Three Blairs*, by Marilyn Tolhurst; and for experienced listeners, a fairy tale parody, *Jeremiah in the Deep Woods*, by Allan Ahlberg. See also listing with *The True Story of the Three Little Pigs* (p).

Dinosaur Bob and His Adventures with the Family Lazardo by William Joyce

HarperCollins, 1988   Pre-S.-4   30 pages

In this dinosaur fantasy book, the Lazardo family brings a dinosaur home from Africa and it proves to be the ultimate pet for home and community—after some initial misgivings by the police department. Also by the author: *George Shrinks* and *Santa Calls* (p).

Here is a list of excellent dinosaur books (fiction and nonfiction): *An Alphabet of Dinosaurs*, by Peter Dodson and Wayne D. Barlowe; *The Dinosaur Question and Answer Book*, by Sylvia Funston; *The Big Beast Book: Dinosaurs and How They Got That Way*, by Jerry Booth; *The Big Book of Dinosaurs*, by Angela Wilkes; three books by Carol Carrick—*Big Old Bones: A Dinosaur Tale*; *Patrick's Dinosaurs*, and *What Happened to Patrick's Dinosaurs*; *Can I Have a Stegosaurus, Mom? Can I Please?*, by Lois G. Grambling; *Little Grunt and the Big Egg*, by Tomie dePaola; *Digging Up Dinosaurs*, by Aliki; *Digging Up Tyrannosaurus Rex*, by John R. Horner and Don Lessem; *Dinosaur Dream*, by Dennis Nolan; *If the Dinosaurs Came to Town*, by Dom Mansell; *The Last Dinosaur*, by Jim Murphy; *Mrs. Toggle and the Dinosaur*, by Robin Pulver; *Pernix: The Adventures of a Small Dinosaur*, by Dieter Wiesmuller; *Time Flies* (wordless), by Eric Rohmann; *Wackysaurus Dinosaur Jokes*, by Louis Phillips; *Why Did the Dinosaurs Disappear?*, by Dr. Philip Whitfield; and *Will's Mammoth*, by Rafe Martin.

Encounter
by Jane Yolen ☆ Illustrated by David Shannon

Harcourt Brace, 1992   Gr. 3-7   30 pages

In observance of the 500th anniversary of Columbus's arrival in the Western Hemisphere, Yolen views the arrival through the eyes of an Indian boy on San Salvador who has a foreboding dream about the newcomers. Portrayed in hauntingly beautiful illustrations, the boy's warnings are rejected by the tribe's elders. A brave and thought-provoking book on imperialism and colonialism. Also by the author: *Sleeping Ugly*; *Good Griselle* (p); and *Greyling* (p). For related titles: see listing with *The Sign of the Beaver* (n).

An Evening at Alfie's by Shirley Hughes
Morrow, 1985   Pre-S.-2   28 pages

This is the classic babysitter story, describing the excitement for little Alfie, his baby sister, and the babysitter on the night the water pipe burst. The series includes: *Alfie's Feet*; *Alfie Gets in First*; *Alfie Gives a Hand*; and the excellent chapter books on the family—*The Big Alfie and Annie Rose Storybook*, and *The Big Alfie Out of Doors Storybook*. Also by the author/illustrator: for toddlers—*Bathwater's Hot*; *All Shapes and Sizes*; *Colors*; *Noisy*; *Out and About*; *Two Shoes, New Shoes*; *When We Went to the Park*. For Pre-K and up: *Angel Mae*; *Dogger*; *Lucy and Tom's Christmas*; *Lucy and Tom's Day*; *The Snow Lady: A Tale of Trotter Street*; *Up and Up* (wordless). For grades 1–3: *Stories by Firelight*.

Frederick by Leo Lionni
Random House, 1967   Pre-S. and up   28 pages

Frederick is a tiny gray field mouse. He is also an allegorical figure representing the poets, artists, and dreamers of the world. While his brothers and sisters gather food against the oncoming winter, Frederick gathers the colors and stories and dreams they will need to sustain their hearts and souls in the winter darkness. Also by the author: *Alexander and the Wind-Up Mouse*; *The Biggest House in the World*; *Fish Is Fish*; *Frederick's Fables: A Leo Lionni Treasury of Favorite Stories*; *Little Blue and Little Yellow*; *Nicholas, Where Have You Been?*; *Swimmy*; *Tillie and the Wall*. For other mice books, see listing under *Anatole* (p).

Frog and Toad Are Friends by Arnold Lobel
HarperCollins, 1970   Pre-S.-2   64 pages

Using a simple early-reader vocabulary and fablelike story lines, the author-artist developed an award-winning series that is a must for young children. Generous helpings of humor and warm personal relationships are the trademarks of the series, each book containing five individual stories relating to childhood. Few author/illustrators sustain as high a quality of work through so many books as did Arnold Lobel. Sequels: *Days with Frog and Toad*; *Frog and Toad All Year*; *Frog and Toad Together*. Also by the author: *Fables*; *Giant John*; *Grasshopper on the Road*; *The Great Blueness and Other Predicaments*; *Gregory Griggs and*

Other Nursery Rhyme People; *Mouse Soup*; *Mouse Tales*; *Owl at Home*; *Uncle Elephant*; and *Whiskers and Rhymes.*

George Washington: A Picture Book Biography
by James Cross Giblin
Scholastic, 1992   Gr. 1-4   40 pages

Magnificently illustrated on large pages, this is an excellent early introduction to biography, written simply but rich with information and anecdote. Giblin is one of the better nonfiction writers for children. See listing with *By the Dawn's Early Light* (p) for an extensive listing of other picture books with historical themes; see *The Day It Rained Forever* (s) for short historical novels.

A Gift for Tia Rosa
by Karen T. Taha ☆ Illustrated by Dee deRosa
Bantam, 1991   K-4   36 pages

Carmela's elderly Hispanic neighbor, Tia Rosa, is teaching her how to knit. Carmela loves her dearly and is grief-stricken when the woman dies. As saddened as she is by the loss, Carmela is even sadder because she didn't have a chance to tell her how much she loved her. And then she discovers a way. A sensitive example of families and neighbors supporting each other in times of loss. Other picture books treating death and loss include: *The Accident*, by Carol Carrick; *The Big Red Barn*, by Eve Bunting; *Everett Anderson's Goodbye*, by Lucille Clifton; *Harry's Mom*, by Barbara Ann Porte; *I Had a Friend Named Peter*, by Janice Cohn; *I'll Always Love You*, by Hans Wilhelm; *I'll See You in My Dreams*, by Mavis Jukes; *My Grandson Lew*, by Charlotte Zolotow; *Nana Upstairs & Nana Downstairs*, by Tomie dePaola; *Remember the Butterflies*, by Anna Grossnickle Hines; *Saying Goodbye to Grandma*, by Jane Resh Thomas; *The Tenth Good Thing About Barney*, by Judith Viorst; *When I Die, Will I Get Better?*, by Joeri and Piet Breebaart; for older students, see the novels listed with *A Taste of Blackberries* (s).

Other books with Hispanic characters or settings: *Baseball in April* (s); *Borreguita and the Coyote*, by Verna Aardema; *El Güero* (s); *The Poppy Seeds* (p); *The Sleeping Bread*, by Stefan Czernecki and Timothy Rhodes; *The Song of el Coqui and Other Tales of Puerto Rico*, by Nicholasa Mohr and Antonio Martorell; *The Tale of Rabbit and Coyote* and *The Iguana Brothers*, both by Tony Johnson; *The Three Little Javelinas*, by Susan Lowell; and *Treasure Nap*, by Juanita Hill.

Good Griselle
by Jane Yolen ✱ Illustrated by David Christiana
Harcourt, Brace, 1994   Gr. 2 and up   42 pages

The evil gargoyles atop the cathedral overhear the stone angels singing the praises of a good woman. They make a bet with the angels that as great as her goodness might be, it could not bring her to cherish an ugly, unlovable child. The story is dramatic, sacred, enchanting, and poetic in its scope, with hauntingly majestic illustrations. Also by the author: *Greyling* (p).

Goodnight Moon
by Margaret Wise Brown ✱ Illustrated by Clement Hurd
HarperCollins, 1947   Tod.–Pre-S.   30 pages

A classic tale based upon the bedtime ritual, sure to be copied by every child who hears it. Also by the author: *The Important Book*; *The Runaway Bunny*; and *Sailor Dog*. Related bedtime books for infants and toddlers: *Before I Go to Sleep*, by Thomas Hood; *Can't You Sleep, Little Bear?*, by Martin Waddell; *Go to Sleep, Nicholas Joe*, by Marjorie Weinman Sharmat; *Good Night, Gorilla*, by Peggy Rathmann; *The Goodnight Kiss*, by Jim Aylesworth; *Goodnight, Goodnight*, by Eve Rice; *I Can't Sleep*, by Philippe Dupasquier; *In the Night Kitchen*, by Maurice Sendak; *Is It Time?*, by Marilyn Janovitz; *Max's Bedtime*, by Rosemary Wells; *Moonlight*, by Jan Ormerod; *The Napping House* (p); *Night Cars*, by Teddy Jam; *Outside the Window*, by Anna Egan Smucker; *The Sandman*, by Rob Shepperson; *Sleep Well, Little Bear*, by Quint Bucchholz; and *Ten, Nine, Eight*, by Molly Bang. For older children, see *Ira Sleeps Over* (p).

Grandaddy's Place
by Helen Griffith ✱ Illustrated by James Stevenson
Greenwillow, 1987   K–3   36 pages

On her first visit to her grandaddy's rural Georgia cabin, a young city girl is frightened by its strangeness. Soon, however, the old man's quiet charm begins to work its magic and a new world opens for the child. The book is divided into short, six-page chapters. Sequels: *Georgia Music*; *Grandaddy and Janetta*.

Other grandparent books: *Always Gramma*, by Vaunda Nelson; *The Always Prayer Shawl*, by Sheldon Oberman; *The Best Present*, by Holly Keller; *Bigmama's*, by Donald Crews; *The Crack-of-Dawn Walkers*, by Amy Hest; *Doesn't Fall Off His Horse*, by Virginia A. Stroud; *Emma*, by

Wendy Kesselman; *Grandad's Magic*, by Bob Graham; *The Grandma Mix-up*, by Emily McCully; *Grandma's House*, by Elaine Moore; *Grandma's Promise*, by Elaine Moore; *Grandma's Secret* (p); *Grandpa's Song*, by Tony Johnston; *Grandpappy*, by Nancy White Carlstrom; *Granny Is a Darling*, by Kady MacDonald Denton; *Knots on a Counting Rope*, by Bill Martin Jr. and John Archambaul; *The Go-Between*, *The Midnight Eaters* (p), *Nana's Birthday Party*, *The Purple Coat*, and *Weekend Girl*, all five by Amy Hest; *Music, Music for Everyone*, by Vera B. Williams; *Not the Piano, Mrs. Medley* (p); *Oma and Bobo*, by Amy Schwartz; *Song and Dance Man*, by Karen Ackerman; *Tales of a Gambling Grandma*, by Dayal Kaur Khalsa; *Tom*, by Tomie dePaola; *The Wednesday Surprise*, by Eve Bunting; *What's Under My Bed?* (p); *When Grandma Came*, by Jill Paton Walsh; *When Grandpa Kissed His Elbow*, by Cynthia DeFelice; *When I Was Scared*, by Helena Clare Pittman; *When I Was Your Age*, by Ken Adams and Val Biro; *Where Does the Sky End, Grandpa?*, by Martha Alexander; *William and Grandpa*, by Alice Schertle; *The Wooden Doll*, by Susan Bonners. See also these novels: *Anna, Grandpa, and the Big Storm*, by Carla Stevens; *My Grandmother's Stories: A Collection of Jewish Folk Tales* (s); *Stone Fox* (s); and *The War with Grandpa*, by Robert K. Smith.

Grandma's Secret
by Paulette Bourgeois ☆ Illustrated by Maryann Kovalski
Little, Brown, 1990   Pre-S.-3   28 pages

A young boy dearly loves his grandmother and their visits together. The only problem is the "bear" that his grandmother says lives in the basement. Related imaginary monster books: *Harry and the Terrible Whatszit*, by Dick Gackenbach; *Donovan Scares the Monster*, by Susan Love Whitlock; *Granny Is a Darling*, by Kady MacDonald Denton; *Monster Mama*, by Liz Rosenberg; *The Real-Skin Rubber Monster Mask*, by Miriam Cohen; *Spooky Poems*, collected by Jill Bennett; *There's a Nightmare in My Closet*, by Mercer Mayer; and *Zerlada's Ogre*, by Tomi Ungerer.

Greyling
by Jane Yolen ☆ Illustrated by David Ray
Philomel, 1991   Gr. 2-4   32 pages

A childless couple takes in an orphaned seal pup, only to discover it is a selkie—a seal in water, a boy on land. They raise him on land, determined to keep him there forever. Then the father is lost at sea; only the boy can rescue him. Also by the author: *The Emperor and the Kite*; *Encounter* (p); *The Faery Flag*; *Favorite Folktales from Around the World* (fa); *Good Griselle* (p); *Honkers*; *Letting Swift River Go*; *Owl Moon*; *Sleeping Ugly*. Related changeling books: *Arnold of the Ducks* (p); *The Boy Who Lived with the Seals* (p); *The Crane Wife*, retold by Katherine Paterson; *Dawn*, by Molly Bang; *Mermaid Tales from Around the World*, retold by Mary Pope Osborne; *The Selkie Girl*, by Susan Cooper; *Sukey and the Mermaid*, by Robert D. San Souci; for older children, *The Animal Family* (n); and *A Stranger Came Ashore* (n).

Gulliver's Adventures in Lilliput
by Jonathan Swift, retold by Ann Keay Beneduce ☆ Illustrated
by Gennady Spirin
Philomel, 1993   Gr. 2 and up   32 pages

Here is an abbreviated children's version of Swift's classic visit to the Lilliputians, retaining much of his adventure and insight. And surely there were never better illustrations to match the story's fantasy.

Harald and the Great Stag by Donald Carrick
Clarion, 1988   K–4   32 pages

When young Harald hears the Baron's huntsmen plan to hunt and kill the Great Stag, the boy purposely leads their dogs astray, only to find himself hunted instead. This story and its companion, *Harald and the Giant Knight*, bring to life the drama of the Middle Ages. For other Carrick books, see *Sleepout* (p). Related deer book: *The Deer in the Hollow*, by Efner Tudor Holmes. Books on the Middle Ages: *The Hero of Bremen* and *Kitchen Knight: A Tale of King Arthur*, both retold by Margaret Hodges; *King Arthur and the Legends of Camelot*, retold by Molly Perham; *The Middle Ages*, by Sarah Howarth; *The Reluctant Dragon* (s); *Robin Hood: His Life and Legend*, by Bernard Miles; *Stephen Biesty's Cross-Sections Castle*; and *Young Merlin*, by Robert D. San Souci. For more experienced listeners: *Otto of the Silver Hand* (n).

Harry in Trouble
by Barbara Ann Porte ☆ Illustrated by Yossi Abolafia
Greenwillow, 1989   K–2   48 pages

This "Harry" easy-reader series is about people as real as the folks next door—grade-schooler Harry, his widower father, and their relatives, neighbors, friends, and teachers. In this book, Harry loses his library card for the third time. Also in the series: *Harry's Dog*; *Harry's Mom*; *Harry Gets an Uncle*; and *Harry's Visit*.

Harry the Dirty Dog
by Gene Zion ✭ Illustrated by Margaret B. Graham
HarperCollins, 1956   Tod.-2   28 pages

This little white dog with black spots just might be one of the most famous dogs in children's literature. All children identify with Harry— partly for his size, partly for his aversion to soap and water, partly for his escapades. Sequels: *Harry and the Lady Next Door*; *Harry by the Sea*; and *No Roses for Harry*. Related books: *Benjy and His Friend Fifi*, by Margaret Bloy Graham; and *Curious George* (p).

Haunted House Jokes
by Louis Phillips ✭ Illustrated by James Marshall
Viking, 1987   K-5   57 pages

Joke books give beginning readers a sense of both accomplishment and satisfaction: From the joke-meister himself, here's a wonderful collection of horror-ible jokes, knock-knocks, and riddles about vampires, ghosts, werewolves, Frankenstein, skeletons, and mummies. Example: What do ghosts drink in the summer? Ghoul-ade! Also by the author: *How Do You Get a Horse Out of the Bathtub?*; *Invisible Oink*; *School Daze: Jokes Your Teacher Will Hate!*; and *Wackysaurus Dinosaur Jokes*. Other popular joke books: Bennett Cerf's three books—*Bennett Cerf's Book of Animal Riddles*, *Bennett Cerf's Book of Laughs*, and *Bennett Cerf's Book of Riddles*; Joan Eckstein's and Joyce Gleit's two super joke books—*The Best Joke Book for Kids* and *The Best Joke Book for Kids #2*; *Buggy Riddles*, by Katy Hall and Lisa Eisenberg; *The Carsick Zebra and Other Animal Riddles*, by David Adler; *Grizzly Riddles*, by Katy Hall and Lisa Eisenberg; and *Halloween Howls: Riddles That Are a Scream*, by Giulio Maestro.

Heckedy Peg
by Audrey Wood ✭ Illustrated by Don Wood
Harcourt Brace, 1987   K-5   30 pages

A determined mother outsmarts a witch who has captured and bewitched her seven children. Also by the author: See listing with *The Napping House* (p). Related books: *A Special Trick*, by Mercer Mayer; *The Whingdingdilly* (p); *The Pumpkinville Mystery*, by Bruce Cole; and *The Widow's Broom*, by Chris Van Allsburg.

Henry Bear's Park by David McPhail
Little, Brown, 1976   Gr. 1–5   48 pages

When Henry Bear's well-to-do father leaves suddenly on a ballooning adventure, he leaves Henry in charge of his newly purchased park. Henry, feeling the importance of filling in for his father, moves into the park as superintendent and excels in the position until the loneliness for his father begins to wear him down. Also by the author: *Andrew's Bath*; *The Bear's Toothache*; *Ed and Me*; *Fix-It*; *Lost!*; *Moony B. Finch, the Fastest Draw in the West*; *The Party*; *Pig Pig Gets a Job*; *Santa's Book of Names*; *Something Special*; and *The Train*. Related father books: *Daddy-Care*, by Allen Morgan; *David's Father*, by Robert Munsch; *Dear Daddy*, by Philippe Dupasquier; *A Father Like That*, by Charlotte Zolotow; *The Year of the Perfect Christmas Tree*, by Gloria Houston; for older children: *My Father's Dragon* (s).

Hershel and the Hanukkah Goblins
by Eric A. Kimmel ✴ Illustrated by Trina Schart Hyman
Holiday, 1989   Gr. 1–5   30 pages

When wicked goblins haunt an old synagogue and prevent the townspeople from celebrating Hanukkah, a clever visitor, yearning for the menorah candles, potato latkes, and merriment of the holidays, offers to break the goblins' spell by outwitting them. Caution: Trina Hyman's goblin illustrations will enchant older children, but use them cautiously with impressionable younger children. Also by the author: *Asher and the Capmakers: A Hanukkah Story*; *The Chanukkah Tree*; *Charlie Drives the Stage* (p); and *The Spotted Pony: A Collection of Hanukkah Stories*. Other Hanukkah books: *In the Month of Kislev: A Story for Hanukkah*, by Nina Jaffe; *Latkes and Applesauce*, by Fran Manushkin; and *The Power of Light*, by Isaac B. Singer.

The House on East 88th Street
by Bernard Waber
Houghton Mifflin, 1962   Pre-S.–3   48 pages

When the Primm family discovers a gigantic crocodile in the bathtub of their new brownstone home, it signals the beginning of a wonderful picture-book series. As soon as the Primms overcome their fright, they see him as your children will—as the most lovable and human of crocodiles. Sequels (in this order): *Lyle, Lyle, Crocodile*; *Lyle and the Birthday Party*; *Lyle Finds His Mother*; *Lovable Lyle*; *Funny, Funny Lyle*; and *Lyle at the Office*. Also by the author: *Ira Sleeps Over* (p). Related books:

Amos: The Story of an Old Dog and His Couch (p); *Dial-A-Croc*, by Mike Dumbleton; *Joshua and Bigtooth*, by Mark Childress; *Zack's Alligator*, by Shirley Mozelle; and Bill Peet books listed with *The Whingding-dilly* (p).

The Hunter by Paul Geraghty

Crown, 1994   Pre-S.-3   26 pages

A lost African girl, finding a baby elephant orphaned by poachers, leads it safely past dangers in the bush to another herd. Along the way, she loses her ambition to become a hunter. Related books: *Jumanji*, by Chris Van Allsburg; *The Gnats of Knotty Pine*, by Bill Peet; *The Magic Finger*, by Roald Dahl; *Polly Vaughn*, by Barry Moser; and *Tiger*, by Judy Allen.

I Can! Can You? by Peggy Parrish

Greenwillow, 1980   Tod.   10 pages

This is one in a series (See and Do Books) that stimulates a baby's language, motor, and social skills though activities suggested by the text. For example, in this book multi-ethnic children are pictured touching toes, wiggling fingers, sticking out tongues—and the child is asked if he can do that activity. All the books in the series have the same title, the difference being a "level" number (1–4) on the cover that refers to the child's maturity level.

Here is a list of toddler books that relate to physical and intellectual concepts children learn best at home in someone's lap:

Labeling their environment—*The Baby's Catalogue*, by Janet and Allan Ahlberg; *Come to Town*, by Anne Rockwell; *Jesse Bear, What Will You Wear?* by Nancy W. Carlstrom; *The First Words Picture Book*, by Bill Gillham; *Three Hundred (300) First Words*, photographed by Geoff Dann; and *Puffin First Picture Dictionary*, by Brian Thompson.

Opposites—*Fast-Slow High-Low*, by Peter Spier; *Here a Chick, There a Chick*, by Bruce McMillan; *Push Pull, Empty Full*, by Tana Hoban.

Colors and counting—*Counting Wildflowers*, and *Growing Color*, by Bruce McMillan; *Ten, Nine, Eight*, by Molly Bang.

Other toddler books: *Spot Looks at Colors*; *Spot Looks at Shapes*; and *Spot's Big Book of Words*, all three by Eric Hill; and these books by Shirley Hughes: *Bathwater's Hot*; *All Shapes and Sizes*; *Bouncing*; *Chatting*; *Colors*; *Giving*; *Hiding*; *Noisy*; *Out and About*; *Two Shoes, New Shoes*; and *When We Went to the Park*; see also listing with *Tom and Pippo Make a Friend* (p); and *Miffy* (p).

I'm a Little Mouse by Noelle and David Carter
Holt, 1991   Inf.-Pre-S.   12 pages

Patterned on the touch-and-feel concepts of Dorothy Kunhardt's *Pat the Bunny*, this book focuses on a mouse instead of a family (thus no ethnic group is ignored). As the mouse meets neighboring creatures, the child reader is invited to touch the textured pages. Related books: *Baby Face: A Mirror Book*, by Gwynne L. Isaacs and Evelyn Clarke Mott; *Kiss the Boo-Boo*, by Sue Tarsky; and *Where's Spot?* (p).

If You Give a Mouse a Cookie
by Laura Joffe Numeroff ☆ Illustrated by Felicia Bond
HarperCollins, 1985   Pre-S.-K   30 pages

In a funny cumulative tale that comes full circle, a little boy offers a mouse a cookie and ends up working his head off for the demanding little creature. Sequel: *If You Give a Moose a Muffin*. For related mouse books, see *Anatole* (p). Related books: See Predictable/Cumulative books listed on page 231.

Ira Sleeps Over by Bernard Waber
Houghton Mifflin, 1972   K-6   48 pages

This is a warm, sensitive, and funny look at a boy's overnight visit to his best friend's house, centering on the child's quandary whether or not to bring along his teddy bear. It makes for lively discussion about individual sleeping habits, peer pressure, and the things we all hold on to—even as grown-ups. In the sequel, *Ira Says Goodbye*, two best friends experience a dreaded childhood pain when Reggie moves away. Waber is also the author of the popular Lyle the Crocodile series that begins with *The House on East 88th Street* (p).

Related books about teddy bears or dolls: *Aki and the Fox*, by Akiko Hayashi; *Babushka's Doll*, by Patricia Polacco; *A Big Day for Little Jack*, by Inga Moore; *Chaska and the Golden Doll*, by Ellen Alexander; *Corduroy* (p); *The Cottage at the End of the Lane*, by Elaine Mills; *Dogger*, by Shirley Hughes; *Good as New*, by Barbara Douglass; *Humphrey's Bear*, by Jan Wahl; *It's the Bear!* and *Where's My Teddy?*, both by Jez Alborough; *Jenny's Bear*, by Michael Ratnett; *The Legend of the Bluebonnet* (p); *Mama Bear*, by Chyng Feng Sun; *Owen* (p); *The Red Woolen Blanket*, by Bob Graham; *Sleep Well, Little Bear*, by Quint Bucchholz; *Theodore* and *Theodore's Rival*, both by Edward Ormondroyd; *This Is the Bear*, by Sarah Hayes; *Tom and Pippo Make a Friend* (p); *Where's My Monkey?*, by Dieter Schubert; *William's Doll* (p); *The Wooden Doll,* by Susan Bonners; and for older children—*Polar: The Titanic Bear*, by Daisy C.S. Spedden.

Highly recommended: the award-winning CD/cassette *Unbearable Bears* by Kevin Roth (Marlboro Records, P.O. Box 808, Unionville, PA 19375) for a collection of favorite teddy bear songs.

The Island of the Skog by Steven Kellogg
Dial, 1973   Pre-S.-2   32 pages
Sailing away from city life, a boatload of mice discover the island of their dreams, only to be pulled up short by the appearance of a fearful monster already dwelling on the island. How imaginations can run away with us and how obstacles can be overcome if we'll just talk with others are central issues in this tale. Also by the author, four retellings of American legends: *Johnny Appleseed*; *Mike Fink*; *Paul Bunyan*; and *Pecos Bill*; also *Best Friends*; *Can I Keep Him?*; *The Christmas Witch*; *The Mysterious Tadpole*; *The Mystery of the Missing Red Mitten*; *Pinkerton, Behave!*; *Prehistoric Pinkerton*; *A Rose for Pinkerton*; *Ralph's Secret Weapon*; and *Tallyho, Pinkerton!*

Jack and the Beanstalk retold by John Howe
Little, Brown, 1989   K-3   30 pages
The classic tale of a boy's battle to outwit the giant atop the beanstalk is retold and illustrated magnificently here with the ultimate in ferocious giants. A tongue-in-cheek sequel can be found in *Jim and the Beanstalk*, by Raymond Briggs. Other giant stories: *Christopher: The Holy Giant*, by Tomie dePaola; *David and Goliath*, adapted by Leonard Everett Fisher; *David's Father*, by Robert Munsch; *The Dragon, Giant, and Monster Treasury*, selected by Caroline Royds; *Giant John*, by Arnold Lobel; *The Good Giants and the Bad Pukwudgies*, by Jean Fritz; *Harald and the Giant Knight*, by Donald Carrick; *The Iron Giant* (s); and *Mary Mary*, by Sarah Hayes.

Jumbo the Boy and Arnold the Elephant
by Dan Greenberg ✫ Illustrated by Susan Perl
HarperCollins, 1989   K-3   48 pages
In a variation on "The Ugly Duckling," a baby boy is accidentally switched with a baby elephant in the hospital nursery. The results are both touching and hilarious before everyone is reunited with the proper parents. Also by the author: *Young Santa* (s).

Katy and the Big Snow by Virginia Lee Burton
Houghton Mifflin, 1973   Pre-S.–2   40 pages

One of the few things that technology has not turned into an antique is the perennial snowplow. This is the little classic about a brave, untiring tractor whose round-the-clock snowplowing saves the blizzard-bound city of Geoppolis. As much as this is the story of persistence, it is also a lesson in civics, as Katy assists the local authorities in pursuing their duties. After reading this story, try Franklyn Branley's *Snow Is Falling*. For other books by the author, see listing with *Mike Mulligan and His Steam Shovel* (p). Related snow books: *Anna, Grandpa, and the Big Storm*, by Carla Stevens; *Grandma's Promise*, by Elaine Moore; *One Snowy Night*, by Nick Butterworth; *The Snowman Who Went for a Walk*, by Mira Lobe; *Snow Company*, by Marc Harshman; *Snow Day*, by Betsy Maestro; *The Snow Lady: A Tale of Trotter Street*, by Shirley Hughes; *The Snowman*, by Raymond Briggs; *A Snowy Day*, by Ezra Jack Keats; *Something Is Going to Happen*, by Charlotte Zolotow; *Up North in Winter*, by Deborah Hartley; and *White Snow Bright Snow*, by Alvin Tresselt.

Ladder to the Sky retold by Barbara Juster Esbensen
Little, Brown, 1989   Gr. 1–5   30 pages

Based upon a Chippewa Indian legend, this tale recounts an Indian nation's fall from grace when it displeases the Great Spirit by climbing the forbidden magic vine to the heavens. While the Great Spirit punishes the tribe with ills never before known, he tempers the suffering by teaching them the secrets of herbal medicines. Interesting parallels can be drawn between this and the Bible stories of Adam and Eve's fall, as well as the Tower of Babel.

Other American Indian tales: *Annie and the Old One*, by Miska Miles; *The Boy Who Lived with the Seals* (p); *Doesn't Fall Off His Horse*, by Virginia A. Stroud; *The First Strawberries: A Cherokee Story*, by Joseph Bruchac; *The Good Giants and the Bad Pukwudgies*, by Jean Fritz; *The Great Buffalo Race*, retold by Barbara Juster Ebensen; *How Rabbit Stole the Fire*, by Joanna Troughton; *Knots on a Counting Rope*, by Bill Martin, Jr., and John Archambault; *The Legend of the Bluebonnet* (p); *The Rough-Face Girl*, by Rafe Martin; *Tonweya and the Eagles and Other Lakota Tales*, by Rosebud Yellow Robe; *Uncle Smoke Stories: Nehawka Tales of Coyote the Trickster*, by Roger Welsch; *Where the Buffaloes Begin*, by Olaf Baker; *USKids History: Book of the American Indians*, by Marlene Smith-Baranzini and Howard Egger-Bovet. See also the Indian tales by Paul Goble: *Crow Chief*; *Death of the Iron Horse*; *Dream Wolf*; *The Girl*

Who Loved Wild Horses; *Iktomi and the Berries*; *Iktomi and the Boulder*; *Iktomi and the Buzzard*; *Iktomi and the Ducks*; *The Lost Children*; *Love Flute*; and *Star Boy*.

The Last Princess: The Story of Princess Ka'iulani of Hawai'i by Fay Stanley ☆ Illustrated by Diane Stanley

Simon & Schuster, 1991   Gr. 2-6   36 pages

The story of the last princess is also the story of America's last state —Hawaii. It is a tragic but important story, showing the proud heritage of the Hawaiian people and one of America's dark historical chapters. Related book: *Encounter* (p). For other historical picture books, see listing with *By the Dawn's Early Light* (p).

The Legend of the Bluebonnet retold by Tomie dePaola

Putnam, 1984   Pre-S.-4   30 pages

Here is the legend behind the bluebonnets that blanket the state of Texas—the story of the little Comanche Indian orphan who sacrificed her only doll in order to end the drought that was ravaging her village. Related book by the author: *The Legend of the Indian Paintbrush*. For other titles relating to American Indians, see listing with *Ladder to the Sky* (p). Tomie dePaola is one of America's most beloved and prolific author/illustrators. His books often deal with the human spirit and are marked by rambunctious humor and warmth. Among his works featuring old legends or retellings: *Big Anthony and the Magic Ring*; *The Clown of God*; *Fin M'Coul*; *Francis: The Poor Man of Assisi*; *The Friendly Beasts*; *Helga's Dowry*; *Jamie O'Rourke and the Big Potato: An Irish Folktale*; *The Knight and the Dragon*; *The Legend of Old Befana*; *The Legend of the Poinsettia*; *Little Grunt and the Big Egg*; *The Prince of the Dolomites*; *Strega Nona*; *Strega Nona Meets Her Match*; and *Strega Nona's Magic Lessons*. Many of his books are autobiographical or based upon the lives of his relatives, including: *The Art Lesson*; *Nana Upstairs & Nana Downstairs*; *Now One Foot, Now the Other*; and *Tom*. His other books include: *The Comic Adventures of Old Mother Hubbard and Her Dog*; *Little Grunt and the Big Egg: A Prehistoric Fairy Tale*; *The Night Before Christmas*; *Oliver Button Is a Sissy*; *Pancakes for Breakfast*; *Tomie dePaola's Book of Bible Stories*; *Tomie dePaola's Mother Goose*; *Tony's Bread*; and *Watch Out for the Chicken Feet in Your Soup*.

Lester's Dog
by Karen Hesse ☆ Illustrated by Nancy Carpenter
Crown, 1993   K–4   30 pages

In rescuing a stray kitten, a young boy and his deaf playmate face down a fierce neighborhood dog and help a heartbroken old man. Related books: *Blumpoe the Grumpoe Meets Arnold the Cat*, by Jean Davies Okimoto; *The Foundling*, by Carol Carrick; and *Uglypuss*, by Caroline Gregoire.

Little Bear
by Else Holmelund Minarik ☆ Illustrated by Maurice Sendak
HarperCollins, 1957   Pre-S.–1   54 pages

This series of books uses the simple but important elements of a child's life (clothes, birthdays, playing, and wishing) to weave poignant little stories about a child-bear and his family. The series has won numerous awards and is regarded as a classic. A former first-grade teacher, the author uses a limited vocabulary at no sacrifice to the flavor of the story. The series includes: *Little Bear*; *A Kiss for Little Bear*; *Father Bear Comes Home*; *Little Bear's Friend*; *Little Bear's Visit.* Also by the author: *No Fighting, No Biting!* Another outstanding bear series is by Frank Asch: *Bear's Bargain*; *Bear Shadow*; *Goodbye House*; *Happy Birthday, Moon*; *Mooncake*; *Moondance*; *Popcorn*; *Sand Cake*; and *Skyfire.* See also Martha Alexander's *Blackboard Bear* books.

The Little Dog Laughed and Other Nursery Rhymes
from Mother Goose
Illustrated by Lucy Cousins
Dutton, 1989   Inf.–Pre-S.   64 pages

Brightly illustrated in primary colors with boldly outlined images (of multi-ethnic characters), this collection of sixty-four Mother Goose rhymes is especially easy for infants and toddlers to view. Other Mother Goose collections include: *Ring-A-Round-A-Rosy*, by Priscilla Lamont; *Michael Foreman's Mother Goose*; *The New Adventures of Mother Goose: Gentle Rhymes for Happy Times*, by Bruce Lansky; *Nick Butterworth's Book of Nursery Rhymes*; *Nicola Bayley's Book of Nursery Rhymes*; *The Random House Book of Mother Goose* and *Whiskers and Rhymes*, both illustrated by Arnold Lobel; and *Tomie dePaola's Mother Goose.*

A Little Excitement
by Marc Harshman ☆ Illustrated by Ted Rand
Dutton, 1989   Gr. 1-4   28 pages

Even though his grandmother has cautioned him against wishing for things he might not be prepared for, young Willie wishes for a little excitement to break the monotony of winter farm days. His wish comes true when his father makes a mistake in banking the stove one night, setting the house afire. The excitement of helping family and neighbors fight the fire isn't quite what Willie had in mind, but it makes for both a touching and exciting story. Ted Rand's watercolors bring to life the frigid winter night and family warmth in an unforgettable fashion. Also by the author: *Snow Company*; *The Storm*; and *Uncle James*. Related picture books about wishes: *Jenny's Bear*, by Michael Ratnett; *Just a Dream*, by Chris Van Allsburg; *The Magic Paintbrush* (p); *The Rainbabies*, by Laura Krauss Melmed; *Shorty Takes Off* (p); *Treehorn's Wish*, by Florence Parry Heide; *The Whingdingdilly* (p); *The Wish Card Ran Out*, by James Stevenson; for older students, *The Wish Giver* (n).

The Little House by Virginia Lee Burton
Houghton Mifflin, 1942   Pre-S.-3   40 pages

This Caldecott Medal winner uses a little turn-of-the-century house to show the urbanization of America. With each page, the reader/listener becomes the little house and experiences the contentment, wonder, concern, anxiety, and loneliness that the passing seasons and encroaching city bring. Many of today's children who daily experience the anxieties of city life will identify with the little house and her eventual triumph. Other books by the author: see *Mike Mulligan and His Steam Shovel* (p). Related books: *Farewell to Shady Glade* and *Wump World*, by Bill Peet; *For the Birds*, by Margaret Atwood; *Just a Dream*, by Chris Van Allsburg; *The Lorax*, by Dr. Seuss; *The Mountain That Loved a Bird*, by Alice McLerran; *Pearl Moscowitz's Last Stand*, by Arthur A. Levine; and *Tattie's River Journey*, by Shirley Murphy.

The Little Jewel Box
by Marianna Mayer ☆ Illustrated by Margot Tomes
Dial, 1986   K-4   30 pages

In this feminist fairy tale, a plucky heroine sets out to seek her fortune, while included in her baggage is a bad-luck cake and a good-luck jewel box. Both play a prominent role in her intrepid, humorous, and very satisfying adventures with a passive "prince" and his scheming father.

Related book: *The Lucky Stone*, by Lucille Clifton. Related heroine books: see listing with *Charlie Drives the Stage* (p).

Little Red Riding Hood retold by Trina Schart Hyman
Holiday, 1983   Pre-S.-3   32 pages

It's hard to imagine a better illustrated version of this famous tale. The artist has given us a child and grandma who are every child and grandmother and a texture so rich you can almost smell the woods. Other versions of Little Red Riding Hood: *Flossie and the Fox*, by Patricia McKissack (African-American version); *The Gunnywolf*, retold by A. Delaney; *Liza Lou and the Yeller Belly Swamp*, by Mercer Mayer, *Lon Po Po*, by Ed Young; and *Ruby*, by Michael Emberley. See also *Jeremiah in the Deep Woods*, by Allan Ahlberg.

Little Tim and the Brave Sea Captain by Edward Ardizzone
Puffin, 1983   K-2   46 pages

Set near an English seaside village, this exciting series by a master illustrator and author combines a sense of drama with warm stories of courage and friendship at sea. The sequels (all published by Oxford in paperback only) should be read in this order: *Tim and Charlotte*; *Tim in Danger*; *Tim All Alone*; *Tim's Friend Towser*; *Tim and Ginger*; and *Tim to the Lighthouse*.

Madeline by Ludwig Bemelmans
Viking, 1939   K-3   30 pages

This series of six marvelous books is about a daring and irrepressible personality named Madeline and her eleven friends, who all live together in a house in Paris. The author's use of fast-moving verse, daring adventure, naughtiness, and glowing color keep it a favorite in early grades year after year. Other books in the series: *Madeline and the Bad Hat*; *Madeline and the Gypsies*; *Madeline in London*; *Madeline's Rescue*; and *Madeline's Christmas*. Related books: *The Three Robbers* (p) and *Zerlada's Ogre*, both by Tomi Ungerer.

The Magic Paintbrush by Robin Muller
Viking, 1990   Gr. 1-5   32 pages

Nib is an illiterate street orphan with the ambition but not the money to become a great artist. When he comes to the aid of an old man being robbed in an alleyway, he is rewarded with a magic paintbrush that will bring to life whatever he paints. Related books: *Dawn* and *Tye May and the Magic Brush*, both by Molly Bang; *The Art Lesson*, by Tomie dePaola; *The Boy Who Drew Cats*, retold by Arthur A. Levine; *Emma*, by Wendy Kesselman; *The Legend of Slappy Hooper*, retold by Aaron Shepard; *Monsters*, by Russell Hoban; *Moony B. Finch, the Fastest Draw in the West*, by David McPhail; *Pumpkin Light*, by David Ray; *The Signmaker's Assistant*, by Tedd Arnold; *The Sign Painter's Dream* (p); and *A Special Trick*, by Mercer Mayer.

The Magnificent Nose and Other Marvels
by Anna Fienberg ✵ Illustrated by Kim Gamble

Little, Brown, 1992   Gr. 2–5   48 pages

Here are five stories (nine pages each) about five girls and boys with extraordinary powers—to build, talk, see, smell, and paint—that lead them on great international adventures. Related book for younger children: *Ten Small Tales* (p).

Make Way for Ducklings by Robert McCloskey

Viking, 1941   Pre-S.–2   62 pages

In this Caldecott Award–winning classic, we follow Mrs. Mallard and her eight ducklings as they make a traffic-stopping walk across Boston to meet Mr. Mallard on their new island home in the Public Garden. Also by the author: *Blueberries for Sal*; *Burt Dow, Deep-Water Man*; *Lentil*; *One Morning in Maine*; and, for older students; *Homer Price* (n) and *Centerburg Tales*. Related books: *Arnold of the Ducks* (p); *Are You My Mother?*, by P. D. Eastman; *Dabble Duck*, by Anne Ellis; *Stellaluna* (p); and *The Story About Ping*, by Majorie Flack.

Matt's Mitt and Fleet-Footed Florence by Marilyn Sachs

Dutton, 1989   Gr. 1–3   40 pages

In this single-volume doubleheader, we are treated to two whimsical baseball stories that were originally published separately. Matt's amazing mitt makes him the greatest fielder of all time, and his daughter Florence's speed afoot is the equal of her dad's fielding. Also by the author: *The Bears' House* (s). Related baseball picture books: *Casey at the Bat* (po); *Elmer and the Chickens vs. the Big League*, by Brian McConnachie; *The Field Beyond the Outfield*, by Mark Teague; *Frank and Ernest Play Ball*, by Alexandra Day; *The Go-Between*, by Amy Hest; *How Georgie Radbourn Saved Baseball*, by David Shannon; *Nate the Great and the Stolen Base*, by Marjorie Weinman Sharmat; *Never Fear, Flip the Dip Is Here*, by Philip Hanft; and *Teammates*, by Peter Golenbock. Fans of Matt and Florence will enjoy Matt Christopher's *Centerfield Ballhawk*. Older students should see listing with *Finding Buck McHenry* (n).

Matthew and the Midnight Towtruck
by Allen Morgan ✯ Illustrated by Michael Martchenko
Annick, 1984   Gr. K-3   26 pages

For any child (or adult) who has wondered what happens to cars and trucks that have been towed away, this first book in a series offers a fanciful answer. Hint: If your clothes shrink in the wash, could the same thing happen to cars? No? Then where do toy cars and trucks come from? Be sure to have some red licorice laces handy for the reading. Others in the series: *Matthew and the Midnight Turkeys* (great for Thanksgiving time) and *Matthew and the Midnight Money Van* (Mother's Day). Also by the author: *Daddy-Care* and *Nicole's Boat*. Related books: *The Amazing Voyage of Jackie Grace* (p); *And to Think That I Saw It on Mulberry Street*, by Dr. Seuss; *Dinosaur Bob and His Adventures with the Family Lazardo* (p); *George Shrinks*, by William Joyce; *Little Tim and the Brave Sea Captain* (p); and *Where the Wild Things Are* (p).

Matthew's Dragon
by Susan Cooper ✯ Illustrated by Joseph A. Smith
Atheneum, 1991   K-3   30 pages

After Matthew's mother turns out the light, the dragon in his book comes alive to take him on a thrilling ride through the night sky—but first there's a dramatic escape from a hungry cat. You'll have a wide-eyed audience for this tale every time. Also by the author, for older students—*Over Sea, Under Stone*. Related books: *The Amazing Voyage of Jackie Grace* (p); *Andy and the Lions*, by James Dougherty; *Maury and the Nightpirates*, by Dieter Wiesmuller; *Where the Wild Things Are* (p); and *The Littles* (s).

Max's Dragon Shirt by Rosemary Wells
Dial, 1991   Pre-S.-K   22 pages

Rosemary Wells is a tuned-in author/parent who has never forgotten the child she used to be, and her books come equipped with built-in enjoyment. In this first book of a series, rabbit Max and his bossy sister Ruby set off to buy him some pants, only to have hilarious circumstances intervene, so that Max ends up with a dragon shirt instead. Also in the series: *Hooray for Max*; *Max's Bath*; *Max's Breakfast*; *Max's Birthday*;

Max's Chocolate Chicken; *Max's Christmas*; *Max's First Word*; *Max's New Suit*; *Max's Ride.* Also by the author: *Benjamin and Tulip*; *Don't Spill It Again, James*; *Good Night, Fred*; *Hazel's Amazing Mother*; *A Lion for Lewis*; *Morris' Disappearing Bag*; *Noisy Nora*; *Shy Charles*; *Stanley and Rhoda*; *Timothy Goes to School*; and *Waiting for the Evening Star.*

The Midnight Eaters
by Amy Hest ☆ Illustrated by Karen Gundersheimer
Simon & Schuster, 1989   K–3   28 pages

Though the doctor says Grandma is too frail, she and her granddaughter sneak downstairs at midnight for snacks and her old picture album of memories. Also by the author: *The Crack-of-Dawn Walkers*; *The Mommy Exchange*; and *The Purple Coat.* For related grandparent books: see the listing with *Grandaddy's Place* (p).

Miffy by Dick Bruna
Methuen, 1964   Inf.-Tod.   24 pages

After Mother Goose, Dick Bruna's books would be my next choice for infants and toddlers. I made sure it was so for my grandchild. When Mr. and Mrs. Rabbit wish and wish for a baby, their wish is granted by an angel. This is the first in a series of books about their wonderful baby Miffy. This is typical of Bruna's titles, an uncomplicated story with boldly colored illustrations. Bruna's books presently are not sold in the U.S., but they are in Canada. Canadian citizens can order from their local bookstore; U.S. citizens can call the Children's Bookstore in Toronto and order his books via the mail and a credit card: telephone—(416) 480-0233. Other books in the Miffy series include: *Miffy at the Seaside*; *Miffy in the Snow*; *Miffy's Birthday*; *Miffy in Hospital*; *Miffy at the Playground*; *Miffy's Dream*; *Miffy at School*; *Miffy's Bicycle*; *Miffy Goes Flying*; and *Miffy at the Zoo.* Related books: see listing with *Tom and Pippo Make a Friend* (p).

Mike Mulligan and His Steam Shovel
by Virginia Lee Burton
Houghton Mifflin, 1939   K–4   42 pages

A modern classic, this is the heartwarming story of the demise of the steam shovel and how one shovel found a permanent home with her master. Also by the author: *Choo-Choo*; *The Emperor's New Clothes*; *Katy and the Big Snow* (p); and *The Little House* (p). Related books: *The Big*

Book of Real Trucks, by Walter Retan; *The Caboose Who Got Loose* and *Smokey,* both by Bill Peet; and *Matthew and the Midnight Towtruck* (p).

The Minpins
by Roald Dahl ✿ Illustrated by Patrick Benson
Viking, 1991 K–4 47 pages

This is one of Dahl's final and most sensitive, most dramatic works. When a small boy disobeys his mother and enters the dark forest, he meets not only the monster she predicted but also tiny matchstick-sized people who inhabit all the trees. The tree creatures enable him to escape, and together they destroy the monster. Also by the author: see the listing with *James and the Giant Peach* (n). Related book: *The Littles* (s).

Miss Nelson Is Missing
by Harry Allard ✿ Illustrated by James Marshall
Houghton Mifflin, 1977 Pre-S.–4 32 pages

Poor, sweet Miss Nelson! Kind and beautiful as she is, she cannot control her classroom—the worst-behaved children in the school. But when she is suddenly absent, the children begin to realize what a wonderful teacher they had in Miss Nelson. Her substitute is wicked-looking, strict Miss Viola Swamp, who works the class incessantly. Wherever has Miss Nelson gone and when will she return? Sequels: *Miss Nelson Is Back* and *Miss Nelson Has a Field Day.* Also by the author: *The Stupids Step Out* (series).

Related school stories: *The Balancing Girl,* by Bernice Rabe; *The Best Teacher in the World,* by Bernice Chardiet and Grace Maccarone; *Captain Abdul's Pirate School* (p); *Crow Boy,* by Taro Yashima; *Daddy-Care,* by Allen Morgan; *I Thought I'd Take My Rat to School: Poems for September to June,* selected by Dorothy M. Kennedy; *If You're Not Here, Please Raise Your Hand* (po); *Mrs. Toggle's Zipper* (p) and *Nobody's Mother Is in Second Grade,* by Robin Pulver; *My Teacher Sleeps at School,* by Leatie Weiss; *The Mystery in the Bottle* and *The Surprise in the Wardrobe,* both by Val Willis; *Poonam's Pets* (p); *The Principal's New Clothes* (p); *Teach Us, Amelia Bedelia,* by Peggy Parrish; and *Thomas' Snowsuit* (p).

Molly's Pilgrim by Barbara Cohen
Morrow, 1983 Gr. 1–4 41 pages

Molly, an immigrant child and the target of her classmates' taunts, discovers she is more a part of America's Thanksgiving tradition than anyone in the class; this book was the basis for the 1985 Academy

Award–winning best short film of the same title. Related Thanksgiving books: *Cranberry Thanksgiving*, by Wende and Harry Devlin; *Matthew and the Midnight Turkeys*, by Allen Morgan; *N.C. Wyeth's Pilgrims*, by Robert San Souci; *Thanksgiving at the Tappletons'*, by Eileen Spinelli; *The Thanksgiving Story*, by Alice Dalgliesh; for older students: *The Hundred Dresses* (s) and *The Thanksgiving Treasure*, by Gail Rock.

Monster Mama
by Liz Rosenberg ☆ Illustrated by Stephen Gammell
Philomel, 1993   K–2   30 pages

Patrick Edward's mother is truly monstrous looking. She cares dearly for her little boy, but avoids others so as not to frighten them. When three bullies pick on her son, she comes out of hiding and proves that looks can be deceiving. Related books: *David's Father*, by Robert Munsch; *Crow Boy*, by Taro Yashima; and *Pumpkin Time*, by Jan Andrews.

Moss Gown
by William H. Hooks ☆ Illustrated by Donald Carrick
Clarion, 1987   Gr. 1–5   48 pages

There are more versions of Cinderella in more cultures than any of other fairy tale. This centuries-old southern version adds elements of King Lear to make an enchanting tale of family rejection and triumph amidst the plantations of the Old South. Other versions: *Ashpet: An Appalachian Tale*, retold by Joanne Compton; *Cinder-elly*, by Frances Minters; *The Egyptian Cinderella*, by Shirley Climo; *Iron John*, adapted by Eric A. Kimmel; *Mufaro's Beautiful Daughters: An African Tale*, by John Steptoe; *Princess Furball*, by Charlotte Huck; *The Rough-Face Girl*, by Rafe Martin; *A Telling of the Tales: Five Stories*, by William J. Brooke; *Ugh*, by Arthur Yorinks and Richard Egielski; *Vasilissa the Beautiful*, retold by Elizabeth Winthrop; and *Yeh-Shen*, retold by Ai-Ling Louie.

Mother Goose—see *The Little Dog Laughed and Other Nursery Rhymes from Mother Goose* (p) and the other titles listed with it.

Mr. Hacker
by James Stevenson ☆ Illustrated by Frank Modell
Greenwillow, 1990   Pre-S.–2   32 pages

In this excellent introduction to the chapter book concept, lonely Mr. Hacker grows weary of noisy and threatening city life and moves to the country. The nine chapters average two pages each. *The Supreme Souvenir Factory* (p) also offers the same chapter pattern. Also by the author: See *What's Under My Bed?* (p). Other picture books broken into chapters: *Andy and the Lion*, by James Dougherty; *The Big Alfie and Annie Rose Storybook*, by Shirley Hughes; *Emily's Own Elephant*, by Philippa Pearce; *Frog and Toad Are Friends* (p); *Ten Small Tales* (p); and *Wagon Wheels* (p).

Mrs. Toggle's Zipper
by Robin Pulver ✯ Illustrated by R. W. Alley
Simon & Schuster, 1990   Pre-S–2   28 pages

When the early primary teacher, Mrs. Toggle, loses the toggle on the zipper to her winter coat enroute to school one day, her class, the school nurse, and the principal all fail to get her out of the coat—until the custodian comes to the rescue. Sequels: *Mrs. Toggle and the Dinosaur*; *Mrs. Toggle's Beautiful Blue Shoe*. Also by the author: *Homer and the House Next Door* and *Nobody's Mother Is in Second Grade*. Other school stories: see listing with *Miss Nelson Is Missing* (p).

The Mysterious Tadpole by Steven Kellogg
Dial, 1977   Pre-S.–4   30 pages

When little Louis's uncle in Scotland sent him a tadpole for his birthday, neither of them had any idea how much havoc and fun the pet would cause in Louis's home, classroom, and school swimming pool. The tadpole turns out to be a direct descendant of the Loch Ness Monster (but what a cuddly monster this is!). For other books by the author, see *The Island of the Skog* (p).

Related books about unusual pets: *Amos: The Story of an Old Dog and His Couch* (p); *Blumpoe the Grumpoe Meets Arnold the Cat*, by Jean Davies Okimoto; *The Boy Who Was Followed Home*, by Margaret Mahy; *Dinosaur Bob and His Adventures with the Family Lazardo* (p); *The New Creatures*, by Mordicai Gerstein; *Patrick's Dinosaurs*, by Carol Carrick; *Poonam's Pets* (p); *The Salamander Room*, by Anne Mazer; *The Secret in the Matchbox*, by Val Willis; and *Uglypuss*, by Caroline Gregoire.

The Napping House
by Audrey Wood ✯ Illustrated by Don Wood
Harcourt Brace, 1984   Tod.–Pre-S.   28 pages

One of the cleverest and most beautiful books for children, this simple tale depicts a cozy bed on which are laid in cumulative rhymes a snoring granny, a dreaming child, a dozing dog, and a host of other sleeping characters until a sudden awakening at daybreak. Also by the author: *Heckedy Peg* (p); *King Bidgood's in the Bathtub*; *The Tickle Octopus*; and by Don Wood: *Little Mouse, the Red Ripe Strawberry, and the Big Hungry Bear*. Related books: see listing of Predictable/Cumulative books on page 231.

Night Cars
by Teddy Jam ☆ Illustrated by Eric Beddows
Orchard, 1989   Tod.–Pre-S.   26 pages

A little boy is rocked to sleep by his father in front of a window overlooking the cityscape. Large color illustrations and rhyming verse mark the night's passage with the passing cars, taxis, garbage and delivery trucks, fire engines, snowplows, and pedestrians. Related books: *A Bed for the Wind*, by Roger B. Goodman; *Before I Go to Sleep*, by Thomas Hood; *Goodnight Moon* (p); *The Salamander Room*, by Anne Mazer; and *The Napping House* (p).

No Jumping on the Bed by Tedd Arnold
Dial, 1987   Pre-S.–2   30 pages

Warned that he mustn't jump on his bed or he might crash through the floor into the apartment below, Walter can't resist the temptation. The exaggerated results are hilarious, and just when you think he dreamed it all . . . Also by the author: *Green Wilma* and *The Signmaker's Assistant*. Related bedtime-ritual books: *Barn Dance!* by Bill Martin, Jr., and John Archambault; *Bedtime for Frances*, by Russell Hoban; *Go to Sleep, Nicholas Joe*, by Marjorie Sharmat; *Grandfather's Pencil and the Room of Stories*, by Michael Foreman; *I Am NOT Going to Get Up Today!*, by Dr. Seuss; *I Can't Sleep*, by Philippe Dupasquier; *I Don't Want to Go to Bed*, by Astrid Lindgren; *In the Night Kitchen*, by Maurice Sendak; *Ira Sleeps Over* (p); *The Magic Rocket*, by Steven Kroll; *Papa's Bedtime Story*, by Mary Lee Donovan; *Switch on the Night*, by Ray Bradbury; *Under the Moon*, by Dyan Sheldon; and *What's Under My Bed?* (p).

Not the Piano, Mrs. Medley
by Evan Levine ☆ Illustrated by S. D. Schindler
Orchard, 1991   Pre-S.–3   26 pages

Grandmothers like to be prepared, but Max's grandma takes it to new limits when she and Max schedule a day at the beach. The list of items she insists upon bringing grows and grows, until pure zaniness breaks through. It's a book you wish had an immediate sequel. Related book: *A Perfectly Orderly House*, by Ellen Kindt McKenzie; *Pigsty*, by Mark Teague; and *Uncle Lester's Hat*, by Howie Schneider. Other grandparent books: See *Grandaddy's Place* (p).

Oh, Brother
by Arthur Yorinks ✸ Illustrated by Richard Egielski
Farrar, Straus & Giroux, 1989   Gr. 1–3   36 pages

Using slapstick and a Dickensian mood, this award-winning author and illustrator team brings us the tale of two bickering twin brothers orphaned in a ship accident in the early 1930s. As they rebound from orphanage to circus to fruit stands, they continue their nonstop quarreling while struggling with the harsh realities of the Depression. A kindly old tailor and fate bring the story to a surprise happy ending. Also by the author: *Hey, Al*; *Ugh!* Related books: *The Christmas Coat*, by Clyde Robert Bulla; *The Hokey-Pokey Man*, by Steven Kroll; *How Pizza Came to Queens*, by Dayal Kaur Khalsa; *A Peddler's Dream*, by Janice Shefelman; and *Peppe the Lamplighter*, by Elisa Bartone.

Old Mother Witch by Carol and Donald Carrick
Clarion, 1975   Gr. 1–6   32 pages

A group of boys out trick-or-treating at Halloween decide to tease the cranky old woman who lives on their street—only to find a frightening surprise waiting for them. The old woman has suffered a heart attack and is lying unconscious on the porch. A young boy's brush with near tragedy and the sobering effect it has upon him will reach all children, perhaps inspiring a new sensitivity toward the elderly in their neighborhoods. For other books by this author, see *Sleep Out* (p). Related books on the elderly: *Always Gramma*, by Vaunda Nelson; *Captain Snap and the Children of Vinegar Lane* (p); *Ella*, by Bill Peet; *A Fruit and Vegetable Man*, by Roni Schotter; *I Know a Lady*, by Charlotte Zolotow; *Grandpa's Song*, by Toni Johnston; *Lester's Dog* (p); *Loop the Loop*, by Barbara Dugan; *Miss Maggie*, by Cynthia Rylant; *Miss Rumphius*, by Barbara Cooney; *Now One Foot, Now the Other*, by Tomie dePaola; *Wilfred Gordon McDonald Partridge*, by Mem Fox; for older students, *Willa and Old Miss Annie* (s). For grandparent books, see *Grandaddy's Place* (p).

Osa's Pride by Ann Grifalconi
Little, Brown, 1990   K–3   30 pages

Unwilling to adjust to her family circumstances, seven-year-old Osa develops a stubborn pride that begins to alienate friends and neighbors in her African village. Finally her grandmother allows Osa to see her foolish self by sewing a story of stubborn pride on a story cloth. Related African titles: *Anansi and the Talking Melon*, retold by Eric A. Kimmel; *Anansi Finds a Fool*, by Verna Aardema; *The Fortune-Tellers*, by Lloyd Alexander; *The House That Jack Built*, by Jenny Stow; *How Many Spots Does a Leopard Have? And Other Tales*, by Julius Lester; *Misoso: Once Upon a Time Tales from Africa* and *Why Mosquitos Buzz in People's Ears*, both by Verna Aardema; *Why the Sky Is Far Away: A Nigerian Folktale*, by Mary-Joan Gerson; *Zomo the Rabbit: A Trickster Tale from West Africa*, by Gerald McDermott; and, for older students, *Bury My Bones But Keep My Words: African Tales for the Retelling*, retold by Tony Fairman.

Owen by Kevin Henkes
Greenwillow, 1993   Pre-S.–K   22 pages

Owen has a favorite blanket that he can't give up, despite every trick of his parents; then one day, as school approaches, his mother hits upon an idea—cutting it up into handkerchiefs. Related books: *Tim and the Blanket Thief*, by John Prater; and *Ira Sleeps Over* (p).

Owl Babies
by Martin Waddell ✵ Illustrated by Patrick Benson
Candlewick, 1992   Tod.–Pre-S.   30 pages

Three young owls awaken to find their mother missing. Their ensuing hours are spent thinking, worrying, imagining, talking, and wishing for her return. And of course she returns, to their great relief and delight. Related books: *Are You My Mother?*, by P. D. Eastman; *Bye Bye Baby*, by Janet and Allan Ahlberg; *Miffy* (p); and *Stellaluna* (p).

The Phantom of the Lunch Wagon
by Daniel Pinkwater
Simon & Schuster/Atheneum, 1992   K–2   30 pages

The mysterious creature that has been "haunting" the local lunch wagon—and scaring away all its customers—turns out to be nothing more than a cat. But the irrepressible Mr. Pinkwater builds a nice creepiness into the tale. Also by the author: *Aunt Lulu*; *The Big Orange*

Splot; and *Guys from Space*. Related books: *Donovan Scares the Monsters*, by Susan Love Whitlock; *Grandma's Secret* (p); *The Little Old Lady Who Was Not Afraid of Anything*, by Linda Williams; *Monsters*, by Russell Hoban; and *The Tailypo*, by Joanna Galdone.

The Pied Piper of Hamelin
retold by Barbara Bartos-Hoppner ✫ Illustrated by Annegert Fuchshuber
HarperCollins, 1987   K-5   26 pages

The consequences of breaking your word are dramatically portrayed here in this 700-year-old tale of enchantment when the Pied Piper rids Hamelin of its rat infestation but is denied his reward. Other versions: *The Irish Piper*, by Jim Latimer; *The Pied Piper of Hamelin*, by Robert Browning, revised by Terry Small; for older students, *What Happened at Hamelin*, a novel by Gloria Skurzynski. For the history of this legend, see *Hey! Listen to This* (a). Related books about mysterious strangers: *Company's Coming*, by Arthur Yorinks; *Dawn*, by Molly Bang; *The Hero of Bremen*, retold by Margaret Hodges; *The Magician*, by Uri Shulevitz; *Old Henry*, by Joan Blos; *The Paper Crane*, by Molly Bang; *Paper John*, by David Small; *The Pumpkinville Mystery*, by Bruce Cole; *The Selkie Girl*, retold by Susan Cooper; *The Stranger* and *The Wreck of the Zephyr*, both by Chris Van Allsburg; *Ty's One-Man Band*, by Mildred P. Walter.

Pink and Say by Patricia Polacco
Philomel, 1994   Gr. 3 and up   48 pages

Based upon an incident in the life of the author/illustrator's great-great grandfather, this is the tale of two fifteen-year-old Union soldiers—one white, one black. The former is wounded while deserting his company, the latter is separated from his black company and stumbles upon the left-for-dead white soldier. The pages and weeks that follow trace this sad chapter in American history about as well as has ever been told for children, beginning with a visit to the black soldier's mother, who is living on a nearby plantation ravaged by the war. There the wounded boy is nursed back to both health and full courage, while discovering the inhumanity of slavery. Patricia Polacco is one of the rising stars in children's literature. Her other books include: *Applemando's Dreams*; *Babushka Baba Yaga*; *Babushka's Doll*; *The Bee Tree*; *Chicken Sunday*; *Just Plain Fancy*; *The Keeping Quilt*; *Meteor!*; *Mrs. Katz and Tush*; *My Rotten, Redheaded Older Brother*; *Picnic at Mudstock Meadow*; *Rechenka's Eggs*; *Some Birthday!*; *Thunder Cake*; and *Uncle*

Vova's Tree. Related books on the Civil War: *Barbara Frietchie*, by John Greenleaf Whittier; *Behind Rebel Lines: The Incredible Story of Emma Edmonds, Civil War Spy*, by Seymour Reitt; *Christmas in the Big House, Christmas in the Quarters*, by Patricia and Fredrick McKissack; *Just a Few Words, Mr. Lincoln: The Story of the Gettysburg Address*, by Jean Fritz; *Thunder at Gettysburg*, by Patricia Lee Gauch; *The Tinderbox*, retold by Barry Moser about a Confederate soldier at war's end; *Which Way Freedom?* by Joyce Hansen; and, for mature readers, *Nightjohn*, by Gary Paulsen.

Poonam's Pets
by Andrew and Diana Davies ✫ Illustrated by Paul Dowling
Viking, 1990   Pre-S.-K   25 pages

When the first-graders put on their pet assembly, the ethnically diverse students arrive with a wide assortment of pets. The biggest surprise comes from the class's smallest, shiest child—who brings her six enormous lions. Related books: *Andy and the Lion*, by James Dougherty; *Andy's Dandy Lions*, by Bill Peet; *The Biggest Bear* (p); *Crow Boy*, by Taro Yashima; *Deer in the Hollow*, by Efner Tudor Holmes; *The Mysterious Tadpole* (p); *Pet Show*, by Ezra Jack Keats; and *Show and Tell*, by Elvitra Woodruff.

See also these stories about black families: *Back Home*, by Gloria Jean Pinkney; *Bigmama's*, by Donald Crews; *Chicken Sunday* and *Pink and Say*, by Patricia Polacco; *Elijah's Angel: A Story for Chanukah and Christmas*, by Michael J. Rosen; *Evan's Corner*, by Elizabeth Starr Hill; *Honey, I Love* (po); *John Henry*, by Julius Lester; *Listen, Children*, by Dorothy Strickland; *Philip Hall Likes Me, I Reckon Maybe*, by Bette Greene; *Seven Candles for Kwanzaa*, by Andrea Davis Pinkney; *Sing to the Stars*, by Mary Brigid Barrett; *So Much*, by Trish Cooke; *Three Wishes*, by Lucille Clifton; *Uncle Jed's Barbershop*, by Margaree King Mitchell; *When I Am Old with You*, by Angela Johnson; and *When Joe Louis Won the Title*, by Belinda Rochelle. See also *Talk That Talk: An Anthology of African-American Storytelling* (a); and the books listed with *Roll of Thunder, Hear My Cry* (n).

The Poppy Seeds by Robert Clyde Bulla
Puffin, 1994   K-2   34 pages

A selfish old man who scorns the friendship and needs of his neighbors is finally reached through the kindness of a Mexican child who attempts to plant poppies in the man's yard. For related books about the elderly, see *Old Mother Witch* (p). For other books with Hispanic characters and settings, see listing with *A Gift for Tia Rosa* (p).

The Principal's New Clothes
by Stephanie Calmenson ☆ Illustrated by Denise Brunkus
Scholastic, 1989   K–4   40 pages

In this modern-day version of the classic tale, a nattily dressed school principal is tricked. The faculty and older students cannot bring themselves to tell him the bad news, but the youngest are happy to oblige. Related book: *The Emperor's New Clothes*, by Hans Christian Andersen, retold by Virginia Lee Burton. Other clothing stories: *The Five Hundred Hats of Bartholomew Cubbins*, by Dr. Seuss; *Froggy Gets Dressed*, by Jonathan London; *The Mitten*, adapted by Jan Brett; *Mrs. Toggle's Beautiful Blue Shoe* and *Mrs. Toggle's Zipper* (p), both by Robin Pulver; *The Purple Coat*, by Amy Hest; *Thomas' Snowsuit* (p); *Uncle Lester's Hat*, by Howie Schneider; and *Your Turn, Doctor*, by Carla Perez, M.D., and Deborah Robison.

Regards to the Man in the Moon by Ezra Jack Keats
Simon & Schuster, 1981   Pre-S.–3   32 pages

When the neighborhood children tease Louie about the junk in his backyard, his father shows him how imagination can convert rubbish into a spaceship that will take him to the farthest galaxies. The next day, Louie and his friend Susie hurtle through space in their glorified washtub and discover that not even gravity can hold back a child's imagination. The settings for Ezra Jack Keats's books are largely inner city, but the emotions are those of all children—the pride of learning how to whistle, or the excitement of outwitting older children. Also by the author: *Apartment 3*; *Goggles*; *Hi, Cat*; *Jennie's Hat*; *John Henry*; *A Letter to Amy*; *Louie*; *Maggie and the Pirate*; *Peter's Chair*; *Pet Show!*; *The Snowy Day*; *The Trip*; and *Whistle for Willie*.

Related books about children's imaginations: *Airmail to the Moon*, by Tom Birdseye; *The Amazing Voyage of Jackie Grace* (p); *The Aminal*, by Lorna Balian; *And to Think That I Saw It on Mulberry Street*, by Dr. Seuss; *Bored, Nothing to Do*, by Peter Spier; *The Beast in the Bathtub*, by Kathleen Stevens; *Because of Lozo Brown*, by Larry L. King; *Benjamin's Barn*, by Reeve Lindbergh; *Grandfather's Pencil and the Room of Stories*, by Michael Foreman; *Harry and the Terrible Whatzit*, by Dick Gackenbach; *James in the House of Aunt Prudence*, by Timothy Bush; *Jumanji*, by Chris Van Allsburg; *The Long Weekend*, by Troon Harrison;

Look Out, Look Out, It's Coming!, by Laura Geringer; *Lost!*, by David McPhail; *The Magic Rocket*, by Steven Kroll; *Roxaboxen*, by Alice McLerran; *Will's Mammoth*, by Rafe Martin; and *Yes, Dear*, by Diana Wynne Jones.

The Samurai's Daughter by Robert D. San Souci
Dial, 1992   Gr. 2–6   30 pages
In this retelling of an ancient legend, a Japanese knight is banished to a faraway island by his emperor. The samurai's daughter, displaying her family's courage and boldness, sails to the island and battles a ferocious sea serpent to win her father's release. Related heroine books: see listing with *Charlie Drives the Stage* (p); for related books on courage, see *The Courage of Sarah Noble* (s).

Santa Calls by William Joyce
HarperCollins, 1993   K and up   38 pages
You could say this book is Santa meets the Wizard of Oz, Jules Verne, the Boxcar Children, and Louis L'Amour. But it's so much more. The art is glorious, Santa never looked better or more important, nor the North Pole so interesting. Three children receive a secret invitation from Santa to visit the North Pole and there they have a grand adventure with a surprise ending. Also by the author: *A Day with Wilbur Robinson*; *Dinosaur Bob and the Adventures of the Family Lazardo*; and *George Shrinks*.

Other Christmas books: *Babushka*, retold by Charles Mikolaycak; *A Certain Small Shepherd*, by Rebecca Caudill; *The Christmas Bear*, by Henrietta Stickland; *A Christmas Carol*, by Charles Dickens, abridged by Vivian French; *The Christmas Coat*, by Clyde Robert Bulla; *Christmas Eve at Santa's*, by Alf Proysen and Jens Ahlbom; *The Christmas Gift*, by Emily McCully; *Christmas in the Big House, Christmas in the Quarters*, by Patricia and Fredrick McKissack; *The Christmas of the Reddle Moon*, by J. Patrick Lewis; *Don't Forget Me, Santa Claus*, by Virginia Mayo; *Elijah's Angel: A Story for Chanukah and Christmas*, by Michael J. Rosen; *Father Christmas*, by Raymond Briggs; *Harvey Slumfenburger's Christmas Present*, by John Burningham; *Just in Time for Christmas*, by Louise Borden.

Other Christmas picture books: *The Legend of Old Befana*, by Tomie dePaola; *The Legend of the Christmas Rose*, by Selma Lagerlöf, retold by Ellin Greene; *Little Jim's Gift*, by Gloria Houston; *Madeline's Christmas*, by Ludwig Bemelmans; *Mama Bear*, by Chyng Feng Sun; *My Prairie*

Christmas, by Brett Harvey; *The Nativity*, illustrated by Julie Viva; *The Night After Christmas*, by James Stevenson; *The Night Before Christmas*, illustrated by Tomie dePaola; *Peter Spier's Christmas*, by Peter Spier; *Petunia's Christmas*, by Roger Duvoisin; *The Polar Express*, by Chris Van Allsburg; *The Reindeer Christmas*, by Moe Price; *Santa's Book of Names*, by David McPhail; *Seven Candles for Kwanzaa*, by Andrea Davis Pinkney; *How the Grinch Stole Christmas*, by Dr. Seuss; *Star Mother's Youngest Child*, by Louise Moeri; *The Worst Person's Christmas*, by James Stevenson; and *The Year of the Perfect Christmas Tree*, by Gloria Houston. For Christmas novels, see *The Best Christmas Pageant Ever* (s).

Shorty Takes Off
by Barbro Lindgren ✣ Illustrated by Olof Landström
R&S Books, 1990   Pre-S.-2   28 pages

Poor Shorty! His cat is lost, his dog ran off, and Mom's mad at him. And that's when he suddenly grows a pair of WINGS! And does that ever change things. Also by the author: *A Worm's Tale*. Related books: *Alec and His Flying Bed*, by Simon Buckingham; *Up and Up* (wordless), by Shirley Hughes; and *The Wing Shop*, by Elvira Woodruff.

The Shrinking of Treehorn
by Florence Parry Heide ✣ Illustrated by Edward Gorey
Holiday, 1971   Gr. 3-8   60 pages

When a young boy mentions to his social-climbing parents that he's begun to shrink, he's ignored. When he calls it to the attention of his teachers, his words fall on deaf ears. Day by day he grows smaller and day by day the adults continue to talk around him and his problem. Finally he must solve it himself. Sequels: *Treehorn's Treasure*; *Treehorn's Wish*; also by the author: *Banana Twist*; *Banana Blitz*; and *The Problem with Pulcifer*.

The Sign Painter's Dream by Roger Roth
Crown, 1993   K-4   38 pages

The talented but grouchy sign painter sees no benefit in helping anyone but himself until George Washington visits him in a dream. An excellent volume for Presidents' Day reading. Related books: *George Washington: A Picture Book Biography*, by James Giblin; see listing with *The Magic Paintbrush* (p); and *Ben's Dream*, by Chris Van Allsburg.

The Silver Pony by Lynd Ward
Houghton Mifflin, 1973   Pre-S.-4   176 pages

A classic wordless book (and the longest ever published for children), this is the heartwarming story of a lonely farm boy and the flights of fancy he uses to escape his isolation. His imaginative trips take place on a winged pony and carry him to distant parts of the world to aid and comfort other lonely children. Also by the author: *The Biggest Bear* (p). Related books: See listing with *Regards to the Man in the Moon* (p). See also the list of Wordless books on page 229.

Six by Seuss: A Treasury of Dr. Seuss
by Dr. Seuss
Random House, 1991   K-4   352 pages

You'll not find a better book bargain (less than $30) anywhere than this collection of six great books in one volume: Beginning with Seuss's first book, *And to Think That I Saw It on Mulberry Street*; as well as *The 500 Hats of Bartholomew Cubbins*; *Horton Hatches the Egg*; *Yertle the Turtle*; *How the Grinch Stole Christmas*; and *The Lorax*. All but *The 500 Hats* are written in Seuss's contagious rhyming verse. For Seuss biographical material, see: "Oh, the Places You've Taken Us," in *The Reading Teacher* (May 1992); and *Dr. Seuss from Then to Now*, a retrospective from Random House and the San Diego Museum of Art.

Other Dr. Seuss books that make excellent read-alouds include: *Bartholomew and the Oobleck*; *The Butter Battle Book*; *Did I Ever Tell You How Lucky You Are?*; *Dr. Seuss's Sleep Book*; *Horton Hears a Who*; *Hunches in Bunches*; *I Am NOT Going to Get Up Today!*; *I Can Lick 30 Tigers Today and Other Stories*; *I Can Read with My Eyes Shut*; *I Had Trouble in Getting to Solla Sollew*; *If I Ran the Zoo*; *If I Ran the Circus*; *The King's Stilts*; *McElligot's Pool*; *Oh, the Places You'll Go!*; *On Beyond Zebra*; *Scrambled Eggs Super!*; *The Shape of Me and Other Stuff*; *The Sneetches and Other Stories*; and *Thidwick the Big-Hearted Moose*. Dr. Seuss fans will enjoy Bill Peet books—see *The Whingdingdilly* (p), as well as *The Red Carpet*, by Rex Parkin.

Sleep Out
by Carol Carrick ✶ Illustrated by Donald Carrick
Clarion, 1973   K-5   30 pages

Christopher and his dog achieve that one great triumph that all children dream of accomplishing: they sleep out alone in the woods one night. This is the first in a series of eight books about Christopher and his family. While the books can be enjoyed separately, they work best when read in sequence. After *Sleep Out*, they include: *Lost in the Storm*—Christopher searches for his lost dog after a long night's storm; *The Accident*—Christopher comes to terms with his grief after his dog is killed; *The Foundling*—Christopher adjusts to the idea of starting life anew after the dog's death; *The Washout*—Christopher and his new dog, Ben, perform a dramatic rescue after a flood; *Ben and the Porcupine*—confronting a neighborhood nuisance; *Dark and Full of Secrets*—Christopher, learning to swim, is rescued by Ben; and *Left Behind*—Christopher is accidentally separated from his classmates during a class trip.

Other books by one or both members of this talented husband and wife team include: *Old Mother Witch* (p); *Big Old Bones: A Dinosaur Tale*; *The Crocodiles Still Wait*; *Harald and the Giant Knight*; *Harald and the Great Stag* (p); *Morgan and the Artist*; *Octopus*; *Patrick's Dinosaurs*; *Paul's Christmas Birthday*; *What Happened to Patrick's Dinosaurs*; and three novels: *The Elephant in the Dark*; *Stay Away from Simon*; and *What a Wimp!*

Somebody Loves You, Mr. Hatch
by Eileen Spinelli
Simon & Schuster, 1991   K and up   30 pages

A definitive book on friendship, it introduces us to a lonely little man—Mr. Hatch—who has no friends. And then one day a box of Valentine chocolates is delivered to him by mistake—changing his world forever. Also by the author: *Thanksgiving at the Tappletons'*. Related friendship picture books: *Chester's Way* (p); *Chin Yu Min and the Ginger Cat*, by Jennifer Armstrong; *Fat, Fat Rose Marie*, by Lisa Passen; *The Giving Tree*, by Shel Silverstein; *Mr. Hacker* and *The Pattconk Brook*, both by James Stevenson; *The Poppy Seeds*, by Robert Clyde Bulla; *Stellaluna* (p); *Teammates*, by Peter Golenbock; *What Goes Around Comes Around*, by Sally G. War; *Will I Have a Friend?*, by Miriam Cohen; and *Will You Be My Valentine?*, by Steven Kroll. For older students: *I Never Knew Your Name*, by Sherry Garland, a book on the suicide of a friendless boy.

So Much
by Trish Cooke ✫ Illustrated by Helen Oxenbury
Candlewick, 1994   Tod.-K   38 pages

As all the guests arrive for Daddy's surprise birthday party, each of them wants to kiss, hug, squeeze, cuddle, toss, roughhouse, and tickle the baby. Using large pages and a demonstrative black family as their vehicle, the author and illustrator give us laughter and excitement, blended with family and affection. See Author/Illustrator Index for other books by Oxenbury. Related book: *Rolling Rose*, by James Stevenson.

Stellaluna by Janell Cannon
Harcourt, Brace, 1993   K–5   44 pages

Separated accidentally from its mother, a baby bat lands in the nest with three baby birds, where it must adapt to bird-ways of resting, sleeping, flying, and (ugh!) eating. Gradually a bond of friendship grows, one that will last when Stellaluna is reunited with her mother. An award-winning celebration of differences and friendship, with a whimsical touch of Mowgli. Related books: see listing with *Arnold of the Ducks* (p).

The Story of Ferdinand
by Munro Leaf ☆ Illustrated by Robert Lawson
Viking, 1936   Pre-S.–2   68 pages

This world-famous tale of a great Spanish bull who preferred sitting peacefully among the flowers to fighting gloriously in the bullring is one of early childhood's classics. Illustrated in a simple black-and-white style, it was the first children's book to make it to *The New York Times* bestseller list—pushing *Gone With the Wind* out of first place. Related books: *Crow Boy*, by Taro Yashima; *The Day Adam Got Mad*, by Astrid Lindgren; *Nice Little Girls*, by Elizabeth Levy; *Oliver Button Is a Sissy*, by Tomie dePaola; and *William's Doll* (p).

The Supreme Souvenir Factory by James Stevenson
Greenwillow, 1988   K–2   56 pages

This picture book with more than the usual amount of text is divided into ten short chapters and is an excellent introduction to the chapter concept. With warmth and humor, the story details the adventures of a timid new factory employee when the old boss is ushered out and his greedy successor replaces all the employees with robots. For other books by the author, see listing with *What's Under My Bed?* (p).

Sylvester and the Magic Pebble by William Steig
Simon & Schuster, 1969   Pre-S.–4   30 pages

In this contemporary fairy tale and Caldecott Medal winner, young Sylvester finds a magic pebble that will grant his every wish as long as he holds it in his hand. When a hungry lion approaches, Sylvester wishes himself into a stone. Since stones don't have hands, the pebble drops to the ground and he can't reach it to wish himself normal again. The subsequent loneliness of both Sylvester and his parents is portrayed with deep sensitivity, making all the more real their joy a year later when they are happily reunited. Also by the author: *The Amazing Bone*; *Brave Irene* (p); *Caleb and Katie*; *Doctor De Soto*; *Doctor De Soto Goes to Africa*; *Farmer Palmer's Wagon Ride*; for older students, *The Real Thief.* Related books: *Arnold of the Ducks* (p); *The Fox and the Kingfisher*, by Judith Mellecker; *Pumpkin Time*, by Jan Andrews; and *The Whingding-dilly* (p); for grades 1–4: *The Chocolate Touch* (n); *Bella Arabella* (s); and *The Wish Giver* (n).

The Tale of Peter Rabbit
See *The Complete Adventures of Peter Rabbit* (p).

The Tale of Thomas Mead by Pat Hutchins
Morrow, 1980   K–3   32 pages

When all the other children were learning to read, Thomas Mead chose not to. "Why should I?" he asked defiantly. The ensuing farcical misadventures with signs, elevators, rest rooms, doors, traffic signals, and the police more than answer that question for him. Related books about reading: *Andy and the Lion*, by James Dougherty; *Arthur's Prize Reader*, by Lillian Hoban; *Aunt Lulu*, by Daniel Pinkwater; *A Bed for the Wind*, by Roger B. Goodman; *Fix-It* and *Santa's Book of Names*, both by David McPhail.

Ten Small Tales
retold by Celia Barker Lottridge ✫ Illustrated by
Joanne Fitzgerald
Macmillan, 1994   Pre-S.-K   63 pages

Though legitimately an anthology, each of these little stories could be used as a picture book. This is one of the few such collections available for preschoolers and kindergartners. The stories are short (three to four pages), simple, but filled with humor, triumphs, and small creatures and children. Related book: *Stories for Under-Fives*, by Sara and Stephen Corrin. See also listing with *Mr. Hacker* (p).

This Time, Tempe Wick?
by Patricia Lee Gauch ✶ Illustrated by Margot Tomes
Putnam, 1974   Gr. 2-4   44 pages

When George Washington's unpaid, poorly clad colonial troops mutiny during their winter encampment, they figure to take advantage of the local citizens. But they meet their match in a tough, nervy local girl named Tempe Wick. Based on fact and legend. Related books: *The Courage of Sara Noble* (s); and *Toliver's Secret* (n). See listing with *By the Dawn's Early Light* (p) for an extensive listing of other picture books with historical themes; see *The Day It Rained Forever* (s) for short historical novels.

Thomas' Snowsuit
by Robert Munsch ✶ Illustrated by Michael Martchenko
Annick, 1985   Pre-S.-4   24 pages

Thomas hates his new snowsuit, much to the dismay of his mother, teacher, and principal—all of whom find him a most determined fellow. But children will find the situation just plain funny! Also by the author: *The Boy in the Drawer; The Dark; David's Father; 50 Below Zero; I Have to Go!; Jonathan Cleaned Up—Then He Heard a Sound; Love You Forever; Millicent and the Wind; Moira's Birthday; Mortimer; Mud Puddle;* and *The Paper Bag Princess.* See listing of clothing stories with *The Principal's New Clothes* (p).

The Three Robbers by Tomi Ungerer
Atheneum, 1962   Pre-S.-1   34 pages

Take three fierce, dark-of-night thieves, one charming little girl, a black cave, trunks of gold, carts and carts of abandoned children, and one majestic castle—what do you have? A tale that will rivet young listeners. Also by the author: *Zerlada's Ogre.*

Tikki Tikki Tembo
by Arlene Mosel ✶ Illustrated by Blair Lent
Holt, 1968   Pre-S.-3   40 pages

This little picture book tells the amusing legend of how the Chinese people stopped giving their first-born sons enormously long first names, and began giving all children short names. Related books with Asian settings: *The Boy Who Drew Cats*, retold by Arthur A. Levine; *Chin Yu Min and the Ginger Cat*, by Jennifer Armstrong; *Crow Boy*, by Taro Yashima; *The Emperor and the Kite*, by Jane Yolen; *The Journey of Meng,* by Doreen Rappaport; *The Magic Purse*, retold by Yoshiko Uchida; *The Rainbow People*, by Laurence Yep; *The River Dragon*, by Darcy Pattison; *The Samurai's Daughter* (p); *Sato and the Elephants*, by Juanita Havill; *The Seven Chinese Brothers*, by Margaret Mahy; *Three Strong Women: A Tall Tale From Japan*, by Claus Stamm; *The Voice of the Great Bell*, by Lafcadio Hearn, retold by Margaret Hodges; and *The Warrior and the Wise Man*, by David Wisniewski.

Tintin in Tibet by Hergé
Little, Brown, 1975   Gr. 2–4   62 pages

When you've been in print for more than sixty years, translated into twenty-two languages, and praised in *The Times* of London and *The New York Times*, you must be special. Tintin is just that. He's the boy detective who hopscotches the globe in pursuit of thieves and smugglers. Loaded with humor, adventure, and marvelous artwork (700 pictures in each issue), Tintin's special appeal for parents who want to assist their child in reading is the fact that each Tintin contains more than 8,000 words. Having heard Tintin read aloud, children will want to obtain his other adventures and read them by themselves, oblivious to the fact that they are reading so many words in the process. Because of the size of the pictures, Tintin is best read aloud to no more than two children at a time. Furthermore, a comic should be read aloud to the child only a few times—to show the child how a comic works. This is similar to the concept of a model train: the parent shows the child how, then turns it over to the youngster to use. Beginning in 1994, Tintin's American publisher began issuing it in hardcover, three comics to a volume.

The Tintin series includes: *The Black Island*; *The Calculus Affair*; *The Castafiore Emerald*; *Cigars of the Pharaohs*; *The Crab with the Golden Claws*; *Destination Moon*; *Explorers of the Moon*; *Flight 714*; *King Ottokar's Sceptre*; *Land of Black Gold*; *Prisoners of the Sun*; *Red Rackham's Treasure*; *The Red Sea Sharks*; *The Secret of the Unicorn*; *The Seven Crystal Balls*; *The Shooting Star*; and *Tintin and the Picaros*. There is also a puzzle/quiz book based upon all the adventures—*The Tintin Games Book*. Methuen in England also publishes a biography of Tintin's creator: *Tintin and the World of Hergé*. Children (grade 4 and up) will be interested in the following books on comic art: *Funny Papers: Behind the Scenes at the Comics*, by Elaine Scott; and *Understanding Comics*, by Scott McCloud. Grade 4 and older will enjoy: *City of Light, City of Dark: A Comic Book Novel*, by Avi.

Tom and Pippo Make a Friend by Helen Oxenbury
Simon & Schuster, 1989   Tod–Pre-S.   12 pages

In this popular series of short, easy-to-understand stories, we follow the neighborhood social adventures of a toddler and his toy monkey. Other books in the series include: *Pippo Gets Lost*; *Tom and Pippo and the Bicycle*; *Tom and Pippo and the Dog*; *Tom and Pippo and the Washing Machine*; *Tom and Pippo Go for a Walk*; *Tom and Pippo Go Shopping*; *Tom and Pippo in the Garden*; *Tom and Pippo in the Snow*; *Tom and Pippo Make a Mess*; *Tom and Pippo Read a Story*; *Tom and Pippo See the Moon*; *Tom and Pippo's Day*. Other books by the author: *All Fall Down*; *Clap Hands*; *Family*; *Friends*; *I Can*; *I Hear*; *I See*; *I Touch*; and *Read a Story*. For children who have outgrown board books, look for Oxenbury's "out and about" series: *Our Dog*; *The Car Trip*; *The Important Visitor*. Related books: *So Much* (p); and *We're Going on a Bear Hunt* (p).

The True Story of the Three Little Pigs
by John Scieszka ☆ Illustrated by Lane Smith
Viking, 1989   K and up   28 pages

For 200 years, we've taken the word of the three little pigs as "gospel truth." But when the author sought the infamous wolf's side of the story, we get an implausible but entertainingly different point of view. Also by the author: *The Stinky Cheeseman*; and the "Time Warp" series of short, zany novels—*Knights of the Kitchen Table*; *The Not-So-Jolly Roger*; and *Your Mother Was a Neanderthal*. Related "three pig" books: *The Fourth Little Pig*, by Teresa Celsi; *The Three Little Javelinas*, by Susan Lowell; *The Three Little Wolves and the Big Bad Pig*, by Eugene Trivizas; and Mary Rayner's five modern tales of a pig family outwitting the wolf: *Garth Pig and the Ice Cream Lady*; *Garth Pig Steals the Show*; *Mr. and Mrs. Pig's Night Out*; *Mrs. Pig's Bulk Buy*; and *Mrs. Pig Gets Cross and Other Stories*.

Other parodies of famous tales include: *Beware of Boys*, by Tony Blundell; *Burgoo Stew*, by Susan Patron; *The Chocolate Touch* (n); *The Cowboy and the Black-eyed Pea*, by Tony Johnson; *Daddy-Care*, by Allen Morgan; *Deep in the Forest* (p); *The Frog Prince*, by Alix Berenzy; *Jack and the Meanstalk*, by Brian and Rebecca Wildsmith; *Jim and the Beanstalk*, by Raymond Briggs; *Jeremiah in the Deep Woods* and *The Jolly Postman*, by Janet and Allan Ahlberg; *The King, the Princess, and the Tinker*, by Ellen Kindt McKenzie; *The Knight Who Was Afraid of the Dark*, by Barbara Shook Hazen; *The Missing Mother Goose: Original*

Stories, Favorite Rhymes, by Stephen Krensky; *Mrs. Goat and Her Seven Little Kids*, by Tony Ross; *The Night After Christmas*, by James Stevenson; *The Not-So-Wicked Stepmother*, by Lizi Boyd; *The Paper Bag Princess*, by Robert Munsch; *Pondlarker*, by Fred Gwynne; *The Princess and the Frog*, by A. Vesey; *The Principal's New Clothes*, by Stephanie Calmenson; *Ruby*, by Michael Emberley; *Sidney Rella and the Glass Sneaker*, by Bernice Myers; *Sleeping Ugly*, by Jane Yolen; *Somebody and the Three Blairs*, by Marilyn Tolhurst; *A Telling of the Tales: Five Stories*, by William J. Brooke; and *Ugh*, by Arthur Yorinks and Richard Egielski.

Truman's Aunt Farm
by Jama Kim Rattigan ✶ Illustrated by G. Brian Karas
Houghton Mifflin, 1994   Pre-S.-2   30 pages

When little Truman's aunt sends him an ant farm, it turns out to be an "aunt" farm—dozens of swarming aunts who cannot do enough to help him. Overwhelmed but pleased by all the affection and attention, Truman is fast running out of room, when he hits upon a solution. See also *The King Who Rained*, by Fred Gwynne. Other books about relatives: *The Go-Between* and *The Purple Coat*, both by Amy Hest; *Great Aunt Martha*, by Rebecca C. Jones; *James in the House of Aunt Prudence*, by Timothy Bush; *The Lemon Drop Jar*, by Christine Widman; *Nana's Birthday Party*, by Amy Hest; *Uncle Lester's Hat*, by Howie Schneider; and *Uncle Willie and the Soup Kitchen*, by Dyanne DiSalvo-Ryan; see also *Pigsty*, by Mark Teague.

Tuesday by David Wiesner
Clarion, 1991   Pre-S.-3   28 pages

In this nearly wordless Caldecott winner, the frogs from a nearby swamp mysteriously float through the air—and through the neighborhood, windows, chimneys, and living rooms. A wonderful book for discussion with young children. An excellent creative-writing-class book for older students. Also by the author: *Free Fall*. See list of Wordless Books on page 229.

The Very Hungry Caterpillar by Eric Carle
Philomel, 1969   Tod.-1   38 pages

What an ingenious book! It is, at the same time, a simple, lovely way to teach a child the days of the week, how to count to five, and how a caterpillar becomes a butterfly. First, this is a book to look at—bright, bright pictures. Then it is something whose pages beg to be turned—

pages that have little round holes in them made by the hungry little caterpillar. And as the number of holes grows, so does the caterpillar. In a slightly more complicated book, *The Grouchy Ladybug*, Carle used pages in off sizes to show the passage of time and growth in size of the ladybug's adversaries. In the middle of it all there's a little science lesson. Also by the author: *Do You Want to Be My Friend?*; *Eric Carle's Treasury of Classic Stories for Children*; *Have You Seen My Cat?*; *A House for a Hermit Crab*; *The Mixed-Up Chameleon*; *The Secret Birthday Message*; *The Very Busy Spider*; and *The Very Quiet Cricket*.

Wagon Wheels
by Barbara Brenner ✫ Illustrated by Don Bolognese
HarperCollins, 1978   Pre-S.–3   64 pages

In four short chapters, this story can be read either as a long picture book or as an introduction to chapter books. Three young black brothers follow a map to their father's homestead on the western plains. The trio braves storms, fires, and famine to achieve their goal. Two other black families' travels are depicted in: *The Drinking Gourd*, by F. N. Monjo, a story of the underground railroad; and, for older students, *The Gold Cadillac*, by Mildred Taylor, a family's car ride through the South in 1950. For related short historical fiction: *The Courage of Sarah Noble* (s); *Charlie's House*, by Clyde R. Bulla; *Going West*, by Martin Waddell; *If You Traveled West in a Covered Wagon*, by Ellen Levine; *The Josefina Story Quilt*, by Eleanor Coerr; *The Lucky Stone*, by Lucille Clifton; *Watch the Stars Come Out*, by Riki Levinson. See also listing with *By the Dawn's Early Light* (p).

We're Going on a Bear Hunt
by Michael Rosen ✫ Illustrated by Helen Oxenbury
Atheneum, 1992   Tod.–K   32 pages

One of the best books of its kind. A family hunts a bear through field, river, swamp, forest, snowstorm (with predictable, appropriate sounds and movement). When they find him, he hunts *them* back home via the same route and sounds. See list of Predictable/Cumulative books on page 231. Related book: *It's the Bear!*, by Jez Alborough.

What's Under My Bed? by James Stevenson
Greenwillow, 1983   Pre-S.–2   30 pages

In this ongoing series, Stevenson gives us a most endearing combination: two innocent but slightly worried grandchildren turn again and again for reassurance to their grandfather, who concocts imaginative tales about his childhood that makes their worries pale by comparison. They've yet to invent the superhero who can equal the hilarious heroics and hair-raising escapades of Grandpa as a child. Also in the series: *Could Be Worse!*; *Grandpa's Great City Tour*; *The Great Big Especially Beautiful Easter Egg*; *No Friends*; *That Dreadful Day*; *That Terrible Halloween Night*; *That's Exactly the Way It Wasn't*; *We Can't Sleep*; *Worse Than Willy!*; *We Hate Rain!*; *Will You Please Feed Our Cat?* Also by the author: *If I Owned a Candy Factory*; *Mr. Hacker* (p); *The Night After Christmas*; *Rolling Rose*; *The Supreme Souvenir Factory* (p); and *The Wish Card Ran Out*.

When the New Baby Comes, I'm Moving Out
by Martha Alexander

Dial, 1979   Pre-S.-1   28 pages

Jealousy surfaces for a little boy as he anticipates the arrival of a new baby in the house and worries that all the attention will be diverted from him. His anger is soothed when his mother tells him the special roles and privileges of big brothers. This is a companion book to *Nobody Asked Me If I Wanted a Baby Sister*. With her gentle humor, Martha Alexander is especially adept at depicting preschoolers' concerns and their eventual resolution. Her books (most are in paperback) and themes include: *I'll Protect You from the Jungle Beasts* (nightmares); *Maybe a Monster* (anxiety); *Move Over, My Outrageous Friend Charlie* (friendship); *Sabrina* (names); *Twerp* (bullying); *We Never Get to Do Anything* (stubbornness). In addition, Alexander has the following books that deal with a blackboard bear that comes to life in aid of a little boy squabbling with older playmates: *Blackboard Bear*; *And My Mean Old Mother Will Be Sorry, Blackboard Bear*; *I Sure Am Glad to See You, Blackboard Bear*; *We're in Big Trouble, Blackboard Bear*; and *You're a Genius, Blackboard Bear*.

Where the Wild Things Are by Maurice Sendak

HarperCollins, 1963   K-3   28 pages

This is the 1963 Caldecott winner that changed the course of modern children's literature. Sendak here creates a fantasy about a little boy and the monsters that haunt all children. The fact that youngsters are not the least bit frightened by the story, that they love it as they would an old friend, is a credit to Sendak's insight into children's minds and hearts. Also by the author: *Higglety Pigglety Pop!*; *In the Night Kitchen*; *Maurice*

Sendak's Really Rosie; *the Nutshell Library* (which includes *Alligators All Around*; *Chicken Soup with Rice*; *One Was Johnny*; *Pierre*); *Outside Over There*; *The Sign on Rosie's Door*; and *We Are All in the Dumps with Jack and Guy*. For the listing of books about bedtime antics, see *No Jumping on the Bed* (p).

Where's Spot? by Eric Hill

Putnam, 1980   Tod.   20 pages

As Spot's mother looks through the house for her missing puppy, the reader and listeners can imitate her search by lifting page flaps to find an assortment of animals in hiding. The flaps are reinforced and the pages durable enough to be handled by young children. The book is an entertaining introduction to household names, animals, and the concept of "No." Also by the author: *Spot's Baby Sister*; *Spot's Birthday Party*; *Spot's First Christmas*; *Spot's First Walk*; *Spot Counts from One to Ten*; *Spot Goes to the Beach*; *Spot Goes to the Circus*; *Spot Goes to the Farm*; *Spot Goes to School*; *Spot Looks at Colors*; *Spot Looks at Shapes*; *Spot Looks at the Weather*; *Spot's First Easter*; and *Spot Sleeps Over*. Other lift-the-flap books allowing active involvement between child and book: *I'm a Little Mouse* (p) and *Kiss the Boo-Boo* (p). Other toddler books are listed with *I Can! Can You?* (p).

Where's Waldo? by Martin Handford

Little, Brown, 1987   K–4   26 pages

Waldo is a hiker on a worldwide trek who plays hide-and-seek with the reader/viewer, who has to find him as he threads his way through thousands of people populating a dozen different landscapes. Children will spend hours searching the pages for Waldo and the list of more than 300 items check-listed at the end of the book. Also note that in each scene Waldo loses one of his twelve personal items. Books like this stretch children's attention spans while polishing visual discrimination. Sequels: *Find Waldo Now!*; *The Great Waldo Search*; *Where's Waldo? in Hollywood*. For early primary children, these books are similar to *Waldo*: *Andy's Pirate Ship*, by Philippe Dupasquier; *What's Missing?*, by Niki Yektai; *Where Is the Green Parrot?*, by Thomas and Wanda Zacharias; and *Where's Wallace*, by Hilary Knight. For older students: *Bamboozled*, by David Legge; *Errata: A Book of Historical Errors*, by A. J. Wood; *Opt: An Illusionary Tale*, by Arline and Joseph Baum; and these visual puzzle books by Jean Marzollo and Walter Wick: *I Spy: A Book of Picture Riddles*; *I Spy Christmas*; *I Spy Fun House*; *I Spy Mystery*; and *I Spy Fantasy.*

The Whingdingdilly by Bill Peet
Houghton Mifflin, 1970   Pre-S.–5   60 pages

Discontented with his life as a dog, Scamp envies all the attention given to his beribboned neighbor—Palomar the wonder horse. But when a backwoods witch changes Scamp into an animal with the feet of an elephant, the neck of a giraffe, the tail of a zebra, and the nose of a rhinoceros, he gets more attention than he bargained for: He ends up a most unhappy circus freak. Happily, all ends well, and tied into the ending is a subtle lesson for both Scamp and his readers: Be yourself! Bill Peet is one of the most popular contemporary author/ illustrators, and his picture books never fail to instruct, stimulate, and amuse children. Many of his books have a fablelike quality, and two of his works—*Wump World* and *Farewell to Shady Glade*—were among the first children's books to call attention to environmental crises during the 1960s.

A sampling of his various themes includes: ambition (*Chester the Worldly Pig*); arrogance (*Big Bad Bruce*); aging (*Encore for Eleanor*); conceit (*Ella*); courage (*Cowardly Clyde*); environment (*The Gnats of Knotty Pine*); hope (*The Caboose Who Got Loose*); loyalty (*Jennifer and Josephine*). His *Bill Peet: An Autobiography* (n) is excellent, with an illustration on every page. (Yes, there are pictures on every page.) Other Bill Peet titles include: *The Ant and the Elephant*; *Buford the Little Big-horn*; *Capyboppy*; *Cock-A-Doodle Dudley*; *Countdown to Christmas*; *Cyrus the Unsinkable Sea Serpent*; *Eli*; *Encore for Eleanor*; *Fly, Homer, Fly*; *How Droofus the Dragon Lost His Head*; *Hubert's Hair-Raising Adventure*; *Huge Harold*; *Jethro and Joel Were a Troll*; *Kermit the Hermit*; *The Kweeks of Kookatumdee*; *The Luckiest One of All*; *Merle the High-Flying Squirrel*; *No Such Things*; *Pamela Camel*; *The Pinkish, Purplish, Bluish Egg*; *Randy's Dandy Lions*; *Smokey*; *The Spooky Tail of Prewitt Peacock*; and *Zella, Zack and Zodiac.*

William's Doll
by Charlotte Zolotow ✶ Illustrated by William Pène du Bois
HarperCollins, 1972   Pre-S.–4   32 pages

William's father wants him to play with his basketball or trains; William, to the astonishment of all, wishes he had a doll to play with. "Sissy," say his brother and friends. But William's grandmother says something else—something very important—to William, his father, and his brother. One of the most prolific (more than fifty books since 1944) and successful authors for children, Charlotte Zolotow is also one of the most beloved. She writes quiet little books with quiet simple sentences, and her work is always illustrated by the best artists. You'll have no trouble finding the many Zolotow books in your library—she has almost the entire "Z" shelf to herself. Here is a partial listing of her popular read-alouds: *Big Sister and Little Sister*; *But Not Billy*; *Do You Know What I'll Do?*; *A Father Like That*; *The Hating Book*; *I Know a Lady*; *I Like to Be Little*; *If It Weren't for You*; *If You Listen*; *Janey*; *May I Visit?*; *Mr. Rabbit and the Lovely Present*; *My Grandson Lew*; *Over and Over*; *The Quarreling Book*; *Some Things Go Together*; *Something Is Going to Happen*; *The Storm Book*; *The Summer Night*; *Timothy Too!*; *When I Have a Little Boy*; and *When I Have a Little Girl*.

The Wretched Stone by Chris Van Allsburg
Houghton Mifflin, 1991   Gr. 2-7   30 pages

When the crew of a clipper ship sailing tropical seas discover a deserted island, they also find a large, luminous, gray stone with one smooth side. When it is brought aboard ship, an eerie change begins to envelop the ship. Fascinated by the rock, the crew members gradually desert their work and leisure activities, spending more and more time gazing in silent numbness at the rock—despite the protestations of the captain. Created by one of today's most important and thought-provoking author/illustrators for children, this is a powerful allegory about the effects of television on society. Van Allsburg's other books include: *Ben's Dream*; *The Garden of Abdul Gasazi*; *Jumanji*; *Just a Dream*; *The Mysteries of Harris Burdick*; *The Polar Express*; *The Stranger*; *The Sweetest Fig*; *Two Bad Ants*; *The Widow's Broom*; *The Wreck of the Zephyr*; and *The Z Was Zapped*, an unusual alphabet book.

SHORT NOVELS

Among the Dolls by William Sleator
Dutton, 1975   Gr. 4-6   70 pages

A spooky psychological thriller about a girl who receives an old dollhouse for a birthday present, then finds herself drawn into the house and tormented by the very dolls she'd mistreated the day before. Also by the author: *The Duplicate*, a haunting science fiction novel, and *Oddballs*, his offbeat autobiographical stories.

Baseball in April by Gary Soto
Harcourt Brace, 1990   Gr. 6 and up   107 pages

One of the freshest new voices in children's books, Soto is a product of a Latino neighborhood in Fresno, California, that featured a cement factory across the street, a junkyard next door, and a raisin factory at the end of the street. This collection of eleven short stories is largely based on his early teen years, filled with the bittersweet laughter and tears found in all adolescent lives. Also by the author: *Living Up the Street*; *Local News*; *Pacific Crossing*; *The Pool Party*; *The Skirt*; *Summer on Wheels*; *Taking Sides*; and *Too Many Tamales*. For a profile of the author, see *Read All About It!* (a).

Be a Perfect Person in Just Three Days!
by Stephen Manes
Clarion, 1982   Gr. 3–6   76 pages

This laugh-out-loud book is far from great literature but very close to the funny bone. A young boy, tired of bearing the brunt of everyone's taunts, begins a do-it-yourself course in becoming "perfect"—with hilarious and surprising results. Sequel: *Make Four Million Dollars by Next Thursday*. Also by the author: *An Almost Perfect Game*; *The Boy Who Turned into a TV Set*; *Chocolate-Covered Ants*; *The Great Gerbil Roundup*; and *Some of the Adventures of Rhode Island Red*. Related books: *The Giant Baby*, by Allan Ahlberg; *The Shrinking of Treehorn*, by Florence Parry Heide; *Sideways Stories from Wayside School* (n); *Skinnybones* (s); and Jon Scieszka's zany "Time Warp" series: *Knights of the Kitchen Table*; *The Not-So-Jolly Roger*; and *Your Mother Was a Neanderthal*.

The Bears' House by Marilyn Sachs
Dutton, 1987   Gr. 4–6   82 pages

A perfect vehicle for a classroom discussion of values, this novel portrays a ten-year-old girl whose mother is ill and can no longer care for her family after the father deserts them. The girl decides to tend the family, while suffering the taunts of classmates because she sucks her thumb, wears dirty clothes, and smells. To escape, she retreats to the fantasy world she has created in an old dollhouse in her classroom. Sequel: *Fran Ellen's House*. Related books: *Bella Arabella* (s); *The Great Gilly Hopkins*, by Katherine Paterson; *Mrs. Fish, Ape, and Me, the Dump Queen* (n); and *The Hundred Dresses* (s).

Bella Arabella by Liza Fosburgh
Four Winds, 1985   Gr. 1–4   102 pages

Neglected by her wealthy, often-married mother, ten-year-old Arabella finds a substitute family and affection among the servants and cats in the family mansion. But the idea of boarding school is too much for her and she conspires with her best friend, Miranda the cat, and turns into a cat, something she discovers is far from pleasant. Related books: For grades 4–6, look for Paul Gallico's *The Abandoned*, a truly great cat story, published by International Polygonics, Ltd, Madison Square PO Box 1563, New York, NY 10159. Related books: *Catkin*, by Antonia Barber; *The Fox and the Kingfisher*, by Judith Mellecker; *The Monster's Ring* (s); *The Wish Giver* (n); and *The Night Watchmen*, by Helen Cresswell.

The Best Christmas Pageant Ever
by Barbara Robinson
HarperCollins, 1972   Gr. 2–6   80 pages

What happens when the worst-behaved family of kids in town comes to Sunday school and muscles into all the parts for the Christmas pageant? The results are zany and heartwarming; a most unusual Christmas story. Sequel: *The Best School Year Ever*. Related humorous novels: see listing with *Sideways Stories from Wayside School* (n). Other Christmas novels: *Christmas with Ida Early*, by Robert Burch; *The Christmas Spurs*, by Bill Wallace; *The Story of Holly and Ivy* (s); *Young Santa* (s); for Christmas picture books, see *Santa Calls* (p).

The Big Lie: A True Story by Isabella Leitner
Scholastic, 1993   Gr. 3 and up   79 pages

A sensitive but straightforward first-person account of one family's Holocaust experience, this is one of the very few books on the subject written for primary grades—but powerful enough to hold older students as well. Related books: See listing with *Number the Stars* (n).

A Blue-Eyed Daisy by Cynthia Rylant
Simon & Schuster, 1985   Gr. 4–8   99 pages

This is the warm yet bittersweet year in the life of an eleven-year-old girl and her family in the hills of West Virginia as she experiences her first kiss, has a brush with death, comes to understand her good but hard-drinking father, and begins to grow into a person you'd love to have as a relative. Also by the author: *But I'll Be Back Again*—her autobiography for older students; *Best Wishes*—her autobiography for younger children; *A Couple of Kooks and Other Stories About Love* (s); *A Fine White Dust*; *Henry and Mudge* (picture-book series); *Missing May*; *The Relatives Came*; *Soda Jerk* (poetry); *Waiting to Waltz: A Childhood* (poetry). Related books: *Bridge to Terabithia* (n); *Ida Early Comes over the Mountain* (n); *Miracle at Clement's Pond* (n); *Little Jim*, by Gloria Houston; and *Sable*, by Karen Hesse.

Chocolate Fever by Robert K. Smith
Dell, 1978   Gr. 1–5   94 pages

Henry Green doesn't just *like* chocolate—he's insane over it. He even has chocolate sprinkles on his cereal and chocolate cake for breakfast. He is a prime candidate to come down with the world's first case of "chocolate fever." Funny with a subtle message for moderation. *Jelly Belly*, also by the author, uses humor and insight to describe the self-image problems of an overweight child. In *Jelly Belly*, as well as in *The War with Grandpa*, Smith paints a powerful picture of the relationship between child and grandparent. Also by the author: *Bobby Baseball*; *Mostly Michael*; and *The Squeaky Wheel*. Related books: *The Chocolate Touch* (n); *Charlie and the Chocolate Factory*, by Roald Dahl; *The Kids' Book of Chocolate*, a book of chocolate history and facts by Richard Ammon. For other food books, see *Never Take a Pig to Lunch and Other Poems About the Fun of Food* (po).

A Couple of Kooks and Other Stories About Love
by Cynthia Rylant
Orchard, 1990   Gr. 8 and up   112 pages

One of today's most versatile writers, Rylant offers us eight short, poignant love stories about memorable and diverse people we come to know and care about deeply. For other titles by the author, see listing with *A Blue-Eyed Daisy* (s).

The Courage of Sarah Noble
by Alice Dalgliesh ☆ Illustrated by Leonard Weisgard
Simon & Schuster/Atheneum, 1986   K–3   54 pages

At the beginning of the eighteenth century, an eight-year-old girl journeyed into the colonial wilderness with her father. With her family's instructions—"Keep up your courage!"—ringing in her ears, she faces the dangers of the forest while Father builds their new cabin. Just when she feels she has confronted all her fears, her father asks her to stay in the nearby Indian village while he returns for the rest of the family. Based on a true incident, the story is an excellent introduction to the historical novel in a short form. Also by the author: *The Bears on Hemlock Mountain*; *The Silver Pencil* (an autobiographical novel); and *The Thanksgiving Story*.

Related books on courage: *The Bear That Heard Crying*, by Natalie Kinsey-Warnock and Helen Kinsey; *Belinda's Hurricane*, by Elizabeth Winthrop; *Brave Irene* (p); *The Cabin Key*, by Gloria Rand; *Captain Snap and the Children of Vinegar Lane* (p); *A Clearing in the Forest: A Story About a Real Settler Boy*, by Joanne Landers Henry; *Harald and the Giant Knight* and *Harald and the Great Stag* (p), both by Donald Carrick; *The Hero of Bremen*, retold by Margaret Hodges; *The Hunter* (p); *Katie's Trunk*, by Ann Turner; *The Lighthouse Keeper's Daughter*, by Arielle North Olson; *The Lily Cupboard*, by Shulamith L. Oppenheim; *A Lion to Guard Us* (s); *The Samurai's Daughter* (p); *Toliver's Secret* (n); *Twenty and Ten*, by Claire H. Bishop; *Wagon Wheels* (p); and *When I Was Scared*, by Helena Cleere Pittman. For historical picture books, see listing with *By the Dawn's Early Light* (p).

The Day It Rained Forever: A Story of the Johnstown Flood
by Virginia T. Gross
Viking, 1991   Gr. 2–5   64 pages

On that rainy day in 1899, Christina and her family were still grieving for the child their mother had lost in childbirth two months earlier. The incessant rain only darkened their sense of loss. Before the day is out, however, the community's dam will burst, sending 20 million tons of water through Johnstown and killing thousands. But on its crest waters will float a small baby who will be rescued by Christina's mother and then brought into the family.

This short volume is part of Viking/Puffin's excellent Once Upon America series that brings alive famous moments and movements in U.S. history through fictionalized children and their families. Other books in the series include: *Beautiful Land: A Story of the Oklahoma Land Rush*, by Nancy Antle; *The Bite of the Gold Bug: A Story of the Alaskan Gold Rush*, by Barthe DeClements; *Child Star: When Talkies Came to Hollywood* and *Close to Home: A Story of the Polio Epidemic*, by Lydia Weaver; *Earthquake! A Story of Old San Francisco*, *Facing West: A Story of the Oregon Trail*, and *Hero Over Here: A Story of World War I*, by Kathleen V. Kudlinski; *Fire! The Beginnings of the Labor Movement*, by Barbara Diamond Goldin; *Hannah's Fancy Notions: A Story of Industrial New*

England, by Pat Ross; *Hard Times: A Story of the Great Depression,* by Nancy Antle; *It's Only Goodbye: An Immigrant Story,* by Virginia T. Gross; *A Long Way to Go: A Story of Women's Right to Vote,* by Zibby O'Neal; *Lone Star: A Story of the Texas Rangers, Night Bird: A Story of the Seminole Indians,* and *Pearl Harbor Is Burning! A Story of World War II,* by Kathleen V. Kudlinski; *Red Means Good Fortune: A Story of San Francisco's Chinatown,* by Barbara Goldin; *The President Is Dead: A Story of the JFK Assassination,* by Virginia T. Gross; and *Tough Choices: A Story of the Vietnam War,* by Nancy Antle. *America Alive,* by Jean Karl, is an excellent illustrated book on American history, covering the Ice Age to George Bush in 112 pages; see also the listing with *By the Dawn's Early Light* (p).

Four Miles to Pinecone by Jon Hassler
Fawcett, 1977   Gr. 4–8   116 pages

Working his grocery-store summer job, Tom recognizes one of the two youths who beat and rob his employer. He wrestles with the question of exposing his friend to the police, turning this simply written tale into a taut drama of family, peer pressure, and personal responsibility. Related books: *Building Blocks,* by Cynthia Voight; *Deadly Game at Stony Creek,* by Peter Zachary Cohen. For older students: *The Foxman,* by Gary Paulsen; and *Scorpions* (n).

The Friendship by Mildred Taylor
Dial, 1987   Gr. 4 and up   53 pages

The Logan children (from *Roll of Thunder, Hear My Cry*) witness the searing cruelty of bigotry during this story set in 1933 in rural Mississippi, where two men (one white, one black) see their one-time friendship destroyed by violence when the black man breaks tradition and calls the other by his first name. Readers should be aware of racial epithets in the context of the story. In the paperback edition, this book is combined with *The Gold Cadillac* in a single volume. For other books by the author and related titles, see listing with *Roll of Thunder, Hear My Cry* (n).

El Güero: A True Adventure Story
by Elizabeth Borton de Treviño
Farrar, Straus & Giroux, 1989   Gr. 4–8   100 pages

In this true story set at the end of the nineteenth century, Mexico's new dictator summons a widely respected judge to his chambers, informing him he was to be exiled instead of executed. He must take his family and move immediately to barren Baja California and conduct his court there. Told through the eyes of the judge's son, El Güero (the blond), the book recounts the hardships of their journey, including the tragic death of his sister from diphtheria. When renegade local troops imprison the judge, the boy crosses desert and mountains through the heart of Indian country to bring help. Related books: *Baseball in April* (s); see also listing with *A Gift for Tia Rosa* (p).

The Half-a-Moon Inn by Paul Fleischman
HarperCollins, 1980   Gr. 2-6   88 pages
   A chilling fantasy-adventure story about a mute boy separated from his mother by a blizzard and later kidnapped by the wicked proprietress of a village inn. Fast-moving, white-knuckle reading. Also by the author, for older students: *The Borning Room* and *The Path of the Pale Horse*. Related books: *A Certain Small Shepherd*, by Rebecca Caudill; *Child of the Silent Night*, by Edith F. Hunter; and *The Widow's Broom*, by Chris Van Allsburg.

Help! I'm a Prisoner in the Library
by Eth Clifford
Houghton Mifflin, 1979   Gr. 1-4   106 pages
   When their father's car runs out of gas in a blizzard, Mary Rose and Jo-Beth are told to stay in the car while Dad goes for help. The two sisters, however, soon leave in search of a bathroom and end up mysteriously locked into an empty old stone library. Before long, the lights go out, the phone goes dead, and a threatening voice cries out, "Off with their heads!" The tension is more dramatic than traumatic, and great fun. Sequels: *The Dastardly Murder of Dirty Pete*; *Just Tell Me When We're Dead!*; *Scared Silly*; *Never Hit a Ghost with a Baseball Bat*. Also by the author: *Harvey's Horrible Snake Disaster*; *The Man Who Sang in the Dark*. Related book: *Old Mother Witch* (p).

Herbie Jones by Suzy Kline
Putnam, 1985   Gr. 1-4   95 pages
   Third-grader Herbie and his irrepressible pal Raymond meet the challenges and trials of third grade—from escaping the bottom reading group to escaping the girls' bathroom. All of it is done with a blend of sensitivity and humor, topped off with some sidesplitting "gross-outs." Also by the author: *What's the Matter with Herbie Jones?*; *Herbie Jones*

and the Class Gift; Herbie Jones and the Monster Ball; Herbie Jones and Hamburger Head. For older students: *Orp; Orp and the Chop Suey Burgers; Orp Goes to the Hoop; Who's Orp's Girlfriend?* See *Sideways Stories from Wayside School* (n) for other humorous novels.

The Hundred Dresses by Eleanor Estes
Harcourt, Brace, 1944   Gr. 3-6   78 pages

Wanda Petronski comes from the wrong side of the tracks and is the object of class jokes until her classmates sadly realize their awful mistake and cruelty. But by then it's too late. Related books: *The Bears' House* (s); *Crow Boy*, by Taro Yashima; *Mandy*, by Julie Edwards; *Mrs. Fish, Ape, and Me, the Dump Queen* (n); *Sara Crewe* (s); and *The Sleeping Bread*, by Stefan Czernecki and Timothy Rhodes.

The Iron Giant: A Story in Five Nights
by Ted Hughes
HarperCollins, 1987   K-4   58 pages

This story has been labeled science fiction, fantasy, a modern fairy tale—take your pick but don't miss it. With suspense dripping from every page, it describes an invincible iron giant—a robot without a master—that stalks the land. Suddenly the earth faces a threat far greater than that from the giant, when an alien creature lands—forcing the iron man into a fight for his life.

Jacob Two-Two Meets the Hooded Fang
by Mordecai Richler
Knopf, 1975   Gr. 3-5   84 pages

For the crime of insulting a grown-up, Jacob is sent to Children's Prison, where he must confront the infamous Hooded Fang. A marvelous tongue-in-cheek adventure story, sure to delight all. Related book: *The Great Piratical Rumbustification*, by Margaret Mahy.

Lafcadio, the Lion Who Shot Back
by Shel Silverstein
HarperCollins, 1963   Gr. 2-6   90 pages

Lafcadio decides he isn't satisfied being a lion—he must become a marksman and man-about-town and painter and world traveler and . . . He tries just about everything and anything in hopes of finding happiness. If only he'd try being himself. A witty and thought-provoking book.

See listing under *Where the Sidewalk Ends* (po) for other books by the author.

A Lion to Guard Us by Clyde Robert Bulla
HarperCollins, 1981   K-4   117 pages

In a simple prose style that is rich in character and drama, one of America's most noted historical writers for children gives us a poignant tale of the founding fathers of the Jamestown colony and the families they left behind in England. Here we meet a plucky heroine named Amanda who is determined to hold fast to her brother and sister despite the grim agonies of their mother's death, followed by poverty and a shipwreck. All the while she clings to the dream that someday she will find the father who left them all behind. In another historical novel, *Charlie's House*, the author portrays a dreamy English boy turned out by his family and eventually indentured to colonial farmers around 1750. Though his story is told with a grim realism, *Charlie's House* is another moving tribute to youthful determination and courage. Related historical books for young listeners: See *The Courage of Sarah Noble* (s). Also by the author: *The Chalk Box Kid*; *Charlie's House*; *The Christmas Coat*; *Daniel's Duck*; *Ghost Town Treasure*; *Last Look*; *My Friend the Monster*; *Pirate's Promise*; *The Poppy Seeds* (p); *Shoeshine Girl*; *The Sword in the Tree*; and *White Bird*.

The Littles by John Peterson
Scholastic, 1970   Gr. 1-4   80 pages

Children have always been fascinated with the idea of "little people"—from leprechauns to Lilliputians, from Thumbelina to hobbits. Unfortunately, much of the famous fantasy literature is often too sophisticated for reading aloud to young children. The Littles series is the exception—fast-paced short novels centering on a colony of six-inch people who live inside the walls of the Bigg family's home and have dramatic escapades with gigantic mice, cats, gliders, and telephones. Also in the series: *The Littles and the Lost Children*; *The Littles and the Terrible Tiny Kid*; *The Littles and the Trash Tinies*; *The Littles Give a Party*; *The Littles Go Exploring*; *The Littles Have a Wedding*; *The Littles Take a Trip*; and *The Littles to the Rescue*. Related picture books: *George Shrinks*, by William Joyce; *The Minpins* (p); *The Story of Imelda Who Was Small*, by Morris Lurie; *Thumbeline*, illustrated by Lisbeth Zwerger; *Tom Thumb*, retold by Richard Jesse Watson; for older students: *The*

Borrowers and *Poor Stainless*, both by Mary Norton; *The Indian in the Cupboard* (n); and *Stuart Little*, by E. B. White.

Lizzie's List by Maggie Harrison
Candlewick, 1993   Gr. 1-3   105 pages

Living alone with her mother, Lizzie compiles a list of what she wants most: a grandmother, grandfather, aunt, uncle, cousins, and a baby. What follows is a tender yet hilarious adventure in reverse adoption. Related book: *The Best Christmas Pageant Ever* (s).

The Monster's Ring by Bruce Coville
Pantheon, 1982   Gr. 2-4   87 pages

Just the thing for Halloween reading, this is the Jekyll-and-Hyde tale of timid Russell and the magic ring he buys that can turn him into a monster—not a *make-believe* monster but one with hairy hands, fangs, and claws, one that roams the night, one that will terrify Eddie the bully, and one that will bring out the worst in Russell. An exciting fantasy of magic gone awry. Sequel: *Jennifer Murdley's Toad*. Also by the author: *Aliens Ate My Homework*; *The Ghost Wore Gray*; *Jeremy Thatcher, Dragon Hatcher*; and *My Teacher Glows in the Dark*. Related books: *Among the Dolls* (s); *Bella Arabella* (n); and *Black and Blue Magic*, by Zilpha K. Snyder.

My Father's Dragon by Ruth Stiles Gannett
Knopf, 1948   K-2   78 pages

Here is a three-volume series bursting with fantasy, hair-raising escapes, and evil creatures. The tone is dramatic enough to be exciting for even mature preschoolers but not enough to frighten them. The narrator relates the tales as adventures that happened to his father when he was a boy. This is an excellent transition series for introducing children to longer stories with fewer pictures. The rest of the series, in order: *Elmer and the Dragon*; *The Dragons of Blueland*. For related dragon books, see listing with *The Reluctant Dragon* (s).

My Grandmother's Stories: A Collection of Jewish Folk Tales by Adele Geras ✿ Illustrated by Jael Jordan
Knopf, 1990   Gr. 3-6   96 pages

What could be more charming or more inviting than a young girl in her grandmother's kitchen, chewing on the delicious stories the woman tells while baking and cooking. Each story/chapter is a moral lesson.

For related food stories, see listing with *Never Take a Pig to Lunch and Other Poems About the Fun of Food* (po).

My Naughty Little Sister
by Dorothy Edwars ✿ Illustrated by Shirley Hughes
Clarion, 1990   K-3   96 pages

In twelve delightful tales, the author looks back fondly on her English childhood and recalls her mischievous, ever-curious sister and the trouble she caused—like the time she and a friend found workers' lunch pails beside the road and had a food fight.

Old Yeller by Fred Gipson
HarperCollins, 1956   Gr. 3-6   117 pages

While Father is away on a cattle drive, the family must fend for itself in this nonstop novel set on a Texas farm in the 1860s. Together with their adopted stray dog, Mother and two sons battle skunks, wild boars, bulls, bears, stubborn mules, and rabies in a tale that tugs on both your attention and your heartstrings. Sequel: *Savage Sam.* An interesting contrast can be made with the pioneer family in *Caddie Woodlawn* (n). See also listing of dog stories with *A Dog Called Kitty* (n).

On My Honor by Marion Dane Bauer
Clarion, 1986   Gr. 5-9   90 pages

When his daredevil best friend drowns in a swimming accident, Joel tells no one and returns home to deny the reality and truth of the tragedy. This gripping drama of conscience and consequences is also a story of choices—the ones we make and those we refuse to make. Also by the author: *Rain of Fire.* Related books for older students: *Jumping the Nail,* by Eve Bunting; *Killing Mr. Griffin* (n); and *Wolf Rider* (n).

Owls in the Family by Farley Mowat
Little, Brown, 1961   Gr. 2-6   108 pages

No child should miss the author's reliving of his rollicking boyhood on the Saskatchewan prairie, where he raised dogs, gophers, rats, snakes, pigeons, and owls. It is an era we will never see again. Mowat would grow up to become a world-famous author and naturalist (writer of *Never Cry Wolf,* book and film). Also by the author: *Lost in the Barrens*; and for older readers and adults, his irreverent, entertaining autobiography: *Born Naked.* Related books: *Capyboppy,* by Bill Peet; *Gentle Ben* (n); and *My Side of the Mountain* (n).

The Reluctant Dragon
by Kenneth Grahame ✲ Illustrated by Ernest H. Shepard
Holiday, 1938   Gr. 3-5   54 pages

The author of the classic *Wind in the Willows* offers us here a simple boy-and-dragon story. The dragon is not a devouring dragon but a reluctant one who wants nothing to do with violence. The boy is something of a local scholar, well versed in dragon lore and torn mightily between his desire to view a battle between the dragon and Saint George and his desire to protect his friend the dragon. For experienced listeners. Related books: *The Book of Dragons*, by E. Nesbit; *The Dragon, Giant, and Monster Treasury*, selected by Caroline Royds; *The Dragonling*, by Jackie French Koller; *The Dragons Are Singing Tonight*, by Jack Prelutsky; *Everyone Knows What a Dragon Looks Like*, by Jay Williams; *Matthew's Dragon* (p); *My Father's Dragon* (s); *The River Dragon*, by Darcy Pattison; *Saint George and the Dragon*, retold by Margaret Hodges; and *The Story of Ferdinand* (p).

Rip-Roaring Russell by Johanna Hurwitz
Morrow, 1983   K-2   96 pages

In this delightful introduction to chapter and series books, we follow little Russell, his younger sister Elisa, and their friends through preschool, kindergarten, and primary grades, and we meet the neighbors in their New York apartment house. Few authors have their finger on the subtle pulse of childhood the way Hurwitz does. No one can resist loving the characters in her books. After this first book, the series reads in this order: *Russell Sprouts*; *Russell Rides Again*; *Russell and Elisa*; *E Is for Elisa*; and *Make Room for Elisa*. Another lighthearted series by the same author for slightly older children is the Aldo series—*Aldo Applesauce*; *Much Ado About Aldo*; *Aldo Ice Cream*; and *Aldo Peanut Butter*.

Related titles: *Ramona the Pest* (n); and this series by Janice Lee Smith about Adam Joshua and his primary grade classmates—(in order) *The Monster in the Third Dresser Drawer*; *The Kid Next Door and Other Headaches*; *The Show-and-Tell War*; *It's Not Easy Being George*; *Nelson in Love*; *There's a Ghost in the Coatroom*; *The Turkey's Side of It*; *Serious Science*; and *The Baby Blues*.

Sara Crewe by Frances Hodgson Burnett
Scholastic, 1986   Gr. 3-6   79 pages

This tale, as powerful today as it was nearly one hundred years ago when it was written, is the story of the star boarder at Miss Minchin's exclusive London boarding school, who is suddenly orphaned and becomes a ward of the cruel headmistress. Friendless, penniless, and banished to the attic as a servant, Sara holds fast to her courage and dreams—until at last she finds a friend and deliverance in a heartwarming surprise ending. Try comparing this story with that of the orphan child in *Peppermints in the Parlor* (n). *Sara Crewe* was expanded by the author into an equally successful longer novel, *A Little Princess*; both are for experienced listeners. Also by the author: *The Secret Garden*. For a profile of the author, see *Hey! Listen to This* (a). Related books: *Mandy*, by Julie Edwards; and *Understood Betsy* (n).

Skinnybones by Barbara Park

Knopf, 1982   Gr. 3-5   112 pages

Author Barbara Park is one of the funniest voices writing for middle-grade children. Her characters may not always be lovable, but they are remarkably alive and interesting as they deal with losing ball games, moving, camp, or sibling rivalries. But best of all, they are funny; not cutesy or caustic, but genuinely and interestingly funny. Typical is Alex Frankovitch of *Skinnybones*, who is an uncoordinated smart aleck who throws tantrums; he's also a laugh a minute. Sequel: *Almost Starring Skinnybones*. Also by the author: *Beanpole*; *Buddies*; *Dear God, Help!*; *Love, Earl*; *Don't Make Me Smile*; *The Kid in the Red Jacket*; *Operation Dump the Chump*; *Maxie, Rosie and Earl—Partners in Grime*; *My Mother Got Married—and Other Disasters*; and *Rosie Swanson, Fourth-Grade Geek for President*. See also books listed with *Sideways Stories from Wayside School* (n).

Soup by Robert Newton Peck

Knopf, 1974   Gr. 4-6   96 pages

Two Vermont pals share a genius for getting themselves into trouble. The stories are set in the rural 1930s when life was simpler and the days seemed longer. But the need for a best friend was just as great. Sequels: *Soup and Me*; *Soup Ahoy*; *Soup for President*; *Soup in Love*; *Soup in the Saddle*; *Soup on Fire*; *Soup on Ice*; *Soup on Wheels*; *Soup's Drum*; *Soup's Goat*; *Soup's Hoop*; *Soup's Uncle*; for older children, *A Day No Pigs Would Die* (n). Related books: *Homer Price* (n); *The Great Brain* (n); *The Not-Just-Anybody Family*, by Betsy Byars.

Stargone John by Ellen Kindt McKenzie
Holt, 1990   Gr. 1-5   67 pages
   In the midst of a turn-of-the-century one-room schoolhouse, six-year-old John meets the new teacher on his first day at school. Her iron-willed and ironhanded approach to teaching sends the introverted child even deeper into his imaginary cave, where he is determined to stay until his teacher leaves. John eventually saves the day and learns to read—thanks to secret lessons from the town's retired but blind school-mistress. Related book: *Caddie Woodlawn* (n).

Stone Fox by John R. Gardiner
Crowell, 1980   Gr. 1-7   96 pages
   Here is a story that, like its ten-year-old hero, never stands still. It is filled to the brim with action and determination, the love of a child for his grandfather, and the loyalty of a great dog for his young master. Based on a Rocky Mountain legend, the story describes the valiant efforts of young Willy to save his ailing grandfather's farm by attempting to win the purse in a local bobsled race. The figure of Stone Fox, the towering favorite for the race, is an unusual departure from the Indian stereotype in children's literature. Also by the author: *Top Secret*. Related books: *Bristle Face*, by Zachary Ball; *Old Yeller* (s); *Shiloh*, by Phyllis Naylor; and *Where the Red Fern Grows* (n).

The Stories Julian Tells by Ann Cameron
Pantheon, 1981   K-3   72 pages
   The author takes six short stories involving Julian and his brother and weaves them into a fabric that glows with the mischief, magic, and imagination of childhood. Though centered on commonplace subjects like desserts, gardens, loose teeth, and new neighbors, these stories of family life are written in an uncommon way that will both amuse and touch young listeners. Sequels: *Julian, Dream Doctor*; *Julian's Glorious Summer*; *Julian, Secret Agent*; *More Stories Julian Tells*. Related book: *Philip Hall Likes Me, I Reckon Maybe*, by Bette Greene.

The Story of Holly and Ivy by Rumer Godden
Viking, 1985   K-5   31 pages
   This is the loving tale of a lonely runaway orphan girl, an unsold Christmas doll, and a childless couple on Christmas Eve. But with Rumer Godden's talent combined with Barbara Cooney's lustrous illustrations, it is unforgettable. The true story of *Polar, the Titanic Bear*, by Daisy

C. S. Spedden, makes an excellent companion book. Related books: *Bella Arabella* (s); *Mandy,* by Julie Edwards; and the listing of Christmas picture books with *Santa Calls* (p).

A Taste of Blackberries
by Doris B. Smith ✫ Illustrated by Charles Robinson
HarperCollins, 1973   Gr. 4-7   52 pages

In viewing death from a child's point of view, Mrs. Smith allows us to follow the narrator's emotions as he comes to terms with the death of his best friend, who died as a result of an allergic reaction to bee stings. The sensitivity with which the attendant sorrow and guilt are treated makes this an outstanding book. It blazed the way for many other grief books that quickly followed, but few have approached the place of honor this one holds. Also by the author: *Last Was Lloyd; Return to Bitter Creek.* Related books about death: *Bridge to Terabithia* (n); *A Day No Pigs Would Die* (n); *Dead Birds Singing,* by Marc Talbert; *The Kids' Book About Death and Dying,* by Eric Rofes; and *On My Honor* (s); for younger children, see listing with *A Gift for Tia Rosa* (p).

Terror in the Towers by Adrian Kerson
Knopf, 1993   Gr. 3-6   96 pages

This is one of the Read It to Believe It series of true-life adventure stories, written with a high sense of drama for reluctant readers. This volume describes the courageous victims in the World Trade Center disaster. Other books and subjects in the series include: *Adventure in Alaska* (Iditarod race); *Head for the Hills!* (Johnstown flood); *The Silent Hero* (World War II); *Survive! Could You?* (survival stories); *They Survived Mount St. Helens* (volcano). Related disaster books: *The Day It Rained Forever: A Story of the Johnstown Flood* (s); see also listing of titles with *Hatchet* (n).

The Whipping Boy by Sid Fleischman
Greenwillow, 1986   Gr. 3-6   90 pages

The brattish medieval prince is too spoiled ever to be spanked, so the king regularly vents his anger on Jeremy, a peasant "whipping boy." When circumstances lead the two boys to reverse roles, each learns much about friendship and sacrifice. Painted with Fleischman's broad humor, this is a fast-paced Newbery-winning melodrama with short, cliff-hanger chapters. Also by the author: See *Humbug Mountain* (n).

Willa and Old Miss Annie
by Berlie Doherty ✶ Illustrated by Kim Lewis
Candlewick, 1994   K–3   92 pages

When she moves to a rural village in Great Britain, little Willa has no pals until her elderly and initially frightening neighbor befriends her and introduces her to a succession of homeless animals. Told in two-page chapters, the tale moves swiftly and with poignancy. An excellent introduction to chapter books. For related books about the elderly, see *Old Mother Witch* (p).

Wolf Story by William McCleery
Shoe String Press, 1988   K–3   82 pages

One of the great chapter-book read-alouds, this is a story on two tracks: (1) the affectionate contest of wills between a five-year-old and his father as the latter attempts to tell a bedtime story and the child insists on editing the tale; and (2) the bedtime story itself, in which a crafty wolf tries to outwit an equally determined hen.

Young Santa by Dan Greenburg
Viking, 1991   Gr. 2–7   72 pages

This is a hilarious spoof on the origins of Santa Claus. To get you started, Santa was named in memory of his parents' vacation in Santa Fe, and his father was a refrigerator salesman transferred to the North Pole. It gets better and better, with lots of tongue-in-cheek humor. Also by the author: *Jumbo the Boy and Arnold the Elephant* (p). For other Christmas titles, see *Santa Calls* (p).

NOVELS

The Adventures of Pinocchio
by Carlo Collodi ✶ Illustrated by Roberto Innocenti
Knopf, 1988   Gr. 1–5   144 pages

Unfortunately, most children's familiarity with this 1892 classic comes from the emasculated movie version. Treat your children to the real version of the poor woodcarver's puppet who faces all the temptations of childhood, succumbs to many, learns from his follies, and gains his boyhood by selflessly giving of himself. The Knopf edition, the most lavishly illustrated ever, is the *real* Pinocchio. Related books: *Bella Arabella* (n); *The Bad Times of Irma Baumlein*, by Carol R. Brink; *The Real Thief*, by William Steig; and *The Story of Holly and Ivy* (s).

The Animal Family by Randall Jarrell
Pantheon, 1965   Gr. 3-7   180 pages

In a beautiful allegory on the need for community and family, a lonely hunter brings a mermaid home to his island cabin. Over time he adopts a bear cub, a lynx, and, finally, an orphaned child. Jarrell, an honored poet, wraps this unconventional community in the warm humor and love that permeate the best of families. Though no great plot unfolds, the reader/listener is drawn into the characters so deeply you begin to care for them. As one teacher described the book: "It's like a warm glove." For experienced listeners. Related books: *Beauty and the Beast*, translated by Richard Howard; *The Boy Who Lived with the Seals* (p); *Charlotte's Web* (n); *The Fox and the Kingfisher*, by Judith Mellecker; *Greyling* (p); and *Stories by Firelight*, by Shirley Hughes.

Bill Peet: An Autobiography by Bill Peet
Houghton Mifflin, 1989   Gr. 3-5   190 pages

Though not a novel, this autobiography belongs here because of its size. By far one of the best and most accessible autobiographies (or biographies) for early- and middle-grade students, this Caldecott honor book provides a behind-the-scenes view of how the children's author/ illustrator rose to fame, including a candid discussion of his two decades in the film industry working for Walt Disney. Students will enjoy discovering the roots of their favorite Peet books in his fatherless childhood in rural Indiana, and learning about how he developed the great Disney animation films of the forties and fifties. It is an excellent read-aloud for art classes. For a complete listing of books by the author, see *The Whing-dingdilly* (p).

Black Beauty
by Anna Sewell ☆ Illustrated by Charles Keeping
Farrar, Straus & Giroux, 1990   Gr. 4-8   214 pages

In one of the classic animal novels of all time and the first with the animal as narrator, the author vividly describes the cruelty to horses during the Victorian period, as well as giving a detailed picture of life at that time. For a profile of Anna Sewell, see *Hey! Listen to This* (a). Related books: *Bambi*, by Felix Salten; the Black Stallion series, by Walter Farley; *Danza!*, by Lynn Hall; and *King of the Wind: The Story of the Godolphin Arabian*, by Marguerite Henry.

Bridge to Terabithia by Katherine Paterson
Crowell, 1977   Gr. 4–7   128 pages

Few novels for children have dealt with so many emotions and issues so well: sports, school, peers, friendship, death, guilt, art, and family. A Newbery winner, this book deserves to be read or heard by everyone. Also by the author: *The Great Gilly Hopkins*. Related books: *Miracle at Clement's Pond* (n); *A Taste of Blackberries* (s); *King Kong and Other Poets*, by Robert Burch. See *Tuck Everlasting* (n) and *A Gift for Tia Rosa* (p) for additional titles dealing with the theme of death or dying.

Caddie Woodlawn by Carol Ryrie Brink
Simon & Schuster, 1935   Gr. 4–6   286 pages

You take *The Little House on the Prairie*; I'll take *Caddie Woodlawn*. Ten times over, I'll take this tomboy of the 1860s with her pranks, her daring visits to Indian camps, her one-room schoolhouse fights, and her wonderfully believable family. Try to pick up the 1973 revised edition with Trina Schart Hyman's illustrations. For experienced listeners. Sequel: *Magical Melons*. Also by the author: *The Bad Times of Irma Baumlein*. For a comparative study, see *Introducing Shirley Braverman* by Hilma Wolitzer. Related books: *Hannah's Farm: The Seasons on an Early American Homestead*, by Michael McCurdy; *Sarah, Plain and Tall*, by Patricia MacLachlin; *Understood Betsy* (n); and *Weasel* (n).

The Call of the Wild by Jack London
multiple publishers   Gr. 6 and up   126 pages

This 1903 dog story, set amidst the rush for gold in the Klondike, depicts the savagery and tenderness between man and his environment in unforgettable terms. For experienced listeners. Also by the author: *White Fang*. Related books: *The Bite of the Gold Bug: A Story of the Alaskan Gold Rush*, by Barthe DeClements, is excellent for Gr. 1–3 students; *Gold: The True Story of Why People Search for It, Mine It, Trade It, Steal It, Mint It, Hoard It, Fight and Kill for It*, nonfiction by Milton Meltzer; see *A Dog Called Kitty* (n) for related dog novels.

Captain Grey by Avi
Morrow, 1993   Gr. 4–7   141 pages

A swashbuckling pirate story told in the classic adventure style, it deals with a young boy's determination to free himself from a band of pirates based on the New Jersey shoreline just after the Revolutionary War. For experienced listeners. See Author/Illustrator Index for a list of Avi titles.

Related pirate books: *The Ghost in the Noonday Sun*, by Sid Fleischman; *Maury and the Nightpirates*, by Dieter Wiesmuller; *The Not-So-Jolly Roger*, by Jon Scieszka; and *Pirate's Promise*, by Clyde Robert Bulla; see also *Weasel* (n).

The Case of the Baker Street Irregular
by Robert Newman
Atheneum, 1978   Gr. 4-8   216 pages

   This finely crafted mystery novel is an excellent introduction to the world of Sherlock Holmes for young readers. A young orphan is suddenly pitted against the dark side of turn-of-the-century London when his tutor-guardian is kidnapped. Complete with screaming street urchins, sinister cabdrivers, bombings, murder, back alleys, and a child's-eye view of the great sleuth himself—Sherlock Holmes. For experienced listeners. Sequels: *The Case of the Vanishing Corpse*; *The Case of the Watching Boy*. Related books: *Peppermints in the Parlor* (n); and *The December Rose* (n).

The Cay by Theodore Taylor
Doubleday, 1969   Gr. 2-6   144 pages

   An exciting adventure about a blind white boy and an old black man shipwrecked on a tiny Caribbean island. The first chapters are slow but the story builds with taut drama to a stunning ending. Sequel/prequel: *Timothy of the Cay*. Also by the author: *Sniper*. See *Hatchet* (n) for other survival books.

Charlotte's Web
by E. B. White ✳ Illustrated by Garth Williams
HarperCollins, 1952   K-4   184 pages

   One of the most acclaimed books in children's literature, it is loved by adults as well as children. The tale centers on the barnyard life of a young pig who is to be butchered in the fall. The animals of the yard (particularly a haughty gray spider named Charlotte) conspire with the farmer's daughter to save the pig's life. While there is much humor in the novel, the author uses wisdom and pathos in developing his theme of friendship within the cycle of life. Also by the author: *Stuart Little*. Beverly Gherman's *E. B. White: Some Writer!* is an excellent children's biography of the author. If you are using *Charlotte* as part of your curriculum, a copy of *The Annotated Charlotte's Web*, from HarperCollins, will be invaluable. Related books: *Ace: The Very Important Pig* and *All*

Pigs Are Beautiful, both by Dick King-Smith; *The Animal Family* (n); *Cricket in Times Square* by George Selden; *Lost in the Fog*, by Irving Bacheller; *Pearl's Promise* (n); *Rabbit Hill*, by Robert Lawson; and *Spiders*, by Gail Gibbons.

The Chocolate Touch by Patrick Skene Catling
Morrow, 1979   Gr. 1–4   122 pages

Here is a new and delicious twist to the old King Midas story. Young John learns a dramatic lesson in self-control when everything he touches with his lips turns to chocolate—toothpaste, bacon and eggs, water, pencils, trumpet. What would happen, then, if he kissed his mother? Either before or after reading this story, read the original version, "The Golden Touch" (for fifth grade and up, the tale is included as one of the stories in Nathaniel Hawthorne's *A Wonder Book*). Other related books: *The Adventures of King Midas*, by Lynn Reid Banks; *The Boy Who Spoke Colors*, by David Gifaldi; *Chocolate Fever* (s); *The King, the Princess, and the Tinker*, by Ellen Kindt McKenzie; *The Marvelous Blue Mouse*, by Christopher Manson; and *The Search for Delicious* (n).

The Curse of the Blue Figurine
by John Bellairs
Dial, 1983   Gr. 4–8   200 pages

If you are looking for intelligent alternatives to the Goosebumps series, look no further than the works of John Bellairs. In this book, Johnny Dixon removes a small figurine from the basement of his church, only to be haunted by the evil spirits attached to it. Johnny and his professor friend continue their spine-tingling exploits down twisted tunnels in: *The Mummy, the Will and the Crypt*; *The Revenge of the Wizard's Ghost*; and *The Spell of the Sorcerer's Skull*. Another series by the same author includes young Anthony Monday and the local librarian: *The Dark Secret of Weatherend*; *Mansion in the Mist*; *The Treasure of Alpheus Winterborn*; and *Lamp from the Warlock's Tomb*. The following books were completed by Brad Strickland after John Bellairs' death: *The Drum, the Doll, and the Zombie*; *The Ghost in the Mirror*; and *The Vengeance of the Witch-Finder*. Related books: *The Case of the Baker Street Irregular* (n); *Peppermints in the Parlor* (n); and *The December Rose* (n).

Danny, Champion of the World
by Roald Dahl
Knopf, 1975   Gr. 3-6   196 pages

This is the exciting and tender story of a motherless boy and his father—"the most wonderful father who ever lived"—and their adventure together. Teachers and parents should explain the custom and tradition of "poaching" in England before going too deeply into the story (Robin Hood was a poacher). See *James and the Giant Peach* (n) for other books by the author. Try comparing the experiences of Danny with those of Leigh Botts, a boy in *Dear Mr. Henshaw* (n).

A Day No Pigs Would Die by Robert Newton Peck
Knopf, 1972   Gr. 6 and up   150 pages

Set among Shaker farmers in Vermont during the 1920s, this is the poignant story of the author's coming of age at thirteen, his adventures, fears, and triumphs. As a novel of life and death, it should be read carefully by the teacher or parent before it is read aloud to children. A very moving story for experienced listeners. Sequel: *A Part of the Sky*. Also by the author: the Soup series (s). Related books: *Isaac Campion*, by Janni Howker; *Where the Red Fern Grows* (n); *Words by Heart* (n); and *Old Yeller* (s).

Dear Mr. Henshaw by Beverly Cleary
Morrow, 1983   Gr. 3-6   134 pages

In this 1984 Newbery Medal winner, Beverly Cleary departs from her Ramona format to write a very different but every bit as successful book—perhaps the finest in her long career. Using only the letters and diary of a young boy (Leigh Botts), the author traces his personal growth from first grade to sixth. We watch the changes in his relationship with his divorced parents, his schools (where he always ends up the friendless "new kid"), an author with whom he corresponds over the years, and finally with himself. There is wonderful humor here, but there is also much sensitivity to the heartaches that confront the growing number of Leigh Bottses in our homes and classrooms. Also by the author: *Ramona the Pest* (first of the Ramona series) (n); *The Mouse and the Motorcycle* (first of a series of three). Related books: *Danny, Champion of the World* (n); *Thank You, Jackie Robinson* (n); and *Mostly Michael*, by Robert K. Smith.

The December Rose by Leon Garfield
Viking, 1986   Gr. 6 and up   208 pages

If Dickens were alive today, he'd be Garfield's biggest fan, which is only fair since Garfield is his. Set in Victorian London, this is the gothic tale of a wily chimney sweep who becomes embroiled with a gang of murderous thieves as colorful as Dickens's best. For experienced listeners. For a profile of the author, see *Read All About It!* (a). Related book: *The Case of the Baker Street Irregular* (n).

A Dog Called Kitty by Bill Wallace
Holiday, 1980   Gr. 1–5   137 pages

In this first-person narrative, a young boy struggles to overcome the deep-seated fear of dogs caused by his traumatic experience with a vicious dog during early childhood. Don't be misled by the cutesy title of this book; it is a powerfully moving story of childhood and family. Also by the author: *Beauty*; *Blackwater Swamp*; *Buffalo Gal*; *The Christmas Spurs*; *Danger in Quicksand Swamp*; *Ferret in the Bedroom, Lizards in the Fridge*; *Never Say Quit*; *Red Dog*; *Trapped in Death Cave*; *Shadow on the Snow*; *Snot Stew*; and *Trapped in Death Cave*.

Other great dog stories: *Big Red*, by Jim Kjelgaard; *Call of the Wild* (n); *Danger Dog* and *Soul of the Silver Dog*, both by Lynn Hall; *Dear Mr. Henshaw* and *Strider*, both by Beverly Cleary; *Follow My Leader*, by James B. Garfield; *Foxy*, by Helen Griffith; *Hurry Home, Candy* (n); *Kavik the Wolf Dog* and *Scrub Dog of Alaska*, both by Walt Morey; *Lassie-Come-Home* (n); *Sable*, by Karen Hesse; *Shiloh*, by Phyllis Naylor; *Stone Fox* (s); *Old Yeller* (s); *Where the Red Fern Grows* (n); and *Woodsong* (n).

Finding Buck McHenry by Alfred Slote
HarperCollins, 1991   Gr. 3–6   250 pages

Eleven-year-old Jason, baseball-card collector extraordinaire, is convinced that school custodian, Mr. Mack Henry, is really the legendary Buck McHenry of Negro Leagues fame. Before either of them can stop it, the idea steamrolls out of control. Slote creates a rich blend of baseball history, peer relationships (male and female), family, and race relations while never losing sight of a good story. Other books by this master of the sport novel for this age group: *A Friend Like That*; *Hang Tough, Paul Mather*; *Make-Believe Ball Player*; *Matt Gargan's Boy*; *Moving In*; *Rabbit Ears*; and *The Trading Game*. See also: *The Macmillan Book of Baseball Stories*, by Terry Egan; *The Random House Book of Sports Sto-*

ries, by L. M. Schulman; *Shadow Ball: The History of the Negro Leagues,* by Geoffrey Ward and Ken Burns, with Jim O'Connor—based upon "The Fifth Inning" of Ken Burns's PBS series *Baseball: The American Epic; Teammates,* by Peter Golenbock; and *Thank You, Jackie Robinson* (n).

From the Mixed-Up Files of Mrs. Basil E. Frankweiler by E. L. Konigsburg

Atheneum, 1967   Gr. 4-7   162 pages

A bored and brainy twelve-year-old girl talks her nine-year-old brother into running away with her. To throw everyone off their trail, Claudia chooses the Metropolitan Museum of Art in New York City as a refuge, and amid centuries-old art they sleep, dine, bathe, and pray in regal secret splendor. An exciting story of hide-and-seek and a marvelous art lesson to boot. For experienced listeners. In related runaway books: a city boy hides in the wilderness—*My Side of the Mountain* (n); a city boy hides in the subway system—*Slake's Limbo* (n). See also *The Car,* by Gary Paulsen; *The Golden Days,* by Gail Radley; *Home at Last,* by David deVries; and *Maniac Magee* (n).

Gentle Ben by Walt Morey

Dutton, 1965   Gr. 3-6   192 pages

A young boy adopts a huge bear and brings to his family in Alaska all the joys and tears attendant to such a combination. Though the struggle to save animals from ignorant but well-intentioned human predators is one that has been written many times over, Morey's handling of characters, plot, and setting makes an original and exciting tale. He supports the pace of his story with many lessons in environmental science. Also by the author: *Canyon Winter; Kavik the Wolf Dog;* and *Scrub Dog of Alaska.* For a personal profile of Walt Morey, see *Hey! Listen to This* (a). Related books: *Call of the Wild* (n); *Daisy Rothschild: The Giraffe That Lives with Me,* by Betty Leslie-Melville; *The Midnight Fox* (n); *My Side of the Mountain* (n); and *The Grizzly,* by Annabel and Edgar Johnson.

The Gift of the Pirate Queen by Patricia Reilly Giff

Delacorte, 1982   Gr. 2-4   164 pages

By the time their father's cousin arrives from Ireland, the O'Malley girls and their father have pretty well unraveled without a mother in the house. But within a week, the newcomer helps each of them to "do the hard thing" that will heal their melodramas. Also by the author: The

Polk Street School series for early primary grades. Related books: *Ida Early Comes over the Mountain* (n) and *Understood Betsy* (n).

The Girl with the Silver Eyes by Willo Davis Roberts
Atheneum, 1980   Gr. 4-8   181 pages

There is something about nine-year-old Katie that sets her apart—other than the strange silver pupils in her eyes. Her secret is that she has paranormal powers as a result of her mother being exposed to certain factory chemicals during pregnancy. Written as a suspense story, it's also a powerful study of a child who marches to a different drummer and the pain that comes with the march. Also by the author: *View from the Cherry Tree*. Related books: *A Gift of Magic*, by Lois Duncan; and *The Secret Life of Dilly McBean*, by Dorothy Haas.

Good Night, Mr. Tom by Michelle Magorian
HarperCollins, 1981   Gr. 6 and up   318 pages

This is one of the longest novels in the Treasury; it might also be the most powerful. Adults should preview it carefully before reading aloud. It is the story of an eight-year-old London boy evacuated during the blitz to a small English village, where he is reluctantly taken in by a grumpy old man. The boy proves to be an abused child, terrified of everything around him. With painstaking care, the old man begins the healing process, unveiling to the child a world he never knew existed—a world of kindness, friendships, laughter, and hope. For experienced listeners. Also by the author: *Back Home*. Related books: *Home at Last*, by David deVries; *Mandy*, by Julie Edwards; *North to Freedom* (n); *Slake's Limbo* (n); *Understood Betsy* (n); and *So Far from the Bamboo Grove*, by Yoko Watkins.

Good Old Boy by Willie Morris
Yoknapatawpha Press, 1980   Gr. 5-8   128 pages

If Tom Sawyer had lived in the 1940s, this would have been the story Mark Twain would have written. In this funny and suspenseful boyhood memoir, one of the South's finest writers tells us about growing up in the South. Available through Yoknapatawpha Press, P.O. Box 248, Oxford, MS 38655. Also by the author: *Good Old Boy and the Witch of Yazoo*.

The Great Brain by John D. Fitzgerald

Dial, 1967   Gr. 5 and up   175 pages

This is the first book in a series dealing with the hilarious—and often touching—adventures of an Irish-Catholic family surrounded by Utah Mormons in 1896, told through the eyes of a younger brother. Tom Fitzgerald is part boy genius and part con man, but in command of every situation. The series reads well on many levels, including a perspective of daily life at the turn of the century. For experienced listeners. Sequels (in order): *More Adventures of the Great Brain*; *Me and My Little Brain*; *The Great Brain at the Academy*; *The Great Brain Reforms*; *The Return of the Great Brain*; *The Great Brain Does It Again*; and *The Great Brain Is Back.*

Hatchet by Gary Paulsen

Simon & Schuster, 1987   Gr. 6 and up   195 pages

The lone survivor of a plane crash in the Canadian wilderness, a thirteen-year-old boy carries only three things away from the crash: a fierce spirit, the hatchet his mother gave him as a gift, and the secret knowledge that his mother was unfaithful to his father. All play an integral part in this Newbery Honor survival story for experienced listeners. It's an excellent science class read-aloud. Sequel: *The River.* For a Paulsen profile, see *Read All About It!* (a). Also by the author: *The Car*; *Canyons*; *The Crossing*; *The Foxman*; *The Island*; *Monument*; *Nightjohn*; *The Voyage of the Frog*; *Woodsong* (n). Related survival books: *Canyon Winter*, by Walt Morey; *The Cay* (n); *The Iceberg Hermit*, by Arthur Roth; *Lost in the Barrens*, by Farley Mowat; *Lost in the Devil's Desert*, by Gloria Skurzynski; *My Side of the Mountain* (for younger readers) (n); *The Sign of the Beaver* (n); and *Snow Bound* (n).

Homer Price by Robert McCloskey

Viking, 1943   Gr. 2–5   160 pages

A modern classic, this is a collection of humorous tales about a small-town boy's neighborhood dilemmas. Whether it's the story of Homer's foiling the bank robbers with his pet skunk or the tale of his uncle's out-of-control doughnut maker, these six tales will long be remembered. Sequel: *Centerburg Tales.* For a biographical profile of the author, see *Hey! Listen to This* (a). Related books: *Humbug Mountain* (n); *The Great Brain* (n); *Soup* (s); and *Pinch*, by Larry Callen.

Humbug Mountain by Sid Fleischman
Little, Brown, 1978   Gr. 4-6   172 pages

Reminiscent of Mark Twain and overflowing with humor, suspense, and originality, here are the captivating adventures of the Flint family as they battle outlaws, crooked riverboat pilots, ghosts, and their creditors, on the banks of the Missouri River in the late 1800s. Also by the author: *By the Great Horn Spoon*; *Chancy and the Grand Rascal*; *The Ghost in the Noonday Sun*; *Mr. Mysterious & Company*; *The Midnight Horse*; *The Whipping Boy* (s). Related books: *Homer Price* (n) and *Maniac Magee* (n).

Hurry Home, Candy by Meindert DeJong
HarperCollins, 1953   Gr. 2-6   244 pages

With a childlike sense of wonder and pity, this book is the first year in the life of a dog—from the moment she is lifted from her mother's side, through the children, adults, punishments, losses, fears, friendships, and love that follow. See *A Dog Called Kitty* (n) for related dog stories.

Ida Early Comes Over the Mountain
by Robert Burch
Viking, 1980   Gr. 2-6   145 pages

During the Depression, an ungainly young woman shows up to take over the household chores for Mr. Sutton and his four motherless children. The love that grows between the children and the unconventional Ida is, like her tall tales, a joyous experience. Ida has been rightly described as a "Mary Poppins in the Blue Ridge Mountains." Sequel: *Christmas with Ida Early*. Also by the author: *King Kong and Other Poets* and *Queenie Peavy*. Related books: *The Gift of the Pirate Queen* (n) and *Mrs. Fish, Ape, and Me, the Dump Queen* (n).

In the Year of the Boar and Jackie Robinson
by Bette Bao Lord ✫ Illustrated by Marc Simont
HarperCollins, 1984   Gr. 1-5   169 pages

Over the course of the year 1947, we watch a nine-year-old Chinese immigrant girl as she and her family begin a new life in Brooklyn. Told with warmth and humor and based on the author's own childhood. Shirley Temple Wong's cultural assimilation will ring true with any child who has had to begin again—culturally or socially. To know this little girl is to fall in love with her. (One of the students in Bette Bao Lord's childhood classroom was the future children's novelist, Avi.) Compare this book with Frances Hodgson Burnett's classic *Little Lord Fauntleroy*, in which a poor American boy must move into his grandfather's English estate. Related immigrant experience books: *Lupita Mañana*, by Patricia Beatty (story of an illegal Mexican immigrant family); *Molly's Pilgrim* (p); *Tales from Gold Mountain*, Paul Yee (tales told by Chinese immigrants); *Twist of Gold*, by Michael Morpurgo (nineteenth-century Irish immigrant children); *Where the River Runs*, by Nancy Price Graff (Cambodian immigrant family today in Massachusetts—nonfiction); and *The Witch of Fourth Street*, by Myron Levoy.

Incident at Hawk's Hill by Allan W. Eckert
Little, Brown, 1971   Gr. 6 and up   174 pages

An extremely timid six-year-old who wanders away from his family's farm in 1870 is adopted by a ferocious female badger, à la Mowgli in *The Jungle Book*. The boy is fed, protected, and instructed by the badger through the summer until the family manages to recapture the now-wild child. Definitely for experienced listeners. When reading this aloud, paraphrase a large portion of the slow-moving prologue. For a profile of the author, see *Read All About It!* (a). Related book: Jane Yolen's *Children of the Wolf*, based on true stories of feral children. Also: *Weasel* (n).

The Indian in the Cupboard by Lynne Reid Banks
Doubleday, 1981   Gr. 2-6   182 pages

A witty, exciting, and poignant fantasy tale of a nine-year-old English boy who accidentally brings to life his three-inch plastic American Indian. Once the shock of the trick wears off, the boy begins to realize the immense responsibility involved in feeding, protecting, and hiding a three-inch human being from another time (1870s) and culture. Anyone concerned about the political correctness of the series will feel relieved by reading the review by Native American author Michael Dorris in *The New York Times Book Review* (May 16, 1993). Sequels: *Return of the Indian*; *The Secret of the Indian*; and *The Mystery of the Cupboard*. Related books: *The Littles* (s); *The Borrowers*, by Mary Norton; and *The Steadfast Tin Soldier*, by Hans Christian Andersen.

James and the Giant Peach
by Roald Dahl ✿ Illustrated by Nancy Ekholm Burkert
Knopf, 1961   K–6   120 pages

Four-year-old James, newly orphaned, is sent to live with his mean aunts and appears resigned to spending the rest of his life as their humble servant. It is just about then that a giant peach begins growing in the backyard. Waiting inside that peach is a collection of characters that will captivate your audience as they did James. Few books hold up over six grade levels as well as this one does, and few authors for children understand their world as well as Dahl did. For a profile of the author, see *Hey! Listen to This* (a). Also by the author: *The BFG*; *Danny, Champion of the World* (n); *Charlie and the Chocolate Factory*; *The Enormous Crocodile*; *Esio Trot*; *The Minpins* (p); *The Fantastic Mr. Fox*; *The Giraffe and the Pelly and Me*; *Matilda*; and *The Wonderful Story of Henry Sugar*. Related books: *Big Bugs*, by Jerry Booth; *Mandy*, by Julie Edwards; *Maniac Magee* (n); and *Rabbit Hill*, by Robert Lawson.

Killing Mr. Griffin by Lois Duncan
Little, Brown, 1978   Gr. 7 and up   224 pages

This young-adult novel offers a chilling dissection of peer pressure and group guilt. Because of the subject matter and occasional four-letter words, care should be used in its presentation. The story deals with five high school students who attempt to scare their unpopular English teacher by kidnapping him. When their carefully laid plans begin to unravel toward catastrophe, they find themselves unable to handle the situation. For experienced listeners. Also by the author: *Ransom* and *I Know What You Did Last Summer*. Related books: *Jumping the Nail*, by Eve Bunting; *On My Honor* (s); *Someone Is Hiding on Alcatraz Island* (n); and *Wolf Rider* (n).

Lassie-Come-Home by Eric Knight
Holt, 1940   Gr. 4 and up   200 pages

One of the classic dog stories, it reads so easily, the words ring with such feeling, that you'll find yourself coming back to it year after year. As is the case with most dog stories, there are the usual themes of loss, grief, courage, and struggle—but here they are taken to splendid heights. Set between the Scottish Highlands and Yorkshire, England, in the early 1900s, the novel describes the triumphant struggle of a collie dog to return the 100 miles to her young master. Unfortunately, Hollywood and television have badly damaged the image of this story with their tinny, affected characterization. This is the original Lassie story. Related books: See listing with *A Dog Called Kitty* (n).

The Lion, the Witch and the Wardrobe
by C. S. Lewis

HarperCollins, 1950   Gr. 3-6   186 pages

Four children discover that the old wardrobe closet in an empty room leads to the magical Kingdom of Narnia—a kingdom filled with heroes, witches, princes, and intrigue. This is the first of seven enchanting books called the Narnia Chronicles, which can be read either as adventures or as a Christian allegory. The sequels, in order, are: *Prince Caspian*; *The Voyage of the Dawn Treader*; *The Silver Chair*; *The Magician's Nephew*; *The Horse and His Boy*; and *The Last Battle*. For a profile of the author, see *Hey! Listen to This* (a). *The Land of Narnia*, by Brian Sibley, is an excellent guide to Narnia, C. S. Lewis, and the evolution of the series. Related books: *Gulliver's Adventures in Lilliput* (p); and for older students: See *Martin the Warrior* (n).

Maniac Magee by Jerry Spinelli

Little, Brown, 1990   Gr. 5-9   184 pages

One of the most popular Newbery winners, this is the tale of a legendary twelve-year-old runaway orphan, athlete extraordinaire, who touches countless families and peers with his kindness and wisdom. Could he be a modern Huck Finn? The book deals with racism, homelessness, and community violence in a most effective, almost allegorical manner. Also by the author: *Space Station Seventh Grade* and *Jason and Marceline*. Related books: *The Great Gilly Hopkins*, by Katherine Paterson; *Home at Last*, by David deVries; *Miracle at Clement's Pond* (n); *No Promises in the Wind*, by Irene Hunt; *The Pinballs* (n); *Slake's Limbo* (n); and *Street Child*, by Berlie Doherty.

Martin the Warrior
by Brian Jacques ☆ Illustrated by Gary Chalk

Philomel, 1993   Gr. 4-7   376 pages

In the tradition of *The Hobbit*, but for younger readers, is the Redwall series. Built around an endearing band of courageous animals inhabiting an old English abbey, the books describe their fierce battles against evil creatures. There is high adventure galore, cliff-hanger chapter endings, gruesome behavior by evil outsiders, and rollicking fun. For experienced listeners. *Martin the Warrior* is a prequel, going back to the founding of the abbey, and should be read first, followed by *Redwall*; *Mossflower*;

Mattimeo; and *Mariel of Redwall.* Related books: for Gr. 6 and up: *The Hobbit*, by J. R. R. Tolkien; *Young Ghosts* and *Young Mutants*, both edited by Isaac Asimov, Martin H. Greenberg, and Charles G. Waugh; for Gr. 4–6 students: *City of Light, City of Dark: A Comic Book Novel*, by Avi; *Gulliver's Adventures in Lilliput* (p); *Rabbit Hill*, by Robert Lawson; *A Stranger Came Ashore* (n); and *Weird Henry Berg*, by Sarah Sargent.

The Midnight Fox by Betsy Byars

Viking, 1968   Gr. 4-6   160 pages

From the very beginning, young Tommy is determined he'll hate his aunt and uncle's farm, where he must spend the summer. His determination suffers a setback when he discovers a renegade black fox. His desire to keep the fox running free, however, collides with his uncle's wish to kill it, and the novel builds to a stunning moment of confrontation and courage. For an excellent profile of the author, see her autobiography—*The Moon and I.* Also by the author: *The Animal, the Vegetable and John D. Jones*; *Beans on the Roof*; *Bingo Brown and the Language of Love*; *Bingo Brown, Gypsy Lover*; *Bingo Brown's Guide to Romance*; *A Blossom Promise*; *The Blossoms and the Green Phantom*; *The Blossoms Meet the Vulture Lady*; *The Burning Questions of Bingo Brown*; *The Cartoonist*; *Cracker Jackson*; *The Not-Just-Anybody Family*; *The Pinballs* (n); *Summer of the Swans*; *The T.V. Kid*; *Trouble River*; *Wanted: Mud Bossom*; and *The Winged Colt of Casa Mia.*

Miracle at Clement's Pond by Patricia Pendergraft

Putnam, 1987   Gr. 6 and up   242 pages

Three teens, having discovered an abandoned baby, deposit the child on the front porch of the town spinster—who thinks it is an answer to her prayers, a miracle. When the rest of the town agrees, the pressure is on the three to confess their part. And the longer they delay, the deeper they sink. Rich with humor and deeply textured characters and families, the story is told in the colorful tongue of rural America. Related books: *A Blue-Eyed Daisy* (s) and *Cracker Jackson*, by Betsy Byars.

Mr. Popper's Penguins
by Richard and Florence Atwater ✴ Illustrated by Robert Lawson

Little, Brown, 1938   Gr. 2-4   140 pages

When you add twelve penguins to the family of Mr. Popper, the house painter, you've got immense food bills, impossible situations, and a freezer full of laughs. The short chapters will keep your audience hungry for more. Related books: *Cappyboppy*, by Bill Peet; *Owls in the Family* (s); *Rabbit Hill*, by Robert Lawson; and *The Story of Doctor Doolittle*, by Hugh Lofting.

Mrs. Fish, Ape, and Me, the Dump Queen
by Norma Fox Mazer

Dutton, 1980   Gr. 3-6   138 pages

Living with her homely but loving uncle (the manager of the town dump), Joyce is taunted unmercifully by her classmates. The walls she has built to resist such derision are beginning to weaken when help comes from a most unlikely source—Mrs. Fish, the "crazy" school custodian. For all its candidness in describing the cruelty of the peer group, the book also portrays the powerful effects of love as an anchor in the lives of three people. Related books: *The Bears' House* (s); *The Hundred Dresses* (s); *The Gift of the Pirate Queen* (n); *Mandy*, by Julie Edwards; *Sara Crewe* (s); and *Stargone John* (s).

Mrs. Frisby and the Rats of Nimh
by Robert C. O'Brien

Atheneum, 1971   Gr. 4-6   232 pages

In this unforgettable fantasy–science fiction tale, we meet a group of rats that has become super-intelligent through a series of laboratory injections. Though it opens with an almost fairy-tale gentleness, this grows into a taut and frighteningly realistic tale. Two decades after the publication of this book, fiction grows closer to fact, with genetic engineering; see the December 27, 1982, issue of *Newsweek*, "The Making of a Mighty Mouse," p. 67; also "Human Immune Defenses Are Transplanted in Mice," *The New York Times*, September 15, 1988, p. 1. Sequels: *Racso and the Rats of NIMH* and *R-T, Margaret, and the Rats of NIMH*, both by Jane L. Conly (Robert C. O'Brien's daughter). Also by the author: *The Silver Crown*. Related book: *The Twenty-One Balloons* (n).

My Brother Sam Is Dead
by James Lincoln Collier and Christopher Collier

Simon & Schuster, 1974   Gr. 5 and up   251 pages

In this Newbery-winning historical novel, the inhumanity of war is examined through the experiences of one divided Connecticut family during the American Revolution. Told in the words of a younger brother, the heartache and passions hold true for all wars in all times, and the authors' balanced accounts of British and American tactics allow readers to come to their own conclusions. This book makes a good comparative study with *Rain of Fire*, by Marion Dane Bauer, in which a young brother is shocked by the effect World War II had upon his brother. The authors also have written an exciting trilogy that deals with the black experience during the Colonial period: *Jump Ship to Freedom*; *War Comes for Willy Freeman*; and *Who Is Carrie?* Related books on the Revolutionary War period: *David Bushnell and His Turtle*, by June Swanson; *The Fighting Ground*, by Avi; *Sarah Bishop* (n); *The Secret Soldier: The Story of Deborah Sampson*, by Ann McGovern; *This Time, Tempe Wick?* (p); *Toliver's Secret* (s); and *USKids History: Book of the American Revolution*, by Marlene Smith-Baranzini and Howard Egger-Bovet. Related war books: *Otto of the Silver Hand* (n) and *So Far from the Bamboo Grove*, by Yoko Watkins.

My Daniel by Pam Conrad
HarperCollins, 1989   Gr. 4-7   137 pages

As an eighty-year-old grandmother leads her grandchildren through the natural history museum toward the dinosaur room, she recounts the one great adventure of her life: when, at age twelve, she and her sixteen-year-old brother Daniel discovered the bones of a giant brontosaurus on their Nebraska farm. It is these same dinosaur bones she is going to view now in the museum—for the first time since the death of her beloved brother sixty-eight years ago. Each room of the museum serves as another chapter in a poignant tale that leads us back to a time when dirt-poor farmers and greedy bone hunters and paleontologists scoured the dry ground of the West for their fortune. Also by the author: *Prairie Songs*; *Prairie Visions: The Life and Times of Solomon Butcher*; *Holding Me Here*. Related book: *Digging Up Tyrannosaurus Rex*, by John R. Horner and Don Lessem—an excellent picture book on the discovery and recovery of the first complete *Tyrannosaurus rex* skeleton.

My Side of the Mountain by Jean George
Dutton, 1959   Gr. 3-8   178 pages

A modern teenage Robinson Crusoe, city-bred Sam Gribley describes his year surviving as a runaway in a remote area of the Catskill Mountains. His diary of living off the land is marked by moving accounts of the animals, insects, plants, people, and books that helped him survive. For experienced listeners. Sequel: *On the Far Side of the Mountain*. Also by the author: *Julie of the Wolves*. For related survival or wilderness books, see listing with *Hatchet* (n).

North to Freedom by Anne Holm
Harcourt, Brace, 1974   Gr. 4 and up   190 pages

This is a magnificent and unforgettable book. Picture a twelve-year-old boy, raised in an East European prison camp, who remembers no other life. Suddenly the opportunity to escape presents itself, and he begins not only a terrifying odyssey across Europe but also a journey into human experi-ence. David must now deal with the normal experiences and knowledge that had been denied him in prison. There are wondrous but confusing mo-ments when he experiences for the first time: a baby crying, flowers, fruit, the peals of a church bell, children playing, and a toothbrush. Meanwhile, he learns how to smile, the meaning of conscience, the need to trust. For ex-perienced listeners. Related book: *The Big Lie: A True Story* (s).

Nothing But the Truth: A Documentary Novel by Avi
Orchard, 1991   Gr. 7 and up   177 pages

In this Newbery Honor winner, a ninth-grader decides to irritate his teacher until she transfers him to another class. But what begins benignly soon escalates into a slanderous assault on the teacher when parents, faculty, media, and school board members climb aboard. In the end, everyone loses. Told exclusively through documents like memos, letters, and diary entries, this is a dramatic exploration of how freedom of speech can be abused. For other Avi books, see *The True Confessions of Charlotte Doyle* (n). Related book: *Terpin*, by Tor Seidler.

Nothing to Fear by Jackie French Koller
Harcourt, Brace, 1991   Gr. 4 and up   279 pages

In short, this is a good, old-fashioned historical novel that grabs you right by the heart and throat and doesn't let go for 279 pages. Set in the Depression, it follows the travails and triumphs of a poor Irish family—especially young Danny and his mother—as they try to hold on against all odds. This is a brilliant depiction of life in the 1930s, but the acts of love and courage displayed by the Garvey family are repeated daily in many families wherever poverty abides—in any decade and in any country. Also by the author: *Dragonling*; *If I Had One Wish*; *Impy for Always*; *Mole and Shrew*; *Mole and Shrew Step Out*; and *The Primrose Way*. Related books: *As Far As Spring Mills*, by Patricia Pendergraft;

Hard Times: A Story of the Great Depression, by Nancy Antle; *Ida Early Comes over the Mountain* (n); *No Promises in the Wind,* by Irene Hunt; *Oh, Brother* (p); and *Roll of Thunder, Hear My Cry* (n).

Number the Stars by Lois Lowry
Houghton Mifflin, 1989   Gr. 4–7   137 pages

In 1943, as the occupying Nazi army attempted to extricate and then exterminate the seven thousand Jews residing in Norway, the Danish people rose up as one in a determined and remarkably successful resistance. Against that backdrop, this Newbery winner describes a ten-year-old Danish girl joining forces with her relatives to save the lives of her best friend and her family. Also by the author: *A Summer to Die*; *Autumn Street*; and for older readers, *The Giver.*

Related books on the Holocaust, for younger children: *The Big Lie: A True Story* (s); *Hilde and Eli: Children of the Holocaust,* by David A. Adler; *The Little Riders,* by Margaretha Shemin; *Twenty and Ten,* by Claire Bishop. For older students: *Alan and Naomi,* by Myron Levoy; *Hiding to Survive: Stories of Jewish Children Rescued from the Holocaust,* by Maxine B. Rosenberg; *Smoke and Ashes: The Story of the Holocaust,* by Barbara Rogasky; *Tell Them We Remember: The Story of the Holocaust,* by Susan D. Bachrach with the U.S. Holocaust Memorial Museum; and *Terrible Things: An Allegory of the Holocaust,* by Eve Bunting.

Otto of the Silver Hand by Howard Pyle
Dover, 1967   Gr. 5–8   132 pages

First published in 1888 and written by one of the leading figures of early American children's literature, this is an ideal introduction to the classics. Intended as a cautionary tale against the glories of warfare, the narrative describes a young boy's joy and suffering as he rises above the cruelty of the world, while caught between warring medieval German tribes. Though the language may be somewhat foreign to the listener at the start, it soon adds to the flavor of the narrative. For experienced listeners. For a profile on the author, see *Hey! Listen to This* (a). For other books about war, see *My Brother Sam Is Dead* (n). For other medieval books, see listings with *Harald and the Great Stag* (p).

Pearl's Promise by Frank Asch
Delacorte, 1984   K–4   152 pages

Adventure, danger, heartache, tenderness, romance, and courage—all are woven tightly into this fast-moving novel about a pet-store mouse who promises her young brother that she will save him somehow from the snake that is about to make a breakfast of him. Fans of E. B. White will love the spunky Pearl. Related books: *The Mouse and the Motorcycle* and its sequels, by Beverly Cleary; *Rabbit Hill*, by Robert Lawson; and *Stuart Little*, by E. B. White.

Peppermints in the Parlor by Barbara Brooks Wallace

Atheneum, 1980   Gr. 3-7   198 pages

When the newly orphaned Emily arrives in San Francisco, she expects to be adopted by her wealthy aunt and uncle. What she finds instead is a poverty-stricken aunt held captive as a servant in a shadowy, decaying home for the aged. Filled with Dickensian flavor, this novel has secret passageways, tyrannical matrons, eerie whispers in the night, and a pair of fearful but plucky kids. Equally riveting is Wallace's *The Twin in the Tavern*. Other gothic mysteries: *The Case of the Baker Street Irregular* (n); *The Curse of the Blue Figurine* (n); *Sara Crewe* (s); and *The Wolves of Willoughby Chase* (n).

The Pinballs by Betsy Byars

HarperCollins, 1977   Gr. 5-7   136 pages

Brought together under the same roof, three foster children prove to each other and the world that they are not pinballs to be knocked around from one place to the next; they have a choice in life—to try or not to try. The author has taken what could have been a maudlin story and turned it into a hopeful, loving, and very witty book. Short chapters with easy-to-read dialogue. See *The Midnight Fox* (n) for Byars's other books. Related books: *The Golden Days*, by Gail Radley; *Home at Last*, by David deVries; *The Loner*, by Ester Wier; *Maniac Magee* (n); *The Most Beautiful Place in the World*, by Ann Cameron; *Mandy*, by Julie Edwards; *Mrs. Fish, Ape, and Me, the Dump Queen* (n); *No Promises in the Wind*, by Irene Hunt; and *The Story of Holly and Ivy* (s).

Ramona the Pest by Beverly Cleary

Morrow, 1968   Gr. K-4   144 pages

Not all of Beverly Cleary's books make good read-alouds, though children love to read her silently. Some of her books sometimes move too slowly to hold read-aloud interest. But that's not so with the Ramona series, which begins with *Ramona the Pest*. The book follows the outspoken young lady through her early months in kindergarten. All children will smile in recognition at Ramona's encounters with the first day of school, show-and-tell, seat work, a substitute teacher, Halloween, young love—and dropping out of kindergarten. Long chapters can easily be divided. Early grades should have some experience with short novels before trying *Ramona*. Sequels: *Ramona and Her Father*; *Ramona and Her Mother*; *Ramona Quimby, Age 8*; *Ramona Forever*. Also by the author: *Dear Mr. Henshaw* (n); *The Mouse and the Motorcycle* and its sequels. Related books: see *Rip-Roaring Russell* (s).

Roll of Thunder, Hear My Cry by Mildred Taylor
Dial, 1976   Gr. 5 and up   276 pages

Throbbing with the lifeblood of a black Mississippi family during the Depression, this novel depicts the passion and pride of people who refuse to give in to threats and harassments from white neighbors. The story is told through daughter Cassie, age nine, who experiences her first taste of social injustice and refuses to swallow it. She, along with her family, her classmates, and her neighbors, will stir listeners' hearts and awaken many children to the tragedy of prejudice and discrimination. Winner of the Newbery Award. For experienced listeners. Other books in the series about the Logans: *Let the Circle Be Unbroken*; *The Road to Memphis*; and four short novels, *The Friendship* (s); *Mississippi Bridge*; *Song of the Trees*; and *The Well*. Also by the author: *The Gold Cadillac*.

Picture books on African-American history: *Coming Home*, by Floyd Cooper; *Follow the Drinking Gourd*, by Jeanette Winter; *The Lucky Stone*, by Lucille Clifton; *If You Lived at the Time of Martin Luther King*, by Ellen Levine; *A Picture Book of Harriet Tubman*, by David A. Adler; and *Pink and Say* (p).

Novels dealing with African-American history: *A Girl Called Boy*, by Belinda Hurmence; *The Borning Room*, by Paul Fleischman; *Christmas in the Big House, Christmas in the Quarters*, by Patricia and Fredrick McKissack; *Escape from Slavery*, by Doreen Rappaport; *Finding Buck McHenry* (n); *Jump Ship to Freedom*, by James L. Collier and Christopher Collier; *My Name Is Not Angelica*, by Scott O'Dell; *Nightjohn*, by Gary Paulsen; *Out from This Place* and *Which Way Freedom?*, both by Joyce Hansen; *Scorpions* (n); *Sour Land* (n)—the sequel to *Sounder*; *Talk That Talk: An Anthology of African-American Storytelling* (a); *Thank You, Jackie Robinson* (n); and *Words by Heart* (n).

Nonfiction books include: *Dear Benjamin Banneker*, by Andrea Davis Pinkney; *Freedom's Children: Young Civil Rights Activists Tell Their Own Stories*, by Ellen Levine; *Get on Board: The Story of the Underground Railroad*, by Jim Haskins; *The Kidnapped Prince*, by Olaudah Equiano;

Letters from a Slave Girl: The Story of Harriet Jacobs, by Mary E. Lyons; *Marching to Freedom: The Story of Martin Luther King, Jr.*, by Joyce Milton; *The Story of Ruby Bridges*, by Robert Coles; *Now Is Your Time! The African-American Struggle for Freedom*, by Walter Dean Myers; *Rosa Parks: My Story*, by Rosa Parks; *Witnesses to Freedom: Young People Who Fought for Civil Rights*, by Belinda Rochelle; and *The Year They Walked*, by Beatrice Siegel.

Sarah Bishop by Scott O'Dell
Houghton Mifflin, 1980   Gr. 5 and up   184 pages

Based on a historic incident, this is the story of a determined young girl who flees war-torn Long Island after her father and brother are killed at the outbreak of the Revolutionary War. In the Connecticut wilderness, she takes refuge in a cave, where she begins her new life. Sarah Bishop makes an interesting comparative study with two other read-aloud novels dealing with children running away: *Slake's Limbo* (n) and *My Side of the Mountain* (n). Each approaches the subject of the runaway from a different point in time. For experienced listeners. O'Dell's stories often focus on independent, strong-willed young women. For a profile of the author, see *Read All About It!* (a). Also by the author: *Black Pearl*; *Carlotta*; *Black Star, Bright Dawn* (Eskimo girl replaces her father in the famous Iditarod race); *The Hawk That Dare Not Hunt by Day* (the fight to translate the Bible from Latin into the vernacular); *Island of the Blue Dolphins*; *The King's Fifth*; *My Name Is Not Angelica*; *Sing Down the Moon* (s); *Streams to the River, River to the Sea: A Novel of Sacagawea*; *Thunder Rolling in the Mountains*; and *Zia*. For related Revolutionary War titles, see *My Brother Sam Is Dead* (n); also *Weasel* (n).

Scorpions by Walter Dean Myers
HarperCollins, 1988   Gr. 7 and up   216 pages

This award-winning novelist has drawn upon his childhood in Harlem to give us a revealing, frightening, and poignant look at an African-American family facing the daily pressures of urban poverty. While seventh-grader Jamal Hicks struggles to resist the pressures to join a neighborhood gang, he is watching his family torn apart by the crimes of an older brother and a wayward father. Moreover, his relationship with school is disintegrating under a combination of his own irresponsibility and an antagonistic principal. Unable to resist the peer pressure, Jamal makes a tragic decision involving a handgun. Readers-aloud should be aware that some of the book's dialogue is written in black dialect. Also by the author: *Fast Sam, Cool Clyde, and Stuff*; *Fallen Angels*; *Somewhere in the Darkness*; *Malcolm X: By Any Means*. Related books: *Four Miles to Pinecone* (s); *Killing Mr. Griffin* (n); *Make Lemonade*, by Virginia Euwer Wolff; and *The Outsiders*, by S. E. Hinton.

The Search for Delicious by Natalie Babbitt
Farrar, Straus & Giroux, 1969   Gr. 3-7   160 pages

After a nasty argument among the King, Queen, and their court over the correct meaning of the word "delicious," the Prime Minister's adopted son is dispatched to poll the kingdom to determine the choice of the people. This poll brings out people's foolishness, pettiness, and quarrelsome natures: Everyone has his own personal definition of "delicious," and civil war looms. Also by the author: *Tuck Everlasting* (n). Related books: *The Butter Battle Book*, by Dr. Seuss; *Chocolate Fever* (s); and *The War with Grandpa*, by Robert Kimmel Smith.

The Secret Garden
by Frances Hodgson Burnett ☆ Illustrated by Shirley Hughes
Viking, 1989   Gr. 2-5   240 pages

Few books spin such a web of magic about their audiences as does this 1911 children's classic about the contrary orphan who comes to live with her cold, unfeeling uncle on the windswept English moors. Wandering the grounds of his immense manor house one day, she discovers a secret garden, locked and abandoned. This leads her to discover her uncle's invalid child hidden within the mansion, her first friendship, and her own true self. For experienced listeners. For a profile of the author, see *Hey! Listen to This* (a). Also by the author: *Sara Crewe* (s); *Little Lord Fauntleroy*; *A Little Princess*; and *The Lost Prince*. Related books: *Good Night, Mr. Tom* (n); *Mandy*, by Julie Edwards; *The Pinballs* (n); *The Story of Holly and Ivy* (s); and *Understood Betsy* (n).

Sideways Stories from Wayside School
by Louis Sachar
Random House, 1990   Gr. 2-5   124 pages

Thirty chapters about the wacky students who inhabit the thirtieth floor of Wayside School, the school that was supposed to be built one story high and thirty classes wide—but the contractor made a mistake and made it thirty stories high! If you think the building bizarre, wait until you meet the kids who inhabit it. Sequel: *Wayside School Is Falling Down*. For a profile of the author, see *Hey! Listen to This* (a). Also by the author: *The Boy Who Lost His Face*; *Johnny's in the Basement*; *Sixth Grade Secrets*; *Someday Angeline*; and *There's a Boy in the Girls' Bathroom*. Other humorous books: *Skinnybones* (s); *The Best Christmas Pageant Ever* (s); *Fantastic Stories* (a); *Funny You Should Ask: The Delacorte Book of Original Humorous Short Stories*, edited by David Gale; *The Great Brain* (n); *Herbie Jones* (s); *Odds on Oliver*, by Constance Greene; *The Random House Book of Humor for Children*, selected by Pamela Pollack; *The Shrinking of Treehorn*, by Florence Parry Heide; *Tales of a Fourth-Grade Nothing* (n); and *Young Santa* (s).

The Sign of the Beaver by Elizabeth George Speare
Houghton Mifflin, 1983   Gr. 3 and up   135 pages

This is the story of two boys—one white, the other Indian—and their coming of age in the Maine wilderness prior to the Revolutionary War. It is also a study of the awkward relationship that develops when the starving white boy is forced to teach the reluctant Indian to read in order for both of them to survive. Also by the author: *The Witch of Blackbird Pond*. For a profile of the author, see *Hey! Listen to This* (a). Related books on the relationship between white settlers and Indian neighbors: *Clearing in the Forest: A Story About a Real Settler Boy*, by Joanne Landers Henry; *Encounter* (p); *Night Bird: The Story of the Seminole Indians*, by Kathleen V. Kudlinski; *Pueblo Boy: Growing Up in Two Worlds*, by Marcia Keegan; *Sing Down the Moon* (n); *Wait for Me, Watch for Me, Eula Bee*, by Patricia Beatty; *Weasel* (n); *Where the Broken Hearts Still Beat*, by Carolyn Meyer; *Wounded Knee: An Indian History of the American West*, by Dee Brown (adapted for children by Amy Ehrlich).

Sing Down the Moon by Scott O'Dell
Houghton Mifflin, 1970   Gr. 3–6   138 pages

Through the first-person narrative of a fourteen-year-old Navaho girl, we follow the plight of the American Indian in 1864 when the U.S. government ordered the Navahos out of their Arizona homeland and marched them 300 miles to Fort Sumner, New Mexico, where they were imprisoned for four years. Known as "The Long Walk," it is a journey that has since become a part of every Navaho child's heritage. The injustices and the subsequent courage displayed by the Indians should be known by all Americans. The novel also provides a detailed account of daily Indian life during the period. Short chapters are told with the vocabulary and in the style appropriate to a young Indian child. Also by the author: *Sarah Bishop* (n). See listing with *The Sign of the Beaver* (n) for related titles.

Slake's Limbo by Felice Holman
Simon & Schuster/Atheneum, 1984   Gr. 5–8   117 pages

A fifteen-year-old takes his fears and misfortunes into the New York City subway one day, finds a hidden construction mistake in the shape of a cave near the tracks, and doesn't come out of the system for 121 days. The story deals simply but powerfully with the question: Can anyone be an island unto himself? It is also a story of survival, personal discovery, and the plight of today's homeless. This book makes an interesting comparative study with three other books that discuss running away, hiding, and personal discovery: *My Side of the Mountain* (n); *North to Freedom* (n); and *Sarah Bishop* (n).

Snow Bound by Harry Mazer
Dell, 1975   Gr. 5–8   146 pages

Two teenagers, a boy and a girl, marooned by a car wreck during a severe snowstorm, fight off starvation, frostbite, wild dogs, and broken limbs, and overcome personal bickering in order to survive. An excellent example of people's lives being changed for the better in dealing with adversity. Occasional four-letter words in the dialogue. Also by the author: *When the Phone Rang.* Related survival stories: See *Hatchet* (n).

Someone Is Hiding on Alcatraz Island
by Eve Bunting
Clarion, 1984   Gr. 7–10   136 pages

Here's a white-knuckle thriller for reluctant readers but not for the faint of heart. When fourteen-year-old Danny incurs the wrath of a local street gang, he flees in desperation to Alcatraz Island, where he hopes to blend in with sightseers and lose the pursuing gang. Instead they trap him there for the night and the action turns chilling. Also by the author: *Jumping the Nail.* Related books: *Killing Mr. Griffin* (n); *Scorpions* (n); and *Wolf Rider* (n).

Sour Land by William H. Armstrong
HarperCollins, 1971   Gr. 4–8   116 pages

This is the little-known sequel to the Newbery-winning *Sounder,* and a better read-aloud. Here we meet the nameless boy from *Sounder,* now grown, teaching in a small black school, maintaining his goodness while the lethal shadow of racism lurks in the corners. Related books: see *Roll of Thunder, Hear My Cry* (n).

A Stranger Came Ashore by Mollie Hunter
HarperCollins, 1975   Gr. 4-7   163 pages

The handsome stranger who claims to be the sole survivor of a shipwreck off the Scottish coast is really the Great Selkie, come to lure the Henderson family's beautiful daughter to her death at the bottom of the sea. Related books: *The Animal Family* (n); *The Crane Wife*, retold by Katherine Paterson; *Greyling* (p); and *The Selkie Girl*, by Susan Cooper.

Tales of a Fourth-Grade Nothing by Judy Blume
Dutton, 1972   Gr. 3-5   120 pages

A perennial favorite among schoolchildren, this novel deals with the irksome problem of a two-year-old kid brother whose hilarious antics complicate the life of Peter, a fourth-grader. Sequels: *Superfudge* and *Fudge-a-Mania* (Readers-aloud should be cautioned that the latter book deals with the question: Is there a Santa Claus?). Also by the author: *Freckle Juice*. Related books: See listing with *Rip-Roaring Russell* (s).

Thank You, Jackie Robinson by Barbara Cohen
Lothrop, 1988   Gr. 5-7   126 pages

In the late 1940s, we meet young Sam Green, a rare breed known as the True Baseball Fanatic and a Brooklyn Dodger fan. His widowed mother runs an inn, and when she hires a sixty-year-old black cook, Sam's life takes a dramatic turn for the better. They form a fast friendship and begin to explore the joys of baseball in a way the fatherless boy has never known. A tender book that touches on friendship, race, sports, personal sacrifice, and death. Also by the author: *The Carp in the Bathtub* and *Molly's Pilgrim* (p). Related books: *The Cay* (n); *Finding Buck McHenry* (n); *In the Year of the Boar and Jackie Robinson* (n); *Teammates*, by Peter Golenbock; and Manfred Weidhorn's biography, *Jackie Robinson*. "Shadow Ball," inning five of Ken Burns's baseball series for PBS (*Baseball: The American Epic*), available on video, offers an excellent portrayal of the color line being broken in baseball.

Toliver's Secret by Esther Wood Brady
Crown, 1988   Gr. 3-5   166 pages

During the Revolutionary War, ten-year-old Ellen Toliver is asked by her ailing grandfather to take his place and carry a secret message through British lines. What he estimates to be a simple plan is complicated by Ellen's exceptional timidity and an unforeseen shift by the British. The book becomes a portrait of Ellen's personal growth—complete with a heart-stopping crisis in each chapter. Related books: *The Courage of Sarah Noble* (s); *George Washington: A Picture Book Biography*, by James Cross Giblin; *Katie's Trunk*, by Ann Turner; *The Secret Soldier: The Story of Deborah Sampson*, by Ann McGovern; *The Sign Painter's Dream* (p); *This Time, Tempe Wick?* (p); and *USKids History: Book of the American Revolution*, by Marlene Smith-Baranzini and Howard Egger-Bovet.

The True Confessions of Charlotte Doyle by Avi

Orchard, 1990   Gr. 4 and up   215 pages

Winner of a 1991 Newbery Honor medal, this is the dramatic tale of a thirteen-year-old girl who is the lone passenger aboard a merchant ship sailing from England to the U.S. in 1832. The crew is bent on mutiny, the captain is a murderer, and the girl herself is accused of murder, tried by captain and crew, and sentenced to hang. Avi is at his finest with this first-person adventure, exploring history, racism, feminism, and mob psychology. For a profile of the author, see *Read All About It!* (a). See *Wolf Rider* (n) for other books by the author. Related books about young heroines: three books by Scott O'Dell—*Bright Dawn, Dark Star*; *Island of the Blue Dolphins*; and *Sarah Bishop* (n). Other books include: *The Clock*, James Lincoln Collier and Christopher Collier; *Roll of Thunder, Hear My Cry* (n); and *Winning Kicker* (n).

Tuck Everlasting by Natalie Babbitt

Farrar, Straus & Giroux, 1975   Gr. 4-7   124 pages

A young girl stumbles upon a family that has found the Fountain of Youth, and in the aftermath there is a kidnapping, a murder, and a jailbreak. This touching story suggests a sobering question: What would it be like to live forever? For experienced listeners. Also by the author: *The Search for Delicious* (n). For related books that include the theme of death or dying: See listing with *A Taste of Blackberries* (s). For picture books, see listing with *A Gift for Tia Rosa* (p).

The Twenty-One Balloons by William Pène du Bois

Viking, 1947   Gr. 4-6   180 pages

This Newbery winner is a literary smorgasbord; there are so many different and delicious parts one hardly knows which to mention first.

The story deals with a retired teacher's attempts to sail by balloon across the Pacific in 1883, his crash landing and pseudo-imprisonment on the island of Krakatoa, and, finally, his escape. The book is crammed with nuggets of science, history, humor, invention, superior language, and marvelous artwork. For experienced listeners. Be sure to have available either the January 1981 issue of *National Geographic* or *Volcano*, by Patricia Lauber, both of which offer a close-up view of the eruption on Mount St. Helens.

Uncle Shamus by James Duffy
Simon & Schuster/Atheneum, 1992   Gr. 2-6   132 pages

Ingredients for an old fashioned page-turner: Two fifth-graders (a black boy and white girl from "shantytown") befriend a blind ex-convict who is waiting to dig up the money he stole thirty years ago. Add to that a heaping spoonful of warm humanity and you have a delicious book! Also by the author: *Missing*, and its sequel, *The Man in the River*. Related book: *The Friendship* (s).

Understood Betsy by Dorothy Canfield Fisher
Dell, 1987   Gr. 2-6   211 pages

Written in 1917 by one of America's most celebrated writers, this is the classic story of a timid, almost neurotic orphan child (Betsy) being raised by her fearful and overprotective city-dwelling aunts. Then a family illness requires the child be sent to live with stiff-necked rural relatives in Vermont and she must stand on her own two feet, do chores, and speak for herself—all of which causes a heartwarming metamorphosis. As a novel, even as a psychological or historical profile, the book is enormously successful. One of its original intentions was to promote the Montessori method of education. For a profile of the author, see *Hey! Listen to This* (a). Related books: *A Gift of the Pirate Queen* (n); *Good Night, Mr. Tom* (n); *Home at Last*, by David deVries; *Mandy*, by Julie Edwards; *The Midnight Fox* (n); and *The Secret Garden* (n).

Weasel by Cynthia DeFelice
Simon & Schuster/Atheneum, 1990   Gr. 2-6   119 pages

Set in Ohio in 1839, this realistic look at the American frontier focuses on a widower and his two children, as they confront racism, violence, and the elements. Most of the challenge comes in the person of Weasel, a former government Indian fighter who captures both father and son. A fast-paced, first-person adventure story, it also describes the plight of the American Indian and America's own "ethnic cleansing." Also by the author: *Devil's Bridge*; *The Light on Hogback Hill*; *Lostman's River*; and *The Strange Night Writing of Jessamine Colter*. Related books: The following pioneer books by William Q. Steele: *Buffalo Knife*; *Flaming Arrows*; *Perilous Road*; and *Winter Danger*. Related books on the plight of the American Indian: *Night Bird: The Story of the Seminole Indians*, a short novel by Kathleen V. Kudlinski, describing America's war against the Seminole Indians; *The Sign of the Beaver* (n); *Sing Down the Moon* (n); and *Wounded Knee: An Indian History of the American West*, by Dee Brown (adapted for children by Amy Ehrlich).

When the Tripods Came by John Christopher
Dutton, 1988   Gr. 5 and up   151 pages

A updating of H. G. Wells's *The War of the Worlds*, this is the prequel to one of modern science fiction's most popular juvenile series: *The Tripods*. When invaders from space take over Earth and begin implanting brain-control devices among the humans, a group of rebellious teens lay the groundwork for the invaders' destruction. For a profile of the author, see *Read All About It!* (a). The series includes (in order): *The White Mountains*; *The City of Gold and Lead*; and *The Pool of Fire*. Also by the author: *A Dusk of Demons*; *The Prince in Waiting*; *Beyond the Burning Lands*; *The Sword of the Spirits*; *The Lotus Caves*; and *The Guardians*. Related books: *Fallout*, by Robert Swindells; and *The War of the Worlds*, by H. G. Wells.

Where the Red Fern Grows by Wilson Rawls
Doubleday, 1961   Gr. 3-7   212 pages

A ten-year-old boy growing up in the Ozark mountains, praying and saving for a pair of hounds, finally achieves his wish. He then begins the task of turning the hounds into first-class hunting dogs. It would be difficult to find a book that speaks more definitively about perseverance, courage, family, sacrifice, work, life, and death. Long chapters are easily divided, but bring a box of tissues for the final chapters. The author's famous speech about his life story ("Dreams Can Come True") is available on audiocassette; for details write Reading Tree Productions, 51 Arvesta St., Springfield, MA 01118. Related books: See *A Dog Called Kitty* (n) for related dog story titles.

Winning Kicker by Thomas J. Dygard
Morrow, 1978   Gr. 6-8   190 pages

A hard-nosed football coach at the end of a long and successful career is jolted in his final season when a girl makes his high school team as a placekicker, potentially turning the season into a three-ring circus. In a companion novel, *Rebound Caper*, a high school boy, benched by his basketball coach, retaliates by joining the girls' team. The author offers a liberated and sensitive view of the family, school, and community pressures that result. Sure to stir the interest of both sexes and provoke a lively discussion. Nobody writing teenage sports books today is better than Dygard. Also by the author: *Backfield Package*; *Forward Pass*; *Game Plan*; *Halfback Tough*; *Outside Shooter*; *Point Spread*; *Quarterback Walk-On*; *The Rookie Arrives*; *Running Scared*; *Soccer Duel*; *Tournament Upstart*; and *Wilderness Peril*. For younger sports fans, see *Finding Buck McHenry* (n).

The Wish Giver: Three Tales of Coven Tree
by Bill Brittain
HarperCollins, 1983   Gr. 4-8   181 pages

Into the town of Coven Tree comes a mysterious stranger who sets up a tent at the church social, promising wishes-come-true for fifty cents. Three young people in this tiny New England town find out the hard way that sometimes we'd be better off if our wishes didn't come true. There is plenty of homespun merriment and fast-moving suspense here. Other books in the Coven Tree series: *The Devil's Donkey*; *Dr. Dredd's Wagon of Wonders*; and *Professor Popkins Prodigious Polish*. Also by the author: *All the Money in the World*; *The Fantastic Freshman*; *My Buddy the King*; *Shape-Shifter*; *Wings*; and *Who Knew There'd Be Ghosts?* Related books: See *The Curse of the Blue Figurine* (n).

Wolf Rider: A Tale of Terror by Avi
Bradbury, 1986   Gr. 7 and up   224 pages

This is breathtaking, plausible, and nonstop reading and my first recommendation for "reluctant-reader" teens. When fifteen-year-old Andy receives a random phone call from a man claiming he's killed a college coed, nobody believes him. And when everyone writes it off as a prank, Andy sets out to find the anonymous caller, in a race against death and the clock. Be sure to read any version of the tale "The Boy Who Cried Wolf" before reading aloud this book. Few of today's writers for young readers come close to Avi's brilliance and versatility. Also by the author: *The Barn*; *Blue Heron*; *Bright Shadow*; *Captain Grey* (n); *City of Light, City of Dark (a comic book novel)*; *Emily Upham's Revenge*; *The Fighting Ground*; *Man from the Sky*; *Nothing but the Truth* (n); *Something Upstairs*; *A Tale of Ghosts*; *Sometimes I Think I Hear My Name*; *The True Confessions of Charlotte Doyle* (n); and *Windcatcher.* Related books: *Deathwatch*, by Robb White; *Killing Mr. Griffin* (n); and *Someone Is Hiding on Alcatraz Island* (n).

The Wolves of Willoughby Chase by Joan Aiken
Dell, 1987   Gr. 3-6   168 pages

Here is Victorian melodrama in high gear by a master storyteller: a great English estate surrounded by hungry wolves, two young girls mistakenly left in the care of a wicked, scheming governess, secret passageways, and tortured flights through the snow in the dark of night. For experienced listeners. See *Hey! Listen to This* (a) for a profile of the author. Sequels: *Black Hearts in Battersea*; *Nightbirds on Nantucket*; and *The Stolen Lake.* Related books: *Peppermints in the Parlor* (n) and *The Secret Garden* (n).

The Wonderful Wizard of Oz by L. Frank Baum
Numerous publishers   Gr. 1 and up   260 pages

Before your children are exposed to the movie version, treat them to the magic of this 1900 book many regard as the first American fairy tale, as well as our earliest science fiction. (Incidentally, the book is far less terrifying for children than the film version.) The magical story of Dorothy and her friends' harrowing journey to the Emerald City is but the first of many books on the Land of Oz. For a profile of the author and the origin of the series, see *Hey! Listen to This* (a). Sequels: *Dorothy and the Wizard of Oz*; *The Emerald City of Oz*; *The Marvelous Land of Oz*; *Ozma of Oz* (the best of the sequels); *The Patchwork Girl of Oz*; and *The Road to Oz.*

Woodsong by Gary Paulsen
Simon & Schuster, 1990   Gr. 5 and up   132 pages

Using the same gripping tension he infuses into his novels, the author gives us a nonfiction journal about living off the land while training a dog team for the Iditarod. Powerful and breathtaking nonfiction—but not for the faint of heart or weak-stomached. Paulsen also has written of racing the 1,800-mile Iditarod race in *Winterdance*, nonfiction for older readers. For other Paulsen titles, see *Hatchet* (n).

Words by Heart by Ouida Sebestyen
Little, Brown, 1979   Gr. 5 and up   162 pages

A young girl and her family must summon all their courage and spirit in order to survive as the only black family in this 1910 Texas community. The child's spunk, her father's tireless patience, and the great faith in God he leaves with her make this an unforgettable book. For experienced listeners. The slow-moving first chapter can be edited with prereading. Sequel: *On Fire*. Also by the author: *Out of Nowhere*. Related books: See listing with *Roll of Thunder, Hear My Cry* (n).

POETRY

And the Green Grass Grew All Around: Folk Poetry from Everyone
by Alvin Schwartz ☆ Illustrated by Sue Truesdell
HarperCollins, 1992   K–4   148 pages

From a top folklorist comes this delightful collection of more than 250 poems, limericks, chants, jump-rope rhymes, taunts, riddles, and much more—all part of the great American folklore tradition. Truesdell's riotous illustrations add the perfect touch to a book that you'll find your children trying to memorize just for the fun of it. Also by the author: *Scary Stories to Tell in the Dark* (a). Related book: *From Sea to Shining Sea* (a).

Casey at the Bat
by Ernest L. Thayer ☆ Illustrated by Barry Moser
Godine, 1988   Gr. 4 and up   32 pages

This description of a small-town baseball game and local hero is one of the most famous pieces in America's literary quilt, and this centennial edition from Godine includes Barry Moser's illustrations based on the uniforms and settings of the original period. "Casey" is as topical today as it was in 1888. Younger children may prefer the illustrations by Wallace Tripp in the Putnam edition. For a biographical profile of Thayer and the history of the poem, as well as a copy of the lesser-known "Casey's Revenge" by Grantland Rice, see *Read All About It!* (a).

The Cremation of Sam McGee
by Robert W. Service ✶ Illustrated by Ted Harrison
Greenwillow, 1987   Gr. 4 and up   30 pages

Once one of the most memorized poems in North America, it is still wonderful humor and remains the best description of the sun's strange spell over the men who toil in the north. After seeing this edition, it will be hard to ever again hear the words without seeing Harrison's brilliant artwork. Also by the author and illustrator: *The Shooting of Dan McGrew.* Two excellent collections of Service poetry: *Best Tales of the Yukon* (Running Press) and *Collected Poems of Robert Service* (Dodd). For a biographical profile of the poet, see *Read All About It!* (a). Related books: *The Bite of the Gold Bug: A Story of the Alaskan Gold Rush*, by Barthe DeClements, is excellent for Gr. 1–3 students; *Call of the Wild* (n); *Gold: The True Story of Why People Search for It, Mine It, Trade It, Steal It, Mint It, Hoard It, Fight and Kill For It*, excellent nonfiction by Milton Meltzer; and *Lost in the Barrens* by Farley Mowat.

Honey, I Love
by Eloise Greenfield ✶ Illustrated by Diane and Leo Dillon
HarperCollins, 1976   Pre-S.–3   42 pages

Here are 16 short poems about the things and people children love: friends, cousins, older brothers, keepsakes, mother's clothes, music, and jump ropes. Set against an urban background, the poems elicit both joyous and bittersweet feelings. Related books: see listing with *Poonam's Pets* (p).

A House Is a House for Me
by Mary Ann Hoberman ✶ Illustrated by Betty Fraser
Viking, 1978   Pre.-S.–4   44 pages

On the surface this book is a rhyming picture book about the variety of dwelling places people, animals, and insects call home. Below the surface it is an ingeniously entertaining study of metaphor: "cartons are houses for crackers," "a rose is a house for a smell," "a throat is a house for a hum." Also by the author: *Fathers, Mothers, Sister, Brothers: A Collection of Family Poems.*

The House That Crack Built by Clark Taylor
Chronicle, 1992   Gr. 4 and up   30 pages

Patterned after the famous children's chant (see *The House That Jack Built*, by Rodney Peppe), this is the tragic modern version, itemizing the communal pain and suffering that spring from the drug trade. Related book for teens: *Go Ask Alice*, by Anonymous.

The Ice Cream Store
by Dennis Lee ✭ Illustrated by David McPhail
Scholastic, 1991   Pre-S.–2   60 pages

Mr. Lee is regarded as the Shel Silverstein of Canada. This is his latest collection, filled with the colorful, zany, weird, and tender characters that make his poems for primary kids just right. The illustrations here by David McPhail are delicious icing on the cake. Also by the author: *Jelly Belly*.

If I Were in Charge of the World and Other Worries
by Judith Viorst
Atheneum, 1981   Gr. 3 and up   56 pages

If the meter or rhyme in these 41 poems is occasionally imperfect, it is easily overlooked in light of their pulse and timing. In prescribing these short verses "for children and their parents," this contemporary American humorist offers a two-point perspective: Children reading these poems will giggle, then recognize themselves, their friends and enemies, and think, "That's really the way it is!" Parents will recognize in the poems the child they used to be. Also by the author: *Alexander and the Terrible, Horrible, No Good, Very Bad Day* (p); *I'll Fix Anthony*; *The Tenth Good Thing About Barney*; *Alexander Who Used to Be Rich Last Sunday*; *My Mama Says There Aren't Any Zombies, Ghosts, Vampires, Creatures, Demons, Monsters, Fiends, Goblins, or Things*; and *Rosie and Michael*.

If You're Not Here, Please Raise Your Hand:
Poems About School
by Kalli Dakos ✭ Illustrated by G. Brian Karas
Simon & Schuster, 1990   Gr. 1–8   64 pages

I know of no single book that so captures the pulse of elementary school the way this poetry collection does. And no wonder! Dakos is a classroom teacher; she's been down in the trenches with all the silliness, sadness, and happiness. Can't you tell just from the title? Also by the author: *Don't Read This Book Whatever You Do! More Poems About School*. Related books: *I Thought I'd Take My Rat to School: Poems for September to June*, selected by Dorothy M. Kennedy; *Never Take a Pig* to *Lunch and Other Poems About the Fun of Food* (po); and *Somebody Catch My Homework*, by David L. Harrison.

Kids Pick the Funniest Poems
compiled by Bruce Lansky ✫ Illustrated by Stephen Carpenter
Meadowbrook, 1991   K–8   105 pages

Here are the 75 funniest poems as chosen by 300 schoolchildren, from a broad cross section of poets.

Mother Goose—see *The Little Dog Laughed and Other Nursery Rhymes from Mother Goose* (p) and the other titles listed with it.

Never Take a Pig to Lunch and Other Poems About the Fun of Food
selected and illustrated by Nadine Bernard Westcot
Orchard, 1994   K–4   62 pages

In this collection of silly or hilarious poems about food, the compiler has divided the 60 selections into four fun categories: (1) eating silly things; (2) eating foods we like; (3) eating too much; and (4) manners at the table. Included are most of the best children's poets of today and yesterday.

Related books about food: *Burgoo Stew* by Susan Patron; *But No Candy*, by Gloria Houston; *Cranberry Thanksgiving*, by Wende and Harry Devlin; *Dinner at the Panda Palace*, by Stephanie Calmenson; *If You Give a Mouse a Cookie* (p); *Frank and Ernest*, by Alexandra Day; *Gregory the Terrible Eater*, by Mitchell Sharmat; *The Hokey-Pokey Man*, by Steven Kroll; *How Pizza Came to Queens*, by Dayal Kaur Khalsa; *The Hungry Thing Returns*, by Jan Slepian and Ann Seidler; *Jeremy Isn't Hungry*, by Barbara Williams; *Little Salt Lick and the Sun King*, by Jennifer Armstrong; *The Midnight Eaters*, by Amy Hest; *Monkey Soup*, by Louis Sachar; *Olson's Meat Pies*, by Peter Cohn and Olof Landstrom; *Pancakes for Breakfast*, by Tomie dePaola; *Pumpkin Time*, by Jan Andrews; *The Sleeping Bread*, by Stefan Czernecki and Timothy Rhodes; *Stone Soup*, retold by John Warren Stewig; *Thanksgiving at the Tappletons'*, by Eileen Spinelli; and *Uncle Willie and the Soup Kitchen*, by Dyanne DiSalvo-Ryan.

The New Kid on the Block
by Jack Prelutsky ✸ Illustrated by James Stevenson
Greenwillow, 1984   K-4   160 pages

One of today's most prolific poets for children, Prelutsky has collected more than 100 of his most outrageous and comical characters, attempting nothing more than to amuse and please children—which he does with a poem about the taken-for-granted blessings of having your nose on your face instead of in your ear, and the one about Sneaky Sue who started playing hide-and-seek a month ago and still can't be found. Also by the author: *The Baby Uggs Are Hatching*; *The Dragons Are Singing Tonight*; *For Laughing Out Loud*; *The Mean Old Mean Hyena*; *Nightmares: Poems to Trouble Your Sleep*; *The Queen of Eene*; *Ride a Purple Pelican*; *The Snopp on the Sidewalk*; see also his *Random House Book of Poetry for Children* and *Read-Aloud Rhymes for the Very Young* (po).

The Random House Book of Poetry for Children
selected by Jack Prelutsky ✸ Illustrated by Arnold Lobel
Random House, 1983   K-5   248 pages

One of the best children's poetry anthologies ever. Poet Jack Prelutsky recognizes here that the common language of all children is laughter and wonder. The 572 selected poems (from traditional as well as contemporary poets) are short—but long on laughter, imagery, and rhyme, and grouped around fourteen categories that include food, goblins, nonsense, home, children, animals, and seasons. This is an excellent companion to his other anthology, *Read-Aloud Rhymes for the Very Young* (po); see also *The New Kid on the Block* (po).

Read-Aloud Rhymes for the Very Young
collected by Jack Prelutsky ✸ Illustrated by Marc Brown
Knopf, 1986   Tod.-K   88 pages

Here are more than 200 little poems (with full-color illustrations) for little people with little attention spans, to help both to grow. Related books: *A Cup of Starshine*, collected by Jill Bennett; and *Whiskers and Rhymes*, by Arnold Lobel. For older children, see the Prelutsky collection *The Random House Book of Poetry for Children* (po).

Side by Side: Poems to Read Together
collected by Lee Bennett Hopkins ✩ Illustrated by
Hilary Knight
Simon & Schuster, 1988   Pre-S.-2   80 pages

Teacher, poet, and anthologist Lee Bennett Hopkins assembles tradi-
tional and contemporary poets to be read aloud to young children. Cov-
ering the seasons, holidays, animals, and lullabies, the 57 poems also
include several of the classic narrative poems for young children like
"Poor Old Lady," "The House That Jack Built," and "A Visit from St.
Nicholas." With Hilary Knight's double-page artwork, it is a superb book.
Other Hopkins collections: *April Bubbles Chocolate: An ABC of Poetry*;
Good Books, Good Times!; *Surprises*; *More Surprises*; *The Sky Is Full of
Song*; and for adults, *Pass the Poetry Please*, the definitive handbook on
introducing poetry to children.

Sing a Song of Popcorn: Every Child's Book of Poems
selected by Beatrice Schenk deRegniers, Eva Moore,
Mary M. White, and Jan Carr
Scholastic, 1988   K-5   160 pages

What distinguishes this volume from other excellent poetry collections
is that each of the nine sections has been assigned to a different Caldecott Award–winning illustrator, including Maurice Sendak, Trina
Schart Hyman, and Arnold Lobel. Thus both the sounds and sights in
this book make it outstanding.

Where the Sidewalk Ends by Shel Silverstein
HarperCollins, 1974   K-8   166 pages

Without question, this is the best-loved collection of poetry for children, selling more than two million hardcover copies in twenty years.
When it comes to knowing children's appetites Silverstein is pure genius.
The titles alone are enough to bring children to rapt attention: "Band-
aids"; "Boa Constrictor"; "Crocodile's Toothache"; "The Dirtiest Man in
the World"; "If I Had a Brontosaurus"; "Recipe for a Hippopotamus
Sandwich." Here are 130 poems that will either touch children's hearts
or tickle their funny bones. Silverstein's second collection of poems, *A
Light in the Attic*, was the second children's book to make *The New York
Times* bestseller list, where it remained for 186 weeks. Also by the author: *The Giving Tree*; *Lafcadio, the Lion Who Shot Back*; and *Who
Wants a Cheap Rhinoceros?*

ANTHOLOGIES

City of Gold and Other Stories from the Old Testament
retold by Peter Dickinson ✷ Illustrated by Michael Foreman
Otter/Houghton, Mifflin, 1992   Gr. 5 and up   185 pages
   Winner of the Carnegie Medal (England's Newbery Award), here are
33 magnificent retellings of Bible stories, as common folk might have
told them at the time. For example, David and Goliath is told in the
vernacular by a sergeant training recruits in the Babylonian army. Related books: *Tomie dePaola's Book of Bible Stories* (for younger listeners)
and *Does God Have a Big Toe?* (a).

Classics to Read Aloud to Your Children
by William Russell
Crown, 1984   K and up   40 pages
   Recognizing that not all great literature can be comfortably read aloud
and that suitable classics often are found in separate volumes requiring
hours of searching out, Russell offers in one book 38 selections of the
very best classic poetry, fairy tales, myths, short stories, and novels. Each
selection is prefaced with a brief paragraph about the story, an estimate
of the reading time, and notes on any unusual vocabulary in the text.
Related books: *A Wonder Book*, by Nathaniel Hawthorne.

Does God Have a Big Toe? by Marc Gellman
HarperCollins, 1989   Gr. 1-7   88 pages
   Along with being a mother lode of wisdom and inspiration, the Bible
through the centuries has been a rich source of literature and inspiration
for those who look for the common thread of story in all life. Because
the Bible lends itself to such diverse interpretation, scholars often create
stories of their own to explain it. In this case, Rabbi Marc Gellman has
taken 20 biblical episodes and given us 20 midrosh—"new stories about
old stories." Its success is largely due to Gellman's original wit and the
reverence he maintains throughout. Also by the author: *Where Does God
Live? Questions and Answers for Parents and Children*, with Msgr. Thomas Hartman. Related books: *City of Gold and Other Stories from the
Old Testament* (a); *The Diamond Tree: Jewish Tales from Around the
World*, retold by Howard Schwartz and Barbara Rush; *My Grandmother's
Stories: A Collection of Jewish Folk Tales* (s); and *Zlateh the Goat and
Other Stories*, by Isaac B. Singer.

Extraordinary Origins of Everyday Things
by Charles Panati
HarperCollins, 1987 Gr. 6 and up 442 pages

Panati writes what I call "readable reference books," filled with short but fascinating stories (500 in this volume alone) on the origins of the things and customs we cherish—like the Boy Scouts, the Barbie doll, pretzels, and the can opener. For experienced listeners. Also by the author: *Panati's Browser's Book of Beginnings; Panati's Parade of Fads, Follies, and Manias;* and *The Origins of Our Most Cherished Obsessions.* Related books: *Paul Harvey's "The Rest of the Story"* (a); *Ever Wonder Why?,* by Douglas B. Smith; *Know It All!,* by Ed Zotti; and *Mistakes That Worked,* by Charlotte Foltz Jones.

The Family Read-Aloud Holiday Treasury
selected by Alice Low ✵ Illustrated by Marc Brown
Little, Brown, 1991 K–5 150 pages

Here's a story or poem for every calendar occasion—from Valentine's Day to Labor Day, from summer days to back-to-school days—religious and secular, as well as multi-ethnic, with contributions from famous authors. Related books: *Free to Be . . . You and Me,* edited by Carole Hart, Letty C. Pogrebin, Mary Rodgers, and Marlo Thomas; *The Read-to-Me Treasury,* edited by Sally Grindley; and *Ten Small Tales* (p).

Fantastic Stories
by Terry Jones ✵ Illustrated by Michael Forman
Viking, 1992 Gr. 2–5 128 pages

An alumnus of Oxford University and Monty Python, Jones writes tales that were best described by a critic who called them a mix of the brothers Marx and Grimm. They are funny, weird, lovable, intriguing, and always fantastic. Forman's illustrations only enrich the package. Also by the author: *Terry Jones's Fairy Tales.* Related book: *Sideways Stories from Wayside School* (n).

Great Lives: Human Rights by William Jay Jacobs
Atheneum, 1990 Gr. 6 and up 266 pages

This is one in a series of biographical anthologies covering the entire curriculum. Written by respected historians, each contains more than 25 biographies approximately 15 pages long, and each volume focuses on a particular area, such as human rights. Others in the series: *American Government; Exploration; Medicine; Invention and Technology; Nature and the Environment; Painting; Science; Sports;* and *World Government.*

Hey! Listen to This: Stories to Read Aloud
by Jim Trelease
Penguin, 1992   K–4   410 pages
 Here are 48 stories from the top authors of yesterday and today. Ideal for reading aloud, they are arranged in categories like school days, food, families, folk and fairy tales, and animals. The selections include entire chapter excerpts as well as complete stories. There are full-page biographical profiles of the authors and stories. Also by the author: *Read All About It!* (a), an anthology for grades 5 and older; and *The Read-Aloud Handbook*.

Little Golden Book Story Land: 40 of the Best
Little Golden Books Ever Published
Western, 1992   Pre-S.–K   254 pages
 Some of America's better writers and illustrators for children began their careers creating those inexpensive little Golden Books. Here are many of them under one roof, along with offerings from Disney and Sesame Street, including the classic *Pokey Little Puppy* and *Sailor Dog.* Related book: *The Random House Book of Easy-to-Read Stories* (a).

Only the Heart Knows How to Find Them: Precious Moments
for a Faithless Time by Christopher de Vinck
Viking, 1991   Gr. 7 and up   217 pages
 Teacher, father, and award-winning newspaper columnist, de Vinck explores the heartbeat of the human condition as it is found in family, school, and community in his columns and essays, always leaving us with important thoughts. De Vinck makes even the deepest of concepts more accessible for most of us by using story or anecdote. Also by the author: *Songs of Innocence and Experience: Essays in Celebration of the Ordinary.* Related book: *Everything I Know in Life I Learned in Kindergarten*, by Robert Fulgham.

Paul Harvey's "The Rest of the Story"
by Paul Aurandt
Bantam, 1978   Gr. 6 and up   234 pages
 This collection of essays from broadcaster Paul Harvey's five-minute radio show, *The Rest of the Story*, is perfect for teachers and parents

trying to win older students to the art of listening. Nearly all of these pieces deal with famous people past and present. The person's name is saved for the last few lines of the tale and serves as an O. Henry punch line. The 81 stories average four minutes in length. Other books in the series: *Destiny* and *More of Paul Harvey's "The Rest of the Story."* Another book of short, anecdotal nonfiction—especially for history or social studies classes: *Extraordinary Origins of Everyday Things* (a).

People Who Make a Difference by Brent Ashabrenner
Dutton, 1989   Gr. 5 and up   129 pages

One of the best nonfiction writers for children, the author gives us 14 moving profiles of ordinary people (a multi-ethnic selection) who have done extraordinary things to change their communities for the better. My personal favorite is the "Helping Hands" chapter about tiny capuchin monkeys trained to assist quadriplegics in their daily needs. An excellent social studies read-aloud. Also by the author: *Always to Remember: The Story of the Vietnam Veterans Memorial* and *Into a Strange Land: Unaccompanied Refugee Youth in America.*

The Random House Book of Easy-to-Read Stories
Random House, 1993   K–2   249 pages

If you're looking for a book bargain for beginning readers, this is it! Sixteen selections from longtime favorite easy-reader books, with the original art and stories by such authors as Dr. Seuss, the Berenstains, Marc Brown, Tomie dePaola, and Richard Scarry. These same books, bought separately, would cost more than $100; this anthology is approximately $20.

The Random House Book of Humor for Children
selected by Pamela Pollack ✶ Illustrated by Paul O. Zelinsky
Random House, 1988   Gr. 3–7   309 pages

Here are 34 short stories and novel excerpts centered around children and humor, featuring many famous authors in children's fiction—from Mark Twain and Rudyard Kipling to Robert McCloskey and Beverly Cleary. Though each stands on its own, they are a terrific way to lure children into the author's complete work. This is part of an excellent series by Random House that includes: *The Random House Book of Fairy Tales*, adapted by Amy Ehrlich; *The Random House Book of Ghost Stories*, edited by Susan Hill; *The Random House Book of Poetry for Chil-*

dren (po); and *The Random House Book of Sports Stories*, selected by L. M. Schulman.

Read All About It! by Jim Trelease
Penguin, 1993   Gr. 5 and up   487 pages

For parents and teachers at a loss for what to read to preteens and teens, here are 50 selections—from classics to newspaper columns, fiction and nonfiction, humor and tragedy. Each story is introduced by a biographical profile of the author—like the story behind the long-lost Harper Lee (*To Kill a Mockingbird*). Also by the author: *Hey! Listen to This* (a), an anthology for grades K-4.

Scary Stories to Tell in the Dark
collected by Alvin Schwartz ✬ Illustrated by Stephen Gammell
HarperCollins, 1981   Gr. 5 and up   112 pages

Dipping into the past and present, the author presents 29 American horror stories and songs guaranteed to make your listeners cringe. The text includes suggestions for the reader-aloud on when to pause, when to scream, even when to turn off the lights. The selections run the gamut from giggles to gore and average two pages in length. In addition, a source section briefly traces each tale's origin in the U.S. (Discretion is advised because of the subject matter.) Sequels: *More Scary Stories to Tell in the Dark* and *Scary Stories 3: More Tales to Chill Your Bones*. Also by the author: *All of Our Noses Are Here and Other Noodle Tales*; *And the Green Grass Grew All Around: Folk Poetry for Everyone* (po). Related book: *The Dark Way: Stories from the Spirit World* (fa).

Talk That Talk: An Anthology of African-American Storytelling
edited by Linda Goss and Marian E. Barnes
Touchstone, 1989   Gr. 4 and up   492 pages

This anthology of nearly 100 stories brilliantly represents the oral tradition in African-American culture, including sermons, truth tales, poetry, biography, humor, and ghost tales, from the famous to the not-so-famous. Related books for younger listeners: *Bury My Bones But Keep My Words: African Tales for the Retelling*, retold by Tony Fairman; and *The People Could Fly: American Black Folktales*, by Virginia Hamilton (fa).

A Treasury of Children's Literature
edited by Armand Eisen
Houghton Mifflin, 1992   Pre-S.–4   302 pages

Sumptuously illustrated with more than 200 full-color illustrations, this is a collection of more than 40 classic pieces of children's literature—from the most popular folk and fairy tales, to nursery rhymes and excerpts from classic novels like *Peter Pan* and *Pinocchio*. At $25, it is one of the best bargains on the market today.

FAIRY AND FOLK TALES

Andersen's Fairy Tales
translated by L. W. Kingsland ✿ Illustrated by Rachel Birkett
Oxford University Press, 1985

This includes twenty-six of Andersen's best-known tales in a single volume, complete with color and black-and-white illustrations. A Puffin paperback edition by the same name, edited by Naomi Lewis, is also excellent. Be sure to introduce children to Andersen's amazing but largely unknown artwork in *The Amazing Paper Cuttings of Hans Christian Andersen*, by Beth Wagner Brust.

Individual Andersen tales: *The Emperor's New Clothes*, illustrated by Virginia Lee Burton; *The Little Mermaid*, adapted by Anthea Bell; *The Nightingale*, retold by Naomi Lewis; *The Princess and the Pea*, illustrated by Dorothee Duntze; *The Snow Queen*, adapted by Naomi Lewis; *Thumbeline*, translated by Anthea Bell; *Seven Tales*, by Eva Le Gallienne; *The Snow Queen*, retold by Naomi Lewis; *The Steadfast Tin Soldier*, illustrated by Fred Marcellino; *The Tinderbox*, retold by Barry Moser, who places it in Tennessee with a Confederate veteran returning home; *The Ugly Duckling*, retold by Troy Howell; and *The Wild Swans*, retold by Deborah Hautzig.

The Dark Way: Stories from the Spirit World
by Virginia Hamilton
Harcourt Brace, 1990   Gr. 4 and up   145 pages

Twenty-five tales of the supernatural from around the world, featuring imps, elves, ghosts and phantoms, witches, monsters, and fairies. For experienced listeners. Related book: *Scary Stories to Tell in the Dark* (a).

The Fairy Tale Treasury
edited by Virginia Haviland ✴ Illustrated by Raymond Briggs
Dell, 1986   Pre-S.-4   191 pages
Former head of the children's department at the Library of Congress, Haviland has collected thirty-two of the most popular tales from Grimm, Andersen, Jacobs, and Perrault, with full-color art by Raymond Briggs.

Favorite Folktales from Around the World
edited by Jane Yolen
Pantheon, 1986   Gr. 6 and up   pages
Here are excellent versions (unillustrated) of more than 150 classic tales from forty different cultures, including a bibliographic history on each tale, edited by one of today's most prolific children's authors. For experienced listeners.

From Sea to Shining Sea: A Treasury of American Folklore and
Folk Songs compiled by Amy Cohn
Scholastic, 1993   Gr. 1-6   273 pages
The editor and publisher of this magnificent volume have used the term "folklore" in this sense: the lore—fact and fiction—that make up a unique people called Americans. More than 300 years' worth of songs, poems, stories, tall tales, celebrations, legends, trickster tales, riddles, sports, animal lore, and stories of our wars and our struggles. To give you an idea of the sweep of this volume (illustrated by eleven Caldecott Medal winners), "Yankee Doodle" is here; so is Martin Luther King Jr.'s "I Have a Dream" speech and Abbott and Costello's "Who's on first?" routine. Related book: *And the Green Grass Grew All Around: Folk Poetry from Everyone* (po).

Household Stories of the Brothers Grimm
translated by Lucy Crane ✴ Illustrated by Walter Crane
Dover paperback, 1963
This collection of fifty-three tales contains the Grimms's most popular works in a translation that is easily read aloud and includes more than 100 illustrations. The maturity and listening experience of your audience should determine their readiness to handle the subject matter, complexity of plot, and language of these unexpurgated versions.
Picture book Grimm titles: *The Bear and the Bird King*, retold by Robert Byrd; *The Elves and the Shoemaker*, retold by Freya Littledale;

The Four Gallant Sisters, retold by Eric A. Kimmel; *Hansel and Gretel*, retold by Rika Lesser; *Iron John*, adapted by Eric A. Kimmel; *Rapunzel*, retold by Barbara Rogasky; *Rumpelstiltskin*, retold by Paul O. Zelinsky; *Sleeping Beauty*, retold by Trina Schart Hyman; *Snow White & Rose Red*, illustrated by Gennady Spirin; *Tucker Pfeffercorn* ("Rumpelstiltskin" set in the American south), retold by Barry Moser.

For preschool children being introduced to the fairy tale for the first time, *The Three Bears and Fifteen Other Stories* (fa) is an excellent collection.

The Maid of the North: Feminist Folk Tales from Around the World by Ethel Johnston Phelps

Holt, 1981   Gr. 2 and up   174 pages

A collection of 21 fast-moving tales with witty, resourceful, and confident heroines (not heroes) from seventeen different cultures. Also by the author: *Tatterhood and Other Tales*. Related book: *Wise Women: Folk and Fairy Tales from Around the World*, retold and edited by Suzanne I. Barchers. For related heroine picture books, see listing with *Charlie Drives the Stage* (p).

Michael Foreman's World of Fairy Tales by Michael Foreman

Arcade, 1991   K-5   142 pages

One of the handsomest collections. Foreman offers 22 tales from around the world, with brief background introductions for each tale. His illustrations are brilliant, matching each story's dramatic tension.

The People Could Fly: American Black Folktales by Virginia Hamilton

Knopf, 1985   Gr. 3-6   174 pages

Rich with rhythm, energy, and humor, these 24 stories were kept alive by slave storytellers and include Bruh Rabbit, Gullah, and freedom-trail adventures, illustrated by Caldecott winners Leo and Diane Dillon. Related books: *Tales of Uncle Remus* (fa); and for older students—*Talk That Talk: An Anthology of African-American Storytelling* (a).

The Rainbow Fairy Book retold by Andrew Lang

Morrow, 1993   K-4   285 pages

Andrew Lang was a successor to the Brothers Grimm, collecting the best fairy tales from a variety of cultures and publishing them in a popular series that largely remains in print today, almost 100 years later. This volume is a collection of the 31 best from those books, including translations of Grimm, Andersen, and Perrault, as well as tales from India, England, Russia, China, Africa, Lapland, and Spain. His other collections (all in Dover paperback): *The Arabian Nights Entertainments*; *The Blue Fairy Book*; *The Brown Fairy Book*; *The Crimson Fairy Book*; *The Green Fairy Book*; *The Grey Fairy Book*; *The Lilac Fairy Book*; *The Olive Fairy Book*; *The Orange Fairy Book*; *The Pink Fairy Book*; *The Red Fairy Book*; *The Violet Fairy Book*; and *The Yellow Fairy Book*.

The Tales of Uncle Remus
retold by Julius Lester ☆ Illustrated by Jerry Pinkney
Dial, 1987   Gr. 1–6   **151 pages**
   Just as captured slaves adapted their African folk tales to a Southern locale, Professor Julius Lester has moved them off the plantation and into the twentieth century without losing any of their wit, wisdom, or flavor. This celebrated black author has replaced Joel Chandler Harris's heavy dialect with a more contemporary and accessible Southern tongue in the mouth of an Uncle Remus who might be sitting on the front porch telling these 48 tales to his grandchild. Sequels: *More Tales of Uncle Remus*; *Further Tales of Uncle Remus*; *The Last of the Uncle Remus Tales*. Also by the author: *How Many Spots Does a Leopard Have? And Other Tales*; *John Henry*; *The Knee-High Man and Other Tales*. Related books: *The People Could Fly: American Black Folktales*, by Virginia Hamilton (fa); see also listing with *Roll of Thunder, Hear My Cry* (n).

The Three Bears and 15 Other Stories
by Anne Rockwell
HarperCollins, 1975   Pre-S.-1   **117 pages**
   A collection of unthreatening but entertaining famous fairy tales for younger children, profusely illustrated by the author.

Appendix

A Note for Doomsayers Who Think Things Have Never Been Worse

The early chapters of this book include some worrisome statistics that reinforce the need to change the way we attempt to raise readers in this culture. But at no point do I intend such statistics to serve as a negative comparison with the students of the past. Indeed, if you are among the many who think today's schools and students are appreciatively inferior to those of, let's say, 1941—think again. I know *I* have since seeing the research. On the other hand, if you believe there's nothing to worry about, think again.

For nearly twenty-five years we've been harangued about the sorry state of today's students when compared with yesterday's. Every time a national education report is issued, there's a feeding frenzy among pessimists and hearse-followers. There was, for example, the national survey of adult literacy that led the news in September 1993—the one that showed that almost one half of the adult U.S. population cannot function adequately in reading or math.[1] Instead of focusing on the intent of such studies, too many used it to declare today's students are less intelligent —dumber, if you will—than their predecessors.

The first thing to understand is the strong inclination of some people to burn their neighbor's house down in order to make their own house look better. When this is transferred to generations, we end up with insecure older citizens imagining their childhoods as better, smarter, and more civilized than the present one. (I might add that the same temptation is present when comparing the families of yesteryear with today's—see "The American Family and the Nostalgia Trap," by Stephanie Coontz, in *Phi Delta Kappan*, March 1995.) Let's see how the schools compare.

Here's a handful of headlines that read like today's newspaper:

- *Yale Review* laments the admission of poorly prepared students.
- Of 331 students at the University of Wisconsin, only 41 attend regular classes.
- Half of Harvard freshmen fail entrance examination.
- Of nearly 400 universities in the United States, only 65 are without preparatory (remedial) departments.
- Over one half of students enrolled at Harvard, Princeton, Yale, and Columbia do not meet entrance requirements; developmental (remedial) courses are established.

Each of those headlines occurred *before* 1908.[2] I could fill this entire page with similar headlines. The great institution of American education didn't turn sour in the last twenty-five years. If the truth be known, it has never been as great as the previous generation thought it was.

The people who worry about the current lack of high standards might want to consider these findings by a dismayed and reform-minded university president: "The school admitted students without any evidence of academic requirements; the classes were not graded; students entered any time and attended lectures then in progress; the school never examined the students, who left after eighteen months of lectures—with a degree." The school? The most prestigious law school in America—Harvard Law—in 1869![3]

But even where there were high standards in the past, they often were imposed to keep the elite in and the rest out. Only in the last thirty years has American education made a sincere effort to welcome any student other than the healthy and wealthy into high school and college. On June 9, 1992, *The Wall Street Journal* reprinted the 1885 entrance exam for Jersey City (N.J.) High School (available at your local library on microfilm). It's so difficult, I estimate many college graduates today would struggle with it, so it's no surprise that less than 10 percent of the eighth-graders in the 1885 population even attempted it.

Those who bemoan today's video culture in favor of the days of yore when families sat around the open hearth reading into the night should consider the lament of Dartmouth professor of English C. F. Richardson in 1906: "Everybody ought to own books. A house without books has been well called a literary Sahara; and how many of them there are! We are a 'reading people'; but nothing is easier to find than homes in which the furniture, the pictures, the ornaments—everything, is an object of greater care and expense than the library. Is it any wonder that their inmates, whatever their so-called wealth or comfort, are intellectual starvelings?"[4]

Until 1890, most rural areas of America had no high schools and the urban centers had no standard curriculum. In Massachusetts, which boasted the most developed public school system, only 1 in 10 high schools had college preparatory courses in 1890. By 1920, the situation had improved to where the average student completed *just one year* of high school and only 20 percent graduated that year. The graduation rate did jump dramatically during the 1930s—thanks to the Great Depression, which eliminated millions of jobs that adolescents would have left school to fill.[5] By 1940, we could boast the following:

- The school dropout rate was 76 percent[6] (compared to 11 percent in 1994[7]).
- Only 5 percent of the population had a college diploma (26 percent today).
- Only 8 percent of the black population had a high school diploma (75 percent graduation rate in 1993[8]).

1941 All-Star S.A.T. Team

And that brings us to the momentous year of 1941—the golden year selected by the College Board as the "average" year's score for the S.A.T.—500 points for either math or verbal. Each succeeding year's test takers would be measured against that score. And when the scores began to decline in the 1960s and continued to do so until the 1980s, many of us associated the drop with a lowered interest in reading and more time in front of the television. Those may have been contributing factors, but they were minor next to a greater cause, largely ignored until the 1990s. It was a reason so obvious and powerful, it forced a dramatic revamping of the S.A.T. scoring system in 1994.

Who exactly were the S.A.T. class of 1941, the "whiz kids" who allegedly made today's kids' scores look so paltry? When "education archeologists" began digging, they came up with surprising answers. For one thing, they were 10,654 in number. Moreover, they were 98 percent white, 40 percent from private schools, and 60 percent male.[9] We also know the Depression was still affecting the nation. The only people who could afford college in 1941 were the wealthy. The S.A.T. class of 1941 was 10,654 rich white guys who became the national average for a half century.

So it's little wonder the scores declined when the S.A.T. opened its door to average students—when class enrollment reached more than 1.2 million, with 83 percent from public schools, 52 percent women, 30 percent minorities (many from the lower socioeconomic levels), and 46 percent from families whose income was $40,000 or lower.[10] The S.A.T. class of 1941 was *not* an average class—it was an all-star team and not representative of seventeen-year-olds in 1941. The class of 1994 was a far truer national average.[11]

A further advantage to the class of 1941's scores was their experience of a peculiar decade in which the U.S. had its lowest immigration rate in a hundred years. Students of the 1990s come from a decade (1980–90) in which immigration figures were the highest in a century.[12] The 1990 census put the number of foreign-born nationals living in the United States at 7.9 percent of the population—an all-time high.[13] By 1994, Massachusetts suburban school districts like Brookline could count 27 different languages being spoken by its students, while Miami, Florida, averaged 44, and Anaheim, California, included 67 different languages.[14]

If you were disappointed at the poor showing by U.S. seventeen-year-olds and college seniors in the general history exam sponsored by the National Endowment for the Humanities in the late 1980s, you can take some solace in this headline from *The New York Times* front page on April 4, 1943: "Ignorance of U.S. History Shown by College Freshmen." The study included 7,000 college freshmen, and when a follow-up exam was given to college seniors and military college freshman, they also failed it.[15]

As one writer put it, the high school of 1940 might have been a superficially pleasanter, quieter place than the high school today, but we need to remember that 49 percent of the students were informally excluded in 1940—the "pregnant, handicapped, learning disabled, emotionally disturbed, poor, and minority."[16]

Another often-heard argument is that corroded standards have caused today's college diploma to be worth less academically than were those of the past. True, the bottom 25 percent of today's *college* graduates are no more literate than the average *high school* graduate—unable to decipher a city bus schedule. But the 1992 national adult literacy survey showed that older college graduates, ages fifty-five or higher, were even *less* literate at the same task.[17]

Good News and Bad

Considering all of the above, along with the social chaos from which many of today's children come to school, it's a miracle we've managed the following:

- The U.S. leads the world in bachelor's degrees—26 percent, versus: Canada—25 percent; Japan—21 percent; Great Britain—14 percent; and West Germany (before unification)—13 percent.[18]
- In a 1993 report from the International Organization for Economic Cooperation and Development (twenty-five industrialized nations), U.S. students ranked near the top in literacy.[19]
- The S.A.T. class of 1993 had a record percent of students scoring above 650 in math.[20]
- The 1994 high school senior classes sent a record 63 percent of their members on to advanced education.[21]
- The 1994 U.S. team won the International Math Olympiad, besting sixty-eight other countries with six perfect scores, the first time that had ever been done by any country.[22]
- The number of bachelor's degrees in engineering, computer science, physical science, and mathematics has increased by more than 75 percent in the last twenty years, despite a decline in the college-age population.[23]
- Today's public school faculties are the best educated in U.S. history. In 1961, only 23 percent of teachers had master's or doctoral degrees; by 1992, that figure had climbed to 53 percent.[24]
- A 1994 study from the Rand Corporation showed that student scores (especially those of minorities) had risen significantly during the last twenty years, and contrary to popular opinion, no

negative impact could be found in student scores when children of single or working mothers were isolated for evaluation.[25]

That's the good news—that today's students are not inferior to the ones in 1941, and in some ways even better. Now for the bad news: the kids may be the same, but the world is not. It's a whole lot more complicated now than in 1941.

When the nation's economy was based upon natural resources, heavy industry, and agriculture, it wasn't what was in a farmer's or miner's *hands* and *head* but what was in his *soil* that determined his income. And then America moved to a "service" economy based upon what was in a person's head—how to create and deliver products that solve people's problems or make their lives easier: computers, cellular phones, medical technology, planes, and cars. At that point, people's intellectual ability became more important than their strength, and their paychecks began to reflect the difference.

The simple demonstration of this might be the family automobile. In 1948, if something went wrong with it, you got a push down to the corner garage, where a high school dropout fixed it. In those days, a family car contained only 150 feet of wiring.[26]

A 1994 car is a world apart. To begin with, 83 percent of its moving parts are controlled by computers, and its wiring stretches for one mile instead of 150 feet. Since most four-year college graduates are not interested in doing auto repair, such tasks are left to the rest of the populace—which still constitutes the nation's majority. But can this majority read and understand the manuals required for such tasks? Apparently not. In 1994, the Environmental Protection Agency estimated that the U.S. had a shortage of 60,000 automotive technicians and the average technician is six to eight years behind in training.[27] The last time I asked my mechanic, he was averaging four weeks of out-of-shop training a year in order to stay abreast of changes.

If Americans are to manage in a more complicated world, our thinking must be deeper and more complicated. Nothing trains the mind as quickly and as thoroughly as reading. Reading is our life preserver. Reading as much or as well as folks did in 1941 isn't good enough anymore.

Notes

Introduction

1. Ina V. S. Mullis and others, *NAEP 1992 Trends in Academic Progress*, Office of Educational Research and Improvement (Washington, DC: U.S. Department of Education, June 1994). See also Paul E. Barton and Richard J. Coley, *America's Smallest School: The Family*, Policy Information Center (Princeton, NJ: Educational Testing Service, 1992).
2. "Schools Getting Tough on Guns in the Classroom," *The New York Times*, August 31, 1994, pp. A1, B8.
3. Kimberly J. McLarin, "Fear Prompts Self-Defense as Crime Comes to College," *The New York Times*, September 7, 1994, pp. A1, B11.
4. Stephanie Strom, "Shootings Lead Chain to Ban Toy Guns," *The New York Times*, October 15, 1994, p. A9. The toy store chain is Toys "R" Us.
5. *The Wall Street Journal*, July 30, 1987, p. 1.
6. Hilary T. Holbrook, "Sex Differences in Reading: Nature or Nurture?" *Journal of Reading*, March 1988, pp. 574–77.
7. A. D. Gross, "Sex Role Standards and Reading Achievement: A Study of an Israeli Kibbutz System," *The Reading Teacher* 32 (1978): 149–56.
8. Hilary T. Holbrook, "Sex Differences in Reading: Nature or Nurture?" Also J. Downing and C. K. Leong, *Psychology of Reading* (New York: Macmillan, 1982).
9. "Teaching Survey Shows Lack of Men, Minorities," Associated Press, July 7, 1992.
10. "Clubhouse Kids," *USA Today*, June 1, 1990, p. C8.
11. David Laband and Bernard Lentz, "The Natural Choice," *Psychology Today*, August 1986, pp. 37–43.
12. J. Santrock, "Relation of Type and Onset of Father-Absence to Cognitive Development," *Child Development* 43 (1972): 455–69.
13. Janelle M. Gray, "Reading Achievement and Autonomy as a Function of Father-to-Son Reading" (master's thesis, California State University, Stanislaus, CA, 1991).
14. Henry J. Parkinson, *Two Hundred Years of American Educational Thought* (New York: David McKay, 1976), 59–102.
15. Mary A. Foertsch, *Reading In and Out of School*, U.S. Department of Education/Educational Testing Service (Princeton, NJ: Educational Testing Service).
16. Richard C. Anderson, Elfrieda H. Hiebert, Judith A. Scott, Ian A. G. Wilkinson, *Becoming a Nation of Readers: The Report of the Commission on Reading* (Champaign-Urbana, IL: Center for the Study of Reading, 1985). See also Diane Ravitch and Chester Finn, Jr., *What Do Our 17-Year-Olds Know?* (New York: Harper & Row, 1987).
17. "Students Cite Pregnancies as a Reason to Drop Out," Associated Press, in *The New York Times*, September 14, 1994, p. B7.

18. Melissa Lee, "When It Comes to Salary, It's Academic," *The Washington Post,* July 22, 1994, p. D1. The Census Bureau reports the following lifetime earnings:

No high school diploma	$609,000
High school diploma	$821,000
Some college	$993,000
Associate's degree	$1,062,000
Bachelor's degree	$1,421,000
Master's degree	$1,619,000
Doctorate	$2,142,000
Profession—doctor, lawyer	$3,013,000

See also Gerald W. Bracey, "The Fourth Bracey Report on the Condition of Public Education," *Phi Delta Kappan,* October 1994, p. 123; Robert B. Reich, "The Fracturing of the Middle Class," *The New York Times,* August 31, 1994, p. A19. Reich notes that a male with a college degree will earn 83 percent more than his counterpart with only a high school diploma.

19. Every time a student's family income increases by $5,000, the student's SAT score (either math or verbal) rises; for each $5,000 decrease, the score drops. This holds true every year and for every ethnic group. See Christopher de Vinck, "An Open Book," *The College Board Review* 159 (Spring 1991): 9–12. See also *USA Today* chart, August 19, 1993, p. 3D.

20. Eugene Rogot, Paul D. Sorlie, and Norman J. Johnson, "Life Expectancy by Employment Status, Income, and Education in the National Longitudinal Mortality Study," *Public Health Reports* 107 (July–August 1992): 457–61. See also Jack M. Guralnik and others, "Educational Status and Active Life Expectancy Among Older Blacks and Whites," *The New England Journal of Medicine,* July 8, 1993, pp. 110–16.

21. Harold L. Hodgkinson, *The Same Client: The Demographics of Education and Service Delivery Systems* (Washington, DC: Institute of Educational Leadership/Center for Demographic Policy, 1989), p. 15.

22. Edward B. Fiske, "Can Money Spent on Schools Save Money That Would Be Spent on Prisons?" *The New York Times,* September 27, 1989, p. B10.

23. From Harold L. Hodgkinson's *The Same Client,* here are the top ten states for high school graduation rates (1989 report) and their national ranking in per capita prison population:

Minnesota	1	49th
Wyoming	2	28th
N. Dakota	3	50th
Nebraska	4	40th
Montana	5	33rd
Iowa	6	43rd
Wisconsin	7	39th
Ohio	8	24th
Kansas	9	22nd
Utah	10	41st

Chapter 1: Why Read Aloud?

1. Mary A. Foertsch, *Reading In and Out of School*, Educational Testing Service/Education Information Office (Washington, DC: U.S. Department of Education, May 1992), pp. 6–7, 35, 36.

2. Richard C. Anderson, Elfrieda H. Hiebert, Judith A. Scott, Ian A. G. Wilkinson, *Becoming a Nation of Readers: The Report of the Commission on Reading* (Champaign-Urbana, IL: Center for the Study of Reading, 1985), p. 23.

3. Ibid., p. 51.

4. Edward B. Fiske, "The Global Imperative," *The New York Times*, Education Life, Section 4A, April 9, 1989, p. 18.

5. Ellen Graham, "Retooling the Schools," *The Wall Street Journal Reports: Education*, March 31, 1989, pp. R1–3.

6. Edward B. Fiske, "Impending U.S. Jobs 'Disaster,'" *The New York Times*, September 25, 1989, pp. A1, 12.

7. Steven Greenhouse, "The Coming Crisis of the American Work Force," *The New York Times*, June 17, 1992, p. A14.

8. Julie Amparano Lopez, "System Failure," *The Wall Street Journal Reports: Education*, March 31, 1989, p. R12.

9. Tom Lowry, "Blue-Collar Blues," *The New York Daily News*, August 7, 1994, pp. C6–8.

10. "Business Teaching 3 R's to Employees in Effort to Compete," *The New York Times*, May 1, 1988, p. 1; "Defect Rate 50% from USA Schools," *USA Today*, October 27, 1987, p. B1.

11. *Literacy: Profiles of America's Young Adults*, National Assessment of Educational Progress (Princeton, NJ: Educational Testing Service, 1987).

12. "Illiteracy Seen as Threat to U.S. Economic Edge," *The New York Times*, September 7, 1988, p. B8.

13. "Foreign-Aid Agency Shifts to Problems Back Home," *The New York Times*, June 26, 1994, pp. 1, 18.

14. "Tougher Military Entrance Standards Slashing Number of Black Recruits," Knight-Ridder News Service, in *Honolulu Sunday Star-Bulletin & Advertiser*, February 9, 1994; "Military Recruiting Nears Record High for Quality," *Education Week*, November 30, 1994, p. 5.

15. Ivars Peterson, "More Get Equivalency Diploma Amid Questions About Its Value," *The New York Times*, October 21, 1992, pp. A1, B8.

16. Edward A. Gargan, "India Among the Leaders in Software for Computers," *The New York Times*, December 29, 1993, pp. A1, 7.

17. Ina V. S. Mullis and others, *NAEP 1992 Trends in Academic Progress*, Office of Educational Research and Improvement (Washington, DC: U.S. Department of Education, June 1994). See also *America's Smallest School*, Policy Information Center (Princeton, NJ: Educational Testing Service, 1992).

18. Ibid.

19. Archie Lapointe, "The State of Instruction in Reading and Writing in U.S. Elementary Schools," *Phi Delta Kappan*, October 1986, pp. 135–38.

20. *A Profile of the American Eighth Grader: National Education Longitudinal*

Study of 1988, National Center for Education Statistics (Washington, DC: U.S. Department of Education, June 1990).

21. Richard C. Anderson, Linda Fielding, and Paul Wilson, "Growth in Reading and How Children Spend Their Time Outside of School," *Reading Research Quarterly*, Summer 1988, pp. 285–303.

22. Ina V. S. Mullis and others, *NAEP 1992 Trends in Academic Progress.*

23. Jacques Barzun, *Begin Here* (Chicago, IL: University of Chicago Press, 1991), pp. 114–16.

24. Consumer research study on book purchasing 1991, done by the American Booksellers' Association in conjunction with the Book Industry Study Group and the Association of American Publishers.

25. Nicholas Zill and Marianne Winglee, *Who Reads Literature?* (Cabin John, MD: Seven Locks Press, 1990).

26. Alex S. Jones, "Study Finds Americans Want News but Aren't Well Informed," *The New York Times*, July 15, 1990, p. 13.

27. 1987 Roper Organization report for Television Information Office; also *Presstime*, American Newspaper Publishers Association, September 1987.

28. "We Daydream About One Life, Live Another," *USA Today*, May 13, 1986, p. A1. (Based on the D'Arcy Masius Benton & Bowles survey.)

29. Thomas Jefferson in letter to Col. Charles Yancey, January 6, 1816.

30. Gordon Rattray Taylor, *The Natural History of the Brain* (New York: E. P. Dutton, 1979), pp. 59–60.

31. Ibid.

32. Keith E. Stanovich, "Matthew Effects in Reading: Some Consequences of Individual Differences in the Acquisition of Literacy," *Reading Research Quarterly* (Fall 1986): 360–407; Richard L. Allington, "Oral Reading," in *Handbook of Reading Research*, P. David Pearson, editor (New York: Longman, 1984), pp. 829–64; Warwick B. Elley and Francis Mangubhai, "The Impact of Reading on Second Language Learning," *Reading Research Quarterly* 19 (Fall 1983): 53–67; Mary A. Foertsch, *Reading In and Out of School.*

33. Mary A. Foertsch, *Reading In and Out of School.*

34. Warwick B. Elley, *How in the World Do Students Read?* (Hamburg: International Association for the Evaluation of Educational Achievement, July 1992). Available from the International Reading Association, Newark, DE, $16/$12 (US).

35. Elton G. Stetson and Richard P. Williams, "Learning from Social Studies Textbooks: Why Some Students Succeed and Others Fail," *Journal of Reading*, September 1992, pp. 22–30.

36. Christopher Hitchens, "Why We Don't Know What We Don't Know," *The New York Times Magazine*, May 13, 1990, p. 32.

37. Keith E. Stanovich, "Matthew Effects in Reading: Some Consequences of Individual Differences in the Acquisition of Literacy."

38. Courtney B. Cazden, *Child Language and Education* (New York: Holt, Rinehart and Winston, 1972).

39. Psychologist Burton L. White, interviewed in "Training Parents Helps Toddlers," *The New York Times*, October 2, 1985, p. C1.

40. George A. Miller and Patricia M. Gildea, "How Children Learn Words," *Scientific American*, September 1987, pp. 94–99.

41. *Starting Points: The Report of the Carnegie Task Force on Meeting the Needs of Young Children*, Carnegie Corporation of New York (New York: Carnegie Corporation, 1994), p. 5.

42. "How Frequently Do You . . . ?" *Education Week*, PTA/Dodge national parent survey, April 4, 1990, p. 22.

43. Richard C. Anderson et al., *Becoming a Nation of Readers*, pp. 74–76; see also C. Fisher, D. Berliner, N. Filby, R. Marliave, L. Cohen, M. Dishaw, and J. Moore, *Teaching and Learning in the Elementary Schools: A Summary of the Beginning Teacher Evaluation Study* (San Francisco: Far West Regional Laboratory of Educational Research and Development, 1978).

44. Mary A. Foertsch, *Reading In and Out of School.*

45. "In School: A Photocopier Salesman Does His Job Too Well, and the Taxpayers Foot the Bill," *The New York Times*, June 29, 1994, p. A12.

46. *1992 NAEP Reading Assessment*, National Assessment of Educational Progress (Princeton, NJ: Educational Testing Service, 1993).

47. K. Jackym, Richard L. Allington, and Kathleen A. Broikou, "Estimating the Cost," *The Reading Teacher*, October 1989, pp. 30–35.

48. Richard Allington, "If They Don't Read Much, How They Gonna Get Good?" *Journal of Reading*, October 1977, pp. 57–61. See also: Richard Allington, "Sustained Approaches to Reading and Writing," *Language Arts*, September 1975, pp. 813–15.

49. M. Nystrand and A. Gamoran, "From Discourse Communities to Interpretive Communities: A Study in Ninth-Grade Literature Instruction" in *Exploring Texts: The Role of Discussion and Writing in the Teaching and Learning of Literature*, G. Newell and R. K. Durst, eds. (Norwood, MA: Christopher-Gordon, 1993), pp. 91–111.

50. H. J. Walberg and S. Tsai, "Matthew Effects in Education," *American Educational Research Journal* 20 (1984): 359–73; Keith E. Stanovich, "Matthew Effects in Reading: Some Consequences of Individual Differences in the Acquisition of Literacy"; following R. Merton, "The Matthew Effect in Science," *Science* 159 (1968): 56–63.

51. Olga Emery and Mihaly Csikszentmihalyi, "The Socialization Effects of Cultural Role Models in Ontogenetic Development and Upward Mobility," *Child Psychiatry and Development and Human Development* 12 (Fall 1981): pp. 3–18.

52. Bruno Bettelheim, *The Uses of Enchantment: The Meaning and Importance of Fairy Tales* (New York: Knopf, 1976), pp. 3–6.

53. Robert Penn Warren, "Why Do We Read Fiction?" *The Saturday Evening Post*, October 20, 1962, pp. 82–84.

54. *Time*, February 1, 1988, pp. 52–58. Tom O'Neill, Jr., is now principal of the Bigelow Middle School in Newton, Massachusetts, after ten years at Lewenberg. For his work at Lewenberg, O'Neill was named one of the inaugural recipients of the Heroes in Education award, presented by Reader's Digest to educators with original and effective methods. The award included $10,000 to the school.

55. All three articles were found in *The Asbury Park Press*, May 16, 1994, pp. 1, 6, 7, 14.

56. Eugene Rogot, Paul D. Sorlie, and Norman J. Johnson, "Life Expectancy by Employment Status, Income, and Education in the National Longitudinal Mortality Study," *Public Health Reports* 107 (July–August, 1992): pp. 457–61. See also Jack M. Guralnik and others, "Educational Status and Active Life Expectancy Among Older Blacks and Whites," *The New England Journal of Medicine*, July 8, 1993, pp. 110–16.

57. "Homeless as a Child, Harvard-Bound Now," Associated Press, in *The New York Times*, June 4, 1994, p. 7.

Chapter 2: When to Begin Read-Aloud

1. These remarks were made during a half-hour interview (on September 3, 1979) with Dr. Brazelton, conducted by John Merrow for *Options in Education*, a co-production of National Public Radio and the Institute for Educational Leadership of the George Washington University.

2. Anthony J. DeCasper and Melanie J. Spence, "Prenatal Maternal Speech Influences Newborns' Perception of Speech Sounds," *Infant Behavior and Development* 9 (2): 133–50 (1986).

3. Marjory Roberts, "Class Before Birth," *Psychology Today*, May 1987, p. 41; Sharon Begley and John Carey, "The Wisdom of Babies," *Newsweek*, January 12, 1981, pp. 71–72.

4. Dorothy Butler, *Cushla and Her Books* (Boston: The Horn Book, 1980).

5. One year after my first meeting with Mrs. Kunishima, *Reader's Digest* made her family's story its lead article: "The Family That Wouldn't Be Broken," by John Pekkanen, *Reader's Digest*, December 1993, pp. 45–50.

6. Vera Propp, "All Babies Are Born Equal."

7. Jacques Barzun, *Begin Here* (Chicago: University of Chicago Press, 1991), pp. 114–16.

8. Laura A. Petitto and Paula F. Marentette, "Babbling in the Manual Mode: Evidence for the Ontogeny of Language," *Science* 251 (March 1991): 1493–96; see also Natalie Angier, "Deaf Babies Use Their Hands to Babble, Researcher Finds," *The New York Times*, March 22, 1991, p. A1, B6.

9. Jerome Kagan, "The Child: His Struggle for Identity," *Saturday Review*, December 1968, p. 82. See also Steven R. Tulkin and Jerome Kagan, "Mother-Child Interaction in the First Year of Life," *Child Development*, March 1972, pp. 31–41.

10. Further examples of "concept attention span" can be found in Kagan, "The Child," p. 82.

11. Deirdre P. Madden, Ph.D., Speech and Theater Department, Baldwin-Wallace College, Berea, OH 44017.

12. These two became the seminal studies for read-aloud research: Dolores Durkin, *Children Who Read Early* (New York: Teachers College Press, 1966), and Margaret M. Clark, *Young Fluent Readers* (London: Heinemann, 1976). See also Anne D. Forester, "What Teachers Can Learn from 'Natural Readers,' " *The Reading Teacher*, November 1977, pp. 160–66.

13. Ina V. S. Mullis and others, *NAEP 1992 Trends in Academic Progress*, Office of Educational Research and Improvement (Washington, DC: U.S. Department of Education, June 1994). See also Paul E. Barton and Richard J. Coley, *America's Smallest School: The Family*, Policy Information Center (Princeton, NJ: Educational Testing Service, 1992), pp. 12–19.

14. In a study of Israeli kindergarten children, high-achieving readers owned ten times as many books as did the low achievers. See Chapter 8; also Dina Feitelson and Zahava Goldstein, "Patterns of Book Ownership and Reading to Young Children in Israeli School-Oriented and Nonschool-Oriented Families," *The Reading Teacher*, May 1986, pp. 924–30.

15. G. Robert Carlsen and Anne Sherrill, *Voices of Readers: How We Come to Love Books* (Urbana, IL: National Council of Teachers of English, 1988).

16. Richard C. Anderson, Elfrieda H. Hiebert, Judith A. Scott, Ian A. G. Wilkinson, *Becoming a Nation of Readers: The Report of the Commission on Reading* (Champaign-Urbana, IL: Center for the Study of Reading, 1985), p. 51.

17. The survey's results were shared privately with me and therefore the name of the community cannot be used.

18. In the interests of fairness, four different factors were taken into account by reading specialist Kathy Nozzolillo in determining the Harris-Jacobson reading level for the script: semantic difficulty; syntactic difficulty; vocabulary; and sentence length.

19. Miriam Martinez and William H. Teale, "Reading in a Kindergarten Classroom Library," *The Reading Teacher*, February 1988, pp. 568–72.

20. "[SIC]," *Harper's*, May 1990. From a White House transcript.

21. Robert McCrum, William Cran, and Robert MacNeil, *The Story of English* (New York: Viking, 1986), pp. 19, 20, 32.

22. "In Sweden, Proof of the Power of Words," *The New York Times*, December 8, 1993, C17.

23. Warwick B. Elley and Francis Mangubhai, "The Impact of Reading on Second Language Learning," *Reading Research Quarterly* 19 (Fall 1983): 53–67. When ESL students in the Fiji Islands were successfully exposed to an intensive pleasure-oriented book project, researchers found their scores rose in the other classroom subjects as well.

24. Carl B. Smith and Gary M. Ingersoll, "Written Vocabulary of Elementary School Pupils," ERIC document ED323564, pp. 3–4.

25. John Holt treats this concept at length in his essay "How Teachers Make Children Hate Reading," *Redbook*, November 1967.

26. Arthur Applebee and others, *NAEP 1992 Writing Report Card*, Educational Testing Service (Washington, DC: U.S. Department of Education, 1994).

27. Adam Woog, "How Tony Hillerman Won the West," *USAir Magazine*, September 1993, pp. 61–3, 113.

28. Roger C. Schank, *Tell Me a Story: A New Look at Real and Artificial Memory* (New York: Scribners, 1990).

29. Peter Johnson, "No. 1 Show Keeps Ticking After 25 Years," *USA Today*, November 12, 1993, pp. 1–2.

30. Daniel Goleman, "Jurors Hear Evidence and Turn It into Stories," *The New York Times*, May 12, 1992, pp. C1, 11.

31. Robert Coles, "Gatsby at the Business School," *The New York Times Book*

Review, October 25, 1987, p. 1; "There's a Lot to Be Learned from Literature, Owners Find," *The Wall Street Journal*, May 20, 1985, p. 29; see also Robert Coles, *The Call of Stories: Teaching and the Moral Imagination* (Boston: Houghton Mifflin, 1989).

Chapter 3: The Stages of Read-Aloud

1. Grace B. Martin and Russell D. Clark III, "Distress Crying in Neonates: Species and Peer Specificity," *Developmental Psychology* 18:1 (1982): 3–9.
2. Otto Friedrich, "What Do Babies Know?" *Time*, August 15, 1983, pp. 52–59.
3. Nancy Rubin, "Learning How Children Learn from the First Moments of Life," *The New York Times Winter Survey of Education*, January 10, 1982, Section 13, pp. 36–37.
4. Daniel Goleman, "Researchers Trace Empathy's Roots to Infancy," *The New York Times*, March 28, 1989, p. C1.
5. Carolyn Rovee-Collier, "The Capacity for Long Term Memory in Infancy," *Current Directions in Psychological Science*, August 1993, pp. 130–35.
6. "Building a Better Brain for Baby," *The New York Times*, April 17, 1994, pp. E1, 6. See also "New Evidence Points to Growth of the Brain Even Late in Life," *The New York Times*, July 30, 1985, p. C1.
7. "Rapid Changes Seen in Young Brain," *The New York Times*, June 24, 1986, p. 17.
8. "The Experience of Touch: Research Points to a Critical Role," *The New York Times*, February 2, 1988, p. C17.
9. Linda Lamme and Athol Packer, "Bookreading Behaviors of Infants," *The Reading Teacher*, February 1986, pp. 504–9; Michael Resnick and others, "Mothers Reading to Infants: A New Observational Tool," *The Reading Teacher*, May 1987, pp. 888–94.
10. "Talking to Baby: Some Expert Advice," *The New York Times*, May 1987, p. C20.
11. Bess Altwerger, Judith Diehl-Faxon, and Karen Dockstader-Anderson, "Read Aloud Events as Meaning Construction," *Language Arts*, September 1985, pp. 476–84.
12. Kornei Chukovsky, *From Two to Five*, trans. Miriam Morton (Berkeley, CA: University of California Press, 1963), pp. 7, 9.
13. David Crystal, *Listen to Your Child* (New York: Penguin, 1986), pp. 16–18.
14. Dorothy White, *Books Before Five* (Portsmouth, NH: Heinemann, 1984), p. 2.
15. Bruno Bettelheim, *The Uses of Enchantment: The Meaning and Importance of Fairy Tales* (New York: Knopf, 1976), pp. 17–18.
16. David Yaden, "Understanding Stories Through Repeated Read-Alouds: How Many Times Does It Take?" *The Reading Teacher*, February 1988, pp. 556–60.
17. Renee Stovsky, "No! No! Not Again!" *St. Louis Post-Dispatch Magazine*, September 5, 1993, p. 8.
18. "Preventing Summer Learning Losses," *The Harvard Education Letter*, June 1988, pp. 5–7; Barbara Heyns, *Summer Learning and the Effects of Schooling* (New York: Academic Press, 1978).

19. Joannis K. Flatley and Adele D. Rutland, "Using Wordless Picture Books to Teach Linguistically/Culturally Different Students," *The Reading Teacher*, December 1986, pp. 276–81; Donna Read and Henrietta M. Smith, "Teaching Visual Literacy Through Wordless Picture Books," *The Reading Teacher*, May 1982, pp. 928–52; J. Stewig, *Children and Literature* (Chicago: Rand McNally, 1980), pp. 131–58.

20. Miriam Martinez and William H. Teale, "Reading in a Kindergarten Classroom Library," *The Reading Teacher*, February 1988, pp. 568–72; see also Gail Heald-Taylor, "Predictable Literature Selections and Activities for Language Arts Instruction," *The Reading Teacher*, October 1987, pp. 6–12; Lynn K. Rhodes, "I Can Read! Predictable Books as Resources for Reading and Writing Instruction," *The Reading Teacher*, February 1981, pp. 511–18.

21. Eli M. Bower, "The Magic Symbols," *Today's Education* 57 (January 1968): 28–31. See also: Vincent R. Rogers, "Laughing with Children," *Educational Leadership*, April 1984, pp. 46–50.

22. G. K. Chesterton, *Orthodoxy: The Romance of Faith* (New York: Doubleday-Image, 1990), pp. 46–65.

23. "Seeing Rise in Child Abuse, Hospitals Step in to Try to Stop the Battering," *The New York Times*, April 5, 1994, p. A18.

24. Ibid.

25. Ann Jones, "Crimes Against Women," *USA Today*, March 10, 1994, p. 9A.

26. "Utah Has a Change of Heart on Guns: It's Curbing Them," *The New York Times*, October 14, 1993, p. 1.

27. Frank J. Huml, "Is Social-Skills Training One 'Missing Link'?" *Education Week*, March 16, 1994, p. 45; according to a 1993 Justice Department report.

28. Perri Klass, "A Bambi for the 90's, Via Shakespeare," *The New York Times*, June 19, 1994, Section 2, pp. 1, 20–1.

29. Gilbert Highet, *Man's Unconquerable Mind* (New York: Columbia University Press, 1954), pp. 19–20.

30. Moylan's explanation was contained in a response journal she kept for a children's literature class with Dr. Mary Lickteig, University of Nebraska–Omaha; used by permission.

31. Book orders for Moll's *Children and Books I: African-American Story Books and Activities for All Children* should be addressed to: Moll, 4104 Lynn Avenue, Tampa, FL 33603. Another outstanding resource for educators is the series of books on using literature in the classroom written by Carol Otis Hurst for SRA: *Once Upon a Time . . . An Encyclopedia for Successfully Using Literature with Young Children; Long Ago and Far Away* (using literature with upper grades); *In Times Past* (history through literature); *Carol Otis Hurst's Picture Book Guide for Kindergarten and Preschool*; and *Carol Otis Hurst's Picture Book Guide for First and Second Grades*.

32. Mary A. Foertsch, *Reading In and Out of School*, National Center for Statistics/U.S. Department of Education (Princeton, NJ: Educational Testing Service, 1992), pp. 10–11.

33. Mary Budd Rowe, "Wait Time: Slowing Down May Be a Way of Speeding Up!" *Journal of Teacher Education* 37:1 (1986).

34. James V. Hoffman, Nancy L. Roser, and Jennifer Battle, "Reading Aloud in the Classroom: From the Modal toward a 'Model,' " *The Reading Teacher*, March 1993, pp. 496–503.

35. Judy Pearson and Richard West, "College Kids Compliant in Class," *Communication Education*, January 1991.

36. For kindergarten statistics, "New York Chancellor Seeks to Broaden Teachers' Roles," *The New York Times*, August 22, 1988, p. A1; third-child statistics, see Harold Hodgkinson, *All One System* (Washington, DC: Institute for Educational Leadership, 1985).

37. William F. Coughlin, Jr., and Brendan Desilets, "Frederick the Field Mouse Meets Advanced Reading Skills as Children's Literature Goes to High School," *Journal of Reading*, December 1980, pp. 207–11.

38. Patricia Greenfield and Jessica Beagles-Roos, "Radio vs. Television: Their Cognitive Impact on Children of Different Socioeconomic and Ethnic Groups," *Journal of Communications*, Spring 1988, pp. 71–92.

39. Sven Birkerts, "Close Listening," *Harper's*, January 1993, pp. 86–9.

40. Robertson Davies, *One Half of Robertson Davies* (New York: Viking, 1977), p. 1.

41. Edgar Allan Poe short story, "The Fall of the House of Usher."

42. Keith Baker, " 'Have You Been Dead?' Questions and Letters from Children," *The Reading Teacher*, February 1993, pp. 372–75.

43. Unpublished manuscript, used by permission of Jeff Smoker.

44. Nicholas Zill and Marianne Winglee, *Who Reads Literature?* (Cabin John, MD: Seven Locks Press, 1990).

45. Patrick J. Groff, "Where Are We Going with Poetry for Children?" *Horn Book Reflections* (Boston: The Horn Book, 1969), p. 181.

46. Jean Little, "After English Class," from *Hey World, Here I Am!* (New York: Harper, 1986).

47. Garrison Keillor radio interview on *The Larry King Show*, February 23, 1993.

48. Karen S. Kutiper, "A Survey of the Adolescent Poetry Preferences of Seventh, Eighth, and Ninth Graders" (doctoral dissertation, University of Houston, 1985). See also: "Using Junior High Readers' Poetry Preferences in the Classroom," by Karen S. Kutiper and Richard F. Abrahamson, in *Literature and Life: Making Connections—Classroom Practices in the Teaching of English*, P. Phelan, ed. (Urbana, IL: National Council of Teachers of English, 1990).

Chapter 5: Read-Aloud Success Stories

1. Arthur Tannenbaum, Everybody Wins Foundation, 10 Park Avenue, Suite 20G, New York, NY 10016; (212) 679-4063.

2. *Mademoiselle*, December 1984.

3. Cindy Visser, "Football and Reading Do Mix!" *The Reading Teacher*, May 1991, p. 711.

4. "An Expert Urges Multiple Reforms," *The New York Times*, July 7, 1983, p. C1.

5. Peter Cohen, James Kulik, and Chen-Lin Kulik, "Educational Outcomes of Tutoring: A Meta-Analysis of Findings," *American Educational Research Journal* 19:2 (1982); *The Harvard Education Letter*, March 1987. See also: Martha D. Rekrut, "Peer and Cross-Age Tutoring: The Lessons of Research," *Journal of Reading*, February 1994, pp. 356–62.

6. Louise Sherman, "Practically Speaking: Have a Story Lunch," *School Library Journal*, October 1986, pp. 120–21.

7. Jill Locke, "Pittsburgh's Beginning with Books Project," *School Library Journal*, February 1988, pp. 22–24.

8. For information, send correspondence and SASE to Read for Life, c/o 15011 Lipson Avenue, Visalia, CA 93291.

9. For information, contact Read-Aloud Delaware, P.O. Box 25249, Wilmington, DE 19899.

10. For information, contact Read-Aloud West Virginia, West Virginia Education Fund, 1520 Kanawha Valley Building, Charleston, WV 25301, ATTN: Ms. Sue B. McKain, Coordinator.

11. For information, contact either Sue Berg, Director, Governor's Council for Literacy and Lifelong Learning, Hawaii State Public Library System, 465 South King Street, Honolulu, HI 96813; or Jack Bates, Star-Seigle-McCombs, 1001 Bishop Street, Pacific Tower, Honolulu, HI 96813.

12. *Life*, November 30, 1962; for an excellent portrait of Frank Boyden, see John McPhee's biography, *The Headmaster* (New York: Farrar, Straus and Giroux, 1966).

13. Personal interviews. See also: "A Soothing 'Late Show' for Troubled Teen-Agers," *The Los Angeles Times*, January 28, 1993, pp. A1, 12.

14. For information, contact MOTHEREAD, INC., Bldg. 2, Suite 335, 4208 Six Forks Road, Raleigh, NC 27609; (919) 781-2088.

15. Personal interview. See also: Hazel Fisher, "Children's Literature," *Higher Faculties: Faculty Development Newsletter*, Bucks County Community College, 176 (March 1992).

16. Joyce L. Epstein, "Parents' Reactions to Teacher Practices of Parent Involvement," *Elementary School Journal* 86:3 (1986): 277–94.

17. In September 1994, Michel Marriott joined the staff of *Newsweek*.

Chapter 6: Home, School, and Public Libraries

1. Dina Feitelson and Zahava Goldstein, "Patterns of Book Ownership and Reading to Young Children in Israeli School-Oriented and Nonschool-Oriented Families," *The Reading Teacher*, May 1986, pp. 924–30; see also Dolores Durkin, *Children Who Read Early* (New York: Teachers College Press, 1966); Anne D. Forester, "What Teachers Can Learn from 'Natural Readers,' " *The Reading Teacher*, November 1977, pp. 160–66; and Jeanne Chall and Catherine Snow, *Families and Literacy: The Contribution of Out-of-School Experiences to Children's Acquisition of Literacy*, National Institute of Education, 1982, ED 234 345.

2. Warwick B. Elley, *How in the World Do Students Read?* International As-

sociation for the Evaluation of Educational Achievement (Hamburg: International Association for the Evaluation of Educational Achievement, July 1992). Report available from the International Reading Association publications department, Newark, DE, $16/$12 (US).

3. Viking Brunell and Pirjo Linnakylä, "Swedish Speakers' Literacy in the Finnish Society," *Journal of Reading*, February 1994, pp. 368–75.

4. See Chapter 7 for an exception to this Finnish TV pattern.

5. Donald Bissett, "The Amount and Effect of Recreational Reading in Select Fifth-Grade Classes" (doctoral dissertation, Syracuse University, 1969). See also: Miriam Martinez and William Teale, "Reading in a Kindergarten Classroom Library," *The Reading Teacher*, February 1988, pp. 568–72.

6. Jann Sorrell Fractor, Marjorie Ciruti Woodruff, Miriam G. Martinez, and William H. Teale, "Let's Not Miss Opportunities to Promote Voluntary Reading: Classroom Libraries in the Elementary School," *The Reading Teacher*, March 1993, pp. 476–84.

7. Richard Anderson, Linda Fielding, and Paul Wilson, "A New Focus on Free Reading: The Role of Trade Books in Reading Instruction," in *Contexts of School Based Literacy*, ed. T. E. Raphael (New York: Random House, 1986).

8. Richard K. Moore, "Letters to the Times," *The Los Angeles Times*, September 8, 1990, p. B6.

9. "School Libraries Struggle to Survive in California," *The New York Times*, June 10, 1993, p. A7.

10. Frank Deford, "A Gentleman and a Scholar," *Sports Illustrated*, April 17, 1989, pp. 87–99.

11. *Sports in Literature*, edited by Bruce Emra (Illinois: National Textbook Company, 1988). Available in hardcover and soft; (800) 323-4900; Illinois: (708) 679-5500.

12. *Book Links*, American Library Association, 50 East Huron Street, Chicago, IL 60611.

13. Mary E. S. Root, "Not to Be Circulated: A List, Prepared by Mrs. E. S. Root, of Books in Series Not Circulated by Standardized Libraries," *Wilson Library Bulletin* 3.1 (1929): 446.

14. Pamela Harper, "After a Long Search, He Finds a Real Treasure," *Santa Barbara News Press*, December 7, 1988, p. B5.

15. Jann Sorrell Fractor et al., "Let's Not Miss Opportunities to Promote Voluntary Reading."

16. Elizabeth Larson, "Library Renewals," *Reason*, March 1994, p. 39.

17. William Ecenbarger, "How Stupid Can We Get?" *Reader's Digest*, April 1994, pp. 17–27.

18. Anthony Brandt, "Literacy in America," *The New York Times*, August 25, 1980, p. 25.

19. Pete Hamill, "D'Artagnan on Ninth Street: A Brooklyn Boy at the Library," *The New York Times Book Review*, June 26, 1988, p. 48.

20. "Clinic-Based Intervention to Promote Literacy," *American Journal of Diseases of Children* 145 (August 1991): 881–84.

Chapter 7: Television

1. Patricia Sellers, "Children in Crisis: 'I'm the Luckiest Person I Ever Met,'" *Fortune*, August 10, 1992, p. 90.

2. Television Bureau of Advertising (477 Madison Avenue, New York, NY 10022), January 1988 report for 1987 viewing.

3. Robert Kubey and Mihaly Csikszentmihalyi, *Television and the Quality of Life* (Hillsdale, NJ: Erlbaum, 1990). See also: Robert Kubey, "A Body at Rest Tends to Remain Glued to the Tube," *The New York Times*, August 5, 1990, p. H27.

4. "Cable Challenger for PBS as King of the Preschool Hill," *The New York Times*, March 21, 1994, p. 1, D8.

5. "Incentives for Inmates: Television Sets in Cell," *The New York Times*, April 4, 1988, p. B3.

6. "Parental Discipline," *Education Week*, May 19, 1993; a Bruskin/Goldring research project.

7. Pete Hamill, "Crack and the Box," *Esquire*, May 1990, pp. 63–65.

8. "Parents Do Care," *Reading Today* (IRA bimonthly), February/March 1993, p. 22.

9. Daniel Goleman, "Studies Reveal TV's Potential to Teach Infants," *The New York Times*, November 22, 1994, p. C1.

10. "TV 'Profoundly' Influences Children's Lives, Survey Shows," Cox News Service, September 26, 1991; based upon Yankelovitch Youth Monitor national survey for Corporation for Public Broadcasting.

11. Paul E. Barton and Richard J. Coley, *America's Smallest School: The Family*, Policy Information Center (Princeton, NJ: Educational Testing Service, 1992), pp. 20–5; this report ($5.50) provides an overview of research done with television and student scores by the National Assessment for Educational Progress, including original research resources.

12. "TV's Up; Viewing Goes Down," *USA Today*, May 25, 1989, p. 1.

13. Paul E. Barton and Richard J. Coley, *America's Smallest School*, pp. 20–25.

14. Paul Copperman, *The Literacy Hoax: The Decline of Reading, Writing, and Learning in the Public Schools and What We Can Do About It* (New York: Morrow, 1980), p. 166.

15. Paul E. Barton and Richard J. Coley, *America's Smallest School*, pp. 20–25.

16. Ibid.

17. California Department of Education, "Student Achievement in California Schools, 1979–80 Annual Report," P.O. Box 271, Sacramento, CA 96802.

18. Arthur Applebee and others, NAEP 1992 Writing Report Card, Educational Testing Service (Washington, DC: U.S. Department of Education, 1994).

19. M. Morgan and L. Gross, "Television and Educational Achievement and Aspiration," in *Television and Behavior: Ten Years of Scientific Progress and Implications for the Eighties*, ed. D. Pearl, L. Bonlithilet, and J. Lazar (Rockville, MD: NIMH, 1982).

20. U.S. Census Bureau report release October 6, 1993; see: "Census Sees Falling Income and More Poor," *The New York Times*, October 7, 1994, p. A16; "Few Feel Economic Rebound," *USA Today*, October 7, 1994, p. 2A.

21. Elizabeth Kolbert, "TV Viewing and Selling, by Race," *The New York Times*, April 5, 1993, p. D7; report based on Bozell advertising agency study.

22. "Zapping of TV Ads Appears Pervasive," *The Wall Street Journal*, April 25, 1988, p. 29.

23. Donald Hayes and Dana Birnbaum, *Developmental Psychology* 16 (September 1980): 410–16. See also *Psychology Today*, June 1982, pp. 78–79.

24. "The American Media: Who Reads, Who Watches, Who Listens, Who Cares," Times Mirror Center for the People and the Press, July 15, 1990.

25. Neil Postman, *Teaching as a Conserving Activity* (New York: Delacorte, 1980), pp. 77–78.

26. Wilbur Schramm, Jack Lyle, and Edwin B. Parker, *Television in the Lives of Our Children* (Stanford, CA: Stanford University Press, 1961).

27. Michael Liberman, "The Verbal Language of Television," *The Journal of Reading*, April 1983, pp. 602–9.

28. Patricia Greenfield and Jessica Beagles-Roos, "Radio and Television: Their Cognitive Impact on Children of Different Socioeconomic and Ethnic Groups," *Journal of Communication*, Spring 1988, pp. 71–91.

29. Postman, *Teaching as a Conserving Activity*, p. 208.

30. Ceil Cleveland and Ryan Vollmer, "Channel Fever," *Notre Dame Magazine*, Summer 1992, pp. 21–25.

31. Joel Urschel, "TV: Checking for Intelligent Life on Earth," *USA Today*, November 4, 1993, p. 12A.

32. Frank Mankiewicz and Joel Swerdlow, *Remote Control: Television and the Manipulation of American Life* (New York: Times Books, 1978), pp. 6, 15–72.

33. Board Report 18-A-94, "Mass Media Violence and Film Ratings: Redressing Shortcomings in the Current System," pp. 1–2 (Chicago: American Medical Association, 1994); other citations in the above: Surgeon General's Scientific Advisory Committee on Television and Social Behavior, "Television and Growing Up: The Impact of Televised Violence" (Washington, DC: U.S. Government Printing Office, 1972); National Institute of Mental Health, "Television and Behavior: Ten Years of Scientific Progress and Implications for the Eighties," Vol. I, Summary Report (Washington, DC: U.S. Government Printing Office, 1982; American Psychological Association, "Violence and Youth: Psychology's Response" (Washington, DC: American Psychological Association, 1983); American Psychiatric Association, "Position Statement on TV Violence" (Washington, DC: American Psychiatric Association, December 1993); A. J. Reiss and J. A. Roth, eds., *Understanding and Preventing Violence* (Washington, DC: National Academy Press, 1993); V. C. Strasburger and G. A. Comstock, eds., *Adolescent Medicine: Adolescents and the Media, State-of-the-Art Reviews* (Philadelphia, PA: Hanley & Belfus, 1993).

34. Ibid.

35. Neil Hickey, "How Much Violence? What We Found in an Eye-Opening Study," *TV Guide*, pp. 10–23, August 23, 1992; Neil Hickey, "New Violence Survey Released," *TV Guide*, August 13, 1994, pp. 37–39. See also: "Television Gets a Closer Look as Factor in Real Violence," Elizabeth Kolbert, *The New York Times*, December 14, 1994, p. 1.

36. Wally Bowen, "Media Violence," *Education Week*, March 16, 1994, pp. 60.

37. Carl M. Cannon, "Honey, I Warped the Kids," *Mother Jones*, July/August, 1993, pp. 16–21.

38. B. Drummond Ayres, Jr., "Crowd, with Disbelief, Still Cheers for the Juice," *The New York Times*, June 19, 1994, p. A21.

39. Bob Greene syndicated newspaper column, July 2, 1994.

40. Bob Keeshan's remarks were made during an interview on September 24, 1979, with John Merrow, for *Options in Education*, a co-production of National Public Radio and the Institute for Educational Leadership of the George Washington University.

41. "Gadgets That Help Parents Wean Kids from TV-itis," *U.S. News and World Report*, September 20, 1993, p. 79.

42. Susan B. Neuman and Patricia Koskinen, "Captioned Television as 'Comprehensible Input': Effects of Incidental Word Learning from Context for Language Minority Students," *Reading Research Quarterly* 27 (1992): 95–106; P. S. Koskinen, R. S. Wilson, L. Gambrell, and C. J. Jensema, *ERS Spectrum: Journal of School Research and Information* 4 (2), 9–13; Patricia S. Koskinen, Robert M. Wilson, Linda B. Gambrell, Susan B. Neuman, "Captioned Video and Vocabulary Learning: An Innovative Practice in Literacy Instruction," *The Reading Teacher*, September 1993, pp. 36–43; Robert J. Rickelman, William A. Henk, and Kent Layton, "Closed-Captioned Television: A Viable Technology for the Reading Teacher," *The Reading Teacher*, April 1991, pp. 598–99.

43. Pirjo Linnakylä, "Subtitles Prompt Finnish Children to Read," *Reading TODAY* (IRA bimonthly), October/November 1993, p. 31.

44. Rosemarie Truglio, Aletha Huston, and John Wright, "The Relation Between Children's Print and Television Use to Early Reading Skills," Center for Research on the Influences of Television on Children, Department of Human Development, University of Kansas, 1988.

45. "Statewide: 'Whittling Away,'" *Texas Monthly*, June 1992, pp. 84–85.

46. "Little Help from a School TV Show," *The New York Times*, April 23, 1992, p. A18. The first report was called: "Taking the Measure of Channel One: The First Year"; the second report, "Channel One: The School Factor." Both are available for $10 (prepaid) from the Institute for Social Research, University of Michigan, Ann Arbor, Michigan 48106; (313) 763-5325. See *Phi Delta Kappan*, February 1995, for an in-depth look at the Channel One dilemma.

47. "Channel One More Often Used in Poor Schools, Study Finds," *Education Week*, October 27, 1993, p. 5.

48. "40 Days Without a Teacher," *The Chadron Record*, October 1, 1991, p. 4.

49. "The American Media: Who Reads, Who Watches, Who Listens, Who Cares," Times Mirror Center for the People and the Press Media, July 15, 1990.

50. John Tierney, "Sound Bites Become Smaller Mouthfuls," *The New York Times*, January 23, 1992, pp. A1, 10.

51. Sven Birkerts, "Close Listening," *Harper's*, January 1993, pp. 86–91.

52. Helen Aron, "Bookworms Become Tapeworms: A Profile of Listeners

to Books on Audiocassette," *Journal of Reading,* November 1992, pp. 208–12.

Chapter 8: Sustained Silent Reading: Reading-Aloud's Natural Partner

1. Warwick B. Elley, *How in the World Do Students Read?* (Hamburg: International Association for the Evaluation of Educational Achievement, July 1992). Available from the International Reading Association, Newark, DE, $16/$12 (US).

2. Ina V. S. Mullis et al., *NAEP 1992 Trends in Academic Progress,* ETS/Office of Educational Research and Improvement (Washington, DC: U.S. Department of Education, June 1994); also found in Paul E. Barton and Richard J. Coley, *America's Smallest School: The Family,* Public Information Center (Princeton, NJ: Educational Testing Service, 1992).

3. Richard Anderson, Linda Fielding, and Paul Wilson, "Growth in Reading and How Children Spend Their Time Outside of School," *Reading Research Quarterly,* Summer 1988, pp. 285–303.

4. John I. Goodlad, *A Place Called School: Prospects for the Future* (New York: McGraw-Hill, 1984), p. 107.

5. Robert A. McCracken, "Instituting Sustained Silent Reading," *Journal of Reading,* May 1971, pp. 521–24, 582–83.

6. Stephen Krashen, *The Power of Reading* (Englewood, CO: Libraries Unlimited, 1993).

7. S. Jay Samuels, "Decoding and Automaticity: Helping Poor Readers Become Automatic at Word Recognition," *The Reading Teacher,* April 1988, pp. 756–60; Richard Anderson et al., "Growth in Reading."

8. Richard C. Anderson et al., *Becoming a Nation of Readers* (Champaign, IL: Center for the Study of Reading, 1985), p. 119.

9. Mark Sadoski, "An Attitude Survey for Sustained Silent Reading Programs," *Journal of Reading,* May 1980, pp. 721–26.

10. Richard Allington, "If They Don't Read Much, How They Gonna Get Good?" *Journal of Reading,* October 1977, pp. 57–61.

11. Richard Anderson et al., "Growth in Reading," p. 152.

12. Edward Fry and Elizabeth Sakiey, "Common Words Not Taught in Basal Reading Series," *The Reading Teacher,* January 1986, pp. 395–98.

13. D. Hayes and M. Ahrens, "Vocabulary Simplification for Children: A Special Case of 'Motherese,' " *Journal of Child Language* 27 (1993): 329–33.

14. Mihaly Csikszentmihalyi, "Literacy and Intrinsic Motivation," *Daedalus,* Spring 1990, pp. 115–40.

15. Robert A. McCracken and Marlene J. McCracken, "Modeling Is the Key to Sustained Silent Reading," *The Reading Teacher,* January 1978, pp. 406–8. See also Linda B. Gambrell, "Getting Started with Sustained Silent Reading and Keeping It Going," *The Reading Teacher,* December 1978, pp. 328–31.

16. Martha Efta, "Reading in Silence," *Teaching Exceptional Children,* Fall 1978, pp. 12–24.

17. "As long as there are math classes, there will be prayers in schools," someone once said. But how civilized prayer makes the student body is another

thing. Looking at the film footage of the students and parents taunting and cursing black students as they integrated public schools during the 1950s, I find it sobering to think they were coming from classrooms where we still opened the day with daily prayers.

18. G. Robert Carlsen and Anne Sherrill, *Voices of Readers: How We Come to Love Books* (Urbana, IL: National Council of Teachers of English, 1988).

19. Stephen D. Krashen and Kyung-Sook Cho, "Acquisition of Vocabulary from the Sweet Valley Kids Series: Adult ESL Acquisition," *Journal of Reading*, May 1994, pp. 662–67. Similar results were accomplished in the Sponce English Language Program at the University of Southern California–Los Angeles using Harlequin romances—see "Pleasure Reading Helps, Even If Readers Don't Believe It," by Rebecca Constantino, *Journal of Reading*, March 1994, pp. 504–5.

20. Warwick B. Elley and Francis Mangubhai, "The Impact of Reading on Second Language Learning," *Reading Research Quarterly* 19 (Fall 1983): 53–67.

21. Jacques Barzun, *Teacher in America* (Garden City, NY: Doubleday, 1954), pp. 60–62, 136. Barzun wrote this while he was a professor of history at Columbia University. He went on to become provost, and today is one of academe's Old Guard.

22. Susan Ohanian, "Literature Has No Uses," in *Who's in Charge? A Teacher Speaks Her Mind* (Portsmouth, NH: Heinemann, 1994), pp. 163–68.

23. Viking Brunell and Pirjo Linnakylä, "Swedish Speakers' Literacy in the Finnish Society," *Journal of Reading*, February 1994, pp. 368–75.

24. Stephen Krashen, "Comic-Book Reading and Language Development," a monograph from Abel Press, P.O. Box 6162, Station C, Victoria Station, BC, Canada V8P 5L5; Emma Halstead Swain, "Using Comic Books in Teaching Reading and Language Arts," *Journal of Reading*, December 1978, pp. 253–58. See also Larry Dorrell and Ed Carroll, "Spider-Man at the Library," *School Library Journal*, August 1981, pp. 17–19.

25. Archie—1.8 grade level; Spider-Man—4.4; and Batman—6.4; from Krashen, *The Power of Reading*, p. 53.

26. Leslie Campbell and Kathleen Hayes, "Desmond Tutu," interview from *The Other Side's Faces of Faith*, pp. 23–26. For a copy of this booklet, write to 300 Apsley St., Philadelphia, PA 19144.

27. Mark Mathabane, *Kaffir Boy* (New York: Macmillan, 1986).

28. Arthur Schlesinger, Jr., "Advice from a Reader-Aloud-to-Children," *The New York Times Book Review*, November 25, 1979.

29. Alex S. Jones, "To Papers, Funnies Are No Joke," *The New York Times*, April 8, 1991, pp. D1, 8.

30. Barbara Heyns, *Summer Learning and the Effects of Schooling* (New York: Academic Press, 1978). See also: Doris R. Entwistle and Karl L. Alexander, "Summer Setback: Race, Poverty, School Composition, and Mathematical Achievement in the First Two Years of School," *American Sociological Review* 57 (1992): 72–84; Barbara Heyns, "Schooling and Cognitive Development: Is There a Season for Learning?" *Child Development* 58 (1987): 1151–60; Larry J. Mikulecky, "Stopping Summer Learning Loss Among At-Risk Youth," *Journal of Reading*, April 1990, pp. 516–21.

31. Pat Ordovensky, "Kids Do Retain More of Lessons," *USA Today*, August 28, 1991, p. 5A.

32. Barbara Heyns, *Summer Learning and the Effects of Schooling*.

33. Hank Whittemore, "The Most Precious Gift," *Parade Magazine*, December 22, 1991, p. 4.

34. Robert Rothman, "In 25 Years, Little Has Changed on Schools' Reading Lists," *Education Week*, June 7, 1989, p. 6; as this book went into production, the College Board issued the results of a new survey of high school assigned texts, showing little had changed since 1989—see Hunter M. Breland, Robert J. Jones, and Laura Jenkins, *The College Board Vocabulary Study* (Princeton, NJ: The College Board, 1995).

35. Susan Ohanian, "A Not-So-Tearful Farewell to William Bennett," *Phi Delta Kappan*, September 1988, pp. 11–17.

36. Nicholas Zill and Marianne Winglee, *Who Reads Literature?* (Cabin John, MD: Seven Locks Press, 1990), pp. 20–33.

37. Sven Birkerts, "Writing for Reading," *Erato/Harvard Book Review*, Winter and Spring, vols. 11–12, 1989; a publication of the Harvard College Library's Poetry Room.

38. Connie C. Epstein, "The Well-Read College-Bound Student," *School Library Journal*, February 1984, pp. 32–35.

39. Robert Anderson et al., "Growth in Reading," pp. 285–303.

40. Dennis Kelly, "A Novel Approach: Turn Off TV," *USA Today*, March 19, 1991, p. 6D.

41. Sid T. Womack and B. J. Chandler, "Encouraging Reading for Professional Development," *Journal of Reading*, February 1992, pp. 390–94.

42. Stanley I. Mour, "Do Teachers Read?" *The Reading Teacher*, January 1977, pp. 397–401. This study was somewhat skewed in favor of teachers because the subjects were more motivated professionally as graduate students. If anything, the results would be worse with teachers not as professionally involved. Included in the numbers were 202 females and 22 males; 6 counselors; 6 principals; 5 supervisors; most of the teachers (145) were elementary level; see also Kathleen Stumpf Jongsma, "Just Say Know!" *The Reading Teacher*, March 1992, pp. 546–48.

43. Nicholas Zill and Marianne Winglee, *Who Reads Literature?*

44. Jeanne Jacobson, "I Couldn't Read This Week Because My Mother Was Busy," *Journal of Reading*, March 1988, pp. 496–97.

45. Mary W. Williams, personal letter to the author, used by permission.

46. Krashen, *The Power of Reading*, pp. 76–78, for an overview of research on writing as a boost for intelligence.

47. W. E. Nagy, P. Herman, R. Anderson, "Learning Words from Context," *Reading Research Quarterly* 20 (1985): 233–53.

48. Stephen Krashen, *Writing: Research, Theory and Applications* (Torrance, CA: Laredo Publishing Company, 1984); also Krashen, *The Power of Reading*.

49. For the anti-incentives: Alfie Kohn, *Punished by Rewards: The Trouble with Gold Stars, Incentive Plans, A's, Praise, and Other Bribes* (Boston: Houghton Mifflin, 1993); see also: Edward Miller, "Letting Talent Flow: How Schools Can Promote Learning for the Sheer Love of It," *The Harvard Education Newsletter*, March/April 1994, pp. 1–8.

50. For the pro-incentives, Mihaly Csikszentmihalyi, "Literacy and Intrinsic Motivation," *Daedalus*, Spring 1990, pp. 115–40. See also: M. Csikszentmihalyi, K. Rathnude, and S. Whalen, *Talented Teenagers: The Roots of Success and Failure* (New York: Cambridge University Press, 1993).

51. "The Profits of Reading," *Newsweek*, November 20, 1991, p. 67.

52. Copies of IRA's Guidelines for Commercial Reading Products can be obtained by writing IRA Public Information Office, 800 Barksdale Road, P.O. Box 8139, Newark, DE 19714-8139.

53. Barnaby J. Feder, "Hooked on Ad Claims," *The New York Times*, Education Section, pp. 42–43, January 5, 1992.

54. " 'Hooked on Phonics' Marketer Settles FTC Charges of Overly Broad Learn-to-Read Claims," *FTC News*, December 14, 1994.

55. For information on "What Is Reading?," contact Pamela Perkins, Ph.D., Literacy Possibilities, P.O. Box 220, Orange, CA 92666-0220; (714) 538-2990.

56. "Most Frequently Challenged Books 1992–93," *Forum: A Bulletin of the People for the American Way* 3 (4), p. 1 (October 1993).

57. Gladys Hunt and Barbara Hampton, *Read for Your Life: Turning Teens into Readers* (Grand Rapids: Zondervan, 1992).

58. Michael Dirda, "One More Modest Proposal," *The Washington Post Book World*, August 15, 1993.

Appendix

1. "Half of Adults Lack Skills to Function Fully in Society, Literacy Study Finds," *The New York Times*, September 15, 1993. See also: Irwin Kirsch and others, *Adult Literacy in America*, and *1992 National Adult Literacy Survey* (both—Princeton, NJ: Educational Testing Service/National Center for Educational Statistics, 1993).

2. Monica Wyatt, "The Past, Present, and Future Need for College Reading Courses in the U.S.," *Journal of Reading*, September 1992, pp. 10–20; article contains a page-long list of headlines on remedial education from 1828 to the present.

3. Henry J. Perkinson, *Two Hundred Years of American Educational Thought* (New York: David McKay, 1976), p. 141.

4. C. F. Richardson, "The Home Library," *Self Culture for Young People*, Andrew Sloan Draper, editor in chief (St. Louis, 1906), p. 35.

5. Daniel P. Resnick, "Historical Perspectives on Literacy and Schooling," *Daedalus*, Spring 1990, pp. 15–32.

6. "Educational Attainment in the U.S.," *Education Week*, November 22, 1989, p. 3.

7. "Students Cite Pregnancies as a Reason to Drop Out," *The New York Times*, September 14, 1994, p. B7. When people calculate the current dropout rate at 26 percent, they are including immigrants who never "dropped in" to U.S. schools to begin with, never mind dropped out.

8. "Educational Attainment in the U.S.," 1989, p. 3; "Gains for Blacks in Education," *USA Today*, November 21, 1994, p. D1. Based upon U.S. Census Bureau reports.

9. "SAT Increases the Average Score, by Fiat," *The New York Times*, June 11, 1994, pp. 1, 10.

10. "1994 Profile of SAT and Achievement Test Taker," The College Board, (Princeton, NJ: Educational Testing Service/National Center for Educational Statistics, 1994).

11. The less select you are about who takes a test, the lower the scores will be. That was true in 1941 and it is true today. Typical is the difference in verbal scores in 1994 between the state (Utah) with the fewest students taking the SAT and the one with the most students (Connecticut):

State	Student's Rank in High School	Parents w/Income of $50,000 or More	SAT Verbal
Utah (4%)	68% in top 5th	78%	509
Connecticut (80%)	35% in top 5th	51%	426

SOURCE: "National and State College-Bound Senior Profiles, 1994" (The College Board/Educational Testing Service, Princeton, NJ, 1994). The majority of Utah students do not take the SAT; they take the ACT, since their state colleges and universities prefer that test. The students who take the SAT are by and large smart and/or wealthy enough to attend out-of-state colleges and universities. Thus, another academic all-star team. Connecticut, on the other hand, draws from a far broader cross section of average students and its scores pale beside the all-stars'.

12. John B. Kellogg, "Forces of Change," *Phi Delta Kappan*, November 1988, pp. 199–204.

13. "Census Data Find More Are Falling Behind in School," *Education Week*, June 10, 1992, pp. 1, 9.

14. William Celis III, "Schools Pay for Diversity in Languages of Students," *The New York Times*, September 11, 1994, pp. 37, 53.

15. This and other performance studies are compared in "The Condition of Education: Why School Reformers Are on the Right Track," by Lawrence C. Stedman, *Phi Delta Kappan*, November 1993, pp. 215–25. See also: "Correction," *Phi Delta Kappan*, February 1994, p. 504.

16. "Backtalk/Remembering 1940—The Author (Mike Males) Responds," *Phi Delta Kappan*, December 1992, pp. 351–52.

17. Paul E. Barton and Archie Lapointe, *Learning by Degrees: Indicators of Performance in Higher Education*, Policy Information Center, Educational Testing Service (Princeton, NJ: Educational Testing Service/National Center for Educational Statistics, 1995), pp. 3–7, 36, 52–55.

18. Gerald W. Bracey, research psychologist and policy analyst for the National Education Association, has developed this same theme more extensively in his essay "Why Can't They Be Like We Were?" *Phi Delta Kappan*, October 1991, pp. 105–17.

19. *Education in States and Nations* (National Center for Education Statistics, Report No. 93-237, 1993). See also: Gerald W. Bracey, "The Fourth Bracey Report on the Condition of Public Education," *Phi Delta Kappan*, October

1994, pp. 115–27; William Celis III, "International Report Card Shows U.S. Schools Work," *The New York Times*, December 12, 1993, pp. A1, 26.

20. George W. Bracey, "The Fourth Bracey Report on the Condition of Public Education," p. 118.

21. "High School Graduates Facing Dead-End Jobs," *The New York Times*, May 30, 1994, p. A1, 26.

22. Chastity Pratt, "U.S. Math Team: Perfect," *The Washington Post*, July 20, 1994, p. A1.

23. Daniel Tanner, "A Nation 'Truly' at Risk," *Phi Delta Kappan*, December 1993, pp. 288–97; the article highlights, among other things, the government-suppressed report "Perspectives on Education in America," Final Draft, Sandia National Laboratories, Albuquerque, NM, April 1992, which reports the state of American education is not as bad as the government claims.

24. "Teaching Survey Shows Lack of Men, Minorities," Associated Press, July 7, 1992.

25. David W. Grissmer, Sheila Nataraj Kirby, Mark Berends, and Stephanie Williamson, *Student Achievement and the Changing American Family*, Rand Corporation, MR-488-130 (Santa Monica, CA: Rand Corporation, 1994).

26. Electrical Component Application Partnership, reported in "USA Snap-shots," *USA Today*, September 9, 1994, p. A1.

27. "A Few Good Mechanics," Associated Press, July 6, 1994; news story responding to EPA report, as well as report from National Institute for Automotive Service Excellence, Herndon, VA.

Bibliography

Adams, Marilyn Jager. *Beginning to Read: Thinking and Learning about Print—A Summary.* Champaign-Urbana: University of Illinois, Center for the Study of Reading, 1990.

Adler, Mortimer. *Paideia Problems and Possibilities.* New York: Macmillan, 1983.

Anderson, Richard C., Elfrieda H. Hiebert, Judith Scott, and Ian A. G. Wilkinson. *Becoming a Nation of Readers.* Champaign-Urbana, Ill.: Center for the Study of Reading, 1985.

Applebee, Arthur N., Judith A. Langer, and Ina V. S. Mullis. *Who Reads Best?* Princeton, N.J.: National Assessment of Educational Progress, 1988.

Applebee, Arthur, Judith Langer, Ina Mullis, Andrew Latham, and Claudia Gentile. *NAEP 1992 Writing Report Card.* Princeton, N.J.: National Assessment of Educational Progress, 1994.

Ashton-Warner, Sylvia. *Spearpoint: "Teacher" in America.* New York: Vintage, 1974.

Atwell, Nancy. *In the Middle: Writing, Reading and Learning with Adolescents.* Portsmouth, N.H.: Heinemann, 1987.

Barton, Paul E., and Richard J. Coley. *America's Smallest School: The Family.* Princeton, N.J.: Educational Testing Service, 1992.

Barzun, Jacques. *Begin Here.* Chicago: University of Chicago Press, 1991.

———. *Teacher in America.* Garden City, N.Y.: Doubleday, 1954.

Bennett, Steve and Ruth. *Kick the TV Habit.* New York: Penguin, 1994.

Bettelheim, Bruno. *The Uses of Enchantment: The Meaning and Importance of Fairy Tales.* New York: Knopf, 1976.

Breland, Hunter M., Robert J. Jones, and Laura Jenkins. *The College Board Vocabulary Study.* Princeton, N.J.: The College Board, 1995.

Bruner, Jerome S. and Sylvia K., editors. *Play—Its Role in Development and Evolution.* New York: Penguin, 1976.

Butler, Dorothy. *Cushla and Her Books.* Boston: The Horn Book, 1980.

Carlsen, G. Robert, and Anne Sherrill. *Voices of Readers: How We Come to Love Books.* Urbana, Ill.: National Council of Teachers of English, 1988.

Carson, Ben. *Gifted Hands: The Ben Carson Story.* Grand Rapids, Mich.: Zondervan, 1990.

Carter, Betty, and Richard F. Abrahamson. *Nonfiction for Young Adults: From Delight to Wisdom.* Phoenix: Oryx Press, 1990.

Cazden, Courtney B. *Child Language and Education.* New York: Holt, Rinehart and Winston, 1972.

Chesterton, G. K. *Orthodoxy: The Romance of Faith.* New York: Doubleday-Image, 1990.

Chukovsky, Kornei. *From Two to Five.* Translated by Miriam Morton. Berkeley: University of California Press, 1963.

Clark, Margaret M. *Young Fluent Readers.* London: Heinemann, 1976.

Collins, Catherine, and Douglas Frantz. *Teachers Talking Out of School.* Boston: Little, Brown, 1993.

Copperman, Paul. *The Literacy Hoax: The Decline of Reading, Writing, and*

Learning in the Public Schools and What We Can Do About It. New York: Morrow, 1980.

Crystal, David. *Listen to Your Child.* New York: Penguin, 1986.

Csikszentmihalyi, M., K. Rathnude, and S. Whalen. *Talented Teenagers: The Roots of Success and Failure.* New York: Cambridge University Press, 1993.

Cullinan, Bernice E., ed. *Children's Literature in the Reading Program.* Newark, Del.: International Reading Association, 1987.

Cullinan, Bernice E., with Mary K. Karrer and Arlene M. Pillar. *Literature and the Child.* 2nd ed. New York: Harcourt Brace Jovanovich, 1989.

Davies, Robertson. *One Half of Robertson Davies.* New York: Viking, 1977.

deSalvo, Nancy. *Beginning with Books: Library Programming for Infants, Toddlers, and Preschoolers.* North Haven, Conn.: Shoe String Press, 1993.

Downing, J., and C. K. Leong. *Psychology of Reading.* New York: Macmillan, 1982.

Durkin, Dolores. *Children Who Read Early.* New York: Teachers College, 1966.

Elkind, David. *The Hurried Child: Growing Up Too Soon Too Fast.* Reading, Mass.: Addison-Wesley, 1981.

———. *Miseducation: Preschoolers at Risk.* New York: Knopf, 1987.

Elley, Warwick B. *How in the World Do Students Read?* Hamburg: International Association for the Evaluation of Educational Achievement, 1992.

Emra, Bruce, ed. *Sports in Literature.* Lincolnwood, Ill.: National Textbook Company, 1988.

Fader, Daniel N., and Elton B. McNeil. *Hooked on Books: Program and Proof.* New York: Berkley, 1968.

Fadiman, Clifton, and James Howard. *Empty Pages: A Search for Writing Competence in School and Society.* Belmont, Calif.: Fearon Pitman and the Council for Basic Education, 1979.

Foertsch, Mary A. *Reading In and Out of School.* Princeton, N.J.: National Assessment of Educational Progress, 1992.

Goodlad, John I. *A Place Called School: Prospects for the Future.* New York: McGraw-Hill, 1984.

Goodman, Ken. *What's Whole in Whole Language?* Portsmouth, N.H.: Heinemann, 1986.

Goodman, Kenneth, Patrick Shannon, Yvonne Freeman, and Sharon Murphy. *Report Card on Basal Readers.* New York: Richard Owen, 1988.

Grissmer, David W., Sheila Nataraj Kirby, Mark Berends, and Stephanie Williamson. *Student Achievement and the Changing American Family.* Santa Monica, Calif.: Rand Corporation, 1994.

Grissmer, David W., Irwin Kirsch et al. *Adult Literacy in America.* Princeton, N.J.: Educational Testing Service, 1993.

Healy, Jane. *Endangered Minds.* New York: Simon & Schuster, 1990.

Hennings, Dorothy Grant. *Beyond the Read-Aloud: Learning to Read Through Listening to and Reflecting on Literature.* Bloomington, Ind.: Phi Delta Kappan, 1992.

Herndon, James. *How to Survive in Your Native Land.* New York: Simon & Schuster, 1971.

Heyns, Barbara. *Summer Learning and the Effects of Schooling.* New York: Academic Press, 1978.

Hodgkinson, Harold L. *The Same Client: The Demographics of Education and*

Service Delivery Systems. Washington, D.C.: Institute for Educational Leadership, 1989.

Hopkins, Lee Bennett. *Pass the Poetry, Please!* New York: Harper & Row, 1987.

Huck, Charlotte, Susan Hepler, and Janet Hickman. *Children's Literature in the Elementary School.* 5th ed. New York: Harcourt Brace College Publishers, 1993.

Hunt, Gladys. *Honey for a Child's Heart.* 3rd ed. Grand Rapids, Mich.: Zondervan, 1989.

Hunt, Gladys, and Barbara Hampton. *Read for Your Life: Turning Teens into Readers.* Grand Rapids, Mich.: Zondervan, 1992.

Kimmel, Margaret Mary, and Elizabeth Segel. *For Reading Out Loud!* New York: Delacorte, 1988.

Kobrin, Beverly. *Eyeopeners! How to Choose and Use Children's Books About Real People, Places, and Things.* New York: Viking Penguin, 1988.

Kohn, Alfie. *Punished by Rewards: The Trouble with Gold Stars, Incentive Plans, A's, Praise, and Other Bribes.* Boston: Houghton Mifflin, 1993.

Krashen, Stephen S. *The Power of Reading.* Englewood, CO: Libraries Unlimited, 1993.

———. *Writing: Research, Theory and Applications.* Torrance, Calif.: Laredo Publishing Company, 1984.

Lapointe, Archie E., Nancy A. Mead, and Gary W. Phillips. *A World of Differences.* Princeton, N.J.: Educational Testing Service, 1988.

Leonhardt, Mary. *Parents Who Love Reading, Kids Who Don't: How It Happens and What You Can Do About It.* New York: Crown, 1993.

Liggett, Twila C., and Cynthia Mayer Benfield. *Reading Rainbow Guide to Children's Books.* New York: Citadel Press, 1994.

Lipson, Eden Ross. *The New York Times Parent's Guide to the Best Books for Children.* Rev. ed. New York: Times Books, 1991.

Mankiewicz, Frank, and Joel Swerdlow. *Remote Control: Television and the Manipulation of American Life.* New York: Times Books, 1978.

McCracken, Robert A., and Marlene J. *Reading Is Only the Tiger's Tail.* Kimberley, B.C.: Classroom Publications, 1985.

McCrum, Robert, William Cran, and Robert MacNeil. *The Story of English.* New York: Viking, 1986.

Mullis, Ina V. S., John A. Dossey, Jay R. Campbell, Claudia A. Gentile, Christine O'Sullivan, and Andrew Latham. *NAEP 1992 Trends in Academic Progress.* Washington, D.C.: Office of Educational Research and Improvement, U.S. Department of Education, June 1994.

National Commission on Excellence in Education. *A Nation at Risk: The Imperative for Educational Reform.* Washington, D.C.: U.S. Department of Education, 1983.

Nell, Victor. *Lost in a Book: The Psychology of Reading for Pleasure.* New Haven, Conn.: Yale University Press, 1988.

Ohanian, Susan. *Who's in Charge? A Teacher Speaks Her Mind.* Portsmouth, N.H.: Heinemann, 1994.

Paulin, Mary Ann. *More Creative Uses of Children's Literature.* North Haven, Conn.: Shoestring Press, 1993.

Perkinson, Henry J. *Two Hundred Years of American Educational Thought.* New York: David McKay, 1976.

Postman, Neil. *Amusing Ourselves to Death.* New York: Viking, 1985.

Postman, Neil, and Steve Powers. *How to Watch TV News.* New York: Viking Penguin, 1992.

Prescott, Orville. *A Father Reads to His Children: An Anthology of Prose and Poetry.* New York: Dutton, 1965.

Raines, Shirley C., and Robert J. Canady. *Story S-T-R-E-T-C-H-E-R-S.* Mt. Rainier, Md.: Gryphon House, 1989.

——. *More Story S-T-R-E-T-C-H-E-R-S.* Mt. Rainier, Md.: Gryphon House, 1991.

——. *Story S-T-R-E-T-C-H-E-R-S for the Primary Grades.* Mt. Rainier, Md.: Gryphon House, 1992.

Ravitch, Diane, and Chester E. Finn, Jr. *What Do Our 17-Year-Olds Know?* New York: Harper & Row, 1987.

Reed, Arthea J. S. *Comics to Classics: A Parent's Guide to Books for Teens and Preteens.* New York: Penguin, 1994.

Rideau, Wilbert, and Ron Wikberg. *Life Sentences: Rage and Survival Behind Bars.* New York: Times Books, 1992.

Rudman, Masha. *Children's Literature: An Issues Approach.* New York: Longman, 1984.

Rudman, Masha, and Anna M. Pearce. *For Love of Reading: A Parent's Guide to Encouraging Young Readers from Infancy Through Age 5.* Mt. Vernon, N.Y.: Consumers Union, 1988.

Sabine, Gordon, and Patricia Sabine. *Books That Make a Difference: What People Told Us.* North Haven, Conn.: Shoestring Press, 1983.

Schank, Roger C. *Tell Me a Story: A New Look at Real and Artificial Memory.* New York: Scribners, 1990.

Schramm, Wilbur, Jack Lyle, and Edwin B. Parker. *Television in the Lives of Our Children.* Stanford, Calif.: Stanford University Press, 1961.

Singer, Dorothy G., Jerome L. Singer, and Diana M. Zuckerman. *Use TV to Your Child's Advantage: A Parent's Guide.* Reston, Va.: Acropolis Books, 1990.

Smith, Charles A. *From Wonder to Wisdom: Using Stories to Help Children Grow.* New York: Plume, 1990.

Smith, Frank. *Insult to Intelligence.* New York: Arbor House, 1986.

——. *Understanding Reading.* 3rd ed. New York: Holt, Rinehart and Winston, 1982.

Stevenson, Harold W., and James W. Stigler. *The Learning Gap.* New York: Summit Books, 1992.

Taylor, Gordon Rattray. *The Natural History of the Mind.* New York: E. P. Dutton, 1979.

White, Dorothy. *Books Before Five.* Portsmouth, N.H.: Heinemann Educational Books, 1984.

Wiener, Harvey S. *Talk with Your Child.* New York: Viking, 1988.

Winkel, Lois, and Sue Kimmel. *Mother Goose Comes First.* New York: Henry Holt, 1990.

Winn, Marie. *The Plug-in Drug.* New York: Penguin, 1977, 1985.

——. *Unplugging the Plug-in Drug.* New York: Penguin, 1987.

Yolen, Jane. *Touch Magic.* New York: Philomel, 1981.

Zill, Nicholas, and Marianne Winglee. *Who Reads Literature?* Cabin John, Md.: Seven Locks Press, 1990.

Subject Index for the Text

(See Author—Illustrator Index for books listed in Treasury)

Author-Illustrator Index for the Treasury

Italics are for illustrator only; * after page number gives location of a group of books by an author or illustrator.

384 AUTHOR-ILLUSTRATOR INDEX

FOR THE BEST IN PAPERBACKS, LOOK FOR THE

ALSO AVAILABLE FROM JIM TRELEASE:

FROM PENGUIN • HIGHBRIDGE AUDIO:

☐ **THE READ-ALOUD HANDBOOK audiocassette**
Jim Trelease shares his extensive knowledge and shows how reading aloud to children can create life long book-lovers and readers. This inspirational audiocassette—a must for every parent—is accompanied by a booklet listing read-aloud titles recommended by Trelease.

Read by the author. Abridged; 3 hours on 2 audiocassettes
                              ISBN 0-453-00835-6   *$16.95*

AND FROM PENGUIN BOOKS

☐ **HEY! LISTEN TO THIS**
   Stories to Read Aloud
This delightful anthology brings together forty-eight read-aloud stories—from folktales like *Uncle Remus* to favorite classics like *Charlotte's Web*—that parents and teachers can share with children ages five to nine.
                    416 pages   *ISBN 0-14-014653-9*

☐ **READ ALL ABOUT IT!**
   Great Read-Aloud Stories, Poems, and Newspaper Pieces
   for Preteens and Teens
This wonderfully diverse treasury of fifty read-aloud pieces will turn young people on to the many pleasures of reading—sparking their interest with selections ranging from an autobiographical sketch by Maya Angelou to "Casey at the Bat" to a moving story about two Holocaust survivors.
                    496 pages   *ISBN 0-14-014655-5*